The Downhill Rocket from North Overshoe

John S. Leech

The Downhill Rocket from North Overshoe by John S. Leech
Published by Amazon Kindle Direct Publishing

Contents

Chapter 1

I was not unhappy as I grew up in Brookline, although I was not joyful either. We, my parents and I, lived in a modestly comfortable house on a street that was leafy and quiet. The summer when I was around 12 there was even some talk about having me take sailing lessons down on the Charles, which I would not have minded doing. It would have gotten me out of the house, and who knows — I might have met some kids I fit in with. Then, when it was time to start seventh grade, I switched schools to Boston Latin.

Boston Latin is the oldest school in America, and it's the school you would want to go to if you wanted to study Latin. In fact if you went to Boston Latin you *would* study Latin; it is a requirement. I could never see any practical purpose in memorizing those Latin declensions. Have you forgotten what declensions are? Here is the brush up: they are the inflections of nouns, pronouns, and adjectives for categories such as case and number. Remember *hic haec hoc*? How about *horum harum horum*? I wish I didn't.

I was as willing to learn as the next kid, maybe even more so, and my marks were excellent, but there are limits to my tolerance for studying anything as wildly impractical as that. My parents had promoted the idea of going to Boston Latin because it was to pave the way for my admission to Harvard and I was willing to go along even though I had no particular desire to go to Harvard, or any other college or university for that matter. Remember I was a seventh grader; all I wanted was a friend or two.

By spring of that year, Boston Latin, its declensions, and its role as a springboard to Harvard became moot. At dinner one evening my father and mother broke the news to me that Dad had accepted a new job and we would be moving.

I had known before a word was spoken that strange doings were afoot. Although our home had a dining room, it sat idle except for the few times when relatives were joining us. Otherwise we ate at the kitchen counter, lined up in a single wing formation with Dad in the center.

On this night of nights I saw that our three places were set on the glossy dining room table. After taking our seats — Dad at the head of the table flanked by Mom and me — there was a brief and uncomfortable silence. It was the end of the week and the table was spread with our traditional Friday evening meal of a salad, deep fried codfish balls, baked beans, and brown bread, but neither of my parents were making a move toward any of it. Instead, Mom gave Dad a significant look and Dad, on cue, sat up a little taller. He took a quick breath and leaned in toward me. "Carl," he said, "we want to talk with you about my job. My career."

I glanced at my mother and realized she was looking at me nervously. Watching for my reaction. I kept my mouth neutral and looked back to my father.

Ice broken, Dad picked up speed. "I like my work, but in order to become a partner I would need to bring in more clients to the firm, and in order to do that I would need to be much more social than I am comfortable with." He sat back in his chair and crossed his arms over his chest. "Rotary clubs, social events, entertaining, I am not suited for that sort of thing, and neither is your mother. I am much more comfortable right here." He ran his hand across the soft white linen tablecloth as his voice trailed off.

I knew by 'here' he meant home with Mom and me. They were waiting for me to say something, I could tell. "And even more comfortable eating in the kitchen," I offered.

At this I saw Mom smile slightly. Dad pressed on.

"Because of this I have bumped up against my ceiling here, and the truth is that Brookline is an expensive place to live. Recently I've been offered an opportunity to switch to another job. Mom and I have discussed it, and we think, well we have decided–" At this point Dad paused, seeming to fumble for the right words.

"Dad," I said, "whatever it is you want to tell me, just say it. Dinner is getting cold." I waved a hand toward the codfish balls.

Another smile from Mom. Dad seemed to relax somewhat and plowed ahead. "Okay, okay. You've heard me talk about our client Miss Grant up in New Kensington, and you know I've gone there several times to work on her tax matters. Well, she wants to hire me to work for her on a full-time basis. It's a wonderful opportunity and a substantial jump in pay, but we will have to move there."

Now it was time for the one-boy peanut gallery to be heard from. I looked at Mom's face. She hadn't said anything, but I could see she was onboard; the concern in her furrowed forehead wasn't with the plan itself but with what I might think of it. I looked to Dad. His eyes were bright, hopeful. Excited about the future. Sensing that all the decision making was already done, I was surprised to realize that I did not mind the thought of being uprooted. Finding it easy to be a good sport, I reached for the brown bread and nonchalantly responded, "How is the sailing up there?"

My parents knew my offbeat sense of humor and I could hear them both exhale audibly with relief. At once they rose from their seats and rounded the table to hug me.

Dad was a mid-level associate with a downtown accounting firm, and the Miss Grant he had mentioned was a lady who owned a quarry up north. A year or two earlier, Dad had become the firm's third CPA; and the first non-partner, to be assigned to Miss Cora Grant, after she had — for one reason or another during the preceding decade — deemed each of the two previous partners unacceptable. The thinking within the partnership was that sending my dad up to see Miss Grant in person was the accounting equivalent of a slap shot from center ice in the closing seconds — a last-ditch attempt to hold onto what had long been a highly-profitable account.

Much to the surprise of the firm's executive suite, Miss Grant had found my father (and thereby the firm) to be worthy of retention. Even more surprising, in March she had offered Dad a position as her chief financial officer. Dad, after consulting with my mother, accepted the offer.

All this and more was explained to me as I ate my way through the beans and fish. We had three months to settle all matters there in Brookline and move to our new home town: New Kensington.

Although I had heard Dad mention New Kensington in connection with the work he had done there on behalf of Miss Grant, I didn't know where it was other than that it was somewhere up north. Curious about the whereabouts of what was to be our new home I got out a map.

Our soon to be new home town turned out to be quite a way further north, not quite into the mountains but close enough so that winters there would be cold and snowy with plenty of slush during the spring melt. I quickly came to think of New Kensington as North Overshoe. Goodbye MTA, hello snowshoes.

Chapter 2

In the next few months I learned that Miss Grant was not your run-of-the-mill rock breaker. She was the latest of several generations of Grants who had operated quarries in New Kensington since the early eighteen hundreds. She would also be the last; she had no children or living relatives.

Originally from Scotland, her ancestors had found work in a local quarry and eventually acquired control of it. Business had prospered from early on; granite was widely used in every aspect of life. Gravestones, of course, but breakwaters were also a major source of revenue. Having a breakwater built could turn a seaside town into a snug port and anchorage and greatly improve the local economy. And who could ask for a better material with which to build a school, church, or library than New Kensington's own stolid, durable, confidence-building gray native rock?

As the quarry business grew, the Grants purchased large amounts of timberland, some of which was actual forest and some of which had been purchased at near giveaway prices from companies who had clear cut the land and had no further use for it.

And so as one generation of Grants passed and the next generation assumed command of the ancestral holdings, New Kensington grew from a frontier outpost into a viable, if small, town, largely due to the success of the Grant's expanding businesses but also due to donations and financing from the Grants. I would later learn that some people attributed these far sighted investments to Miss Grant's grandfather Malcolm Grant… while others credit the philanthropic spirit of her great grandfather Roy Grant. In one respect the town was in total agreement-- None of this was due to the actions of Miss Grant's father, Hammy. Whatever the motivation, the town we moved into had a full-scale school system, a first-class library, and a respectable array of shops, stores, and restaurants. There were two bars, one bank — owned by guess who — and a viable main street through the center of all this, named, with Yankee straightforwardness, Main Street.

Main Street also had a modest business section, which was where Grant Holdings was headquartered. Inside the largest building, fortress-like and constructed of New Kensington's favorite material, was to be my father's new command post. The main quarry was three miles north of the town, but only the director of operations was headquartered there. This suited my father, as he was used to a necktie sort of environment — a quiet building with central heat and air conditioning. He was perfectly content to have a three mile buffer zone between his desk and the blasting, crushing, dust, and noise that went with the quarry operations.

Miss Grant maintained an office on Main Street but she seldom put it to use. Instead she preferred to oversee her varied business matters from an office within her grand private residence, Sycamore Hall. When Miss Grant wanted to speak with my father in person, he would make the short drive to her home.

And so it was that our small family came to move from Brookline to New Kensington in the summer before I was to start eighth grade. We bought a house just outside the downtown area, Dad set up his office inside the Grant Holdings building, and Mom joined a book club, which met weekly at the town library. I passed my time reading, mostly fiction, but intrigued by what I understood to be the main business of Grant Holdings, I also started in on a textbook covering the basics of geology. When I became restless I would ride around on my bike, and in that way I became somewhat familiar with my new hometown.

Then school started. Within the first day I discovered that New Kensington's school system had a very direct method of assigning its students to classrooms, courses of study, and teachers. Based on a blend of previous grades (in my case transcripts), aptitude test results, and the just plain subjective opinion of a dragon-like administrator named Mrs. Griffin, the students were placed into one of three classifications: A, B, or C. In this respect, Mrs. Griffin functioned something like the fictional Sorting Hat at Hogwarts.

According to this system, the students in the A group were thought to be college material. Those in the C group were expected to enter the workforce or become housewives upon graduation (if they indeed got that far). Those in the B group were in a sort of academic no man's land; overachievers could be moved up into the A group and, conversely, slackers faced the possibility of falling in with the C's.

My immediate impression was that this was a harsh system, both cruel and overly subjective. However, as I became accustomed to life in this small town school system I realized that my fellow eighth graders did not seem to mind it. The A group students readily accepted that they were given more homework than those in the B group were given, and far from feeling stigmatized, the C's seemed to be entirely content, almost like baseball players mired deep in the Red Sox minor league system but happy to be playing at their level.

I did not mind school at all; I never had. The teachers seemed to be nice, some more so than others, but that was a constant at my previous schools too.

Other students ignored me for the most part and I was used to that. Kids form impressions based primarily on what they see and secondarily on what they hear. Being somewhat shorter than average and tending toward pudginess I knew that these eighth graders had quickly determined I was a nebbish.

In class I followed my long standing personal guideline of only raising my hand to answer a question once per class, and if I was called on to answer I would keep my commentary brief and to the point.

The only exception to this was a spur-of-the-moment decision I made one day during the second week of my new English class. As part of this class, my fellow A's and I were learning about foreign phrases that were in common use. When I was called on to define the expression 'bête noire,' I stood up, walked to the blackboard, and wordlessly drew a stubby, horned monster, complete with fangs and evil, slanted eyes.

This got some laughter from the class, and the teacher, while giving me a motherly pat on the arm, simply said "Perfect."

It turned out to be perfect in more ways than one. When the class ended and I was gathering my books for the trek to Algebra class, Sally Bain walked up to me, smiled, and said "Hi Carl. That was a neat drawing you made. Very cute."

At least that is what she may have said. I did not really hear a word of it because being on the receiving end of a smile from Sally Bain was a benumbing experience. Sally Bain was a girl who sat in the second row of my first period class and I'd been taken with her since the first day of school. It was clear that I was not the only boy who felt that way when I saw the way she turned heads. She had long blonde hair pulled into a ponytail , sky blue eyes, and a perfect figure head to toes and front to back. On that particular day she was wearing a white and yellow striped dress that fit her perfectly. Sally was a walking, talking dream and no doubt the launcher of hundreds, maybe thousands of teen aged fantasies.

On top of this Sally was funny and easy going. She didn't seem full of herself the way so many other eighth grade girls seemed to be. While it wasn't unusual for some of her cheerleader friends to act superior to their less popular classmates, Sally seemed to enjoy being around those of us who were not athletes or cheerleaders. Everyone seemed to want to be her friend. When Sally floated between classes there seemed to be an invisible tide that swept her and several friends along the corridors of New Kensington junior high. To my amazement, by Sally's anointment I was now a fringe member of her entourage of friends and admirers; all it took was a smile from Sally Bain and her daily 'Hi Carl" to be widely, if only moderately, tolerated.

Widely tolerated was as much as I could ever have said about my social status back in Brookline, so it felt like something of a victory that within my first few weeks in my new school I was back to where I had previously been; not popular but not an outcast either.

I was soon finding myself on speaking terms with several other of my fellow eighth graders. Among them a boy named Jack Hathaway. Jack was tall and lean but not skinny — he had that naturally athletic look, although at that time I didn't actually know if he played sports. He had dark hair, gray, friendly eyes, and although not exactly handsome he somehow looked attractive.

Our first interaction was hardly notable. I knew who he was because on my first day of school I was leaving Algebra class and not sure where to go for my next class, which was History. I must have looked as indecisive as I felt because Jack was in the Algebra class also and stopped and asked me what my next class was. When I said History. he smiled and said "Oh, you've got Mr. Barrett. Come on, I'll show you where his room is." When we got to Mr. Barrett's room he introduced me to Mr. Barrett by saying that I had just moved to New Kensington from down around Boston so I probably hadn't been taught how to read. When both of them shared a gentle laugh at this I replied "No, but I am willing to learn." They both laughed harder at this and somehow it made me feel welcome. After this, whenever our paths happened to cross Jack would never fail to smile and say hello. It was almost a nothing moment, and yet I sensed immediately that I liked Jack. He seemed very down to earth . . . I wanted to be his friend.

I didn't put it together that day, but I'd already met Jack's father. Like most of the students in my class, Jack Hathaway had lived in New Kensington his whole life, as had his father. Jack's grandfather had started the town's hardware store, cleverly named Hathaway Hardware, and Jack's father was now the owner and operator of it.

Shortly after we moved into our new home, my mother had sent me to Hathaway Hardware to buy some picture hooks. The hardware store was just on the outskirts of town, set on an oversized lot that ran back to a wooded area, so that the property had ample parking, then a field that had originally been used to grow corn. Mr. Hathaway allowed the field to be used for all sorts of worthy causes--pumpkin patch, Christmas tree sales to benefit charities, farmers markets, you name it., and then past the field was the edge of the woods. The store was an easy bike ride from our house.

When I entered the store, Mr. Hathaway was behind the sales counter, along with an older lady. Like Jack, he was tall and rangy with gray eyes, but Mr. Hathaway's hair was salt and pepper. He did not look like Gary Cooper but somehow, he reminded me of that well-known actor, as he had stood; tall and resolute, playing the part of the sheriff in the movie High Noon.

As I stood inside the entrance I saw aisles of hardware paraphernalia in front of me. Each was numbered, but what I needed was a sign directing me towards picture hooks.

Sensing my indecision Mr. Hathaway asked me if he could help me find something. When I told him I was seeking picture hooks for my mother, he came out from behind the counter and led me to where they were located.

I hesitated, stumped by the wide array of choices.

"What sort of project do you need them for?" Mr. Hathaway asked warmly. "What is your mother hanging?"

I frowned, considering the mental image of framed photos and prints and knick knacks scattered around the living room floor, propped up against the couch and leaning against one of the walls.

"Uh," I said. "There's a bunch. Some are like this–" I began using my hands to mime the outlines of a portrait and Mr. Hathaway laughed.

"Let's do this," he said. "I'll send you with a variety and you just bring back what you don't need." He plucked a handful of hooks from several little bins and we walked back toward the cash register.

I handed him my mother's cash in exchange for a small brown paper bag full of hooks, then he extended a hand across the counter. "I'm Tom Hathaway," he said as we shook. "I am going to guess you're part of the Smith family that just moved here."

I felt surprised — somewhat flattered — and told him that I'd be entering eighth grade. He said his son Jack would be a classmate of mine and that he'd tell him to keep an eye out for me. I left the hardware store with the impression that Mr. Hathaway was a nice man, and in time I found that my first impression was correct.

Chapter 3

Apparently Sally Bain was also taken with Jack, because I soon began to notice that Jack stood first among Sally's many boy admirers. I would often see the two of them chatting away before and after school and, more significantly, every day during lunch period they sat side-by-side eating their meal together and; seeing that it was cafeteria food, for better and for worse. Each time I scanned the crowded cafeteria for an empty seat, the sight of them invariably sent a twinge of envy through me, though I wasn't sure what it was I was longing for: that kind of closeness with Sally, camaraderie with Jack, or simply somebody to eat lunch with.

Then came the fateful day, the day of my first and only brawl. At least I always think of it as my brawl even though I was a relatively inactive participant.

At the end of an otherwise routine school day I was milling around with a number of other kids while we waited to board the school bus that would take us home. The ever-lovely Sally Bain rode the same bus that I did, and I happened to be standing near her. Also nearby was a ninth grader by the name of Arnold O'Grady.

Arnold O'Grady was large for his age and one of the few students in the C section who were unhappy with school. He showed this dissatisfaction on a daily basis by being rude, making fun of smaller kids, and in general making a nuisance of himself. He most definitely was not part of Sally's circle of friends.

As Sally was chatting away cheerfully, Arnold pushed his way in front of her and said "I want to feel your boobs."

This, of course, was a major breach of New Kensington protocol and Sally's small entourage gave a collective gasp. Sally's reply was an instantaneous and loud, "Get away from me you churl!"

I will never know how Sally came up with the word 'churl,' but having said it she stepped back from her offender and turned dramatically so her back was to him.

Then, in rapid order, this: Arnold yelled, "Stuck up!" and reached out and gave Sally's ponytail a sharp yank. Sally shouted, "Ouch! Stop that!" Finally alert, I stepped between the two of them so that I was facing Sally's back. I started gently pushing her away from the freshly identified churl.

As I did this, Arnold threw a punch which mostly missed me but did make partial contact with the back of my head, causing me to stumble forward towards Sally. Sally happened to turn back towards me at that very moment and, seeing my face about to bump into her face, she very sensibly ducked.

The result of this was Sally's hairline making hard contact just below my left eye. I had been head butted by an uncrowned beauty queen.

Dazed, I collapsed at Sally's feet; my only thought; weirdly out of context, being to note that her sneakers were spotless. That was the moment that Jack entered the fray. Because Jack's house was on the outskirts of town, he was waiting for a different bus, so he had been standing a short distance away when Arnold began harassing Sally.

However, once Jack noticed what was going on, he sprinted over and ran full throttle into Arnold. Fists were flying even before they crashed to the ground.

This was the real brawl, but before it could reach whatever the conclusion may have been, our afternoon bus monitor, Mr. De Santo jogged over. "KNOCK IT OFF," he roared, yanking Jack up and off Sally's oppressor.

As students began drifting back into their own clusters and I regained my footing, I discovered a cut over my cheek bone and under my left eye as a result of Sally's unwitting head butt. Mr. De Santo saw this, as did Jack and Sally, and after giving me a brief look over he told me to go see the school nurse for what turned out to be a watered-down medical inspection. Sally produced a few tissues from her purse and, with Sally on one side and Jack on the other, back we went into the school and into the nurse's small office, where the petite woman we called Nurse Mary cleaned and bandaged my cut. In Nurse Mary's professional opinion I did not need any stitches, and the three of us were sent on our way.

By the time we returned from the nurse's office the busses had left. Jack's father would have been at the hardware store, but Sally or I could have gone back into the school and called our parents for rides home. However, Sally had a better idea. "I want to walk home with my two heroes," she announced. She bumped her way into a central position between Jack and me and linked arms with us.

Off we went and I could not remember ever being in a better mood as we made our way towards Sally's house. As we strolled along, Sally was polishing her version of the brawl, which she dubbed "The battle at the bus stop." Arnold O'Grady became "that huge freshman pig" who had "tried to pinch my breasts and then rip my scalp off." Even though I was "less than half his size," I had managed to hold him off "valiantly" until Jack "tackled him and beat him up."

This review of what had happened took all sorts of liberties with the facts, but so what, I was walking a beautiful girl home and she was squeezing my arm and referring to me as a valiant hero. As if this wasn't enough, on the other side of this beautiful girl was one of the more popular boys in junior high and the three of us were laughing and chattering like long time best friends.

I could have gone on like that for hours, but all too soon we were at Sally's house. She gave Jack a quick hug and then put her hands on my ears and kissed me on the band-aid before giggling and scampering into her house.

Jack and I stood there briefly looking at Sally's front door. Then Jack turned towards me and laughed. "You are blushing."

"I am not!"

"Okay, your face is just always red when girls kiss you."

With that Jack bumped my shoulder with his and we walked on towards my house, which was close by. I wanted to change the subject from Sally's kiss. "That O'Grady kid IS a pig," I said, "but, you know, he does have an eye for boobs."

With that Jack burst out laughing. I joined in, and we two battle-hardened comrades strode on.

Jack's house was out on the edge of town where the woods began, so I asked him if he'd like my mother to give him a ride the rest of the way.

Jack thanked me, saying that he would like to but his dad would be expecting him to show up at the hardware store, adding that sometimes he would help with the work there if they were busy.

So we headed off in different directions. I was disappointed. I knew that my mother would take one look at my bandage and would want a full explanation. Having Jack there with me would be an ideal visual aid as I described the battle. Also, My mother would be pleased to meet him, I knew that she worried about my lack of close friends and Jack would make an excellent impression. Not only that, if we walked to my house we would have had more time to hang around together; I wanted our friendship to last.

Chapter 4

The battle at the bus stop had served me well; it would prove to be the point at which Sally, Jack, and I did become friends. The next weekend, Jack invited me to come to his house, offering to "show me around." This invitation was extremely welcome. Until then I was not at all sure that the sense of companionship I had felt when we walked home from school after "The Battle," as Sally had put it, was shared by Jack. Considering that my social calendar was a total blank I quickly agreed, and on Saturday afternoon I hopped on my bike and rode to the Hathaways' house, where I saw that the front yard was nicely landscaped.

The property had originally been a farm and from the moment I walked into the entry hall I sensed that it had a warm, lived in feel. Jack walked me through a formal dining room and into the kitchen, where he poured each of us a glass of lemonade. As he was doing that I looked out a picture window and saw that the backyard was a well kept lawn and behind that there was a thick hedge. Past the hedge was an open field which I later learned had been a victory garden during the war. Beyond the field there was a somewhat tumbled down stone wall, and finally, past that I could see a densely wooded area which I was soon to learn ran on into a state forest.

Mr. Hathaway was at the hardware store, but Jack led me from the kitchen through a different door, past the entry hall and a wide staircase to our right and into the living room to meet his sister Nancy. She was reclining on one of the two matching green couches, reading a book. She didn't seem to notice us at first (I suspected this was an act) and I stepped closer to see what she was reading. *To Kill a Mockingbird* – I'd just finished the same book that summer.

"This is my sister, Nancy," Jack said, his voice loud and sharp, clearly relishing the opportunity to break his sibling's concentration. "She's a seventh grader at our school."

Nancy set the book on her chest and glared at Jack before even looking toward me. Her face softened slightly as she rose and moved toward where we were standing. I felt immediately impressed, even a little intimidated, by her noticeably perfect posture and the way she extended her hand to shake mine; the gesture seemed so grown up, despite her being a year younger than Jack. Her grip was somehow firm and soft at once. As we said hello, she eyed me with an extremely direct gaze. It was if I had 100 percent of her attention.

Nancy had the same grey eyes as Jack and their father, though her hair was even darker. Black, in fact. She had a slim, athletic build, like a feminine version of her brother. She was my height, and though She wasn't flashy and might not stand out in a crowd, there was something extremely likeable about her face. Her mouth curled ever so slightly at the corner as she spoke. "You must be a good friend," she said. "Jack does not bring many kids here. I hope you're ready for a hike."

I turned to Jack, my eyes wide. "Hike?"

With what was intended to be a reassuring smile Jack replied that he was going to show me a beautiful spot in the forest that was just a short walk away. When I asked if I could ride my bike there I heard a quick snort from Nancy.

Jack, picking up on my lack of enthusiasm for straying into the forest, told me that there was a marked trail and that I would like it.

But I did NOT like it and replied "I am from a city and the only trees that I have ever had to deal with have been between a street and the sidewalk."

Nancy had returned to the couch where she had been reading. She stood and came to me again. With another of her focused looks she said "It will be okay Carl, Jack knows these woods inside and out and you will be safe."

I was boxed. I might have insisted that we stay indoors and play a board game if it had just been Jack, but I was not going to show a seventh-grade girl that I was fearful of what lay beyond the hedge, so

I said "Now that I know how safe I'll be, what are we waiting around for?"

Before we went out the back-door Jack slung on a backpack. Noticing my look of concern, Jack said that he never went into the woods without taking along some basics.

We passed through a gate in the hedge, crossed the field, stepped over the stone wall and entered the great unknown.

After following Jack for a short distance and seeing no sign of a marked trail I said "You never said that the trail was invisible."

Jack turned towards me and said "See that tree?"

"I see hundreds of trees, all I see are trees"

"The one right in front of us has a blaze mark right at head level."

"You mean that scrape?"

"That's the one. My grandfather blazed this trail with a hatchet when my dad was a kid. All you would have to do is go from one mark to the next to get to where we are going."

"Fine; how would I get back?"

"Good question. Trail blazers always mark both sides of each tree so the trails can be read in two directions."

With that Jack started walking and I followed along. Jack was not a clumsy kid, but in the woods he seemed to become as graceful as Hawkeye. My next question was "How far are we going and how long will it take?"

"It's not far; takes maybe an hour or so."

"Fine, then you don't need to rush."

"I'm not, we are going slowly so you can get used to being a woodsman."

"Oh."

And with that we continued deeper into the unknown, with me craning my neck to see if I could spot the blaze marks, which in most cases were being swallowed up as the bark slowly grew back. Reading my mind, Jack said that someday he would re-blaze the trail.

Somehow, I became almost relaxed. The ground was uneven and there were several small hills and one or two small streams which we crossed by balancing on logs, which I presumed had been thoughtfully put in place by Grandfather Hathaway.

In time we came to a fairly steep decline that sloped from our left to our right and I heard the sound of running water. We stepped into a clearing and I saw what Jack had brought me to see.

We were at the bottom of a valley, which, due to reading my geology book, I knew had probably been carved by a glacier. As the glacier retreated it left behind all sorts of debris; everything from pebbles to boulders, some of which were huge.

This low place in the valley was the natural drainage for the surrounding slopes, and the sound of running water that I had heard came from a medium sized stream.

Slightly to our left and at shoulder height there was a flat rock that had large boulders on each side which pinched the stream in on itself. Directly past these boulders there was a vertical drop of about five feet. The result was a beautiful clear mini waterfall which landed into an oblong pool that was maybe 5 feet across and twice that long, at which point the stream fell off again and broadened out as it continued on its way.

Neither one of us said a word as I took in what I was seeing. After a short pause Jack said, "Well?"

I turned slowly around. There was a small grassy area where we were standing, and two smooth rocks just the right size for sitting. The best I could come up with was "This is beautiful, you could almost go swimming here."

"Good idea; in fact, that's what we are going to do next."

"That's a joke, right?"

"Nope."

"I don't have a bathing suit. I don't have a towel."

"We don't NEED bathing suits out here, and hmm, look what is in here!"

With that Jack pulled a towel out of his backpack and started to undress.

"I don't think my mother — never mind."

With that I started to undress as fast as I could, intending to jump in and out before I could change my mind. With my best Indian war cry I took the leap. Jack was only a second behind.

The water was numbingly cold. After splashing around for a few seconds I Looked downwards in mock horror and turned to Jack, who smiled and said “Don’t worry; cold makes things contract. It feels great when you come out.”

“Perfect, that’s all I needed to know.” And with nothing further to prove I scrambled out and grabbed the towel before Jack could get it. After dressing we sat on the smooth rocks. Jack was right, it did feel great to get out of the chilly pool and into the much warmer early Fall air. Jack then said quietly “My grandfather proposed to my grandmother here.”

“I would bet that she said, ‘Okay, but you have to promise not to make me jump into that pool ever again.’”

With a laugh Jack picked up his backpack, draped the wet towel over the top of it and slung the pack on. We were homeward bound.

When we passed through the hedge gate I saw that Nancy was standing on the back porch, leaning against a support column, right foot crossed behind her left ankle. Looking at me she asked “How was it?”

“Fine; next time we are going to Canada.”

Chapter 5

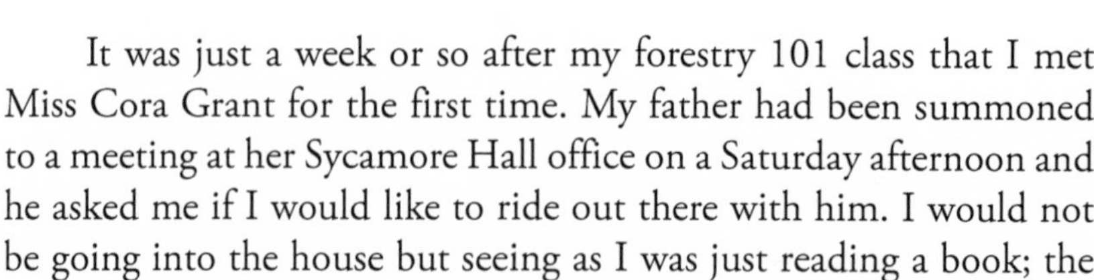

It was just a week or so after my forestry 101 class that I met Miss Cora Grant for the first time. My father had been summoned to a meeting at her Sycamore Hall office on a Saturday afternoon and he asked me if I would like to ride out there with him. I would not be going into the house but seeing as I was just reading a book; the geology text as a matter of fact, Dad though I could just as easily read it in the car while I waited for him to come back out.

That is exactly what we did. The drive was a pretty one and the leaves were just starting to change from green into their Fall colors. Before long Dad turned between the round granite boulders that marked the start of Sycamore Hall's driveway and our tires were crunching the gravel driveway as we passed between the namesake trees.

At the front of the main house the driveway widened into a car park. Dad got out, saying that he did not expect the meeting to last much more than half an hour. I settled in, content to continue reading the geology text.

Geology is an interesting science, and by skipping the aspects of mineralogy that dealt with physics I was able to keep it light but informative. I was reading about zones of subduction, which caused me to think of the section of Boston known as the combat zone. Time passed quickly.

My dad's meeting with Miss Grant was dragging on and I had an increasing problem; I had to pee.

One thing was certain, I was NOT going to knock on the front door of the very imposing Sycamore Hall and ask whoever opened it if I could use the bathroom. Suppose Miss Grant answered the door herself? Was I going to introduce myself and ask for bathroom directions?

Certainly not. Not when there was a simpler solution. One side of the car faced the house, the other side was close to the plants and shrubs that the driveway looped around at the car park. I quickly solved the problem and went back to the zones of subduction.

It was a good thing that I had not decided to tough out my bathroom need, because the meeting with Miss Grant took more than an hour. Eventually my dad returned to the car, and somewhat to my surprise Miss Grant walked out with him.

I slid out of the car and was introduced to Miss Cora Grant, my father's boss and the doyenne of Grant Holdings.

Miss Grant was slightly on the tall side and her erect posture made her seem even taller. She was wearing dark slacks, a tan sweater, and had a tweed sport coat over it. Her features were regular and her gray hair was pulled back in a no-nonsense sort of way.

As my father introduced us, I could tell that I was being assessed by a pro.

Her first words to me were "Hello Carl, I am glad to meet you. If I had known that you were here I would have invited you in. You have been out here for quite some time; would you like to come in and use the bathroom?"

I turned slightly, glancing towards the plantings, and said "No thank you, I'm fine now."

I happen to have a somewhat twisted sense of humor and as soon as I blurted this out I regretted it. However, Miss Grant merely gave a slight smile and said "Thankfully those are hardy perennials. Still, next time your father comes here please come in with him, the library is an excellent place to read geology texts."

Apparently, Miss Grant recognized my text book by its shape and color, as she had not looked directly at my book when we were introduced. If my father had noticed the brief interplay between me and his boss that dealt with my urinating on her "Hardy perennials" he let the matter rest; with relief, no doubt.

For better or worse I have a lifetime habit of speaking my mind. In this case Miss Grant had picked up on it and apparently approved.

I say that because later that Fall my father was again called to Sycamore Hall and Miss Grant specifically asked that he bring me along. Apparently, I was going to be shown into the library, where I would be able to read in comfort and also have access to indoor plumbing.

Sycamore Hall had been built by Miss Grant's great grandfather as the seat of the Grant lairds, and it had been built in a style that had suited the times as they were then. It was situated on the furthest part of a road that looped out of town, squared off at the Grant property, and then swung back into the town.

The roadside frontage of the property was marked by a fieldstone wall which curved inward in a quarter circle on both sides of the entrance to the driveway, at which point the fieldstone wall gave way to twin granite fieldstone structures, roughly square, rising to six feet. These entrance markers were topped with flat slabs sufficiently thick to be inscribed "Sycamore Hall" on one side of the driveway, and "Grant" on the other. Atop these were two rough hewn granite balls approximately five feet in diameter.

From there a gravel driveway ran between two parallel rows of sycamore trees and up to the main house, as well as a large garage off to the right side. The garage had a dormer windowed second floor which served as a residence for Miss Grant's driver, who did double duty, as he was also in charge of overseeing the upkeep of the surrounding grounds, which were extensively landscaped.

The hall itself was built in the Georgian style with the ground floor constructed of small and medium sized fieldstones. At the front of the house the driveway opened up into the car park, and then continued around the oblong area of groomed bushes and shrubs before reconnecting with the main part of the driveway.

Viewed from the front the hall appeared to be built in the form of a rectangle, two and a half stories tall. However, later I learned that the hall had wings which went back from each side of the house, so that the overall shape of the house was that of a squared off U, with a grassy courtyard in the area between the wings.

The front of this very large house as well as the wing on the left side were for general use, while the right wing contained the kitchen and pantry, behind which was a small dining area and a living room for servants, with a stairway leading up to the servants bedrooms.

Our doorbell ring was answered by a formidable looking middle-aged woman who in time I learned was the housekeeper. Immediately past the door was a long, wide hallway, to the right of which was a smaller room; later identified as the "cloak closet". We were shown into the first room on our left, which was Miss Grant's office and where she greeted us.

As she came around her desk she told me–not asked–that she would show me around the ground floor of her home before settling me in the library. With that she started the tour.

"This room is now my office as you can see. When my great-grandfather built this house there was not much in the way of a public school system here so we had tutors; and this was used as a school room. We still call it that."

She lead us out of the school room and down the wide hall past a large fireplace.

"Behind this fireplace there is a cutting room with a side door that leads out to the garden. Next is the gun room, and here is the library."

We dutifully entered the library, the walls of which were lined with bookshelves and which was furnished with comfortable chairs, a desk, and a leather couch that looked to weigh at least 1000 pounds. I noticed a relatively small (by Sycamore Hall standards) door on the left side of the library wall. Without having seen my quick glance at it Miss Grant said, "That door leads into the cutting room."

She then took us through a different door on the back right side of the library and into an enormous living room. This room had a huge fireplace on it's far wall which was flanked by matching couches facing each other. There were assorted seating areas, and tables behind each of the couches both of which held Tiffany lamps.

I took all this opulence in wordlessly. After a moment Miss Grant's dry summary was "Barely sufficient for my needs."

Past the living room and down a step there was a screened in porch with wicker furniture. After glancing at it we returned to the main hallway through a set of double doors, walked past an impressive grandfather clock, and then past a wide staircase where a shorter hallway to our left lead into a dining room that could have comfortably seated 16; probably more.

This concluded my tour of Sycamore Hall, as Miss Grant summarized the remainder of the house's ground floor beyond the dining room as being a pantry, the kitchen, and the servants wing.

She then walked us back to what I would thereafter always think of as the School room, saying to me "Carl, you may make yourself comfortable in the library." And then, after a meaningful pause added, "There is a bathroom off the cloak room."

Chapter 6

The school year passed fairly quickly. Jack was an End on the junior high football team, Sally, predictably, was a cheerleader, and I, equally predictably, did nothing.

Earlier I have said that I didn't mind school. In fact I liked it, except for one thing, which was our daily Physical Education class. No matter the activity, whether it was tag football, basketball, or softball, I was equally maladroit and unhappy.

However, the friendship between Jack, Sally, and I continued and even strengthened. Before long it was time for the Christmas vacation.

Jack's father had a tradition of hosting a pre-Christmas party for the people who worked at Hathaway Hardware. The party was at the Hathaway's home, and the families of the employees were also invited. Jack had invited Sally and I to join the party, and naturally we quickly said yes.

I learned that before Mrs. Hathaway passed away she would prepare all sorts of dishes and put them out as a buffet. Since her death Mr. Hathaway had continued the party and the buffet, but hired one of our local restaurants to cater the meal.

Mrs. Bain gave Sally and me a ride to the Hathaway's and the party apparently had gotten off to an early start because as we approached the door we could hear many people talking at once; the sure sign of a successful Christmas gathering.

I, coached by my mother, was wearing a pair of slacks, a button-down shirt and a sports coat. Sally, who apparently had an endless closet, wore a pretty green dress, and Jack looked semi-preppy in pressed khaki pants with a heavy sweater.

Nancy was also wearing slacks and a sweater and after some preliminary wandering around greeting the other guests the four of us fixed ourselves plates of food and sat partway up the stairs to dig in.

After a little time, Mr. Hathaway came to the foot of the staircase and asked Nancy to go up to his bedroom and bring down a book that he wanted to loan to the wife of one of his employees.

Nancy said "Sure," put her plate down on the stair she had been sitting on, and ran up the stairs so fast that her feet were a blur. The lady who was to receive the book watched Nancy zip away and commented "My, she certainly is nimble."

As simply as that Nancy had a nickname, Nimble Nancy, or Nim for short. I was never sure if Nancy cared for the nickname, but it definitely suited her.

As the party was breaking up and Sally and I were waiting for Mr. Bain to give us a lift home and I was thanking Mr. Hathaway for inviting me to the party, he surprised me by asking if I would like to come skiing with them the week after Christmas.

For me this was a classic good news/bad news situation. The good part of the invitation was the part about going on a vacation with the Hathaway family. The bad news was the word skiing.

I turned to Jack for input. With a smile he told me that they had owned a cabin at a ski resort to our north for many years. He went on to say that there was plenty of room and that I would have fun.

I told him that I was all for having fun, but that I did not know anything about skiing, did not have any equipment, and hated frostbite. Jack smiled and said that frostbite was part of the fun. Once the laughter died down I agreed to come along.

Nimble Nancy walked to the door with me and said that basic skiing was not hard and that she would help me get started.

And so several days later we were off to the Hathaway's cabin in the mountains. The cabin was more than what I had expected it to be. There was a porch (covered with snow) on which was a large stack of firewood. Inside there was a main room, a cozy fireplace, tables, supporting furniture, a kitchen on one end and two bedrooms and a bathroom on the opposite end. There was also a partial upstairs where there was a large bunk room and another bathroom. Jack and I were to be in the bunkroom while Nancy and Mr. Hathaway had the downstairs bedrooms.

Mr. Hathaway had brought along plenty of groceries. We started a fire and settled in. I was thinking that ski trips were very nice, so long as I didn't have to ski.

At dinner we went over the plans for the next day. Right after breakfast someone from the ski resort was going to pick Nancy up and take her to the slopes so that she could get in some early runs before the general public arrived. Later the three of us would drive over and Jack and Mr. Hathaway would supervise my getting set with rental skis, boots, and poles. Once that was taken care of they were going to enroll me in a beginner ski class that would last until we were all to meet at the base lodge for lunch.

All this made sense to me except for the part about Nancy leaving early, so I asked why she would not be driving to the resort with us.

Mr. Hathaway replied quietly that Nancy was an expert skier, that everyone who worked on the ski slopes knew her, and that she liked to get up to the top of the mountain when the first workers went up so that she could ski as fast as she wanted without having to dodge around crowds of slower skiers.

I looked at Nancy; she looked at me and tilted her head slightly in acknowledgement. With a laugh Jack said that Nancy was crazy good on skis and had been right from her start.

The next morning at the resort I was processed through the equipment rental and Jack and Mr. Hathaway supervised my clumsy way to the base of the bunny slope and into my beginner's class. Once they saw that I was where I should be they went off on their way and I found myself in the care of a pleasant college aged girl. Soon we were learning how to walk uphill and to snowplow down. My low expectations were exceeded, and by the time the class ended and it was time to meet the Hathaways for lunch I had conquered the bunny slope several times.

Feeling pretty good about this I went to the spot where we had agreed to meet. As I looked up the slope for the Hathaways I soon saw Nancy, who stood out in her bright yellow jacket and matching cap. Nancy didn't seem to ski; she flowed. Even though that part of the ski slope was busy Nancy found pathways effortlessly. As I watched her someone nearby said "Wow, who's that kid?" In reply another skier said "Her name's Nancy; she's some sort of prodigy."

At lunch all talk was of skiing. Mr. Hathaway and Jack had skied some of the easier black runs, which I had already learned were for advanced skiers. Nancy had been taking some runs on something called "Widow Maker", and I entertained them with tales of how I had out shone several 5-year olds.

I also repeated the conversation I had heard wherein Nancy had been called a prodigy.

The general afternoon plan was for me to get more experience on the wide and gentle front slope. After assuring Mr. Hathaway and Jack that I would be fine on my own they agreed on where they would be skiing.

Then Nancy said that she was going to take me up to Old Tote Road. The other Hathaways agreed, although Mr. Hathaway seemed surprised.

I was anything but sure I wanted to ski anywhere with Nancy after seeing her ski and said so. Nancy put her hand on my sleeve and told me that I would be fine and that settled it. I looked at my trail map.

Old Tote Road started at the very top of the mountain, as did several other trails. However, the others went down the front of the mountain; "Our" run went off to the side, then all around the edge of the ski property, and eventually curved back and ended on the far side of my new pal, the Bunny Slope.

Although I had become fairly comfortable with the ski equipment and the gentle slope where I had spent the morning, the chair lift that went to the mountaintop was intimidating and I did not relish the thought of getting onto it in the company of Nimble Nancy.

She read my thoughts, and when it was our turn to be whisked away she greeted the lift operator by name and said "Beginner", looking in my direction. With a smile the operator slowed the lift to a crawl long enough for me to sit down, and we settled in for the long ride to the top.

As we rode along among the tree tops we chatted away. I had come to think of Nancy as being a girl of few words, but one on one I found her to be interesting and perceptive.

Of course when we got off the lift at the top I fell just sliding down the exit ramp. Nancy was unperturbed and helped me up and we turned towards the start of our task at hand; the Old Tote Road. It looked benign, not particularly steep, and comfortably wide. Before we began our descent, Nancy roughed out our strategy; we would make wide curves, go nice and slow, and stop often.

So it was said and so it was done. I only fell twice and laughed both times. Before I knew it we were back at the base.

At that point I planned on thanking Nancy for the help and seeing her off to whatever terrifying trail she might feel like zipping down, but to my astonishment she asked if I wanted to do it again. My answer was a big “Yes” and off we went. This time I only fell once even though our curves were narrower. The young prodigy was a skilled instructor.

Once we were back at the base again I told her that I was done for the day and that she had helped me a lot. With a wave and a smile, she was off. I headed for the base lodge, content to relax there until the Hathaways joined me for the ride back to the cabin.

Overall the day had been a big win for me. I had found a sport that I didn’t hate, a first for me, and I was very relaxed with the Hathaway family and the comfortable cabin. True, I was sore the next day but I thought of it as a mark of honor. The rest of the mountain stay passed quickly and before we came home I was a bona fide (but somewhat retarded) intermediate level skier.

Chapter 7

The rest of our eighth grade school year passed in a routine way for the most part; a few more visits with the Old Lady, one more walk into the forest with Jack (but on a different trail this time); I was increasingly at home in "North Overshoe."

One constant was my dislike for our P.E. sessions, and when Spring arrived our activities centered around softball games. I would always play Right Field–deep Right Field, where the flow of the game usually left me alone. When I had to take my turn at bat my policy was to swing at every pitch; that way it was over quickly.

Then on one otherwise routine day, as the softball teams were being sorted out I had a moment of inspiration and it came from the most improbable of sources; a boy named Alves.

I do not even remember Alves's first name, not that it mattered, everyone called him Alves, usually preceded by an adjective such as "That damn Alves."

Alves was not a bad kid and he was certainly not crazy, it was just that he could be relied on to do self-destructive things. As a result, when he was mentioned it was likely to be as "That crazy Alves". In the terms of today it would be said that he had attention deficit disorder. Back then everyone accepted that he was half nuts and let it go at that.

On the day that turned out to be so pivotal for me, while the P.E. instructor was dividing us into two teams Alves threw the catcher's mask up onto the top of the slanted screen behind home plate.

The instructor, mildly exasperated but unsurprised, yelled, "All right Alves, climb up there and get it down, then go run laps until the bell rings."

Alves retrieved the mask and headed off to the nearby track. As I watched him start jogging around the track I had an epiphany; I would be less unhappy working my solitary way around the track than I would be playing softball, or more accurately, doing my best to avoid playing.

Instantly I formed my exit strategy. I went to the P.E. instructor and said, "Coach, I don't really like playing softball, do you think my team would miss me if I just go run some laps instead? I will get more exercise that way."

The instructor said, "Sure, if that's what you want go right ahead."

When I arrived at the track Alves was waiting for me and said, "Smith! I never would have expected to see you here, what the hell did you do?"

"Nothing; I just got tired of hitting home runs and decided to work on my blazing speed." With that I took off full throttle.

My version of full throttle was less that supersonic, and Alves easily cruised along with me. Within 10 or 15 seconds I was winded and stopped. Alves; who was frequently banished from P.E. activities offered these words of advice: "I usually run 100 steps, then walk 100, then run another 100. You are in such terrible shape you should try 25/75."

This was advice from the school's leading head case but it was better than no plan at all, so that is what I started doing. I found that I did not mind the running-walking very much. I preferred it to dodging fly balls and whiffing. From then on through the end of the school year I would ignore the P.E. activity *de jour* and head directly to the track, sometimes with Alves as a wingman or if he had managed to behave himself I would run alone. I even set a goal for myself, I was shooting for what I named 'The Alves ratio'; 100/100. I had not made it by June, but my stride and speed; having no direction to go but up, had improved considerably.

Chapter 8

School ended for the Summer and soon thereafter Dad had another of his meetings with Miss Grant; the Old Lady.

By then I had picked up some of the nicknames that the townspeople had for her. "Boneyard" was one, along with it's cousin "Bone Ass." Others were "The Queen", Queenie", "Her Highness", "Smiley" (this was sort of a reverse play as Miss Grant did not waste much time smiling), Gravel Gertie, and my particular favorite: "Fig Tits."

All this aside Miss Grant was widely respected. Although she had no official position in the town's political structure she had wide influence partly due to her ownership of the bank, the quarry, a theatre, several buildings in the main part of town, a number of farms in the surrounding area, considerable undeveloped land in and outside the town, and thousands of acres of timberland.

The fact that the Grant name was on several of the town's properties added to the impression of wealth and power. The Grant family had been prime benefactors to New Kensington for generations and everyone knew it.

For this particular meeting Dad told me that Miss Grant had asked him to bring me along with him. Both of us were wondering what she had up her sleeve, as we knew that she never so much as took a breath without having a plan for its use. Not knowing what to expect, off we went.

The housekeeper, a battleship of a woman, greeted us at the door and escorted us to the Schoolroom, where Miss Grant sat at her desk, expressionless.

After motioning us to take seats in front of the desk she looked at us with her chin cupped between her thumbs and forefingers for a few seconds and then spoke.

"Carl, your father knows some of what I am going to be talking about today and some of it he does not. I expect that it will all, or mostly all, be new to you. I want to tell you something about our family history here in New Kensington."

Without realizing it I found that I had been somewhat tense. I relaxed; If she had summoned me for nothing more than a verbal stroll through her family scrapbook that was fine with me. I like a good story, in print or verbal, and I was thinking that this should be interesting.

Miss Grant began. "My grandfather Malcolm Grant was born in 1865 right here in New Kensington. At that time the quarry was well established and was a thriving business under the oversight and control of my great-grandfather Roy Grant. We also owned the town bank and several other local businesses. It was Roy Grant who had this house that we are sitting in built. Great grandfather Roy had a good head for business."

Miss Grant continued: "Roy passed away in 1900 and the ownership of what we now know of as Grant Holdings passed to my grandfather Malcolm Grant, who was 35 at that time. Grandfather Malcolm was also very well suited for business and the scope and value of our properties increased greatly while he was the family's decision maker."

My father Hamilton was born in 1885. Everyone called him Hammy and if he ever had a serious thought in his head it was quickly stifled. Father managed to squeak through prep school and our family's money and connections got him into Yale, where he lasted part way through his sophomore year. During the short time he was there he majored in tennis, golf, and parties. I am not sure if he flunked out or was expelled; he always claimed that both of these things occurred simultaneously.

"Grandfather Malcolm had long since recognized that Hammy was born to be a good-natured friend to all mankind who could always be counted on to know where the next party was. Grandfather Malcolm also knew that Hammy was useless when it came to business, or for that matter, anything serious. Hammy was put on a liberal allowance, which was chronically overdrawn, and allowed to roam. Hammy was gifted in that regard, and in the course of his wanderings he met my mother; sweeping her off her feet. I was born in 1910." After a pause Miss Grant added this footnote to history: "Probably the result of too much champagne and too little planning."

At last a glimpse into Miss Grant's thoughts on these matters. I didn't try to hide my smile at this self-depreciation on the Old Lady's part. I knew she would notice my appreciation of her dry humor.

The family saga continued: "My parents were not exactly bad parents so much as they were absent parents. Grandfather and grandmother took care of my upbringing and I knew that they loved me. As for my parents, well, they loved me too, but usually from a distance. I will say this; they always were home for Christmas. You should have been here in those days. The decorations, the heaps of gifts, the guests, the meals, the parties, this house seemed enchanted then." This last comment was made almost wistfully. I couldn't contain myself and interjected this when she paused in thoughtful reflection. "What happened to your parents?"

"They were killed in a car wreck. Hammy's car hit a patch of ice in the Alps and their car went over a cliff. That was in 1925 when I was 15."

This time it was my father who spoke, saying "That must have been very hard on you."

"It was and it wasn't. My grandparents had raised me and before long I was off to college. Grandfather had already been grooming me to eventually take control of our investments, and like him and his father I had an affinity for business. When Grandfather passed away in 1940 I was 30 and ready to inherit our businesses and investment portfolio."

She then asked "Carl, has this been boring for you?"

"Are you kidding? It's fascinating. Do you have any relatives?"

"None. I was an only child. There were some great uncles and aunts; all long gone. There may be some distant cousins but if there are they have been out of the picture for decades. I am the last of the Grants."

Blunt as always, I then asked "What will happen when you die?"

With that Dad turned to me and in a scolding tone said "Carl!"

With a small hand motion Miss Grant waved away my father's objection to the interjection "That is an excellent question and I do not have the answer yet so I can't die until I do."

With that she turned to me and asked "Carl, what are your plans for this Summer?"

I was blindsided by this and after a pause for thought I said "Plans? I don't have any plans. I am 14, 14-year olds don't plan, we take things as they come." I then added "there has been some talk around the house of a trip to Cape Cod."

Miss Grant, leaning forward slightly focused her steady eyes on me and replied "Go ahead and take that vacation to the Cape. For the rest of the Summer I have a job for you."

What I had been thinking of as a review of the Grant's family history had taken a sudden and totally unexpected ninety degree turn. Clearing my throat, I said, "Job; what do you mean?"

"What do you think I mean? I want you to work for me this summer."

Me? Work? A job? None of my classmates had lined up summer jobs; at least so far as I knew. Suddenly I felt a swell of pride; Carl Smith, former nebbish, soon to be a breadwinner!

"What sort of a job, Miss Grant?"

"I want you to start learning something about the operations of our businesses. You will be starting at our gravel facility, then up where the cutting is done, and after that I will likely move you into sales or maybe the bank."

That sounded more like a complex checkerboard move than a job; a series of cameo appearances. Was I to be Grant Holdings version of a 14-year-old Scarlet Pimpernel?

"It does not sound like I will have much time to learn any of these."

The doyenne of the Grant empire continued to roll out surprises." I expect that you will pick up some understanding of the way things are done as you move around, but that will be a secondary consideration."

I looked towards my father for some clue as to where this conversation was taking us, but I saw by his stiff posture that he was as astonished by this as I was.

So I asked the obvious question; “Then what is the primary consideration?”

Miss Grant; arms on her desk with palms down then leaned forward and dropped the bombshell. “I want as many people as possible to see and understand that I have my eye on you, and I want the conclusion drawn that in time you will be given more responsibilities.”

With this she cocked an eyebrow and I saw the faintest of smiles. She knew that I was stunned.

I WAS stunned; stunned wordless as my mind went into overdrive trying to assimilate what she had said. I leaned back in my chair, fingertips on my temples.

“Carl, I know this is all unexpected. I plan on being around for many more years but at some time I need to have a plan for succession in place. I believe that you are smart, honest, have a quick grasp of things, and have both your feet on the ground. You would be surprised how few people can be described in those terms. I see excellent potential in you and if I am wrong I want to know sooner rather than later.”

She then added “But I am not wrong often.”

Chapter 9

Within the Smith household Miss Grant's wishes were close to scripture. We took our family vacation to Cape Cod shortly after school ended for the summer, and the first Monday following our return I reported as ordered to the gravel operation; overseen by Mr. Jim Curci.

Mr. Curci was waiting for me when my mother dropped me off a little before 8 o'clock. He did not waste any words, saying "I was told to teach you something about what we do here. What I DON'T know is why."

"That makes two of us Mr. Curci."

"All right then, here is what we are going to do; for the next two weeks you are going to follow me everywhere I go. If I go to the crusher, follow. If I head for the sorter, follow. If I take a crap, hand me the tissue."

"How many sheets?"

Thankfully Mr. Curci turned out to have a sense of humor, and with a laugh and a smile we headed off to what I learned was the sorter. The day passed fairly quickly.

When mother picked me up at 5 she immediately asked how my first day of work had gone.

"Gravel is more important than most people realize" I started "Did you know that most of the roads in Russia are paved with gravel?"

Mother was impressed; "You learned all that in one day?"

There was more. I went on to inform her that gravel could be as large as 2 ½ inches in diameter; larger than that and it was no longer gravel, becoming cobble. I then asked her if she knew what the size category below gravel was known as.

"No, but I have always wanted to know."

"Sand!"

"Oh stop!"

"It's true! I can't wait until tomorrow!"

My summer as a fledgling employee of Grant Holdings passed quickly as I hop-scotched from one part of the businesses to the next. I learned a little with each of my cameo appearances, but not much. I did get to meet some of her supervisors such as Jim Curci. All of them had specific but limited responsibilities; the closest to what I thought of as upper management was my father, who as I said earlier, was the chief financial officer of the holding company.

None of my job activities held the attention of my friends Jack and Sally. When we were together we went to movies, had ice cream at the drugstore, and sometimes just walked around doing nothing in particular.

One Saturday late in the summer we decided to have a picnic in the park. I had asked Nimble Nancy if she wanted to come and she did, so the four of us found a table and settled in. As we were finishing up our sandwiches Nancy told us that she had been offered a scholarship to attend the Mountainside Ski Academy. We were all surprised; even Jack had known nothing of this and said so.

Nancy then explained that this was a big decision for her, and that Mr. Hathaway wanted her to take some time before she decided if she wanted to accept the scholarship. Nim went on to explain that the Mountainside Ski Academy, or 'Mountainside' as it was usually referred to, was 90% ski and 10% academy. It was supported by the U.S. Ski Federation and was a proving ground for our best young skiers.

Most of the students at the academy had hopes of eventually making the U.S. Ski Team. There would be considerable travel, training, and supervision by top level instructors. In short, this was her ticket to big time skiing.

When she finished filling us in on this Sally asked her if she had made up her mind about going. In reply, Nancy looked towards me and said "Not yet; what do you think I should do?"

Before I could give an opinion–not that I had formed one at that point Sally scooted up next to Jack, saying that Nancy and I should ride our bikes back to the Hathaway's house and talk it over on the way. As she was saying this she twitched her head towards me. I got the message; she wanted us out of the way so she could be alone with Jack.

Nancy and I took the hint and mounted up. As we pedaled along I asked how much she would miss her father, brother, and friends if she accepted the scholarship offer.

"I will miss Jack and Dad very much, I love them." She then stopped her bike and went on to say that since her mother had passed away things had never been the same at their house. She knew that her dad was very lonely. After a pause she took a breath and said "As for friends, none of them are close, the only person besides my family that I will miss is you."

I knew that it was my turn to say something, I just did not know what. By then I was walking my bike also. After a step or two I said "I will miss you too Nancy, but I think you should go. You are a wonderful skier and you love it. Besides, if things do not work out you can always come back."

"NO! If I go I am going in with both feet and I will MAKE it work out. I want to make the Olympic team and this is my way to do it."

Chapter 10

That fall Sally, Jack, and I entered high school. Jack, with his height and natural speed was an end on the football team. Sally decided that cheerleading was not for her, saying that she would rather be in the stands, and that the cheerleaders were too catty anyway.

As for me, when we were weighed and measured as school began I found that I had grown three inches over the summer. Also, most of my pudginess had been stretched away. We still had physical education daily, but I always went directly to the track to work on my Alves ratio.

Sally and I sat together for the first football game of the season, and part way through the game she told me that she had a date that night with Bob Souther, who I knew was a junior who played basketball.

To me this seemed like a betrayal. I pointed toward the field and asked "What about Jack?" Sally was ready with her answer. "I can't sit around forever waiting for Jack to ask me out; my phone has been ringing a lot lately." She then added in a less defiant tone "Maybe this will let him know that I don't want to sit at home like an old maid."

I could see this not going over well at all with Jack. I asked "Will this be a car date?"

"Yes indeed, we are going to a movie."

With eyes turned to slits I said "Traitor!"

As we had learned in junior high science class, for every action there is a reaction. The grapevine at New Kensington high school worked as efficiently as the gravel sorter at the quarry and the news of Sally's car date made it to Jack at the speed of sound.

Jack was both angry and hurt. Feeling like the guy in the middle of this I was upset but had no idea what to do about it. Result: I did nothing. Jack refused to talk to Sally, and Sally retaliated by going on another date with a different boy. Somebody had to do something and do it soon or our three-way friendship would be as dead as the last Dodo.

I already knew Sally's position; she had made it clear when we were in the bleachers watching the football game, so I went to Jack.

"You like Sally, right?"

"I used to until she stabbed me in the back."

"She has not stabbed you in the back, she has had two dates and the only reason she agreed to go out with those guys is because the boy she wants to go out with hasn't asked her out."

"I was going to ask her out but it is not that easy. I have football practice, homework, and I do not have a driver's license."

To me these seemed like weak reasons; excuses. "Jack, wake up! The most beautiful girl in school is crazy about you! Stop sulking, do something, and do it quick before this gets out of control!" I then added "Do not let some warped sense of pride keep you from something both of you want." Then I threw in "I just wish it was me she wanted."

Jack said nothing for a while, then he quietly said "She's not just beautiful, she's funny, kind, and lots of other good things." Then, after another pause "You are right about the pride though, but okay, I'm going to fix things if I'm not too late."

"You are late, but not too late. Call her and don't waste time."

Chapter 11

The next afternoon Sally called. "What are you doing?"

"Nothing. I *was* thinking, but I stopped about five minutes ago."

"Well don't move, I am on my way."

This was unusual to say the least, Sally had never come to our house. In a short time she was knocking on our door. Clearly she had something on her mind, but with her usual charm she greeted my mother and complimented her kitchen. We then sat down in the living room.

Sally came directly to the point; "Jack asked me out."

"Good."

"He wants to take me into the jungle!"

Jungle? I had no idea what she was talking about "What jungle is that?"

"The big one behind his house"

Ahh, realization. "I wouldn't call that a jungle, woods maybe, or a forest."

"He's taking me on the mah jong death march!"

This struck me as uproarious and both of us started laughing. Once order was restored I told her that the only death march I knew of had been in Bataan and that I doubted if there had ever been a mah jong march of any sort.

Sally was not ready to let go. "I am thinking of the snakes; cobras!" with that she raised her right arm, flattened out her hand, and made darting motions toward me.

Sally could always get me laughing and she weakly joined in. I told her that there had been cobras there in the forest but the bears had eaten them all.

Sally was taken aback. "Bears?"

"Well where else would they be, it is a forest you know."

This got me a light punch on the arm. "Carl, I know you are teasing but this is important to me. I can take a little groping and I am fine in a back seat with a boy, but this is going to be our first date and it has to be wonderful. The only thing I want biting me is Jack, not a bat or something."

Sensing that Sally was actually worried I decided to be more helpful. "I have been into those woods with Jack and there is nothing to worry about. Jack is like an Indian in there; you will be perfectly fine."

Sally, 100% girl, then said "I don't know what to wear."

"Probably a nice dress, low heels, Coppertone would be the right fragrance."

"I'm going to kill you!" Then more laughter.

"Just wear what you would if you were walking with him to the drug store, or better yet, ask Jack."

"I will; what else can I do but be a good sport and hope for the best. He said that we would have a picnic. If the whole thing is a disaster I will make him promise to let me plan our next date."

"You are assuming there will be a second date."

With that Sally stood up and held both of my hands. Looking me in the eyes she said "He's the only boy for me Carl. You know that, right?"

"Yes, I know that."

With a smile Sally said "I can still see a scar from when my head hit your cheek"

"That's because I wanted a scar and picked the scab. When is the big date?"

"Sunday. I will give you a full report if I come back alive." Pause; smirk. "Well, maybe not too full a report."

And with one of her great smiles and a giggle she was off.

Chapter 12

Sunday turned out to be one of New England's lovely Indian Summer days; perfect for a picnic in the woods. Late in the afternoon there was a knock on our door. It was Sally; no phone call this time, I was going to get my report before she even went home.

She was wearing faded jeans, a sweatshirt (New Kensington Blasters), sneakers that were somewhat muddy and a baseball cap. I noticed that her hair was slightly damp. She headed directly to the living room couch, sprang onto it, and thumped the cushion next to her. I sat there as ordered.

Sally was as excited as I had ever seen her and she started right in. "Carl, that forest is beautiful, have you seen it? Oh yes, I remember he's taken you in. Aren't those blaze marks cute? We had a wonderful time just following them along and we talked about everything."

I asked about snakes.

"No, nothing." (Huge grin); "just us! We followed the trail. Jack had this big backpack and then we found a waterfall and a tiny pond."

Just to keep the conversation going I said "What a surprise." Sally continued: "Jack thought of everything. He had sandwiches and chips in his backpack and guess what, he even had cokes for us already cooling in the little pond; he'd put them there yesterday. He is so sweet! He had a blanket for us and everything was perfect."

Sally paused, shut her eyes and smiled at the recollection. I lead her back into conversation. "Then you packed up and walked back out?"

Sally turned her head slightly, touched a finger to her hair, and said "Carl, you can't tell anyone this."

"I wouldn't even tell my cat."

"You don't have a cat!"

"There might be one under the couch."

"If there was I would have sneezed by now. Please stop talking. I just had to kiss him. We were sitting on those Indian rocks and it was SHAZAM! Then he said that we should have a dip in the pond, in our birthday suits!"

"Naturally you were outraged."

"I know you are joking, best idea I ever heard. I told him to shut his eyes while I undressed but I was afraid that he might not peek so I pretended to step on something sharp and yelled."

This was getting me depressed. Sally went rattling on: "Don't look so shocked, I only let him see my haunch. Then I jumped in."

I had a good picture of the waterfall scene. "Let me guess; when Jack was undressing you peeked."

"I had my fingers over my eyes, but somehow two of my fingers wouldn't quite fit together."

I took a slow, deep breath and asked her to skip the rest of the details. Sally; always intuitive, put a hand on my knee and said "Carl, I want you to be as happy as I am, we will find you a girlfriend who will love you."

"Good; maybe a Hollywood starlet will show up, or your long lost twin."

Sally gave a light laugh and wrapped up the story of the big woods date by saying that they didn't spend much time in the water as it was freezing cold. They toweled off and got dressed under modest conditions and walked back to civilization arm and arm.

"At the end of the woods we kissed and I told him that if he loves me he has to call me tonight."

"What if he forgets?"

Sally got up, saying that she had to get home. At the door she turned and said "He won't forget; he's hooked!"

Chapter 13

The school year rolled on. Sally and I went to all the home football games, which both of us enjoyed regardless of which team won. When Jack was in the games he seemed to be able to make all the hard catches but drop most of the easy ones. Sally was the perfect fan-slash- girlfriend; delighted with his catches and amused by his bobbles.

When Christmas vacation was about to begin Nimble Nancy was allowed a short break from the Ski Academy so she was at home with Jack and Mr. Hathaway. One afternoon while I was at their house and hanging out with Jack, Nancy wanted to show us the workout equipment she had arranged for Mr. Hathaway to set up for her in the garage.

The garage had originally been a barn so there was plenty of room for her exercise equipment: weights of various sorts, a low padded bench, a very large ball, and something attached to a wall that looked like half of a stepladder. I asked her what it was supposed to be.

"It's for abdominal work; like this" and with that she grabbed hold of the sides, whipped her legs up above her head so that she was upside down facing out, and hooked her ankles through a canvas loop near the top rung. She then let go with her hands, clasped them behind her head, and started doing vertical sit-ups, giving me a view of her pale and cute tummy. I told her to stop before she ruptured something.

With a laugh she unhooked her feet and somersaulted down on to the barn floor. "Carl, I do that hundreds of times a day up at the academy. How about this?"

She then put her hands on top of the large ball and hopped up on it, balanced there like a mountain goat. Then, singing one of those oddly catching songs from Sesame Street, she started shifting her weight from one foot to the other.

This looked to be nearly impossible and also dangerous and I told her so. "Nancy are you crazy; you are going to fall!'

Misquoting Dr. Seuss, and giggling, Nancy replied "Have no fear little fish I will not let you fall as I hop all around while I'm up on this ball!"

Jack didn't seem to be concerned by this but I was. I got as close to the ball as I dared and held up my hand. "Please, I'm worried, come down."

"I will if you make me a promise."

"What?"

"I'll tell you later."

"Okay, anything, just come down."

I had said the magic words. With that she sprang off the ball, lightly catching my hand as she did. Turning towards me and with a big smile she said "You are going to take me to the Christmas dance!"

I was horrified and wordless. She had to be talking about the school Christmas dance, which was socially a big deal there at North Overshoe high school. I have no idea what my face looked like at that moment but it certainly amused Jack, who was convulsed with laughter.

What had I done? I had never been to a dance, had never even had a date, and my only dancing experience had been back in sixth grade; eight of the worst hours of my life, forced to attend Miss Prudence's dancing school, from which I should have been expelled due to total ineptitude.

All I could say was "But I don't know how to dance."

Jack was still close to tears of laughter but Nancy, who was still holding on to my hand, had turned serious. "Carl, everyone can sing and everyone can dance. What you mean is that you can't dance well. We can fix that with a little practice."

"How about a movie instead?"

"NO! We're going to the dance! You promised."

With this Nancy managed to look both stubborn and hurt at the same time. I had a doom-like fear of failure, but a promise is a promise.

"Okay, the dance it is but I will probably step on your toes all night."

Nancy stepped in front of me, and with one of her clear eyed direct looks said "Carl, do you like me?'

"Yes, of course I do. The problem isn't you it's the dancing."

"Carl, remember when you couldn't ski. I took you up on the Tote Road trail and we found out that you COULD ski?"

I had to smile. She was right.

Chapter 14

For the next few days I would spend some time at the Hathaway's house learning how to dance with Nancy. We started with the basic box step, a term (but not the steps) that I remembered from my misspent hours at Miss Prudence's. I was a nervous wreck when we began.

Nancy had found a long-playing record of rumbas for us to use as practice. We started out side by side doing the 'slow-quick-quick-slow' routine. I eventually relaxed a bit. Mr. Hathaway was at work and Jack was under strict orders to stay far away from us. Before we quit for the day I was doing well enough to be able to dance with Nancy; holding her stiffly in the approved position; left hand flat across the base of her spine, right hand holding her left hand up about at chin level.

By the end of our second session we had mastered the underarm turn. Up would go my right hand and Nancy, nimble as always, would glide under our raised arms and end up back at the starting point. It was the Old Tote Road revisited; I could do a basic dance; at least with Nancy I could.

Next; and thankfully last, came Swing. In a way it was easier, just one, two, rock-step, over and over. Somewhat to my amazement she had me able to pull off two maneuvers, the Sugar-Push and something where she went from my right side to my left side, then back to where we started from.

Still I had questions. What if the band doesn't cooperate and play rumbas and swing for example? And, horror of horrors, what if some guy wants to cut in and leaves me to dance with a girl who is unaware of my limited portfolio of dance moves?

Nancy was reassuring. "We will not be dancing every dance, just a few, and only the ones we are comfortable with. As for the cutting in, I doubt if it will happen but if someone tries I will just smile a big smile and say that you promised that you would only dance with me."

She went on: "Anyway we won't be staying at the dance that long."

This was news to me, and good news at that. "Well, you seem to have thought everything out."

"Carl," she said, "I am a planner. Before I ski a mountain, I go all over it very slowly and carefully. In fact, if I can I will walk down it before there is any snow just to see exactly what the topography is. I hear skiers talk all the time about attacking the mountain. I want to befriend it. Most of the other skiers at the academy get by just on talent. Not me, I'm going to make the Olympics and I won't get there by cutting corners."

I was looking at a very determined girl. I asked her why we were going to all the bother of teaching me entry level dancing if we were not going to stay at the dance for very long. What was her plan in that regard?

Smiling a puckish smile, she made things clear. "Oh, I just want us to strut our stuff a little and let everyone know that we're around. Then you can walk me home."

One surprise after another! "Are we going to the dance in sneakers?"

"Nope, here is what I think we should do. One of your parents brings you to pick me up and takes us to the dance in our dancing clothes. We also have walking home clothes in bags that we take in with us. When we are ready to leave we change in the bathrooms, leave our dancing stuff in your locker, you walk me home, and my dad will drive you back to your house. What do you think about that?"

That was the question of the day; what DID I think of the whole 'First date and going to the Christmas Dance with Nancy Hathaway' plan? After all the entire evening had been Nancy's idea from start to finish and I had been swept along like a leaf in a high wind. I thought for a few seconds and then said "Want to know what I would like to change?"

I was then on the receiving end of Nancy's total attention grey-eyed stare: "What?"

Smiling and with my palms up at shoulder height I sprinkled my holy water on the plan: "Nothing!"

That tease got me a pretend kick on a shin and she walked me towards the door. As I was leaving she told me that this was going to be her first date too and asked if I had known that.

Not only had I not known that, I had not even thought about it. "Well, it will be a breakthrough for both of us. Remember to pack something warm for the walk home."

"Don't worry about that, I am a girl of the mountains!"

Everything considered and taking into account several things that could have gone wrong but didn't, our outing to the Christmas Dance followed Nancy's plan fairly well. I showed up at the appointed time looking just the way my mother thought a high school freshman going to a dance should look; navy blazer, gray slacks, unruly hair slicked into submission by a healthy slug of Dr. Ellis's Hair Trainer, bag of warm clothes to change into for the walk back, and, thanks entirely to my mother's vision, a flower thing for Nancy to slip onto her wrist.

Nancy, I had to admit, looked nice. Black sleeveless dress with skinny straps that was fairly tight above her waist and loose from there down, shoes that blended in with the dress, and a string of pearls that turned out to be a legacy from her mother. She looked less like Jack's younger sister and more like a pretty girl that I was lucky to be going out with.

Once at the dance we sat with Jack and Sally. One of my lesser worries was that we would be sort of social wallflowers, but any time you were with Jack and Sally you could count on there being plenty of kids around; basking in Sally's glow. Sally Bain at a high school dance was the roundest peg in the roundest hole; absolutely beautiful and in high spirits.

Our dancing followed Nancy's plan; picking our spots we box stepped our way through two rumbas. The underarm turns went almost as practiced, just one minor glitch that Nancy smoothed over, and two swings.

I almost enjoyed the swings. Okay, I did enjoy them. Nancy was such a natural athlete that she took all the attention away from me, which was just what I wanted.

After our fourth and final dance we sat with Jack and Sally for a few minutes. Then Nancy gave me a nudge and asked if I was ready to change and go. As we said our goodbyes Sally gave me a hug and whispered in my ear that I had done great; adding "Handsome too!"

She was stretching the truth of course, but still I was feeling pretty good about myself as I changed into my walking-Nancy-home togs.

We hung our battle gear in my locker (New Kensington High School had excellent full length lockers for each student) and set off towards the Hathaway's; Nancy wearing corduroy pants with a ski jacket and cap. I was suitably bundled.

We chatted for a while about the dance and the kids that we had seen there and talked with. We both agreed that the attraction between Jack and Sally was made to last. Then Nancy asked me if I had any plans for the summer.

Actually, I did; or at least I knew what I was not going to do. I told her that if Miss Grant asked me to work for her again, bouncing around Grant Holdings like a ping pong ball, I was going to politely say no.

Nancy, always one to get to the bottom of things, asked why, seeing as it would clearly lead me toward bigger and better things within the Grant empire.

Not that I had given much thought to summer activities, but I told her that Miss Grant's assignments seemed to be more suited to someone older. I thought a better summer job for me would be selling burgers and ice cream at the local drug store lunch counter.

Nancy approved of that idea, saying that it would be more fun selling ice cream cones than sorting gravel. "Besides," said Nancy, "Miss Grant isn't going any place, you could always work for her in another year or two."

We continued the walk. There was almost no traffic and we were warm enough in our winter jackets. After a minute or so of comfortable silence Nancy said that her future plans were somewhat in doubt. Speaking in her usual matter-of-fact way she told me that she was being considered for the junior National Ski Team. That team had a lower age limit of 16 and Nancy would be only 14, but she was already a better downhill skier than any girl at the Academy and the coaches of the junior national team wanted her to be a skier full time.

I could see that this would be a very big step indeed. I asked her about schooling.

Nancy told me that they would provide tutors, which were on the staff anyway for the older team members. She said "This is what I have been wanting ever since I first put on skis, but now that it might actually happen I'm scared."

After a few steps taken in silence I asked her what she was afraid of, would the ski slopes be steeper?

"Maybe; I don't know, but it isn't that. The Ski Academy is mostly about skiing but it is still a school. There are teachers, classrooms, bedtimes; there are rules. If I join the junior national team it will be like a full-time job. I'd be traveling a lot and I wouldn't be home much at all."

"You're not home much as it is."

"Yes, but this is still a big step. Those team coaches are very intense. I feel like I will have to grow up in a hurry."

"Could you quit if you want to?"

"Oh sure, but if I say I will do it I'm not quitting. I like to do what I say I am going to do"

"Okay, I know your dream is making the Olympic Team. Could you say no to the Junior Team and still make the Olympics?"

"I don't think so–no. I have ability but I would need training, the best coaching, and a lot more experience. I need to ski against the best; world class girls."

At that point I suddenly felt sorry for Nancy. Besides being a ski prodigy, to me she was my best friend's little sister. A girl who called her father Daddy and had been seen wearing bunny rabbit slippers. It seemed she was about to be yanked away and into an adult world. All I could think of to say was that it was a big step. Not very profound.

"Do you think I should go? Jack says I should; Daddy says to wait a year or two."

"I think the skier should go and the girl should stay"

Nancy the girl put her head on my shoulder for a step or two as an answer. She then asked if I wanted her to go. I told her of course not, as there was no one else around for me to take to the Spring Dance; not that I knew if there even was such a thing.

By then we were almost to her house. Before we went in, and while I was worrying about what to do in the way of concluding our date, Nancy solved the problem for me by giving me a nice hug and a lip-kiss. Then, while I was still stunned, she gently pulled both of my ears, said that she had been wanting to do that all night, and with a big wink ran into the house.

Mr. Hathaway gave me a ride home and asked how I had liked the dance. I told him that things had gone well but that his daughter had pulled my ears.

I had never heard Mr. Hathaway laugh as hard as he did then. It was infectious and I joined in the mirth. As he let me out at our house he told me that it was a very good sign when a girl pulls a boy's ears, and with another laugh he drove away.

Chapter 15

The remainder of our freshman year passed uneventfully. Late in May Miss Grant summoned me to her home office, this time without my father riding shotgun. Miss Grant asked me if I wanted something to drink and I asked for a Coke.

No" said my hostess, "Have tea, it's better for you."

"If you were going to have me drink tea then why did you offer me a choice?"

"I wanted to give you a chance to make the right choice. When you didn't I took corrective action."

I had to laugh and shake my head. I did not really care what I drank and besides, she was almost always right. Tea was served.

After she had a sip she told me that she was going to review her plan for my summer work. That was just what I had expected; I was ready for a counter attack with a plan of my own. I had already spoken with the owner of the downtown drug store about working at the lunch counter and he had agreed to take me on. I was looking forward to serving ice cream to my fellow New Kensington Blasters, and how hard could cooking hamburgers and making chicken salad sandwiches be? I had a mental image of me passing butterscotch sundaes to an assortment of pretty girls.

If I had expected resistance from Miss Grant I was mildly surprised. With one of her level, all knowing looks she said "I see."

I had come to like Miss Grant a great deal, plus I didn't want to burn my bridges, which, unburnt, might lead to bigger and better things within Grant Holdings at some future time. I clarified my reasoning.

"I liked my experiences working for you last summer but, for this summer at least, I want to mix with the drug store crowd and learn the sandwich and ice cream trade."

Miss Grant raised her eyebrows and twisted her right wrist and hand from side to side, indicating that she could see both sides, another summer of learning things about the workings of Grant Holdings versus burgers and ice cream.

She then cocked her head slightly to the side and said "Are you interested in hearing what I had in mind for you?"

There was only one answer for that question of course, but beside the obvious 'Yes' suddenly I was curious to learn what she had up her sleeve. I replied "I am; please tell me."

"Oh, never mind, it's not important"

This was a Miss Grant first; she was actually teasing me! Two can play that game. I looked as shrewd as I possibly could as I replied "I'll give you a nickel."

"All right then, I'll tell you. I was going to have you get your feet wet in real estate."

"Real estate; what do you mean?"

Never a lady to tolerate foolish questions, she replied "What do you mean what do I mean? You know what real estate is don't you?"

"You wanted me to sell houses?" I was nonplussed.

Miss Grant clarified her thoughts. She explained that the previous year the holding company had sold several acres to a technology company, which was building a headquarters for itself and that once it was ready the company would be re-locating there from it's current location, which was near route 128 west of Boston.

This was a fairly small company, and New Kensington was big enough to be able to handle the infrastructure needs and housing demands of the company and it's employees.

However, the reasons behind the re-location, which included high taxes and housing costs near the Boston area, were not unique to this particular company. More would likely follow, but only if New Kensington could handle the inflow.

And that would be the itch which Grant Holdings would be scratching. Certainly it owned enough land to meet all needs; many thousands of acres.

Chapter 16

But I went my own way that summer. I worked flexible hours at the drugstore, sometimes from early morning to just past the busy lunchtime and other days at different hours, depending on who might be going on vacation or be out sick. The job was not difficult. In fact the reason that I had the job was that a kid could do it.

My pal Jack was helping out at the hardware store as needed, and Sally would pour some of her sunshine on both of our work stations quite often. Mostly she hung around with her girlfriends during the days. Of course she and Jack spent plenty of time together; movies and just plain boyfriend/girlfriend things.

However, the major news that summer was that Mr. Hathaway found a woman! So far as anyone knew, Mr. Hathaway had not been involved in any way with anyone since Mrs. Hathaway had passed on, so this was big news indeed, not only for Jack and Nancy but for the entire town.

Every year Mr. Hathaway would go to a trade show; always in a major city; New York, Chicago, Las Vegas, places such as those. I never knew anything about what went on at these conventions. I had no interest in knowing. If anyone had asked me I would have guessed that they learned the latest trends in sharpening saw blades and whatever might be new with screwdrivers.

This particular gettogether was in Seattle, not that it mattered where it was. What DID matter was that, as always, there were professionals on hand to do the many things that need to be done to assure that things run smoothly. In the case of this particular confab there was a team of four women handling the details. These women, known as event planners, were led by Kathleen McKay; known to all as Kathy.

During this and similar events these women worked very long hours and were always around keeping the ship on course, so to speak. Several times Kathy and Mr. Hathaway had short conversations, and towards the conclusion of the convention Mr. Hathaway managed to get Kathy aside and asked her if she could find time to spend an hour or two with him.

The answer was some version of thanks but I can't. Kathy did not have any time to spare while the show was still going on, and as soon as it ended she had just enough time to catch her plane back to Chicago, where her office was.

Mr. Hathaway then surprised her by asking if he could catch the same plane and sit beside her for the flight. Kathy describes her reaction this way: "I have been to so many of these trade shows and there are always these lover boys; half of them with wives at home, who try to charm the pants off me. Then along comes this hardware guy, somehow reminding me of Gary Cooper, who wants to ride home with me.

"I was so used to brushing these guys off I almost did it this time too, but then I thought, why not? I said if you are serious, sure."

They had a fruitful conversation on the plane and agreed to have dinner together that night. At dinner Mr. Hathaway asked her what her plans were for the next day, and when Kathy said that she had a day to run errands and get her clothes clean before she had to return to work in her office the following day, he said that if she would wash the clothes he would fold. Before he returned home they had agreed on a time for Kathy to come visit him in New Kensington.

Mr. Hathaway told Jack and Nancy at dinner a few nights after he was back from the convention that he had met a woman that he liked very much while he was in Seattle and that she would soon be coming for a visit; staying in the Hathaway's guest room.

If Mr. Hathaway had been concerned over how his children would react to the big news he should not have been; Jack and Nancy were delighted; Jack pumping his dad's hand and Nancy hugging his neck. They wanted to hear all about this mystery woman from the midwest.

Chapter 17

Kathy flew into Boston on a Thursday afternoon where she was met by Mr. Hathaway, and together they drove back to New Kensington. Before she left on Sunday to return to Chicago she had charmed Jack (who she later said was a pushover), Nancy, who started out more skeptical and ended up totally on board, and everyone else that she met during her short visit; including me.

Kathy was a little above average in height, slim and trim. She had medium brown hair cut short, light brown eyes, never seemed to be wearing makeup, (Sally later told me that Kathy wore makeup but that only another girl could see it) and had a knack for understanding what was going on in an instant. That must have been a very helpful trait to have for a person who earned a living by keeping conventions on track.

It turned out that Kathy was not from Chicago. She had grown up outside Dallas, gone to Cornell, and then taken a job in New York working for an advertising agency. While there she, in her words, got whirlwinded out of her senses and into marriage by a good-looking wordsmith who turned out to be all hat and no cattle (a Texas expression no doubt.) Almost before she knew it she was 26, divorced, and working at a job she could barely tolerate in a city that she disliked intensely.

It had not been much of a switch from the advertising business to event planning and coordinating, and Kathy found Chicago and it's people to be more to her liking. She had been there and doing that for the past 6 years.

When Nancy, always direct, asked Kathy if she had other boyfriends since leaving New York Kathy had said yes, but although they all looked different, eventually they all ended up seeming the same.

Apparently Kathy and Nancy had gone on a short trip to a grocery store together, which gave them time for girl talk. Nancy had then said that her dad was not at all like other men, and Kathy had looked at her and replied "I don't think so either; that's why I am here."

The Saturday afternoon of Kathy's visit was a beautiful August day. I was working at the drug store and Nancy came in and sat at the counter. This was a mild surprise, as Nancy's days were always organized and she seldom took time for loitering at the lunch counter.

I asked her what she was doing and if she wanted ice cream or something. It turned out that Mr. Hathaway had taken Kathy for a hike into the woods. Nancy had gotten the impression that it would be fine with them if no one was home when they got back.

I fixed Nancy a dish of coffee ice cream; her go-to flavor. She tapped the bottom of her spoon on the ice cream and said "Kathy seems really smart and she's pretty."

I asked if something was bothering her and the answer was yes. "I hope things work out between them and I think they will but I don't want Dad to be hurt."

I asked how old her father was and Nancy said that he was 40. Then after a pause she said, "I guess he can figure things out for himself. Anyway, I won't be around."

I knew that was true; Nancy was set to join the National Junior Ski team at their headquarters on the first of the month.

Chapter 18

As things turned out Nancy's concern was unfounded. Mr. Hathaway was not only not hurt, he seemed to be enchanted by Kathy and the feeling was mutual. Romance was in full bloom in fact. Mr. Hathaway soon made a weekend visit to Chicago and Kathy came back to New Kensington several times. She even took to wearing a New Kensington 'Blasters' sweatshirt; she was all in!

There was a proposal, an acceptance (we were told her exact words were "Hell yes"), and they were married the following spring in Chicago; the location chosen, according to Kathy, because it was mutually inconvenient for her family and friends in Dallas and Mr. Hathaway's New Kensington followers.

Sally summarized the courtship this way: "Once he took her into that enchanted forest it was all downhill; there was no other way things could have turned out."

Kathy left her job and jumped into life in New Kensington, where she hit the ground in full stride. The bed in the master bedroom was replaced before they were back from their honeymoon. Sally's comment: "That was a given; the bed was toast."

All of the rugs went bye-bye as well as a good part of the furniture, and the windows got a total makeover. Kathy wanted to have more light in the house, pointing out that things were dark enough here in North Overshoe (she loved my nickname for her new home town) during the winter without making things worse.

The kitchen escaped mostly intact, other than a new fridge. Kathy was bemused by the magnitude of the late Mrs. Hathaway's array of cooking paraphernalia. She remarked to Jack: "Is there anything that she didn't have? Was there anything that she didn't cook? I don't even know what half these things are, let alone how to use them."

While this was going on Kathy was active on another front; she put herself in charge of modernizing the hardware store's record keeping system, which was still being done as it had always been done; that is by hand entries in ledgers and on 3 by 5 cards. Her dry comment; "Where is the ink well and the goose quill pen?"

Mr. Hathaway could not have been happier with these changes, saying that he knew the house needed a facelift but did not know where to start. As for the bookkeeping changes, he had always thought record keeping to be the worst part of owning the store.

But that was by no means all that Kathy had in mind. The lady who worked at the store ringing up the sales was a retired school teacher named Mrs. Gurnsey. She was well into her 70's and had arthritic feet. Sensing that the situation called for diplomacy, she spoke with Jack (thinking that anything coming from Jack would be less official than it would be coming from his father) asking if he thought there was a way that she could ease into Mrs. Gurnsey's position without creating ill will.

Because Jack sometimes worked at the store he knew the old lady well and agreed to feel her out about the possibility of a retirement. Mrs. Gurnsey quickly said that she had been thinking of finding a way to cut back but had not wanted to leave Jack's father without a replacement on hand.

And so it came to pass that Mrs. Gurnsey would work the cash register for the first 3 hours for 5 days a week. That left Kathy's mornings mostly free to manage the house, run errands, and also to do bookkeeping. In the afternoons she would work behind the counter at the hardware store.

Chapter 19

Time passed. I spent another summer working at the drugstore, but only after Mrs. Grant convinced me to pledge that I would work for Grant Holdings thereafter. Jack and Sally continued to be almost inseparably, and Jack was dropping fewer passes on the football field.

I liked the drugstore job; low key suited me just fine, and I got to know quite a few of the townspeople. I met housewives buying suntan oil, teenagers goofing off, and many blue-collar workers as they took work breaks. This is the way I came to know the town's police force, and even the chief; Chief Hale; an interesting man who had previously been a homicide detective in Newark. He once told me that compared to some of the things he had seen in New Jersey, New Kensington seemed like Disney World.

We did not see much of Nancy. She always came home for Christmas and usually for one or two other brief visits during the year. The rest of the time she was with her ski team and in a state of semi-perpetual winter as the team often went wherever there was snow.

Just before Christmas of our sophomore year Jack gave me a heads up; Nancy had a Christmas present for me. The implication was clear, I had better be sure to have a gift for her. The best idea I could come up with was a world atlas, which I had the store wrap in seasonal colors.

Fortunately Sally intervened. "You are giving her a book? Do you think she is a librarian?" With her guidance we picked out some perfume for her, although I still kept the atlas to give her.

On Christmas Day I was invited to join the Hathaway's for a late afternoon dinner. That dovetailed nicely with my family's tradition of having our holiday meal around noon.

Kathy had the house beautifully decorated inside and out; it had been a huge hit at the yearly Hathaway Hardware Christmas party. Trust an event planner to get Christmas right.

After the meal Kathy sent Nancy and me into the living room, where the tree stood aglow; and in what I now clearly see was a pre-arrangement, Jack; with Sally naturally, and Mr. and Mrs. Hathaway stayed behind to clear the table.

That is when Nancy and I exchanged our gifts. Wisely, I gave her the atlas first, followed by the perfume.

Nancy liked the atlas, pointing out some of the places her team had been, but the perfume was the bigger hit. She smelled it with strong approval, dabbed some behind her ears and asked me if I liked it on her, leaning in toward me as she did.

When I leaned in for a whiff Nancy gave me a kiss and then said quietly "Thank you Carl". She then added "I like it when you blush".

I certainly didn't and told her it was embarrassing. Nancy smiled slightly and said that was because I hadn't been kissing girls, and she didn't want that to change.

I then opened her gift to me. Beneath the wrap was a medium sized box. Inside it, wrapped carefully in tissue was a carving of some sort of bird, the likes of which I had never seen. The bird; now mine, was bright scarlet from it's head to the midpoint of it's body where the colors changed on a diagonal line; where the wings were. From there down the bird was black. The carving came with a base and a short stick which was to be stuck into a hole in the bird's scarlet belly with the other end in the base. It was a beautiful bird, the question was: what was it?

Nancy told me that the team had spent a day in Peru and that is where she had seen it in an art gallery window and bought it for me. The carving was of a Cock-of-the-Rock; the Peruvian national bird.

After this she asked if I liked it, and the truth was that I had taken an immediate shine to the bird, and I told her so.

"That's good Carl. I want you to put it where you will see it every day. I am always traveling and I want you to remember me."

I had no answer for that and none seemed to be expected. Nancy slid close to me, my arm found itself over her shoulders, and together we used the atlas to look up places where her team would be going in the coming year.

Chapter 20

That spring, as expected, I was asked to come to Sycamore Hall. I had no doubt that Miss Grant remembered my promise to work for her in the coming summer and I was curious to learn what she had in mind for me.

Naturally we started with tea being served. In truth, I had consumed so many cokes that I had made for myself at the drug store fountain that I had come to prefer water. I was fine with tea.

Miss Grant's desk was as impressive as everything else in Sycamore Hall; large, dark and, based on my visits, the surface was usually close to bare.

That day was no exception; however, we were seated on the other side of the desk and across the room in matching leather chairs with a low table in front of us. She came straight to her desired topic.

"Now as you certainly will recall I had wanted to get you acquainted with the real estate business and it is increasingly important to our holding company and to this community that we not fall behind in this."

She then paused, reaching down beside her chair to bring up a rolled-up map which she spread out on the table.

The map was of New Kensington as well as the surrounding area and was colored according to what sort of development the zoning code allowed. Residential, business, industrial, agricultural, and so forth.

After securing the map's edges with two books she continued: "That first tech company that we spoke of earlier is now up and running here." An elegantly manicured finger helped me locate the spot, not that I needed it to be pointed out; everyone in town was aware of the new building and the cerebral appearing men and women who worked there.

She leaned back slightly and turned towards me. "Carl, when my ancestors started here this was a frontier. There was the quarry, the town; primitive then, a road to get in and out, and a rail spur to transport our granite. Over the years the quarry prospered and we used the profits to diversify our business interests. We started the bank, and some of the businesses that you know in town. When the early timber companies were finished clear cutting the forests near here and to our north we bought tens of thousands of acres from them for almost nothing. Now all that is reforested. We do some timbering ourselves now; not a lot. It is a commodity type business and the profit margins are not exciting"

She paused again and seemed to be reflecting. She was turning out to be quite a historian and I felt drawn in.

"My grandfather Malcolm had been investing in stocks for many years and so had his father; my great-grandfather Roy Grant. These investments were very profitable. However, my grandfather smelled trouble in 1928 and liquidated all of the family's stock portfolio. Our bank did the same, switching into short term U.S. government bonds.

"In brief, grandfather had battened down the hatches. Within a year the stock market crashed and a long and terrible economic depression followed.

"Our bank had loaned money to quite a few of our local businesses and also had mortgages on a large number of homes and farms here and in the surrounding area. Many of these businessmen, homeowners, and farmers became unable to meet the required loan terms and mortgage payments and the bank was forced to foreclose; meaning that the bank then became to owner of the businesses, homes, and farms. This was happening all across the United States. Banks were financially pinched too and had no choice other than to sell these foreclosed properties on courthouse steps for pennies on the dollar."

Talk about bringing history to life! Having been born in 1910 Miss Grant remembered these events with her usual cut and dried clarity. It was as if I was listening to a war veteran describing firsthand the landing at Normandy.

Looking now towards the fireplace but no doubt seeing the past as it had unfolded, Miss Grant continued.

"But our bank was so strongly capitalized that we had choices as to what to do about defaulted loans and mortgages. Grandfather Malcolm instructed our bank president to call in the homeowner, business owner, or farmer for a talk. Could they continue to make payments if the interest rate was reduced? Did they even want to try to stick it out until better times? Were they interested in staying on as renters if the bank took title to the property? The townspeople found our bank; which had always been strict in regard to lending standards, to be very flexible in dealing with problem loans."

I pictured this as an analogy. Harvard was difficult to get accepted into, but once a student was admitted the school did it's best to keep them there through graduation.

Miss Grant's tutorial went on: "The bank examiners did not like any bank to hold assets that were not easily liquidated, and so my grandfather often bought foreclosed properties from the bank. All of the homes he bought were sold when the economy improved and so were many of the downtown buildings, although we still own several.

"The farms did not recover as well, which is why we still own about a dozen. Even so they have turned out to be successful investments because as the town has expanded the farmland has become much more valuable for development. We have never forced any farming family to give up farming if they want to continue, but as time has passed newer generations have wanted different lifestyles. In this area family farming is a dying business."

And then she shocked me by turning directly towards me and after a pause said "And so is our quarry."

"I thought the quarry was your main business."

"Oh no. When skyscrapers became popular in big cities granite could not compete with steel. Granite is limited in the amount of weight it can support. Also, once a breakwater is in place it will last for over 100 years. Our labor costs continue to increase and our main markets are limited by transportation expense. We will keep the quarry open because it is the town's main employer, but so far as the holding company is concerned we could close it tomorrow and not miss it."

I was having difficulty getting a grip on what she had just said. Before I could get a word out Miss Grant told me not to interrupt.

"I didn't."

"No but you were about to and I haven't told you about how we acquired the First National Bank of Commonwealth Avenue."

"In Boston? You own a Boston bank?"

"There you go interrupting again."

I had not interrupted her before but I didn't want to quibble so I apologized and asked her to continue, which she did.

"As I said, our bank here was rock solid financially due to my grandfather's good judgement and sound business practices. However, the majority of America's banks had been far too aggressive in their lending. When the depression hit, many of these poorly managed banks had to close their doors, which made things worse for the country. In 1932 the chairman of the Federal Reserve Bank of Boston asked grandfather to come to Boston. He went on to say that the First National Bank of Commonwealth Avenue was insolvent and would have to close it's doors within a week unless the Federal Reserve Bank could work out a rescue plan.

"Grandfather agreed to come down to Boston and he brought me along with him. During the train ride Grandfather seemed to be in an unusually good mood.

"He told me that the Federal Reserve Bank of Boston was part of the United States of America's government and had almost unlimited powers when it came to bank supervision. It's chairman, Quincey Hopkins, was faced with a very messy situation. The Commonwealth Bank (as it was called) was one of the biggest banks in Boston; in all of New England in fact. The bank was insolvent, the books were a mess, and the depositors were starting to get wind of the situation; lining up to withdraw their savings. If nothing was done, and done quickly, the Federal Reserve Bank of Boston would have to step in and take control. Mr. Quincey Hopkins did not want to do this because he had already taken over several other banks and had his hands full. Besides; he was basically a lazy bureaucrat.

"Grandfather surmised that Mr. Quincy Hopkins planned to offer him what would be called something like "The chance of a lifetime"; the opportunity to acquire the First National Bank of Commonwealth Avenue."

At this point Miss Grant paused again. A predatory smile on her face as she strolled down memory lane.

She then continued: "I was 22 at that time and had already learned a great deal about my grandfather's way of doing business. I knew he wouldn't fall into such an obviously bottomless financial pit. I asked grandfather what he had in mind.

"I will be willing to take the problem bank off his hands said my grandfather, on the following conditions: first, the Federal Reserve Bank will take over the First National Bank of Commonwealth Avenue and simultaneously sell it to our bank, New Kensington National Bank for one dollar. All of the Commonwealth shareholders get nothing and all of their bondholders get nothing, so we will be buying the bank with no debt and no other shareholders to answer to.

"Second, the Federal Reserve Bank agrees to buy back any of the Commonwealth's loans at book value at any time as we see fit.

"Third, I will choose a new chief Executive officer to run Commonwealth, his salary to be paid for the first three years by the Federal Reserve.

"Fourth, all of Commonwealth's deposits are guaranteed by the Federal Reserve Bank. Nobody who put their hard-earned money into what will then be our bank will lose a penny (pause) even if it wasn't hard- earned."

Shaking her head in admiration of her grandfather's outrageous terms, Miss Grant finished up with this summary: "That afternoon grandfather and I met Mr. Hopkins in his stately office overlooking the Charles River. As grandfather had predicted the deal of a lifetime was for our bank to acquire the First National Bank of Commonwealth Avenue for ten million dollars plus 50 percent of the stock of New Kensington bank. Grandfather calmly listened to

Mr. Hopkins finish explaining what a sweetheart deal he was being offered. He concluded by saying that he had to have an answer by morning, otherwise the Federal Reserve Bank would have to take over the Commonwealth bank at five O'clock on Friday."

I could not stay quiet much longer. I had a mental picture of young Miss Cora Grant waiting for her grandfather's reply; which was simply this; according to Miss Grant: "I'm sorry Quincy, we won't be able to do that."

Mr. Quincy Hopkins had apparently expected some horse trading, and after pointing out the many benefits of his generous offer he with great reluctance lowered the cash amount of the purchase to eight million dollars. When grandfather Grant again turned him down, Mr. Hopkins opened the door that the Grants had been waiting for by asking what Grandfather Grant had in mind.

Miss Grant's words again: "As grandfather listed the conditions under which he would take over the troubled bank Mr. Hopkins became agitated and ended up standing open mouthed; eyes wide in shock."

"Are you insane? You get the bank for a dollar? The building alone is worth millions! And you want us to cover all the loan losses?"

Apparently, this ranting went on for quite a while and at one point Mr. Hopkins; Boston aristocrat and Mayflower descendant, threw his cigar across the room, scattering ashes on Miss Grant's skirt as it tumbled through the air. Finally, exhausted and frustrated by grandfather Grant's unwillingness to change his acquisition offer other than to lower the percentage of the loan buybacks from 100% to 80%, Mr. Hopkins said this: "I will have to talk to Washington about this. I don't know what they will say. They are going to kill me."

Standing to leave, and with Miss Grant at his side, Mr. Malcolm Grant had this to say: "They are going to agree to our terms. It keeps the bank off their books and out of their hair. They have nothing to lose. Please let us know when you hear the decision. We are staying at the Ritz and will be leaving in the morning."

What a story! I asked Miss Grant why her grandfather had agreed to lower the repurchase price of the bad loans. "Because grandfather knew that the Commonwealth Bank had loan loss reserves that would be more than sufficient to cover those losses. He wanted Mr. Hopkins to be able to tell his Washington bosses that he had fought us tooth and nail and that he had barely managed to pull that concession out of us."

Miss Grant and her grandfather had dinner that night in the cavernous main dining room of the Ritz overlooking the park; having already received word that their terms of acquisition had been accepted. As they reviewed the meeting with Mr. Quincy Hopkins and the negotiations, Miss Grant had commented that she thought Mr. Hopkins might have a heart attack when he heard her grandfather's terms.

At that her wise mentor replied: "Cora, most of that was an act. He was relieved that we would take over the bank and would have agreed to almost any offer we made. Then after a pause and with a quiet chuckle he added I thought throwing the cigar was a nice touch."

I asked Miss Grant if the Boston bank was still a part of Grant Holdings. "Oh no," she answered. "We were able to get it back to a profitable state fairly quickly and over time it's deposits and profits increased steadily. Eventually a large California bank that wanted to establish a presence on the east coast made a purchase offer to us that was so attractive that we agreed to sell. Overall, we did well." (another pause, followed by her punchline) "It isn't often we get to turn a one dollar investment into a profit that was well into nine figures."

In the silence that followed I did my mental math. Hmm; one thousand dollars is four figures. A million dollars is seven figures. Good heavens; they had made a profit somewhere in the hundreds of millions on the bank sale!

Miss Grant seemed to have been reading my mind. She then asked if I was ready to hear what her summer plans for me were.

Ready? I was almost drooling. I answered; "You mentioned real estate?"

Chapter 21

Thinking back, I realize that until that meeting with Miss Grant I had been just going along with things when I had agreed to drift around some of her local businesses. Now it made sense; she sincerely intended for me to start learning what made her holding company tick. Furthermore; I wanted to learn about business. I was out of the ice cream cone field and into real estate.

That pivotal conversation took place in April. A few weeks later Jack asked me if I was game for another hike into the woods. My first reaction was "Why?"

In reply Jack told me that we would be going much deeper into the state forest and would be camping overnight at a spot where Indians had lived long ago. I told him that he was making it sound worse, not better.

"Are you scared to try something new?"

We were having lunch at school while this conversation was taking place so Sally, naturally, was with us, plus several of our other classmates were at our table and within earshot.

"Not so much scared as reluctant."

At this one of the nearby boys made the noise of a chicken clucking. Sally chimed in: "You should go Carl; you and Jack always have fun together."

"That's a record I'd like to protect; why don't you go?"

Sally had a ready excuse; "I can't, I'm addicted to flush toilets."

This, of course, brought a round of laughter from the table, including me. Potty humor always sold well within our lunch group. I gave in, saying I would go, but that I was going to bring my homework along. This was a fib and Jack and Sally knew it, but it might have confused some of the other kids who had been listening in. I had something of a reputation as a grind when it came to schoolwork but the truth was that I didn't find the work particularly difficult and I certainly was not enslaved by it. However, if some of my classmates wanted to think that I was a scholar, inclined to take homework into the forest, well that was fine with me.

Chapter 22

Our woods adventure started that Saturday morning, but before we left Jack and I spent some time putting our backpacks together; heavier things towards the bottom. Each of us had a map, a compass, and a police style whistle.

When I asked why I needed the map and compass, considering that I would be following Jack the whole time it was explained to me that they were in my pack only because I would be glad to have them in the unlikely event of our being separated. The whistles were along in case we got lost. They would save us from having to scream our lungs out when a search party tried to locate us.

Jack left a note at home, telling where we were going and when we expected to be back. As we made these preparations Jack told me the woodsman's creed; 'expect the best; plan for the worst.'

Although the spot we were heading for was only a few miles away by direct line the terrain was rugged and it took us several hours to get there; no blazed trail this time. Jack had only been to this Indian campground once before; with his father, and he wouldn't tell me much about it other than a brusque "You'll see when we get there."

I had learned to trust Jack, both because he was a natural in the forest and because he was a person who could always be counted on. I trudged along in his footsteps and let myself enjoy the wilderness.

Eventually we came to a stream, and after following it for 30 minutes or so we reached our target. A low ledge to our right rose up abruptly to a cliff about 50 feet or so in height, and the stream bent sharply away. Between the stream and the cliff there was a flat grassy area, with some rocky debris at the base of the cliff.

"Rule number one," said my guide, "Get the camp set up before it gets dark". Up went the pup tent, out came the air mattresses and sleeping bags. Then Jack assembled a collapsible shovel and started to dig a shallow trench around the tent. "A snake moat?" I questioned.

"Not quite, but if it happens to rain tonight we will be glad we did this; it will keep the water out of the tent."

Eventually we were settled in. A fire was laid (we had matches; none of this rubbing sticks together nonsense) and we had gathered plenty of dead branches to keep it going. I asked Jack why he had said that this had been an Indian campground. Jack lead me to the base of the cliff and had us clear back some of the debris, which would be scree to a geologist. Almost immediately we uncovered several shallow indentations. You could almost call them mini-caves. Neither of us could figure out what the Indians had used these for, but it must have been important if the Indians make the effort to chip them out of solid rock.

Then Jack told me that he and his father had found some broken pottery nearby, and also a few arrowheads. In fact, he started digging around in the area around the cliff base looking for some.

Anyone who has ever gone shelling knows how addictive this sort of searching can be and we each found several. Jack came in with the biggest, it must have been some sort of spear head.

But I claimed first prize; an arrowhead that was about an inch and a half long and seemingly made from flint. The shape was classic and, to my eyes at least, it was gem quality.

We started our dinner preparations around 5 that night. Jack had it all planned in advance. Baking potatoes (farsightedly wrapped in aluminum foil before we left civilization) and for each of us there was a steak. Jack had packed a small, lightweight metal grill which we balanced between two rocks near the fire. We cooked the steaks over hot coals that we raked out from the base of the fire. The potatoes were just pushed into the base of the campfire; we used a stick that was handy to turn them over and around once and that was it. Jack estimated that they would be about done in an hour and he was right, they were. Our utensils were forks and jackknives.

For dessert we had some Toll House cookies that Kathy had baked for us and we washed dinner down with tea that we drank from collapsible tin cups. The cookies had not survived the hike totally intact but they tasted fine in pieces. It may have been the best meal I ever had.

After dinner we sat by our campfire, which Jack had situated against the base of the cliff so that some of the heat would reflect back out towards us. The talk turned to girls; not that I had much to contribute in that specialized area. I asked Jack how things were going with Sally.

He shook his head "That girl," he said, "Has an uncanny way of getting me to do things that I don't want to do. Once she gets me laughing I always give in. Then I end up having a good time anyway. Once, just for the hell of it I held out and refused to go along. It was some sort of shopping thing."

"How did she take it?"

"Fine. She just looked a little disappointed, said she would see me later and headed off. I felt terrible; couldn't get over it. I ran to the store she had gone to and caught up with her. She came close to breaking my neck she hugged me so hard."

We sat quietly for a while. Then I said "Talk about beginner's luck, the first girlfriend you have turns out to be a world's record."

"She is, I don't even fantasize about other girls anymore."

"Hogwash!"

"Well, less than I used to."

Laughter around the campfire.

Then Jack turned the conversational spotlight on me. I had decided to break out of my solitary rut earlier that month and had arranged a date with a seemingly good-natured sophomore named Janie. He asked how the date had gone.

"How did it go? It went nowhere. She seemed terrified of me. It was as if she was glued to the opposite side door of the car."

"That couldn't have been good"

"It wasn't. Some date that was!"

Jack was sympathetic and suggested that I ask someone else out.

"I did, I asked Faith Barnes if she wanted to go out with me last Friday."

Faith Barnes was the class brain. Nothing but A's across the board, perfect penmanship, always had the correct answer ready for any sort of class question. Although she was not at all bad looking there was nothing eye catching about her and she did not seem to have any close friends.

Faith had short hair that was always exactly in place. She had a pale complexion and dressed conservatively; blouses starched, almost nun-like. I had no idea what her personality was like (assuming that she had one) and I doubt if anyone else in the school did either. My thinking was that she had to be totally unlike the seemingly good-natured Janie. After a mid-week school day I had managed to find a time when no one else was around and asked her if she would like to go out with me that Friday.

This was news to Jack; he wanted to know how things had gone, and I told him.

"She said that my asking her for a date was unexpected, and didn't I mean to say Saturday; not Friday?

"I told her no, that I had meant Friday, and why did she think I had meant Saturday? She explained that the Spring Dance was on Saturday, and that seeing as I was asking her for a date she had made the logical assumption that I had intended to ask her to the dance"

Jack smiled and said that sounded like something Faith Barnes would say. I continued telling him of my conversation with Faith.

"I told Faith that dances were too formal for my taste and what I had in mind was maybe for us to sit in the park for a while and get to know each other a little; then get some ice cream.

"Then things started to get weird; she asked me if I planned to kiss her."

Jack was seriously laughing now and said "Then what?" "I told her I didn't really have that kind of a plan, and she seemed upset. She said that if I didn't want to kiss her then why had I asked her out?"

Part of me was thinking that I never should have said anything about this to Jack; it was embarrassing, but After all, I had to hold up my end of the campfire conversation. I went on: "I told her I never said I didn't want to kiss you, and she told me that I had certainly implied it."

By this time Jack was almost rolling into the fire. I wrapped up the story of my conversation with Faith: "She had things so twisted around that all I could think of to say at that point was that I had simply asked her to go out this Friday, and did she want to or not? She looked at me sternly and told me that she had wanted to, but now she wasn't sure."

"Then I said Okay, I guess we should forget it. Next thing I know she's crying!"

Change of mood.

"That's bad" said Jack.

"Yes, very bad,"

I replied. "I hate it when girls turn on the juice. I made sure no one else could see her and told her I was very sorry that I had upset her. She sniffed a few times, told me that I was a nice guy and it wasn't my fault, that she was always over analyzing things. Then she made me promise not to blab about this all over the school. I said I wouldn't. As I started to turn to go she said: "I'm not flat you know."

Jack almost fell off the rock he was sitting on. "What? No!"

I assured jack it was true, and told him that I was still trying to think of an answer to Faith's parting comment.

Later, when we were in the tent and inside our sleeping bags I made sure that Jack would keep what I had said about my conversation with Faith to himself. He agreed, and I knew that he would. Jack would never say anything that could hurt someone.

We blew out the candle and I must have been asleep within 2 minutes.

That should have been it until morning, but the night was far from over. Sometime in the dead of night I was brought bolt upright by an awful scream that came from the woods not too far away from our tent.

"What was that?" I asked Jack.

Jack had been woken also but he was in no way surprised, telling me that there were plenty of animals out in these deep woods that did their hunting at night. The scream we heard was the end of the line for some small animal and a dinner bell for something bigger.

After that I slept fitfully, until there was the sound of branches being shaken in a nearby tree, followed by an extremely loud and unpleasant gargling noise from the tree.

Without being asked Jack told me that it was an owl.

"What happened to hoo-hoo?"

"Hoo-hoo is the storybook owls, we have the real stuff out here."

I fell back asleep thinking 'what next?'

The next morning was overcast. Jack scraped together some embers from our fire, added some small branches, and our breakfast was tea and donuts. Jack thought that rain was likely and that we should get started back. We took down the tent, re-loaded our packs, doused the fire with water from the stream and headed home.

Before long it started to drizzle. Each of us had light ponchos (they took up almost no space in our packs) but before we could stop and dig them out it was too late; the rain was coming down harder and we were already wet. We decided to just keep going. It was late morning when we broke out of the woods behind Jack's house and we were soaked to the skin.

Kathy was there to greet us, saying that we looked like a pair of wet cats. She sent us to the showers, scrounged up something dry for me to wear home, and then wanted to hear all about our journey into the deep woods.

Between the two of us we made a good story of it, with emphasis on the Indian artifacts and the wild kingdom night noises. We edited out all mention of Sally and Faith. Kathy was quite impressed with my prize arrowhead. She cupped it in the palm of her hand, turned it over, hefted it as a jeweler might, and told me that it would make a wonderful necklace for the right girl.

Chapter 23

It was only a short time after our overnight adventure into the deep woods that I had a follow up session with Miss Grant. This time she was behind her desk, and once we had our customary tea in front of us she came, as she usually did, directly to the point, saying that she wanted to give me some details as to what she had in mind for me within Grant Holding's extensive real estate interests.

I quickly learned that Miss Grant had hired a Boston firm that specialized in corporate relocations. Their assignment was to find more white-collar corporations to establish offices in the areas skirting New Kensington; specifically, on land owned by the holding company.

This undertaking was off to a good start. Several corporations were showing serious interest, and Miss Grant had already briefed the town commissioners, the mayor, and the zoning board on her plans and in each instance they were enthusiastic; doubly so when they were informed that Grant Holdings would provide the town with interest free loans to pay for the roads, sewers, and other new infrastructure that the town would need to put in place to accommodate this new corporate growth. These loans would be repaid from the real estate tax revenue which would follow once the new offices were up and in use.

After saying this Miss Grant allowed herself a cunning smile, saying that she had only felt the need to lightly touch the possibility of the quarry's revenue and employment diminishing over the coming years. I asked if she wasn't bearing all the risk with these interest free loans.

"Oh, I don't think so Carl." She said, leaning slightly forward to emphasize her point. "All this will take time and planning. We will have contracts signed by any companies planning on moving here before we call in the steam shovels. Plus deposits; we like deposits; very comforting."

That was a point that I easily understood, and I signaled my acknowledgement with a wide smile.

"Also, Carl, we are going to be making excellent profits when we sell these corporations the land they will be building on. And if they prefer to lease the land from us, well, we don't object to turning vacant land into income producing property. Triple net leases are clean and simple."

She then asked me what else I thought might be needed, and I wondered if our schools would be sufficient once this corporate migration started.

For that I received a well done, but she then asked: "Before that?"

The room fell silent; I was thinking. Then My synapses did their job. "They will need places to live; houses; apartments!"

Miss Grant slapped her desk in approval. "Good thinking Carl, of course! And that is how we are going to put you to work this summer. We are about to build a 20 unit apartment building right here (pointing on a map to a spot near the edge of town) here are the plans and I have already hired a general contractor. Take a wild guess who his assistant is going to be."

It only took one guess, and with big smiles we clinked our tea cups in a toast to my summer assignment.

Chapter 24

Early that June Just as I was starting my assignment as assistant to the general contractor Nancy came back into town for one of her brief visits, and this time she had big news. She was being promoted to our National Ski Team.

Although this was a very big deal Nancy seemed to be of two minds about it, saying that although she was glad to be included with our country's best skiers and the training benefits and other perquisites that came with it, she would once more be the youngest member of the team; this time by 3 years. Also, she knew that although technically she would still be an amateur, in practice she would be working a full-time job and she knew that there would be no allowances made for her relative youth. She was 16, and the following year was an Olympic year.

Suddenly it hit me; she was going to try to make the next Olympic team! I asked her if it was not pushing things along too fast and reminded her that she would only be 21 when the next Winter Olympics rolled around.

I should have known Nancy better than that. She said "No Carl, my downhill times are better than all the girls on the team except for one or possibly two of them and my times are still improving. It's not the racing that concerns me it's everything else that comes with it."

Looking somewhat sad she went on to explain that she was a downhill skier plain and simple and that is what she loved to do. What she was NOT was a business woman, and being on the U.S. National Ski team was a business. She was totally committed to making the upcoming Olympic team and then doing the very best she possibly could when the games took place. Beyond that she was not at all sure that she wanted to devote another four years to the same intense daily grind.

With that she gave me a sly, half sideways smile and said "I may want to see what a normal life is; like yours for instance."

"Like mine? Mine isn't normal at all. I'm 17 and I work for a rich old lady who has me about to start learning how to build apartment buildings. What's normal about that?"

Those clear gray eyes focused directly on me. "That rich old lady is very perceptive. She knows that you are smart, honest and have a wonderful set of values. That's why she is arranging for you to learn how businesses work. One of your best traits is that you are extremely modest, otherwise you would know all that. I have been around the world Carl, and there aren't many people like you and the few who I have met are much older."

Coming from Nancy, one of the most straightforward girls anyone could meet, that was quite a mouthful. All I could think of to say in reply was "Thanks Nancy. You are pretty special yourself, and I'm not talking about what you do on the slopes."

That conversation took place while we were walking from the drugstore to the hardware store. Jack and Sally were with us too, but they had lagged behind us, maybe so that they could have a private conversation or it could have been one of Sally's intuitive moves to allow Nancy and I to be apart from them. When it came to interpersonal relationships Sally was a shining star.

Chapter 25

That summer, the one between our junior and senior years of high school went by quickly. I learned within the first week of my apprenticeship to the general contractor that I would not be able to come close to learning even a fraction of all that went into the construction of an apartment building, even a relatively small twenty unit one. Most of the time I just watched what the general contractor was doing. Sometimes he would explain, other times he would ignore me. I understood; he was always busy and I must have seemed to be an underfoot nuisance.

During the second week that I was tagging around behind him he finished a phone call, turned towards me and asked what I thought about what was going on. At that early stage of the construction the survey had been done, the boundaries staked out and the base of the first floor (called within the trade 'the slab') had been poured. The slab had all sorts of pipes sticking up from it. Water? Electric? At that point I did not know.

I told him that to me the general contractor's job made me think of the conductor of a symphony orchestra, substituting a telephone for a baton.

The general contractor, whose name was Anthony (call me Tony) Farina Said "I like that kid, there may be some hope for you around here. I always think of myself as being a juggler, but I like symphony conductor better. I'm going to tell my wife tonight that she is sleeping with the Arthur Fiedler of the North Woods."

That little conversation loosened things up between us, and from then on Tony usually dragged me along with him whenever he met with the many subcontractors and handled all of the delays and changes that seemed to be a routine expectation for any construction job.

In due course I was called to Sycamore Hall to give Miss Grant a progress report. I told her that constructing an apartment building was a much more complex undertaking that I would have guessed and the trick seemed to be getting the materials on time and having the subcontractors do what they needed to do and also *when* they were supposed to do it.

"Well that is about it in a nutshell Carl. Plus, the architect's plans have to be extremely detailed and precise. The more precise the plans are the fewer the missteps, and missteps cause delays and cost money to correct. Remember that because it is true for many things in life besides construction."

I said that I would certainly remember that, but that in spite of the extensive blueprints Mr. Farina spent a good part of his time making adjustments to the plans in order to keep the project moving along.

"Do you call him Mr. Farina?" she asked me.

"No, he says that he wants me to call him what everyone else does; Tony."

"I thought so. There is no reason to be more formal here with me. If he is Tony there on the job then he should be Tony here between us. You need to relax, don't be so stiff."

"Okay, should I call you Cora?"

"Don't get carried away." However, this was said with a twinkle in her eye.

The next time Tony and I had a minute for general conversation I mentioned what Miss Grant had told me about the value of detailed blueprints. Tony was constantly referring to the set of blueprints that he had close at hand on a large drafting table.

"That's right. One of the things I have found out from working for your old lady is that she always finds talented people to work for her. This architect is a top shelf guy and he normally would not be bothered with a small project like this one. He must smell more projects to come after this one."

I knew better that to repeat exactly what I knew of Miss Grant's long term business plans, but I saw no harm in speaking about what was commonly obvious.

"I think you are right about that" I said. "She has spoken to the city commissioners and the zoning board about bringing in more white-collar businesses to this area and the need for the town to plan for housing needs, infrastructure, and everything that will be necessary for an increase in population."

"Maybe she plans to have you run for mayor."

"No thanks, I don't see myself cutting ribbons and kissing babies."

Chapter 26

The rest of our summer break passed without anything out of the ordinary happening except for one bit of unpleasantness that stood out at the time it happened if only because in general New Kensington was a mellow sort of small town.

One Saturday around noon Jack and I were having some ice cream at the drug store counter when one of the town's police officers tapped Jack on the shoulder and told him to get up; that he needed the seat.

Jack swiveled around on his stool and politely told the officer that he wasn't finished eating but would get up as soon as he finished.

In reply the officer raised his voice and said "I don't have time for you to lick your plate, move your ass."

Jack was never a person who allowed himself to be pushed around and said "Not until I'm finished."

Fortunately, the pharmacist; who was also the owner of the drug store had noticed what was going on. He came over to the officer and said that he had an empty stool down at the end of the counter and that he would be happy to take the officer's order as they went to that seat. As the owner and the officer went to the empty seat the officer said to Jack "I'll remember you, wise guy."

After we left the drug store we walked to Hathaway Hardware so that Jack could see if his father needed any help at the store. As we were walking Jack told me that he had seen that same policeman yell at three elementary school kids for crossing a street without using the marked crosswalk. Specifically, he had called them little brats and when he noticed that Jack was watching he had glared at Jack; asked him what he was staring at, and patted his holster.

When Mr. Hathaway asked how we were and what we had been doing I told him about our encounter with the rude police officer. I knew that Chief Hale was a regular customer of the store and that he and Mr. Hathaway sometimes went fishing together, which is why I brought up the subject.

Mr. Hathaway nodded and told us that he wasn't surprised. That policeman was a new hire named Vincent DiNardo, and that he was the son of Chief Hale's sister-in-law.

DiNardo had been discharged from the Army recently under vague circumstances. He had been in the Military Police force and had gotten into serious trouble for use of excessive force–using a night stick and causing a fractured skull-- while dealing with a prisoner at Fort Leavenworth, where he had been stationed. DiNardo claimed that he was merely defending himself from a violent prisoner but the Army thought differently. Under other circumstances DiNardo would have been faced with a court martial; the military equivalent of a trial.

However, if convicted and sentenced to prison DiNardo, as a former M.P., might well have been murdered, as there was widespread hatred of the military police among the hard core inmates. And so he was offered, and accepted, the chance to leave the Army with a General Discharge, a shady sort of catch-all discharge that differs importantly from the usual Honorable Discharge.

This General Discharge, combined with his abrasive personality, made it difficult for DiNardo to find employment anywhere in the field of law enforcement and Chief Hale's wife had pressured him to give DiNardo a chance. That is what Chief Hale had done. Somewhat against his better judgement, and having a vacancy on the force, he had hired his wife's nephew, but only after giving him strict orders to behave himself and stay out of trouble. It shouldn't have been hard to follow those orders as there was very little crime in New Kensington. Traffic violations, petty larceny, feuds between neighbors, just that sort of thing.

After giving us this background information on officer Vincent DiNardo, Jack's father said "It sounds like he won't fit in here, and if he doesn't the chief won't keep him around for long."

The rest of the summer passed routinely. My job at the apartment construction site became routine and I was learning, although I knew that my knowledge of what was going on was superficial at best.

When I had free time, I hung around with Jack and Sally, although in the evenings they preferred to be by themselves. We also got into the habit of using the gym equipment that Nancy had set up in the Hathaway's barn and often Kathy would join us, saying that Sally was Jack's training partner and she would be mine. I found that after a few sessions I didn't mind doing some of the basic exercises. Sit-ups, curls, bench presses, squats, and; thanks to a piece of pipe Nancy had rigged to hang from a rafter, pull-ups. I knew that I was not ever going to become Muscle Boy, but by the time summer vacation ended and school started I could see and feel a difference in my previously untoned body. Kathy said that she had not been in such good shape since she was a high school cheerleader.

As for Sally, she exercised the least and talked the most. She was a wonderful audience and had the rest of us strutting around. Even Kathy enjoyed Sally's commentary and the two of them became close friends.

Chapter 27

As my summer job was coming to a close I was called to Sycamore Hall for another conference with Miss Grant. Once more I was seated in front of her desk.

She started by saying that the apartment building would be finished in a few more months. Then she asked me what I thought the apartments should rent for. Naturally I had no idea and I told her so. I did not expect to avoid the question that easily; it was like the opening move in a chess match, as so many of my conversations with Miss Grant were.

She then asked me what we (we?) should take into consideration in setting the rent schedule. After thinking for a few seconds, I answered that once the total cost of the building, parking lot, and landscaping were known then it would be easier to know how much rent to charge.

"What about the cost of the land?" She asked with raised eyebrows.

That was a tricky question, Grant Holdings had owned the land for decades. I gave her my go-to short answer; "I don't know."

My reply seemed to satisfy her. She then asked me what other rental apartments in and around New Kensington were priced at. I had a better answer for that question, "I don't know but I can find out if you want me to."

It turned out that she did want me to do exactly that. She went on to explain that we (she used that collective word again) intended to use one of the apartments as a manager's apartment and that the manager would be allowed to live in it rent free in return for general oversight of the building, showing apartments to prospective renters, collecting rents, and seeing to it that things ran smoothly. It would be a nice part time job for a retired person who didn't mind keeping an eye on the place in return for free rent.

Continuing on the subject of rents, Miss Grant pointed out that we would then be faced with a built in 5% vacancy factor and what with renters moving in and moving out there were bound to be times when other apartments were also vacant. The trick would be to price the rents so that our units would be in steady demand. We had advantages in this regard; our apartment would be brand new, besides which we were including a meeting room which the tenants could use for gatherings, and there would also be a nice outside patio with chairs, tables, and a barbeque grill.

On the other hand, Miss Grant was not going to write leases. Instead the tenants would be given renters agreements. These renters agreements would be a series of things that the renters could not do without risking being forced to move out.

I asked if that wouldn't cause some potential renters to go elsewhere.

"I expect that it will, especially if they are likely to violate the terms of the renter's agreement. In those cases we will be better off if they don't move in. I intend to price the rents attractively; so much so that the lack of a lease will be counterbalanced by the other positive factors. The best business arrangements are the ones where both sides are benefiting. I want you to always remember that Carl."

I told her that her reputation for fair dealings should be useful too.

"Yes" she replied "But remember that many of our potential renters will be new to our town and they will not put much weight on the Grant reputation, so here is what I want you to do."

I had developed a habit of carrying a pocket-sized notebook when I was on the job, and at this point I took it out.

"I want you to find out what the other rental apartments go for in and around here, and also how large those one and two-bedroom apartments are. I expect that ours will be larger. Overall, I want our building to be the smart choice, everything considered."

I told her that I could do that and asked when I was to start.

"Why don't you tell Tony that I am stealing you from him and that I have you working on a secret mission. Once you have given me the report you will be done until you graduate."

The secret mission terminology was Miss Grant's sense of humor showing itself, there was nothing secret about my fact-finding assignment, and I had the information she wanted typed (Dad's secretary was given that assignment) and into her hands before the start of our senior year.

Chapter 28

Everyone should have more than one senior year of high school. After working our way up through the ranks, starting in junior high, being a senior seemed as if we had reached a summit. Although the football team lost as often as it won, Jack stopped dropping balls completely. He was scoring touchdowns often, was faster than ever, and had developed a talent for shiftiness that caused defenders to miss tackles. Several smaller colleges were offering him athletic scholarships.

Sally and I were yelling ourselves hoarse at the games and having the time of our lives in the process. Sally told Jack that she didn't care where he went to college just as long as it was co-ed, because wherever he went was where she was going and if she was not accepted there then Jack couldn't go there; and that was cut in stone.

I was there when Sally told Jack this and we both were laughing as she said it, but for once Sally did not join in the merriment. Instead she grabbed Jack's shirt and said "I mean this Jack."

Jack turned serious too, and said "Don't worry, I will never leave you."

Upon hearing that Sally gave him one of her thousand-watt smiles and said "Good; otherwise I would have to make Carl beat you up."

As for my college admission process, it was fairly simple. Although other than having a big role in our senior play (I was perfectly cast as Applegate–the devil–in "Damn Yankees" with Sally hysterically funny and having the time of her life playing Lola) I had avoided most of the school's extra-curricular activities due to their overall pointlessness, and sports, of course, were always out of the question based on a long standing tacit agreement between the school's athletic department and myself.

However, what I did have was a letter of recommendation from Miss Cora Grant; well-known philanthropist and president of Grant Holdings. The letter stated that I had been employed directly by her during my summer vacations as her special assistant, and the letter described me in such glowing terms that I couldn't even recognize myself as being the subject.

That plus excellent marks and SAT scores were sufficient to get me accepted to the college of my choice; Williams. Early admission even.

Williams checked all my boxes. It was small, not too far away, and the students and faculty were bright. Also, the school didn't seem to care what I wanted to study and that was good because I had no thoughts along those lines.

My parents were fine with my college decision process and simply told me that I would do well wherever I went; that if I decided to specialize in any field I could do that in graduate school. As far as they were concerned they just wanted me to make friends and be happy; where did not matter.

Miss Grant's comments were more specific. She told me that Williams was a fine school and all that but she wanted me to take pre-law courses.

Where did that come from? "Pre-law? I don't want to be a lawyer; at least I don't think I do. I know I don't want to work in New York or even Boston grinding out contracts and documents and being under the thumbs of the partners."

"There you go again jumping ahead of me" said my stern-faced mentor. "What do you think I have been training you for, to be one of a hundred junior associates at some revenue-oriented snarl of lawyers?"

This was just the opening I had been waiting for; I asked the big question that I (and my parents) had been wondering about. "No, I don't know what plans you have in mind for me and I would like to know because I really enjoy working for you and if it is not going to be something I think I will continue to enjoy I want to know now and not be even more disappointed later."

Later I came to think of what was said next as 'The big talk.'

Miss Grant slowly stood up and walked to the window; obviously pensive. She then turned away from the window and gave me a slight smile, saying "That is a fair question Carl. I hadn't intended to tell you all that I have in mind for you this soon, but now I think it is time." With that she asked if I would mind taking a walk around the grounds while we talked. Once we were outside she outlined her plans.

"As you know Carl, our holding company is extremely valuable; much more so than people know or suspect. Your father knows, of course, I know, and you have an incomplete idea of what we own, that is about it. Everything is owned by the holding company and the holding company is owned by the Grant Trust.

The trust is totally controlled by it's trustee, and that trustee is me and me alone. In a few words what this means is that although I delegate some authority to people such as your father I am in total control of everything that Grant Holdings owns and I have been since I was thirty years old."

Looking at me from the side, head cocked and one eyebrow raised she said "It's a fairly simple table of organization."

No one had a dryer sense of humor than Miss Grant. She continued.

"For some time I have been looking for someone to take over after I am gone or unable to manage things effectively."

My mind was racing; she couldn't be thinking of me taking over; 18 years old and still in high school? I cut in to ask if she was considering my dad as her successor.

"I did, briefly. Your father is a fine human being and he has a wonderful sense of values but he would be miserable if he had to run the holding company. He does not like supervising people, he does not like making business decisions, and he is best suited doing exactly what I have him doing and not taking his work home with him. Your father is the slippers and pipe, home by the fireside type."

Ignoring the technical point that my father did not smoke I knew she was right. Dad was simply not ambitious.

She came back to her preamble: "I do not have any relatives so regardless of what plans I put in place for eventual relinquishing control I will be the last of the Grants. Whoever my successor is will need to be smart, be able to think long term, and will need to be fair and honest in dealings with people. In all business matters have vision; and above all else have integrity."

With this she stopped walking and turned directly toward me, saying: "That person is going to be you Carl."

Even though I had somehow suspected that this could be coming, suspecting it and hearing it were miles apart. I was stunned and mentally overloaded. All I could do was stammer "No! I can't possible handle all that. I would be so over my head I would have a nervous breakdown within the first week!"

She was ready for this sort of reaction and poked me in the ribs with her elbow. "Settle down! I am not planning on dying soon! You will have plenty of time to finish your education and while you are getting a law degree you will be taking business and finance courses. Almost everything that we do these days requires familiarity with laws and dealing with lawyers.

"Also, starting on the day you graduate from high school you are going to become a full-time paid employee of the holding company. Your first job will be to get a college education and during the summers you will be working right here with me learning what I do and how I do it. How does that sound?"

"It sounds overwhelming. I don't know what to say."

Looking back, I think that Miss Grant was relieved to have had this talk with me. We turned back towards the house, and as we did she looked up at it and said "There it is, Sycamore Hall. Home of the Grant clan for four generations. It has served us well but it is looking like it needs some sprucing up, don't you think?"

I couldn't think about much at all at that point and said so. She hardly seemed to care and went on to say that she would soon re-organize her office so that I would have a desk. She wanted me to be close at hand once I graduated from high school so that I could begin learning how she handled the day to day operations of her various enterprises. She then added "besides, I may decide to take a trip this summer, I am past due for one. If I do then you will be here to keep me informed."

When we arrived back at the Hall she sent me home. "You should tell your parents about what we have discussed. Your father and I will work out a suitable salary for you before too long. In the meantime, you can tell him that one of your fringe benefits as a fulltime employee will be that all of your educational expenses will be paid for. Grant Holdings takes care of it's own!"

And with a hearty laugh she turned into the house saying over her shoulder "From now on call me Cora!"

Chapter 29

Well there it was; my professional future all tied up in a pretty package. A Williams education was far from cheap; had Miss Grant tossed the paid tuition and full time salary in just to be sure that I gave her a quick yes? Was I being manipulated? I decided that it did not matter, I liked everything that she had outlined. Actually, the more I thought about it I realized that I loved it. By the time I finished college and law school I would be in my mid-twenties and would have been working with her for close to ten years. Besides, I could always do something else if I ever changed my mind. I decided that I preferred the word incentivized to the word manipulated.

My parents were very happy, saying that they were proud of me. Dad said that although they could have afforded to pay for my higher education It was nice to know that the holding company would be treating it as one of my fringe benefits. Mom wondered what else might fall into my lap, and I said "What else could I want?"

All in all, it was quite a day for the Smiths. Dad came up with a bottle of champagne and even though I was not a drinker; having immediately thrown up the first time I had a gulp of whiskey, I joined them in a toast to my future.

Meanwhile while winter was settling in around North Overshoe Nancy was becoming an international star throughout the skiing world. She was either winning or coming near to winning her downhill races against the best women skiers in the world, and she was on the cover of Ski Magazine wearing a navy blue warm up suit with USA across the front in big letters, one foot crossed behind the other and holding ski poles across her shoulders and behind her head.

I spent a long time looking at that magazine cover thinking that the pose was almost exactly the way she looked when Jack and I walked out of the woods after he had taken me to see the waterfall. This was the girl who taught me to ski on Old Tote Road. The girl who persuaded me to take her to the dance, who pulled my ears, who gave me "Rocky" (the name I had given my carved Cock of the Rock), and the girl who had kissed me when I gave her perfume at Christmas. Our Nimble Nancy was world famous! More to the point, why was I so sad about it? I remembered the times that she had done her best to let me know that she cared about me and I had been too clueless to tell her my feelings toward her. I had the thought that I had let her slip away without ever even giving her any encouragement.

Chapter 30

We had expected Nancy to be home for Christmas in time to be around for the yearly Hathaway Hardware Christmas Party, an event that I particularly looked forward to. Furthermore, the party had become something of a hot ticket since Kathy had assumed it's supervision. Not only was the food outstanding, she had the house, porch, and driveway looking like a winter wonderland. It was now a two-tree event; the second tree a welcoming beacon out on the porch. The whole evening was in perfect taste and a delightful experience.

Some time around the middle of December I received a letter from Nancy, postmarked Chamonix, France and written on personalized United States Olympic Ski Team stationary no less.

Dear Carl;

I am very sorry to say that I will only be home briefly this Christmas. The coaches, particularly the head coach, want to keep the team together over the holidays and we have been told that other than Christmas day we will be training. If any family members want to see us then they are welcome to visit us here on the 25th. Otherwise we have work to do.

The head coach and I are not on good terms and I am sure that if it were not for my success lately in my event he would have kicked me off the team.

Because I have been getting so much attention lately (I'm sure you have seen or read some of that 'Teen-aged ski phenomenon' stuff) I was able to get a few extra days off. I will be arriving late on the 23rd and will be leaving the morning of the 26th.

Carl, I have so much that I want to talk with you about. I know this is asking an awful lot of you, but will you please meet my flight at the Boston airport on the 23rd? I want to be sure that we have this time to be by ourselves because once we get home things will be hectic so I hope you can say yes.

Dad has my flight information and he knows that I am asking you to pick me up.

Thank you Carl. You don't know what this will mean to me.

Love, Nancy

I would say that I read her letter at least 5 times consecutively. Just when I was feeling that Nancy had gone big time on all of us; cover girl and all that, here comes this mystery letter. What did she want to discuss with me? Well I was going to have to wait to find out.

And she had signed the letter "Love." What was I supposed to make of that? Some people throw that word around carelessly, as if it is just another word. Personally, I feel that is a very powerful word. I almost never use it. I would be unlikely to say that I love any inanimate object, for example. That is just me being my usual buttoned up self; Nancy was probably different, especially now that she had become famous.

Anyway, I was happy to meet her at the airport and told Mr. Hathaway and Kathy that I would be driving down to bring her home.

Nancy's flight was on time and she was one of the first people off the plane. The crew had recognized her and upgraded her to first class. Because she was traveling with a small bag which had been stored in the overhead bin we were able to get through the Logan Airport crowds quickly. Nancy set a brisk pace and had a cap pulled down low. If anyone recognized her they left her alone, and we were soon driving through that claustrophobic tunnel under the harbor and heading towards home.

I was about to ask her what it was that she wanted to discuss with me, but Nancy beat me to the punch. She said "I'm so glad that you came Carl. There are some things that I want to say that are very important, and questions that I need to ask, but before I start please get us out of this terrible traffic so we can concentrate on what we are talking about."

She was right, the streets in Boston are narrow and it was already dark. I was white-knuckling it for another 30 minutes before Nancy turned towards me, hitched her knees up on the seat and spoke.

"Carl, I have a lot to say and some of what you are going to hear I can't discuss with anyone else. You will understand why when you hear it.

"First the skiing. Ever since I first started I have wanted to ski fast. I have always been good at it and loved it. That is why I went to the Ski Academy. I learned a lot there and improved very quickly. When I was asked to join the Junior National team I was told that it was a huge step, but I wanted to take it as a challenge. That is where I became a full-time skier. Lots of travel, heavy duty training, high level coaching, uniforms, team rules. I jumped into all of it and I continued to improve. Soon I was the best on the team."

I knew that Nancy was not telling me this to brag; she was leading up to something and my side of the conversation was mostly nods to show understanding. She went on.

"I found that the best way for me to meet my goals was to keep to myself and focus entirely on my skiing. There was some jealousy, and clashes with a few of the staff, but my times kept improving and I was winning races. Mostly I was left alone.

"Then I was added to our Senior National team, where I am now. This is skiing at the highest level. It is big time and as intense as it could possibly be, particularly with the Olympics coming in just a few months. Our coaching staff will do absolutely anything to win, and that's where trouble started."

I interrupted just to say "Oh-oh."

"Yes; a very big oh-oh. My main competition at the Olympics will be the European women. They are all older than I am and they are, without exception, big. I am in terrific shape and I train extremely hard, but I am not built to weigh 150 pounds or anything close to that. The head coach called me in last Fall and told me that if I wanted to win the Olympic downhill I needed to gain 20 pounds, and that he was going to put me on a high calorie diet to bulk me up. I know my body and what I can and can not do with it and I told the coach that I was already at my perfect weight.

"He started to get angry and yelled that he knew what it would take to win and that I would shut up and do exactly as he said.

"I became angry too, and told him that I was not going to do it, and that I didn't want to have an ass the size of a kettle drum."

I had to laugh a little at the thought of Nancy saying that.

"Then he really had a tantrum. He screamed that I would do exactly what he told me to do or he would throw me off the team.

"I was not going to let him or anyone else make me do something that I knew would hurt my chances of winning and I came right back at him. I said that if he threw me off the team that I knew of half a dozen other countries that would love to have me on their Olympic team and that I was going to win the Olympic downhill race or die trying and I wanted to do it wearing the U.S.A.'s uniform but if not then I would do it for Luxemburg or some other country that would be ecstatic to have me."

She paused to catch her breath.

I asked if that was allowed and the answer was yes; there is no requirement that members of a country's team be citizens of that country.

Nancy had become a little agitated as she told me about this clash with her coach, but she calmed down and added "Besides, we both knew that the Ski Magazine cover story was coming out. If he kicked me off the team he would be crucified by the press and probably be fired. He started swearing and told me to get out of his sight but that was all. Later when I told him that I needed a few days off for Christmas he called me a prima donna but didn't try to stop me from coming here."

I was impressed with the way Nancy had stood up to the coach and told her so. Not only was she a terrific skier she had guts and courage. I was proud of her.

She was quiet for several seconds and then told me that something much worse had happened several weeks ago. She had almost been raped.

"What!" I think I shouted. "Wait till I can get off the road, then tell me everything. Was it that coach?" I pulled into a gas station, stopped, and turned to her.

Nancy was clearly upset. She took a deep breath, let it out, and began: "Carl, when people become national figures as I have we get all sorts of attention. It is flattering in a way, but it is also annoying. The team has procedures that keep people away from us most of the time but we get fan mail, we get yelled at, sometimes ugly things are said, and frankly I do not like being a celebrity. I do not go out at night. I do not socialize, and I do not date. At this stage of my life I'm a skier; that's it.

"Well, we were in Switzerland for a big race and this guy from the Italian team was pestering me for a date. At first I was polite when I brushed him off, but he kept it up and when I was sick of having him following me around and bothering me I told him to get lost and stay lost.

"Then he was angry, called me names and said that he would teach me a lesson in manners that I wouldn't forget.

"A few nights later I walked a little way up the downhill course to see how the grooming looked. Suddenly that Italian lout jumped out of some trees beside the course and started ripping at my clothes and saying that I was going to get it good."

I was horrified at this and of all the impractical thoughts to have I was wishing I could have been there to protect her.

Nancy, speaking quietly, continued. "I tried to fight him off and was kicking his shins. Then he punched me hard in the face. I fell down and when I started to get up he hit me very hard on the side of my head. I just heard a crunch and blacked out.

"I must have been out for a few seconds. When I woke up he had ripped my pants open and was pulling them down around my knees with one hand and opening his pants with the other.

"I was sort of dizzy but I knew I had to do something quickly. I tried to laugh and I asked him how he knew I liked it rough. He said that was good because that was how I was going to get it.

"Then I said that if we were going to have sex then he had to at least kiss me."

I was listening to this awful story with my mouth open as wide as the tunnel we had driven through back in Boston.

Nancy then said "That idiot bent down to kiss me and I got my teeth into his nose, clamped down as hard as I could, and bit the tip off!"

"You WHAT?"

"That's what saved me. He was screaming so loud it could have started an avalanche. He ran off down the slope holding his nose with one hand and his pants up with the other. I pulled my pants back up and went straight to our security office. The guy on duty called our head of security, all our coaches got involved. Everyone was talking at once; it was bedlam."

I wondered why I had not read about it and Nancy told me that the U.S. team and the Italians made a deal to hush it up. The rapist was banned forever from their team and she agreed not to talk about what happened; at least until after the Olympics. The last thing she needed at that point was all the ruckus a story like that would create. She did not want the distraction.

"But just in case the story ever got out and it somehow turned into a 'he said-she said' sort of thing, with him claiming that his nose was slammed in a doorway or some such, I took out an insurance policy. Later that night I went back to where he had attacked me. I had spit out the piece of his nose that I had bitten off once he jumped away from me. When I went back I poked around in the snow and found the piece of nose and I have hidden it in a safe place."

Hearing this astonishing story was overwhelming. I opened my car door, walked around to Nancy's side of the car and opened it. She got out and I hugged her. For a long time I just rocked her back and forth without a word being said.

Finally I was able to say how sorry I was for what she had endured, and how proud I was of her. She quietly said "Thanks so much Carl, that makes the rest of what I want to say much easier for me."

We resumed our drive home and Nancy told me that what she had just told me had to always be just between us. Of course I promised to protect her privacy.

Then she turned towards me again and asked if I had found a girlfriend for myself. This was typical Nancy. Between she and Miss Grant there was never a curve ball thrown. They both always came directly to the point when they had something important to say.

I am fairly candid myself, and after Nancy had spoken so openly about things that were deeply personal I knew this was not a time for tap dancing, and the situation called for more than a simple yes or no.

And so I said "No; no girlfriend. I've tried to get something started once or twice but my heart hasn't been in it. Casual dating around just is not my style. I want something like Jack and Sally have and I don't want to settle for less. I guess I am a one girl sort of guy and I don't have that one girl. I'll probably ask someone to our Senior Prom just so two of us don't have to sit at home that night; that's about it."

In reply Nancy asked me to stop the car again as soon as I could.

As soon as we were off the road and parked we got out of the car, walked around to the trunk and leaned against it. Nancy began by holding both my hands and saying "Carl, I feel the same way as you. I want someone for keeps, not just a guy who seems better than the last four guys who wanted a date with me. I see other girls my age making such obvious mistakes with men I wonder if they have salt for brains. To me, finding the right guy and keeping him is the most important decision I will ever make."

Here there was a long pause. She took a deep breath, let it out slowly, moved in close to me, looked directly up into my eyes and said, "And I have him right here; it's you Carl."

Instinct trumped everything else. I put my arms around her and we had a kiss that said more than anything that I could have thought to say. When I final did say something, it was simply "Wow!"

Nancy started to laugh and cry. She started to talk rapidly, telling me that she had a crush on me since before the time we went to the dance and every time she came home her feelings grew stronger.

As we were once more on the road she continued talking excitedly. She said, "Remember how I have said that I am a planner? Well I have thought out some plans for us, but I didn't know how you felt about me. You hide your feelings. Does your 'Wow' mean what I hope it means?"

I told her that she was right about me hiding my feelings, that she had a big head start on me, and that I had never dared think or hope to have her as my girl, but the more the reality was sinking in the happier I was getting, and what plans had I been swept into?

She laughed and said that it was almost the 24th and she had to leave early on the 26th so about all we would be able to do right away would be to talk about everything; our goals, our futures, and above all else our feelings. When I said " Nancy, you will have to be patient with me. I'm going to have to learn to open up" she said that we would work everything out, and that the important thing was that we were committed to each other.

And that sounded pretty good to me.

Chapter 31

By the time we pulled into the Hathaway's driveway it was past 10 P.M. Nevertheless the Hathaway family plus Sally, who was close to being a part of their family, were waiting for Nancy. After a round of hugs and greetings Nancy sang out for all to hear: "Surprise! I brought my new boyfriend with me!" With that she grabbed my right arm and raised it over my head. "And Here he is!"

A general uproar ensued. Mr. Hathaway did seem to have been taken by surprise and I think that Jack was too. Sally and Kathy later said that they knew it was coming the second they learned that Nancy had asked that I come alone to the airport to pick her up.

I didn't know what to do other than stand there smiling and blushing but it was one of those times when a person does not need to do anything. Sally almost knocked me over with a hug and yelled 'Finally!" Jack pumped my hand and mussed up my hair. He probably said something too; I don't know.

Mr. Hathaway put his long arms on my shoulders and told me that he could not be happier for both of us. Then he wiped away a tear. Maybe he was remembering Nancy's mother.

I think the most level-headed person in the room was Kathy. She held her fire until the jumping around had slowed. Then she held hands with both Nancy and I and told us that she knew the first time she saw us together that we made a perfect match. She then turned to Mr. Hathaway and said "Tom darling, was that a bottle of champagne I saw in the fridge?"

The answer was yes to the question, and Nancy and I were toasted. Sally sat Nancy down and demanded that she tell her exactly how she was able to wake Rip Van Winkle (me) up to the fact that I loved her.

Nancy then did an excellent job of summarizing what went on between the two of us during the drive. This abridged version of what was said was sufficient; everyone was happy and that was what mattered.

Eventually things calmed down. It was late and I had to get home. Jack had left to drive Sally home and Nancy and I walked out to my car, side by side, arms around each other's waists. We made plans for the next day; Christmas Eve, and had a long and wonderful kiss. Nancy said "I love you Carl Smith", and I heard myself unhesitatingly reply "And I love you Nancy Hathaway."

All in all, it had been quite a day.

Chapter 32

My parents were in bed but awake when I got home; unable to sleep until they knew I was safely back from fetching Nancy. When they asked me how the drive went and how Nancy was doing I ducked the questions by saying that everything was fine and that I would fill them in on the details in the morning.

That bought me some time to sort out my thoughts and new status–formerly a non-dater and 100% girl-less; now the proud possessor of a wonderful girlfriend. Not only that; loved and in love!

And oh, those kisses! I never knew what I had been missing.

Nancy was right, we had a great deal to talk about. I had agreed to come see her the next morning before lunch and I was sure that we would be making 'heap big smoke', an expression I thought I had picked up from an old cowboys and Indians movie. What other plans had Nancy cooked up for us?

The first thing I did in the morning was tell my parents that Nancy and I had come to the realization that we had been carrying the torch for each other since the time we went to the dance, or maybe even before that, and once those cards were on the table we had decided to be boyfriend/girlfriend. I tactfully omitted the L word; no point in overloading my parent's emotions all in one breakfast conversation.

I expected them to be happy to hear this and I was right. They were very happy and said that they knew Nancy was a wonderful person. They did, however wonder how we were going to make the relationship work with Nancy being committed to her skiing career.

In answer to that I asked "Do you mean to suggest that having her travel the world while I am here in North Overshoe is less than a perfect situation?"

When the laughter died away I told them that Nancy seemed to have made plans that we had not been able to discuss the previous night, but that they were at the top of our agenda and that I would be going to the Hathaway's house shortly to talk about our future.

But before I could do that I needed to stop at Sycamore Hall. I had planned to drop off a Christmas gift for Miss Grant, and while I was there I intended to tell her about my enhanced status with Nancy.

My gift was a sterling picture frame. Her desk lacked any sign of warmth and I thought that if I gave her a nice frame that she might come up with a photo to put in it that pleased her. What a perfect time to tell her that my love life had finally broken out of the gate! Maybe what she needed to put in the frame was a photograph of Nancy and me.

When I told her that Nancy and I had let our feelings about each other be known Miss Grant gave me an austere hug. She skipped over the obvious questions as to how we would overcome her travel obligations and told me that she wanted to meet Nancy. Naturally she knew all about Nancy's background and her accomplishments and she knew me well enough to be confident that I had chosen wisely. She looked forward to getting to know her.

I said that I wanted to show her off to as many people as possible and Miss Grant in particular but that it might have to wait until her next visit seeing as Nancy was leaving the morning after Christmas due to the need for her to resume her training for the Olympics and it was already Christmas Eve.

I left fairly quickly, as I was eager to see Nancy and continue planning our future.

When I arrived at the Hathaway's everyone was up and about; Nancy looking fresh as a flower in slacks and a light sweater. Kathy, the resident event planner, asked me if I thought my parents would agree to have our family join them for dinner that night as well as for Christmas dinner. She pointed out that we all needed to spend as much time together as we could before Nancy left early on the 26th.

I told her that our family certainly would jump at the chance, and in less than a minute Kathy and my mother were on the phone happily discussing logistics. What could my mother bring? Pies? Extra chairs?

I told Nancy about my short visit to see Miss Grant, and that she wanted to meet Nancy as soon as she could.

"Great" said my new love. She went directly to Kathy when she finished her telephone conversation with my mom and asked if we could handle one more guest for the big Christmas meal; the legendary Miss Cora Grant.

For a woman who was used to riding herd on hundreds of conventioneers at a time one more dinner guest was nothing, and in short order she was on the phone again, this time introducing herself to Miss Grant, apologizing for issuing an invitation on such short notice, but would it be possible for her to join the Smiths and Hathaways for a late afternoon Christmas dinner? We could easily tell by listening to Kathy's end of the conversation that Miss Cora Grant would be delighted to round out our group.

Chapter 33

Kathy had heard my tongue in cheek nickname for New Kensington–North Overshoe–within 24 hours of her first visit and had been amused by it; thinking that it was droll.

This fall she had put her thoughts into action and had ordered a few dozen sweatshirts and tee shirts in various colors and sizes featuring a large unbuckled galosh on the front with "North Overshoe" printed in curved letters over the top. These were to be offered for sale at the hardware store and prominently displayed behind the checkout counter. I was flattered to think that my passing witticism was gathering traction but at the same time doubted that the citizens of our fair town would be willing to pay good money to wear something like that.

I never should have doubted Kathy's ability to read people. Those sweatshirts and tee shirts sold out almost immediately. I barely had time to buy a sweatshirt (in navy, as suggested by Kathy) for Nancy before they were gone and a re-order was placed.

My thinking was to have two presents for her this Christmas, the sweatshirt being a Christmas Eve mini gift. Because the rest of her family already had the sweatshirts and also tee shirts, we had worked it out that these North Overshoe clothes would be kept hidden until after she had opened hers.

For her main gift, which she would open on Christmas day, I was giving her the arrowhead that I had found at the Indian campsite where Jack and I had spent the night.

After Kathy had opined that it would make a fine necklace pendant I had been thinking that I would like to give it to Nancy for Christmas. The unresolved detail was exactly how to turn the Indian artifact into an attractive piece of jewelry.

While this was still undecided I overheard Miss Grant making plans to have the Boston firm of Shreve, Crump, and Low prepare a large order of sterling letter openers which she planned to give as Christmas gifts to many of her employees. I knew that Shreve, Crump and Low had a jewelry department and that Miss Grant was an important client of theirs and had been for many years. I asked her if she would make a call to them, to see if they would tackle the task of turning a perfect arrowhead into a necklace and pendant.

Shreve, Crump, and Low was happy to oblige and asked for it to be sent it to them. I had thought they would somehow drill a small hole near the top of the arrowhead and attach a chain. What they did was much better. The arrowhead came back with a thin gold wire wound twice around the narrow neck of the arrowhead with a custom make clasp attached. Along with it came a beautiful gold chain which I was told had been hand made so that it would be in perfect proportion for the pendant. With it came a beautiful box with a velvet lining.

For this elegant piece of workmanship Shreve, Crump, and Low refused payment. They only asked for permission to use a photograph of the necklace in a promotional brochure for their custom jewelry department.

I quickly agreed to this. My arrowhead; Nancy's necklace, was to become slightly famous.

I spent the next several hours at the Hathaway's home nestled on a couch in front of the living room fireplace, Nancy by my side. It was then when Nancy revealed her long-term plans.

She started with this: "The more I have come to know the inner details of how international skiing competition works, and the more I have become familiar with the people who organize, manage, supervise and coach the competitions and control the skiers, the more I have become sure that after this winter's Olympics I will be done with it all."

She was looking at me earnestly as she was telling me this. There was no anger or disgust as she spoke; just well-expressed certainty.

She continued: "The backstabbing, the duplicity, the win at all cost approach to every aspect of the sport, and the flat out lying is shameful. I have a good chance to win my race. That has been my dream and what has motivated me to accept the grueling training, the constant travel, and the loneliness.

"Even if I don't win I am now just 17 and so well-known and established that I could keep on skiing at this level for another 10 or 15 years if I wanted to. But I don't."

With that said Nancy gave a short nod of her head for emphasis and waited for me to comment. I asked her who was aware that she planned on leaving the team after the Olympics.

"Dad and Jack, and now you. I made Jack promise not to tell Sally. She is a great girl but I am not sure that she could keep this to herself and Jack agrees. I know I can trust Jack. I asked Dad not to tell Kathy, but if she asks him if he knows my plans he has my permission to tell her. She is his wife and I do not think she would talk out of turn."

Keeping this quiet would be quite an accomplishment. Already there had been reporters around New Kensington, seeking background information about Nancy as they scurried around filing stories about 'America's downhill rocket' as one story headline had labeled her.

It was accepted as a foregone conclusion that Nancy would continue her skiing career. Any hint to the contrary would have sent the press into a frenzy.

"My downhill race will be earlier than the giant slalom, so I may compete in that event depending on how things develop. I have skied the giant slalom a few times. It isn't that different from downhill and there would be no reason not to enter that race once the one I really care about is over. But win or lose, after these Olympics I will be a 17 year old retiree."

At that point she stretched her legs (sox but no shoes) out onto my thigh, leaned back against the arm of the couch, and said "What do you think of my plan so far?"

My answer was an easy one; I did not like the idea of her being used and lied to, especially if we were separated. So I said "I love it so far; what will be the follow up?"

With a big smile she said "Money! I think every sports agent in the world wants to guide me to a fortune. Speeches. Corporate appearances. A line of clothes. My own logo. Product promotion. Modeling. Maybe even a centerfold!"

This last was a joke and I knew it but I still couldn't let it slide by without bending her toes and saying "Never!"

"Ouch; okay, I'll keep my clothes on. Then there are the lawyers, the investment advisors, ghostwriters, you name it. My retinue could stretch for miles!"

This last was said with raised eyebrows and arms spread wide.

One good thing about the team's security staff; they were able to keep this swarm of opportunists away from Nancy for the most part, but what would happen after she leaves the team?

Nancy had that angle covered. "I have already decided to sign with one large, full service agency, although they do not know it yet. They have a middle aged married couple who I will have to represent me and they are headquartered in Chicago. I'm going to tell them that I do not want to travel outside the United States and I want plenty of time to be on my own. They will be the only business people I have contact with. That way I can be with you."

This was worth a hug, and for a while we stopped talking. By then we were stretched out side by side on the couch. Looking up I pointed toward the ceiling and said "I can see it now. Your own brand of cereal. Want to ski like Nancy? Eat Zipos!"

Nancy then revealed her exit plan. "I am going to tell this agency that I will do this public relations sort of thing for a maximum of one year; less than that if it becomes too irritating. Eventually I think I would like to have a ski school for young intermediate level skiers who want to get to the next level. Once they are good enough I will advise them where to go next. I'll need quite a bit of money to set this up."

Then she turned to me and said "This all seems to make sense to me Carl, but the most important part of these plans; or any plan, is you."

Suddenly we were very serious. "I have to stay totally focused on these Olympics, just for a few more months. After that, it's us."

Now it was my turn to talk. I started with the conclusion, which was that I knew we could make her ideas work for us. I also said that if there would be problems they would come from outside; too many interests all clamoring for Nancy's time and attention.

Nancy had a ready reply. "Exactly. That is why I am going to hire North Wind; the Chicago agency. The man and woman who will be my representatives know my feelings about this and that I absolutely will not sacrifice my free time in order to ring the cash register. I will make plenty of money, all that I need, without squeezing the last oink out of the pig."

I asked where she had picked up that expression. "From that Chicago couple. It's a good one isn't it?"

I continued. "Miss Grant has offered me a wonderful opportunity, and I don't mean money, although I am confident that there will be plenty of that too.

"The day I graduate this June I will become a full-time employee of Grant Holdings; the operating part of the Grant Trust, which she has total control of. I will be her personal assistant. She and my dad are going to decide what my salary will be, but I have a feeling that it will be generous."

With a twinkle in her eyes Nancy cut in. "Will your ego be hurt if I happen to make more than you?"

"Not at all. Beautiful Olympic stars should make more than personal assistants."

With a smile she said "well, at least for a while. Go on."

"My summer duties are not set, but mainly I will be learning as much as I can about her businesses. Then in the Fall I will be going to Williams which the trust will be paying for. I'll be taking pre-law and business courses. She wants me to get a law degree because just about everything that she does involves legal issues."

"So you will be her lawyer?"

"Among other things, although I think she sees me more as supervising lawyers. I would be more like her vice president. The long-term plan is for me to take over everything when she is no longer able to run things."

"Can you do that from here or would you need to be in Boston or some other big city?"

"I don't see why I would need to ever leave here other than business trips now and then. She does fine without even leaving her house except for going to her office in town from time to time."

"Well that's good. I don't like big cities. Crowds, noise, dirt in the air, washing your face and hands Every time you come in from being outside. I'll take a mountain any day over that."

"Me too. But Nancy, here is what makes me really excited about her offer. Everything she does and plans to do, she does with integrity and as part of a long-term plan. The apartment building that we just built? The first requirement was that it be a good deal for the tenants. That's just one example. I will be doing good things."

Nancy was happy to hear this and summarized: "People will be calling us 'The Goodlies' in no time. Where is everyone? I'm hungry!"

Chapter 34

Everyone turned out to be in the kitchen. Mr. Hathaway was helping Kathy make dinner preparations and Sally was also watching to see how Kathy was putting a lasagna together. That, of course, meant that Jack was also there so I knocked off.

I suspected that the group had agreed to leave Nancy and I to ourselves in the living room. That was considerate, but the kitchen was getting crowded. Kathy pulled a tray of cheese and crackers off a counter and another tray, this one with shrimp and cocktail sauce out of the fridge. She asked; well sort of ordered us, to put it out somewhere in the living room, and to not eat it all before my parents arrived.

Around 5 O'clock my parents did show up and the festivities were under way. My parents were never the life of the party sort of people, but Sally was always at the top of her game in social gatherings and Kathy had been earning her living mingling in disparate groups for years. My parents were surrounded with some really nice people and in no time at all they were right in the thick of the conversations. The prime topic being the new couple; Nancy and Carl.

At the dinner table Nancy was seated across from my parents; I was near Mr. Hathaway and Kathy. Jack and Sally were around the middle, but it seemed that Sally, conversationally, was everywhere.

I had decided to give Nancy her pre-Christmas gift, the North Overshoe sweatshirt, as we sat down for dinner so I had the package stashed under my chair. Once we were all settled in there was an expectant hush, as everyone but Nancy knew about my sweatshirt plan.

I stood up holding the package and, looking at my wonderful girlfriend of 24 hour standing, told her that although it was not quite time for Christmas gifts I had a special little something that was just dying to be unwrapped. With that I handed it across to Nancy.

Nancy has an expressive face, and as she held the wrapped box she managed to look surprised, pleased, and confused all at once. All eyes were on her as she opened it.

Her first comment once she saw the sweatshirt (which was folded so that the galosh was showing) was a drawn out "Whaaat?" Then she looked at me and asked "Did you do this?"

Sally couldn't contain herself and burst into an explanatory description of the sequence. First my coming up with the nickname, North Overshoe. Then Kathy having the vision to have sweatshirts and tee shirts made so that they could be sold at the hardware store. Adding that they had sold out 'lickety-split' and were all over town.

Nimble Nancy was beside me in the blink of an eye. It was uncanny how that girl could flit around the table so fast without tipping anything over. I was hugged, kissed, and told that she loved it and couldn't wait to show it off. With that she pulled it on and strutted around for all to admire. The Hathaway's Christmas Eve dinner was off to a great start.

My parents; homebodies as always, left shortly after dinner. Mr. Hathaway and Kathy refused our half-hearted offers to help with the cleaning up, so we drifted back into the living room, where Jack told me that knowing his sister's tendency to plan things well ahead of time he should have sensed that something was behind her request that I meet her at the airport but had I expected her to throw herself at me on the ride back?

"She didn't throw herself at me." I replied. "She simply let me know her feelings and it is a good thing she did because I have trouble expressing mine. I am still getting used to the fact that we are in love, but it is a great feeling. I am incredibly lucky."

Sally, a romantic to the bone, simply said "Ah; so sweet." Jack's answer was also short; "I'm really happy for both of you, I know that you are right for each other."

I liked Nancy's response the best; a full contact hug and kiss. How could a girl so strong and in such tremendous physical condition feel so soft?

Jack left to drive Sally home. Nancy and I cuddled for a while, although I was all too aware that her father and step-mother were likely to join us any minute. We made our plans for the next day. We would spend the morning with our families, then I would come to the Hathaway's around noon. Nancy and I would exchange our gifts then.

Jack was to visit Sally at the Bain's house and then return to greet my parents and Miss Grant, who had been asked to arrive around 3PM for a 5 o'clock dinner. Sally needed to spend some time with her family, but she would drive herself to the Hathaway's when she could break away; perhaps around 7 o'clock.

When I arrived home my parents were waiting for me. The first thing they said was what a wonderful time they had, how much they admired the Hathaway family, and that they thought that Nancy was both beautiful and delightful. I felt that a "but" was coming and sure enough it did.

But they were a little concerned that our romance seemed very sudden. Was I absolutely sure that Nancy and I were meant for each other? They did not want me to be hurt if she changed her mind, after all, she was world famous and so young.

"Yes" I said. "I am totally sure. The only thing sudden is that she opened up her heart to me on the drive here from Boston and my realization that I loved her but had been afraid to admit it even to myself. I guess it was some form of fear of failure."

I ended by saying "Don't worry about Nancy's commitment. She may be 17 but she is 100 % grounded. She is an expert at thinking things through in advance. I am still having a hard time believing we are in love, but I know that we are."

My parents toddled off to bed. I went outside for a few minutes to clear my head (a process I call 'counting stars'), then I went to bed also.

Chapter 35

The next morning my parents and I gave each other our gifts and my mother fixed my all time favorite breakfast; Johnny Cakes with warm maple syrup and bacon. The rest of America outside of New England does not seem to know about Johnny Cakes; I will never understand why.

I showed up at the Hathaway's house around noon; Nancy's arrowhead necklace nicely wrapped and tucked in a jacket pocket. Nancy met me at the door looking stunning in a short sleeved green velvet dress. We went to the living room where Mr. Hathaway and Kathy were relaxing; a few recently opened gifts scattered here and there.

Under the tree was a medium sized package all by itself. Nancy told me that it was my gift and she added a hint; "It isn't a sweatshirt."

In reply I said "And neither is this." With that I handed her my small package. She wanted me to open my gift first so I did. It was a beautiful briefcase in luxurious soft black leather; my initials in gold letters on the side near the handles. It looked like it would belong in the hands of the president of a major bank.

I was delighted with it and told her so. I hefted it a few times swinging it back and forth.

I said "This looks so good Miss Grant will probably give me a raise the second she sees it!"

Nancy told me that she had bought it before she knew of my future with Grant Holdings but now she was glad she picked it out for me. Then she said "Now I'm going to see what you have for me."

When she had the wrapping off and saw the pretty box that Shreve, Crump, and Low had provided she stopped, gave me a long look and whistled softly, saying "I never know what to expect from you."

Then, when she opened it: "Oh my goodness this is beautiful! Wherever did you find this?" Out of the corner of my eye I saw that Kathy was beaming as she walked over to get a close look at the arrowhead pendant and chain. She said "Who did this Carl, the workmanship is exquisite?"

I then told Nancy how I had found the arrowhead and that Kathy had given me the idea of having it made into a pendant. How the idea had stayed in my head until I learned that Miss Grant was a good customer of Shreve, Crump, and Low, and how she had spoken to their jewelry department about what I had in mind. I told how they were eager to tackle the project, and that they were so tickled with the result that they refused payment provided we allowed them to include a photo of it in a glossy promotional brochure they were preparing.

By this time Nancy had the chain around her neck and was admiring it in a mirror. Even I was impressed. The combination of her dark hair, the velvet dress, the black arrowhead, the gold necklace and wire, all with her very fair skin was stunning. She came to me and said softly that it was the best Christmas gift ever and she adored it.

"More than the sweatshirt?" I asked.

"Yes. I didn't think anything could top that but this is indescribable."

The rest of the afternoon passed quickly. Nancy answered a few questions about the Olympic preparations, the venue, her main competition, and so forth. She spoke about her attitude of staying on good terms with the slopes, as opposed to attacking them, and also mentioned that she was working on using her poles and arms faster right at the start of her races. Mr. Hathaway and Kathy spoke about a big trip they planned on taking in a few weeks to New Zealand and Tasmania. Neither of them had ever been to that part of the world. It was summer down there, and they wanted to do some hiking and explore the natural beauty of those far off places.

I asked about the supervision of the hardware store. Mr. Hathaway replied that the staff could handle things, and anyway, winter was the slowest time of the year for the store; everything would be fine.

My parents arrived promptly at 3 o'clock. They are compulsively early for any and all appointments and it must have been a struggle for them to keep from ringing the Hathaway's bell at quarter of. Before long the bell rang again and Miss Grant filled out the group.

I was used to seeing Miss Grant (It was difficult for me to call her Cora) dressed conservatively; usually in dark colors, but for this holiday occasion she was wearing green slacks (true, they were dark green, but still) a white blouse and a blazer embellished with a gold and enamel Christmas tree on the lapel.

I wanted to say something complimentary about her appearance but everything that came to mind could have been taken as sarcasm so I wisely kept quiet. No comment from me was necessary anyway; the rest of the party greeted her effusively.

My mentor had not arrived empty handed. She produced a very large bottle (I now know it was a magnum of Dom Perignon) of fancy looking French champagne which she handed to Kathy, saying that she had brought it chilled just in case it might fit into her Christmas plans.

Kathy was impressed and asked Cora where she had managed to find a rare bottle of fine champagne on such short notice. With a laugh Cora replied that her father was not usually good at practical things, but that before his untimely death he had stocked Sycamore Hall's wine cellar with hundreds of bottles that were now well aged.

As introductions were made Miss Grant made it clear that she wanted to be called Cora; adding that she hoped that the Hathaways and Smiths would have an easier time with that than "Carl here does."

At the time I was standing next to Nancy, who giggled and poked me in the ribs with her elbow. If I had any thoughts that Cora's presence might cause the gathering to be somewhat more formal that it would have been otherwise I would have been wrong. She was obviously enjoying herself immensely.

While the adults were enjoying Cora's gift; the French champagne, she produced a large rectangular box, wrapped in red and bound with a wide green ribbon. The card attached had my name on it. As she handed it to me she said, "I think you will be putting these to use from time to time."

Once I had carefully removed the wrapping I saw another box inside. In the upper left corner, written in block letters were the words "Rogers Peet."

Inside that box were three beautiful suits; one dark blue, one medium gray, and one a light tan. All of them were made of fine, lightweight wool.

I knew that Rogers Peet was a high end, old line Boston clothing store. As I held up the jacket of the dark blue suit to admire it my mother filled in the background. Cora had called her in October to get all of my sizes, so the suits were custom made and sure to fit.

As I was thanking Cora for the wonderful suits, she replied that it wouldn't do for me to be looking ragged when I was representing Grant Holdings.

I was somewhat overwhelmed by her generosity and as I gave her a hug she held me for a few extra seconds and whispered that there was an envelop in the inside pocket of the gray suit, but I was not to open it until I came back from driving Nancy to the airport the next day. What could that be all about?

In time we sat down to a wonderful Christmas dinner. Mr. Hathaway carved a turkey at an old sideboard, and there were the traditional side dishes; mashed potatoes, peas, stuffing, cranberry jelly, and rolls. Some families like to add other dishes to their Christmas meal, but I was glad that Kathy had stuck to the basics. Why clutter the table with all sorts of items that no one needs or even wants? Besides, I wanted to save some room for pumpkin pie.

The dinner table conversation was spirited and interesting. Kathy told a funny story of a convention of Lawyers who specialized in wills and estates that she had helped organize and oversee. She had expected these lawyers; mostly men, to be serious and dignified. Instead they drank like whales and took a child-like joy in wearing straw cowboy hats that she had thoughtfully provided them with.

Cora recalled Christmases of earlier days at Sycamore Hall. Her father Hammy traditionally became drunk every Christmas, so to counter this her grandmother kept moving the big Christmas meal to progressively earlier times until finally the Grant Christmas dinner was served at noon; about the time when Hammy would be making his first appearance of the day.

While the topic of old times at Sycamore Hall was in play, Cora switched to that very large house's current state. She told our group that over time the house had gradually become tired looking. She recognized that interior decorating was not something that she had a flair for, but that she did not want to bring in someone from outside to tackle the job on the grounds that it would seem impersonal. She then said this: "I want to ask all the women here to do a large favor for me. Would you be willing to come to my home, look around, and tell me what you think we could do to brighten up the place? That way when I do hire a decorator I will be able to point her in the right direction. Nancy, I wish you could be part of this but I know that you have to leave tomorrow morning.

"Jack, I definitely want your Sally to be part of this if she is willing. I will ask her if she has an interest once she gets here."

My mother quickly agreed. For her it was something of a command performance seeing that Cora was her husband's employer. Even so, I could tell that she was pleased with the idea.

Kathy was almost jumping out of her seat with excitement. The chance to have a say in re-doing the interior of New Kensington's largest and most historic home was exactly the sort of assignment that she thrived on.

As for me, I was glad. Sycamore Hall was definitely showing it's years. The cloak room, for example was poorly lit. The rugs had seen better days, and maybe something could be done to transform the gun room. Were there still guns in there? I had not looked.

After dinner, when Sally joined us and was invited to participate in the 'Sycamore Hall Study Group', as Kathy dubbed it, she squealed with delight, saying that she was jumping in with both feet.

Eventually the evening wound down. My parents, predictably, were the first to leave, closely followed by Cora.

After some cleaning up around the dining room and kitchen Kathy and Mr. Hathaway went upstairs. Jack and Sally settled down in the living room, and Nancy and I went out onto the porch.

We did some hugging and kissing and I said that I would be back around 6 A.M. to drive her back to Logan Airport. Then I headed home, my new suits and splendid briefcase in the back seat. I had temporarily forgotten about the mystery envelope that Cora had stashed in the inside pocket of the gray suit.

Chapter 36

I had set my alarm clock for 5 A.M. the next day so I knew I would not oversleep. Nevertheless, whenever I have to wake up earlier than normal I do not sleep well, and I was awake at 3 A.M. and slept fitfully from then on, finally getting out of bed at 4:55.

I pulled up to the front of the Hathaway's house a little before 6. Nancy must have been watching for me, because she came right out, suitcase in hand, and we turned the car towards Boston.

So much had happened since I had picked Nancy up at the airport on the 23rd that I was still having trouble grasping the fact I was in love totally, with Nancy. Furthermore, Nancy; stunning, charming, world famous Nancy was in love with me. I knew it was all true; after all, I had kept my feelings smothered under a layer of insecurities until Nancy bravely told me of her love for me. That had taken great courage; she had put herself way out on an emotional limb. My insecurities had quickly evaporated. I had never felt better; both about myself, and the world in general.

As we drove towards Boston I did my best to make these thoughts and feelings clear to Nancy. She told me that she had been a nervous wreck leading up to her confession of her love for me; worrying that I might not feel the same way she did and reject her. I told her that it took guts to open up the way she had, and Nancy said "Yes, and it certainly paid off didn't it?"

Then, always the planner, Nancy said "But, so far at least, there has been something missing hasn't there?"

I knew immediately what she was referring to. In fact the thought of being intimate with Nancy had been constantly on my mind since our first heavy duty roadside kiss three days earlier. I took my eyes off the road briefly and said to her "Yes; something vital. You had to have felt from our full contact hugs and kisses that my feelings for you are more than platonic. Have you been noticing all the motel signs we have been passing?"

Cars in those days had bench seats. She slid over to me and lightly took my ear in her teeth. "I would have had to be numb from the waist down not to have felt you. I have wanted to yell 'Where is the nearest bed?' several times"

She quickly added "I can't miss my plane, can you wait until after the Olympics?"

"If we have to; but barely."

She pulled out a tissue and blotted her eyes, saying "Oh Carl, I get so emotional. I'm going to miss you something fierce! You have to write to me every day."

"Every single day?"

"I'm thinking–okay, every day might be too repetitive. How about three times a week?"

"Done. Who knows, I may slip in a few extra bonus additions."

"I'll do the same. It is only seven or eight more weeks; then I will be home, win or lose."

"Winning would be best, but regardless, you know where to find me."

At the airport we said goodbye to each other at the curb. Nancy knew from experience that she was less likely to be recognized and swarmed by admirers if she kept her head down and moved fast, and she quickly vanished into the post-Christmas throng of travelers.

The Boston traffic was even worse than usual, but once I was out in the suburbs I could relax somewhat. I spent the remainder of the drive home alternating between thinking of Nancy and her shot at Olympic glory, my steamy thoughts about tending to the matter of what she and I had waiting under the heading of 'unfinished (actually unstarted) business', and also jumping in and out of my mind was the matter of Cora's mystery envelope, which was still tucked untouched in the inside pocket of my new gray suit; now nicely hanging in my bedroom closet.

Intimacy with Nancy was going to have to wait, but not the envelope. Once I was back at my house and had chatted briefly with my parents I went up to my room, took out the envelope, and sat down on the edge of my bed to see what Cora was up to.

Chapter 37

I could tell that there was something inside the envelope besides paper, it was heavy. I tore it open and was astonished to find that there were three diamond rings inside. Three diamond rings! What in the world was this all about. I picked up the phone and called Cora.

She seemed to be unusually pleased with herself when I asked what I was supposed to do with the rings, saying "Why don't you bring them over here and I will explain?" I made myself a turkey and stuffing sandwich (I had missed breakfast and was starving) and the rings and I were soon being shown into the former schoolroom inside Sycamore Hall. Miss Cora Grant was sitting on a couch and motioned for me to sit beside her. I did that, and wordlessly put the rings on the table in front of us; my eyebrows raised. With a 'Cat that swallowed the canary' expression on her face she asked "Have you figured this out yet?"

"Yes; I have figured out that you gave me three suits and one of them had an envelope in a pocket that had three diamond rings in it. Beyond that I have no idea what you mean by doing this. Is this some sort of old Scottish ritual?"

Shaking her head in mock frustration she asked "You love Nancy Hathaway, do you not?"

"Yes, I do. She is amazing. I am crazy lucky that she loves me back."

"And Carl, I know you well enough that I am sure you will always love her. You should; she is perfect for you."

"The rings?"

"You men can be so thick; I'll walk you through this. When two people love each other, what do they do?"

"They get married. But Nancy and I haven't had a chance to even talk about that. I guess we will after the Olympics."

"Progress at last. Now what happens before they get married?"

I had two thoughts simultaneously. One was (from the hormone driven part of my brain) that they start having sex as quickly as possible. The other was that they get engaged. Duh; these were engagement rings! "These are engagement rings aren't they?"

"Congratulations, you have managed to connect the dots. It took you long enough."

She picked up one of the rings. "This was my great grandmother's engagement ring."

She then picked up the ring with the largest diamond. "This was my grandmother's engagement ring. She let my father give it to my mother. He wanted to impress her with a big stone and his allowance wouldn't stretch far enough to buy a diamond of this size, so this was also my mother's engagement ring."

It was really an exceedingly large diamond, beautiful but also clunky; at least to my eyes. Putting that ring back down she picked up the last ring, saying "This fellow was MY engagement ring."

"Yours? I never knew you were married!"

"I never said I was married. I was engaged for a while to a handsome and funny young man named Preston. My father would have loved him. That was the problem, my beau was exactly like my father had been. They were both like champagne bubbles. I knew what my father had been like, that he could never change, and that I couldn't be happy with a man I didn't respect. When I broke off our engagement Preston was a good sport about it and said that he understood. He also said he knew that the first time I caught him cheating on me there would be hell to pay. He wouldn't take back the ring, saying that it wouldn't be right to put it back in circulation, so I have kept it all these years.

"All three of these rings have been gathering dust in a safe deposit box. I have no use for them and I have never wanted to sell them. Frankly the settings are outdated but the diamonds are flawless. I think that before long you will be asking Nancy to marry you and that will call for you to give her a diamond ring, so pick one."

Sometimes things just move too fast for me and this was one of those times. All I could say was that the big one; her mother's and grandmother's was too big. If Nancy put it on it would look like the ring was wearing Nancy. She would look lopsided.

Cora chuckled, saying that she agreed. She pushed that ring aside, leaving two finalists. Of the two I prefered the one that happy-go-lucky Preston had given to Cora. It was large without being too large and had a beautiful sparkle. I said "Your great grandmother's ring gets the silver medal. Yours looks the best to me. Are you sure you want to give it to me? It must be valuable."

"Yes, I am totally sure. And you have good taste in diamonds, that is by far the best of the three."

"I am not sure about the setting though, and I don't even know Nancy's ring size."

"The setting never looked right to me either. Preston must have been crocked when he picked it out. For that there is a three-word solution; Shreve, Crump, and Low. As for her ring size, I had Kathy get Nancy playing with some of her jewelry; Nancy will need a size six."

I refrained from pointing out that her solution had four words, not three. After thanking her for the generous and thoughtful gift I left. As I was driving home I wondered how many people were aware of what a warm-hearted woman Cora was. She was also far sighted; always thinking a step or two ahead and planning so as to assure good outcomes. In that regard she and Nancy were cut from the same bolt of cloth.

Several days later I was once again on the road towards Boston, the diamond ring snug in my pocket. This time I was to meet Shreve, Crump, and Low's manager, as arranged by their important customer Miss Cora Grant. Together we were to select a suitable setting for what would be Nancy's engagement ring. Cora and Nancy were not the only people around who could execute a plan; Preston's gift to Cora, after spending decades in the mothball fleet, would soon be back on active duty.

My meeting with Shreve, Crump, and Low's store manager, Mr. Gilbert (pronounced Gill-Bear) went well. He escorted me into his office and after some preliminary chit-chat he asked if I had any preconceived ideas as to what type of setting I would like to be shown. He had already been given sufficient background information by Cora, so he knew that I had a fine diamond in an outdated setting.

In reply I told him that I knew nothing about selecting ring settings, but that I knew the girl that I was selecting for, and that she would be more inclined to favor simple over fancy. With that I reached into my pocket, pulled out the ring, and placed it on a small dark blue velvet square that was between us on Mr. Gilbert's desk.

Mr. Gilbert picked it up in a respectful way, held the ring in the palm of his left hand and regarded it with an appreciative smile. Other than "Umm" he said nothing for several seconds.

He then said "Tiffany", paused, and added "Definitely from the 1930's. These two smaller diamonds and the squared off edges were all the rage back then and earlier also. These days women prefer gold settings to platinum. May I show you some settings that are more popular today?"

I thought about saying that I hadn't come to buy fishhooks but I minded my manners and meekly replied "Yes please."

I liked the third setting that Mr. Gilbert showed me, but, remembering what Nancy had said earlier about not accepting the fifth guy's advances simply because he seemed better than the previous four, I spent close to half an hour looking at settings that he thought could be suitable while he described what they were and how they would complement the diamond.

In the end I still thought the third setting I had been shown would be the one that Nancy would like the most. Mr. Gilbert nodded his approval, saying "Based on what you have told me I think you have made a wise choice. What would you like us to do with the former setting and the smaller diamonds?"

I certainly had no use for them and I was certain that Cora felt the same. I asked if Shreve, Crump, and Low would be interested in purchasing the leftovers, and the answer was yes. Mr. Gilbert then asked if I would like the proceeds credited against the cost of the new setting, adding that it might very well work out to a net credit.

That simply did not seem right, so we arranged for a bill for the setting to be sent to me (I had some savings from my summer jobs), and the proceeds from the sale of the old setting to be credited to Cora's account there at Shreve.

Given a choice between driving back into Boston in a week or so to pick up my new ring or having it sent to me I chose to have it sent. I was (and remain to this day) a timid driver. "Small Balls", in the lunch table parlance back at New Kensington High. When driving in and around the narrow, twisting streets of Boston they were particularly small. I was not eager to drive there again if it could be avoided.

As I was leaving, Mr. Gilbert; proper Bostonian that he was, said that he would like to ask me a personal question. When I agreed to permit it he asked if he would he be correct in guessing that the young woman I had given the arrowhead necklace to would be the same young woman that I intended to present the engagement ring to?

With equal formality I replied that such a guess would be accurate. His parting words were "Safe travels Mr. Smith."

Chapter 38

My travels turned out to be safe enough as I drove towards home, but once I was past the worst of the traffic I gave thought to this: when would be a good time to propose to Nancy? Should it be soon; right after the Olympics? Why wait? I was completely certain that I would always love her.

Then, on the other hand, I was only 18 and Nancy was 17. A very mature and stable 17 without question, but still there seemed to be no need to rush.

Did being engaged necessitate wedding plans? To me the answer was no. I would be a freshman at Williams in the fall and Nancy would be charming convention attendees and posing for cereal box photos for a year or so after her big race. A long engagement looked to be the smart move; would Nancy agree? I thought so but clearly we would need to talk the matter over. With a smile I pictured Nancy; the master planner, mapping out a strategy for us.

I gave a little thought to what friends, family, and the outside world would have to say. Friends and family knew that Nancy and I were in love and would stay in love; they would be supportive regardless of our decisions. As for the rest of the world? I didn't give a hoot.

In a way it was a shame that I could not convene a special 'when should Carl pop the question' committee. I mentally formed the group: Cora, of course would be there. Kathy was wise to the ways of the world. My parents could always be counted on, and Sally would bring a young woman's modern day perspective to the table. I had fun with that line of thought, but I knew the decision was mine alone to make.

Back in New Kensington things moved along in a routine way for a week or two except for another confrontation between Jack and officer Vincent (Vinny) DiNardo, the town's misfit cop. The former military policeman that Chief Hale had hired against his better judgement as a favor to his sister-in-law and due also to wifely pressure.

On a night that turned out to be fateful Jack and Sally had stopped at a diner on the way home from a movie. They were the only customers in the diner and they were enjoying slices of blueberry pie when officer DiNardo drove a patrol car into the lot and walked in.

Seeing Jack and Sally seated in a booth near the door DiNardo walked up, stood almost on top of them, and said, "I don't feel like sharing a meal with you, Hathaway. Get your ass out of here and take that little broad with you."

Sally could feel Jack tense up and quickly grabbed his elbow with both of her hands, saying "Jack; stay cool!"

Jack took a deep breath and replied "We are still eating so we won't be leaving for awhile."

DiNardo became red in the face and in a loud voice replied, "I said get out!"

While this exchange was going on Maisy; who was serving as both cook and waitress for the diner at that hour spoke up. Raising her voice, she said, "You leave those kids alone Vinny!"

Sally still had a tight grip on Jack's arm which was serving to help Jack keep his temper under control. Twisting around in the booth so that he could see Maisy around Vinny, Jack sounding calmer than he felt I am sure, asked her to call the station and tell the duty officer what was going on.

That served the intended purpose, or at least for that night it did. Vinny turned to Maisy and told her not to bother making the call; he had lost his appetite. Facing back towards Jack and Sally he said in a low voice "Trying to get me fired aren't you? Well I'm from Sicily and I'll get you for this, you little shit." With that he left the diner and drove away.

Sally was deeply upset by the incident and said to Jack "You stay away from that man; he's crazy!"

Jack's hands were shaking due to a surge of adrenalin that had swept through him during the confrontation. When Sally noticed this she held both his hands in hers and leaned her head against his shoulder. After another deep breath Jack replied "You're right; he's off his rocker. Dad is friends with Chief Hale. When I get home I am going to tell Dad what happened. The chief should know about this."

In answer Sally pushed away the uneaten part of her pie saying "I'm coming with you. I want to be sure you tell it right!"

At the Hathaway's house Mr. Hathaway and Kathy were at the dining room table working up a list of things they needed to pack for their upcoming trip to New Zealand and Tasmania, which was to commence in just a few days. Jack, with frequent embellishing interruptions from Sally, told his father what had happened at the diner. Mr. Hathaway and Kathy listened carefully. When Jack and Sally finished Mr. Hathaway was quiet for a moment. Kathy said "Tom, that man is dangerous."

In reply Mr. Hathaway quietly said "You're right; he is dangerous; and unstable to boot. I'm going to have a talk with the chief first thing tomorrow. In the meantime, Jack, I'm going to drive the two of you back to Sally's house and drop her off. I don't want you driving by yourselves while he is out there on duty."

The next morning Mr. Hathaway met with Chief Hale at the police station, telling him of the earlier incident between Jack and DiNardo at the drugstore lunch counter and then the more recent confrontation at the diner. He also told the chief about Jack overhearing DiNardo call the three little boys brats, and then acting belligerent and patting his holster when he noticed Jack nearby.

Part way through the conversation the chief began taking notes. When Mr. Hathaway finished speaking Chief Hale said "This is very serious Tom, and I am glad that you have let me know. I believe every word of it and I am going to interview Maisy just to get her to back up Jack and Sally's version of what went on. I'll also need to speak with Jack and Sally as well as the pharmacist. It is just a formality but I will need their statements.

"Then I'm going to get Vinny in here and listen to him try to talk his way out of the trouble he is in. Whatever he says isn't going to work. Under our agreement with the policemen's union I can't fire him without a hearing, so I will be putting through that paperwork today. I never should have hired him in the first place."

Chief Hale knew that the paperwork had to be in proper order for the hearing. He interviewed Maisy, Jack, Sally, and also the pharmacist, who had a clear recollection of DiNardo ordering Jack to give up his seat at the lunch counter.

Once he had done all this the chief called DiNardo into his office, reviewed the situation as well as the witness's statements and told him that he was being charged with misconduct. There would be a hearing, in accord with union rules, and that once that was out of the way he would be fired.

Sensing disaster, Vinny tried to minimize the situation. "Oh come on Chief, that wasn't anything. I was just teasing the kid. If he can't take a joke then I'll leave him alone. He's trying to get me in trouble over nothing."

The chief leaned forward in his chair and, looking directly in DiNardo's eyes replied "No Vinny, it isn't nothing. We are here to serve and protect the people who live here, not to bully them, not to order them out of restaurants, and not to call them brats, broads, and little shits. I never should have hired you in the first place and I am going to correct that mistake. You should not be wearing our uniform; you are a bad cop."

Desperate, Vinny played his last card; "Aunt Angie will stand up for me!"

Aunt Angie, of course, was the chief's wife Angela and Chief Hale had heard enough. "Aunt Angie wishes she never heard of you. She can't wait till you are out of her sight. Now get out of here."

Then, as soon-to-be-ex-officer DiNardo was leaving, the Chief fired this parting shot "And stop telling people that you are Sicilian. You're American. The part of Italy your great-grandparents came here from is a lot closer to Albania that it is to Sicily. If you have to say anything about your ancestry try telling people you're Albanian for a change."

And that, we thought, settled the officer DiNardo situation, pending the hearing; which was expected to be a brief formality.

The terms of the union agreement had all new patrolmen on a probationary status for their first year of service and Vinny was well short of that. During their probationary period rookie patrolmen could be terminated for almost any reason, and the chief's decision was sure to be upheld.

And so we had reason to assume that DiNardo would no longer be a concern. How wrong we were.

Chapter 39

A few days later Kathy and Mr. Hathaway left for their much-anticipated vacation. They planned to start on the North Island of New Zealand and work their way down to the South Island, taking their time as they did so.

From there the plan was for them to fly to Hobart, Tasmania, where they would rent a car and explore that island at leisure. From there they would fly across the Bass Strait to Melbourne and then return home.

The night before they were to leave There was a Bon Voyage dinner for them at the Hathaway's home; a brainstorm of Sally's. Jack and Sally were to prepare what Sally predicted would be an unforgettable meal, and I was invited to share the feast.

The unforgettable meal turned out to be spaghetti and meatballs, which I thought was just about the limit of Sally's kitchen skills, and we all had a wonderful time. After dinner Kathy performed her interpretation of the New Zealand native's Maori war dance, The Haka, complete with fierce grimaces, and accompanied with uproarious grunts and threatening gestures.

Not to be outdone, Mr. Hathaway retaliated with his version of the same ritual and with that we all joined in, taking turns.

Once this hilarity wound down we voted for best Maori. The unanimous winner was Sally, who besides adding a cross-eyed strut to her performance had thrown in a concluding wide-kneed squat and bicep slap, embellished with a show stopping fart.

Mr. Hathaway had not set any particular time table for their return because he and Kathy didn't know exactly where they would be going or how much time it would take to see and do whatever they might want to experience. Roughly they thought two or three weeks should be sufficient.

While they were away Jack would be on his own and was looking forward to it. He knew how to fix his own breakfast and lunch and could handle a simple dinner.

Mr. and Mrs. Bain expected Jack to be a frequent dinner guest and my parents wanted him to join us as often as possible. It was clear that Jack would not suffer from malnutrition while his father and step-mother were away.

Chapter 40

As I said earlier, New Kensington had an excellent public-school system. Overall the teachers and administrators did their jobs efficiently and well. The head administrator was the town's superintendent of schools, Mr. Clarence Brown. Mr. Brown, in turn, reported to the town's three-member school board; which was chaired and tightly controlled by Mrs. Elizabeth Anderson.

Mrs. Anderson's age was difficult to estimate. Her hair was always tightly lacquered into place; lips and nails flawlessly red. I had never seen her expression change; never a frown, never a smile. Sometime in the distant past there had been a Mr. Anderson, but he had long since fled the town and; so far as anyone could tell, the universe.

There had also been a daughter; Julia. Julia was a pretty girl but had little to say, seemingly colorless; probably downtrodden. When she graduated from New Kensington High she had gone off to college and never returned. Mrs. Anderson lived alone.

It was several days before word of Jack's parents being away on an extended vacation reached the ears of Mrs. Anderson and she interpreted it as a situation that threatened the stable behavior of New Kensington's school aged children.

Mrs. Anderson swung into protective action. She called a postal worker named George, the most malleable of the other two members of what she often referred to as "Her board" and outlined the moral risks that now threatened to lead their students astray. The parental void that currently existed at the home of Mr. and Mrs. Hathaway. The fact that the house was out on the edge of town, with no neighbors close at hand to report whatever wild teen-aged parties might spring up. The potential for drinking! And imagine what that could lead to; Sex orgies!

Clearly something had to be done and done quickly. It was obviously the duty of New Kensington's school board to protect their students and her quickly formed strategy was two pronged. First, the Hathaway's house must be locked up; Chief Hale to be the keeper of the keys. Jack would be allowed to continue to attend school, but only if a set of responsible parents agreed to have him be their house guest until such time as Mr. and Mrs. Hathaway return from their 'extended travels'.

Second; to assure that this action be taken promptly, Jack was to be suspended from school until these protective steps were taken. Surely that would be only for a day or two.

George was uncertain. Did they have the authority to do this?

"Of course we do! We are responsible for the education and well being of all our children. I want your backing on this; do I have it?"

"Well, I guess so."

That was all chairwoman Elizabeth Anderson needed to hear. There was no need to call the third member of the committee, a retired teacher with whom Mrs. Anderson frequently clashed. She finished the conversation with Jellyfish George and called the superintendent of schools, Clarence Brown. She outlined the situation as well as what she described as the school board's decision, and ordered him to suspend Jack, effective the following morning. The suspension to remain until Mr. Brown notified her that the board's conditions had been met and that Jack could be reinstated.

Mr. Brown listened in shock to Mrs. Anderson's plan. When she finished his reply was both simple and direct: "We can't do that Mrs. Anderson."

"We can and we will. This is for the protection of our students."

"You are asking me to suspend one of our students for something he hasn't done and is unlikely to do. Jack Hathaway is one of the most popular kids in the whole school and his girlfriend is maybe even more popular. If you insist on doing this these kids are going to riot."

"If you explain what we are doing correctly the students will understand. It will all be finished in a day or two."

"I don't think it would be legal. I know locking up the house wouldn't be."

"I know what I have authority to do and I am telling you, not asking you. Suspend that boy!"

Mrs. Anderson now had Mr. Brown in a tight spot. If he refused her direct order she might fire him and replace him with someone who would follow her orders. The best reply he could think of was this: "The smart thing to do is first, let Chief Hale know what we intend to do. We may need him to smooth things over and we don't want the newspaper to put what we do in a bad light."

"I don't care what our little bitty newspaper has to say."

"Well I do, everyone in town reads it. Besides, the Hathaways are friends of Cora Grant, and she owns the newspaper."

This information gave Mrs. Anderson pause. Suspending a student was one thing. Crossing swords with Cora Grant was something else, and would definitely be picking a fight with the wrong person.

"All right. I will meet you at the station house in half an hour. Call the chief and tell him to expect us then."

Chapter 41

Half an hour later they were seated in the chief's office. Although Mr. Brown had told Chief Hale what Mrs. Anderson intended to do, the chief played it straight, saying, "All right, what do you want to see me about?'

Doing her utmost to sound calm and reasonable Mrs. Anderson explained why her board felt that it would be prudent to take the steps necessary to avoid the risk of the Hathaway's home becoming a magnet for 'her' students, who were basically good but easily lead astray when presented with opportunities for mischief and sin. She always put her students' welfare first. Besides, Mr. and Mrs. Hathaway might be gone for months.

The chief, despite thinking that he had seldom met a more self-important and mean-spirited woman than Mrs. Elizabeth Anderson, managed to avoid showing his feelings. He leaned back in his chair, cupped his chin between his right thumb and forefinger, and said this:

"No one whose name isn't Hathaway is going to be locking that house. Do either of you know when Mr. and Mrs. Hathaway plan on coming back?"

After learning that neither of them had any information about the Hathaway's travel schedule he said "Let's find out." He walked to his door, leaned out, and slightly raising his voice asked Plugs, the switchboard operator, to call the hardware store and get Jack on the phone. By that time it was close to 4 P.M., and Jack usually helped at the store after school.

Plugs promptly replied that Jack was there but outside helping unload a delivery of lumber. Upon hearing this, Chief Hale asked her which officers were currently on patrol. The answer was Wicks and DiNardo.

This caused the chief to say to Plugs, "I don't want DiNardo anywhere near the Hathaway boy. Tell Wicks to go to the hardware store. Tell him that Jack Hathaway is outside unloading some lumber and to tell him that I would like to know when he expects his father back from his trip. If he could swing by the station I would appreciate it. He will probably have his car there but Wicks can offer Jack a lift if he wants a ride."

For several minutes the chief attended to some paperwork at his desk while Mrs. Anderson and Mr. Brown sat stiffly in chairs across from him. He then went to the door and asked, "Have you heard from Wicks?" The answer was "Vinny said he was just a block away and that he would handle it."

Frowning, the chief said "Excuse me" to Mrs. Anderson and Mr. Brown, and went to the switchboard operator, saying, "Did you hear me say that I didn't want DiNardo anywhere near the Hathaway boy?"

"Yes, but I didn't know you wanted me to broadcast it."

Hearing that the chief, looking exasperated, picked up the police broadcasting microphone and said "Wicks, get over to the hardware store fast and keep an eye on things."

While that was happening Plugs, the switchboard operator, answered a call with her usual greeting; "New Kensington police sta–" then "WHAT? Chief, someone from the hardware store says that Vinny just shot Jack Hathaway!"

The chief was still holding the microphone. He said "Oh God no!" and then "Wicks! We have a report the DiNardo just shot Jack Hathaway. Lights and siren. Disarm DiNardo and be careful; he may have gone crazy! I'm on my way!"

But it was too late to make any difference. Vincent (Vinny) DiNardo had arrived at the hardware store less than two minutes from when he had heard Plugs relay Chief Hale's message. He pulled his patrol car around to the back part of the store where the lumber was kept and saw Jack helping a truck driver unload two by fours. Opening the back door of the patrol car he said "Hathaway, get your ass in here."

Jack didn't move, saying "What are you talking about?"

"I'm talking about you're under arrest. I'm taking you to the station."

Jack didn't believe him. More importantly he didn't trust him. Shaking his head, he said "I'm not getting into that car with you. I'll call Chief Hale and find out what is going on."

Hearing that, DiNardo grabbed Jack's arm, twisted it behind his back, and roughly shoved him into the back seat of the patrol car, slamming the door shut as he did so.

Modern patrol cars do not have door handles on the inside back doors but in those days New Kensington's police cars did have back door handles, although the back doors could be kept locked from the front seats. Officer DiNardo had neglected to lock the back doors after opening them when he pulled into the hardware store parking lot.

When Jack was thrown into the back seat he quickly slid across to the opposite door, opened it, and started running for the hardware store entrance.

Seeing that, DiNardo yelled "Hey!", pulled his revolver, and shot twice. The first bullet missed Jack, grazing one of the customers who had just left the store in the upper arm. The second bullet hit Jack slightly to the left of his spine, tore through his heart and lodged in his aorta. Jack was knocked flat, made one small effort to get up, and fell back dead.

Besides the driver of the lumber truck there were several people in the parking lot who watched this take place. For a second everyone was too stunned to move. Then one man ran to Jack, hoping to be able to help. The others stayed still, watching officer DiNardo to see what he would do next.

Still holding his revolver DiNardo seemed confused. Finding his voice, he said "You saw what happened, my prisoner tried to escape!"

The man who had tried to help Jack turned and said "You son of a bitch, you just murdered this kid!"

Wicks arrived; siren blasting, lights flashing. He carefully approached DiNardo with his gun out. His first words were "Vinny, put your gun down."

Vinny did as he was told. Wicks quickly had Vinny put his hands behind his back, handcuffed him, and locked him in the back of Wicks' patrol car. Once that was done He picked up the car's microphone and reported that officer DiNardo had shot Jack Hathaway and wounded another bystander, that Jack appeared to be in very serious condition, that DiNardo was disarmed, cuffed, and in Wick's car, and that he was waiting for the chief.

By this time the siren of Chief Hale's car could be heard, but it was far too late to matter.

Chapter 42

While this was going on I was doing what I often did after school and before dinner; I was sitting in my room reading. I barely noticed when the phone rang, but I certainly noticed my mother's scream. As I ran downstairs my mother, looking totally shocked, turned to me saying "Oh Carl, that crazy cop just murdered Jack!"

The information was sketchy but validated by several other calls my mother made in quick succession. I sat on our couch with my head in my hands. I was shocked and unable to think. What should I do? Mr. Hathaway and Kathy were somewhere on the other side of the world and Nancy was in Europe, where it was night. She was probably sleeping. Suddenly I thought of Sally. I ran to the phone and called her. The line was busy and I knew what that meant; she knew. I grabbed my car keys, told my mother that I was going to Sally's house, and took off.

Mrs. Bain greeted me at the door, tears rolling down her face. Behind her I heard Sally sobbing pitifully. I hadn't been crying until I saw Sally, but she was a sight to break anyone's heart. We hugged each other and cried our eyes out.

Poor Sally. poor, poor Sally. Sally, the girl who always walked in sunshine, was devastated; crushed. She kept repeating "How could anyone kill Jack? What am I going to do? And then "Help me Carl; please help me!"

Mrs. Bain had called their family doctor who came, took one look at Sally, and gave her a strong sedative. By that time Mr. Bain had arrived home and together the doctor and Mr. and Mrs. Bain helped Sally upstairs and into bed. I had figured out what I needed to do next and it was going to be the hardest thing I would ever have to do.

But first I went up to Sally's bedroom. The sedative had almost knocked her out but she held out her hands for me and God bless her, she told me that I had to call Nancy.

That is the call that I was dreading but I did not want her to hear of Jack's death from anyone else but me. I kissed Sally's cheek and went home.

My first call was the easy one. Or what I should say is that it was easier than what would be my second call; I called Cora.

She had already heard the awful news, someone had called her housekeeper and the housekeeper had told Cora.

As always, she was on top of the situation. After we commiserated briefly she told me that we had to track down Tom and Kathy Hathaway without knowing where they were, other than that they were somewhere in New Zealand. Cora was about to call our senior state senator; a man who had received substantial campaign contributions from Grant Holdings and knew her well. The senator would be asked to contact the Secretary of State and to tell him it was urgent that the Hathaways be located. Once they were contacted they were to be told call Miss Grant immediately due to a family emergency.

Cora told me that she would remain in her house until she could speak with Tom, and that when she did she would break the terrible news to him. She guessed that it might be a day or two before they were located and perhaps another day or two before they would be able to return home. She was also going to contact Chief Hale to keep him informed of the steps she was taking.

My job, my duty, and my responsibility was to reach Nancy by phone and break the news to her that her brother had been murdered.

In this regard there was not a moment to waste. Horrible as this news would be, it would be worse for Nancy to hear it first as a rumor or incomplete information. Or from anyone or any source other than me. I started making calls.

Starting with the main telephone number for the U.S. Olympic committee, eventually, and not without difficulty, I was speaking with the night security guard at the hotel where our ski team was staying.

Naturally he was unwilling to wake Nancy up so that she could take a phone call from someone who claimed to be her boyfriend. I started by apologizing for putting the guard in a difficult position, but there had been a family tragedy and that Nancy had to be informed.

I thought that the guard felt that I was sincere. However, he told me that they got many crank calls and he was not going to disturb Nancy simply on the word of someone he had never heard of.

I shifted gears and told him that the tragedy was going to be national news within a few hours at the latest if it was not already, and when that happened the media would be after Nancy like a biblical plague. It was imperative that Nancy have a chance to prepare for this. I finished by asking how risky it would be for him to call her room and tell her that Carl Smith was calling with an urgent message. I assured him that she would take the call. To further convince him I said that I knew about the recent attack on her by the member of the Italian ski team.

This brought a few seconds of thoughtful silence. The guard made up his mind, saying "We have kept that very quiet, so if she told you about it then (pause) okay. I'm going to knock on her door and tell her that she has an urgent call from Carl Smith. She had better know who you are or I'm going to track you down and knock your teeth down your throat. Hold the phone."

The guard was human. After a short wait Nancy picked up. "Carl, is that you? What's happened?"

It broke my heart to tell her this. "Nancy darling, I have awful news, it's about Jack; he's dead."

I heard Nancy gasp and choke. "No! he can't be dead. Are you sure?"

"I'm positive and I hate having to tell you but the media is going to be jumping all over this. That nasty cop DiNardo found out that the police chief wanted to ask Jack when your father and Kathy were coming back from their vacation. DiNardo tried to arrest Jack and when he wouldn't get into the squad car the crazy bastard shot Jack in the back."

"Oh dear God, how could anyone do this?' Nancy was crying hard. "I can't think! What am I going to do? I have to get home!"

I had been thinking about what she ought to do, and said this: "Yes, even though this is a very bad time to leave the team you have to come home. I hope not for too long. Cora is using her influence to have our government locate your father and Kathy. They will come home as soon as they can be found.

"You are part of a big organization there and you will need to use the support people with the Olympic team. Have them find a way to get you back here right away. In the meantime make sure that they keep the media away from you. Make them understand that you will be back as soon as you can and that you will stay in touch with them."

"Yes, alright. What else?"

"Give my phone number to whoever might need it; Cora's too, she will be staying by her phone around the clock. As soon as you know your flight information let me know; I'll meet the plane. I just wish I was there now for you."

Nancy seemed to rally. She said she would be calling me back and told me that she loved me and would see me soon.

"I love you very much and I will see you at the airport. If that security guard is still around I need to talk to him."

The guard got on the phone saying "Jesus Christ, some nut killed her brother? I'm sorry I didn't believe you at first."

I told him that I knew he was doing what he was there for and gave him my phone number in case anyone needed it. When I put the phone down I felt that I was at the end of my ability to handle things.

My parents had been listening to my side of the conversation and tried to comfort me as best they could. I felt that I had aged five years since hearing the news.

Chapter 43

After my brief but traumatic conversation with Nancy I was drained and emotionally wrung out. My mother made a sandwich for me, and although I had no appetite I put on my winter coat and, sandwich in hand, went out onto the porch. I was trying to think things out and not having any luck.

After 20 or 30 minutes of this I decided to call Cora. Apparently she was at her desk; she picked up on the second ring. I told her about my telephone conversation with Nancy and she told me that our senator had promised to have the State Department contact the New Zealand government and have them take any and all steps to locate Mr. Hathaway and Kathy.

She had also brought Chief Hale up to date on the efforts to contact Jack's parents. Going further, she had arranged for the chief and New Kensington's mayor, William (Billy) Travis, to meet with her at her home later that evening. Cora anticipated that the media would be descending full force on our town and falling all over themselves in search of every crumb of information that in any way concerned the shooting, the town, the Hathaway family, and above all else, how this would affect Nancy and her status as Olympic favorite.

Cora went on to say that although Chief Hale was obviously deeply disturbed by the action of a member of his force and crushed that he had compromised his judgement when he hired DiNardo, she felt that he was still capable of doing his job.

At the meeting with the chief and the mayor she intended to emphasize the need for complete honesty in dealing with the media in all it's forms. Any attempt to sugar coat the ugliness of the situation would be ripped apart, and that stonewalling, hiding, not returning phone calls, or any form of disinformation would only make things worse.

Her plan was for the mayor and the chief to become highly visible so that television reporters and all others covering the story would not resort to scouring the town seeking scraps of gossip. To assist them with this Cora had hired a Boston public relations firm, Kenmore Square Consultants, and a team of four specialists was already on it's way from Boston. They were to drive directly to Sycamore Hall, and she expected them to arrive before Chief Hale and the mayor. She wanted things done professionally and with integrity. In this way the situation stood a reasonable chance to be seen as a horrible tragedy and not simply a bunch of small town bumpkins making a series of dumb judgmental errors.

Having said all this she then suggested that I get some rest. She asked that I call her when I learned Nancy's travel plans. Cora told me that in view of the fact that Nancy would be arriving in town well before Mr. and Mrs. Hathaway, she might prefer to stay at Sycamore Hall until her father and Kathy managed to get here. If that turned out to be the case she would be a welcome guest.

We finished our call and I decided to take her advice and lie down. As I was taking my socks off Nancy called. "Carl, the chairman of the U.S. Olympic Committee has arranged for me to fly home in his personal jet. I'll be in the air as soon as I can get to the airport and the crew is ready. They can fly into the executive airport at the capital and we should be there by mid-afternoon your time tomorrow. Is that okay?"

"Yes, perfect, I'll be waiting for you there. This will save us lots of driving time. Besides, Cora expects that the media will be swarming so it's good that we can avoid Logan. How are you doing?"

"I feel like my brain is half paralyzed, but everyone here is 100% supportive; even our head coach. All he said was that he understands why I have to go, but to please come back as quickly as possible. How are you holding up?"

"I'm spent, and I'm going to get some rest. Cora is organizing the town so that all the national attention does not swamp us."

"She is the one to do it. My roommate is helping me pack. Get some sleep and I'll see you soon. I love you."

"I love you more than ever. Nancy, this couldn't be worse or at a worse time, but somehow we will get through it."

"Together Carl, always together. Bye for now."

I called and gave Cora a quick update, lay down, and was asleep in seconds.

Chapter 44

I said earlier that the superintendent of schools, Clarence Brown, had told Elizabeth Anderson, chairwoman of the school board, that Cora owned the town's newspaper but this was an oversimplification. Three years earlier the man who had owned the newspaper suffered a severe stroke and handling the multiple tasks of being owner, publisher, and editor became much more than he could deal with. He needed to sell the paper quickly so that he and his wife could move into a condo on the west coast of Florida.

There was an eager potential buyer; an assistant editor at the Boston Globe who had all the right credentials. Education, experience, a stable family life, and a desire to live in a small town and be his own boss. There was only one problem–money; he had very little of it.

The paper generated a healthy yearly profit and the seller needed cash. Cora was aware of the situation and stepped in.

She felt that our town needed the newspaper. It had been doing a good job of covering local news: high school sports, obituaries, balanced reporting of New Kensington's political activities, and a useful advertising section.

So Cora bought the newspaper for a fair price and immediately hired the man from Boston, Robert Long, to run it. She started by giving him five percent ownership of the paper, contingent on Mr. Long running the paper for at least 2 years.

She also gave him a series of yearly options to increase his ownership up to 100 percent, so that he could use profits from his yearly bonus to buy out Cora over time.

This was Cora at her classic best. The former owner was able to retire to the land of palm trees and alligators. Mr. Long would realize his goal of being his own boss provided that he ran the newspaper successfully. Cora would make some money as she gradually sold off her ownership interest to the incoming editor and publisher, and the paper; an asset to the town, never missed a publication date. Everyone got what they wanted.

Jack's murder (I was never able to refer to it in other terms such as the shooting or killing, which the media felt the need to do) became a sensation in and around New Kensington and the nation as well. Our Schools were closed, flags flew at half mast, and the town's watering holes did a booming business as people sought companionship and conversation. DiNardo was quickly moved from our town's dinky, two cell police station to a more secure facility at the state capital.

Chief Hale handed his resignation to the mayor on the night of the murder when they met with Cora at Sycamore Hall, and offered to call the governor's office the next day to request that a representative from the state police assume the chief's duties until the town could hire a new chief.

At Cora's suggestion the mayor requested that Chief Hale remain in his position for at least the next several days, which would allow time for the worst of the uproar to die down, but that this delay in the resignation be made public the following morning. This fit with her plan for the town and it's officials to be completely candid and open in it's reaction to Jack being killed by DiNardo.

Our newspaper came out with a special edition (which promptly sold out and required several re-printings), and in his editor's column, aptly named 'The Long View,' Robert Long wrote a piece which he titled "If Only."

In it he listed things that could have saved Jack's life starting with: "If only the Army had court martialed DiNardo instead of turning him loose with a general discharge."

"If only DiNardo hadn't begged his mother to speak to her sister, Angela Hale, and attempt to have Mrs. Hale ask Chief Hale to give DiNardo a chance", and "If only Angela Hale had refused to interfere in a police matter."

"If only Chief Hale had used more of his judgement and less of his heart," and "If only someone had told the chief of officer

DiNardo's earlier improper behavior towards Jack at the drugstore's lunch counter."

And "If only Elizabeth Anderson had kept her nose out of a situation which clearly should not have involved the town's school board."

"If only Ann ('Plugs') McNab had passed verbatim the chief's instruction's to have officer Wicks speak to Jack and that the chief did not want DiNardo near Jack, instead of editing out the crucial last part."

And finally, "If only Jack had stayed in DiNardo's squad car instead of sliding out the far side and running towards the entrance of Hathaway Hardware, then in all likelihood Jack would still be with us."

Chapter 45

As predicted by Cora, the town of New Kensington quickly became a media focal point. Television, radio, magazine reporters; there were squads everywhere thrusting microphones, photographing and filming the town and it's population. Children were stopped in the street so that they could be asked if they knew Jack Hathaway. Teachers were tracked to their homes and doorbells rung: what could they tell the world about Jack?

Various media outposts were maned; the town square became the mayor's *ad hoc* office, where (with constant and much needed assistance from one of Cora's public relations people) the mayor did a surprisingly good job of answering an avalanche of questions.

There were never less than 20 reporters milling around the front of the police station where, to his everlasting credit, Chief Hale, on an hourly basis accepted full blame for hiring Vincent DiNardo.

This deflected some of the media's blood lust as they searched for a prime villain, besides DiNardo. Cora had correctly foreseen this, and two more of her Boston P.R. people were at the chief's side through all this.

It took little time for the media's searchlights to turn towards the chairwoman of New Kensington's school board. Before noon of the day after the shooting there were news vans outside the front door of Mrs. Elizabeth Anderson's home.

She made a brief appearance. Standing in her doorway she said that she had done nothing wrong and that her only concern was for the welfare of her schoolchildren.

Finally the members of the media had opposition. If they had one collective skill that was finely honed it was their ability to smell self-protecting double talk from a mile away. The questions flew like poisoned arrows towards the stone faced Mrs. Anderson.

"Was it helpful to order the suspension of a student who had done nothing wrong?" "Was it her practice to browbeat a fellow committee member into agreeing with her questionable decision?" (Jellyfish George,the unfortunate member of the school board who had agreed to go along with Mrs. Anderson's decision to suspend Jack had already been cornered and done what he could to put the blame on her).

"Why had she not consulted with the third member of her committee?" "Was it her practice to overrule school superintendent Clarence Brown on minor matters such as a student's parents going on vacation?"

And "Is it your belief that no 18 year old can be trusted to behave if left alone while the parents are vacationing, or was there something specific about Jack Hathaway that alarmed you?"

Mrs. Elizabeth Anderson's reaction to this onslaught was to slam her door shut. Several minutes later her garage door opened and she tried for a clean escape. Finding the base of her driveway blocked by a TV van, she cut across her front lawn, scattering media people left and right, as she was filmed fleeing the town.

There was a second side to all this juicy news fodder. It had already been made public that Jack's sister, the beautiful Nancy Hathaway, America's shining Olympic star, was aware of the death of her brother and would be returning to New Kensington as quickly as possible. What was not known was that she was already airborne, and that she was due to arrive at the small executive airport at our state capital that afternoon. The press had missed that one; at least so far, and were misdirecting their efforts toward Logan airport, anticipating a prime photo opportunity when the grieving sister arrived.

So far as I knew the media people had not staked out the Hathaway's house. Why should they? No one was there.

There was one exception to this. A photographer from a tabloid magazine, attempting to photograph Jack's home, set off on foot and made the mistake of taking what he thought would be a shortcut through the woods.

Within minutes he became disoriented and went further into the forest. Several hours later, badly scratched, hysterical, and without his camera, he stumbled into a farmer's back pasture. From there the farmer arranged for him to be taken by ambulance to our local hospital where he was treated for dehydration and frostbite.

Of course the search was on for Tom and Kathy Hathaway in far away New Zealand, and that added more spice to the mix for the millions who were following the developments. Thankfully the New Zealand government was able to locate the Hathaways before they learned about Jack. Mr. Hathaway was given the message to call Miss Cora Grant to receive an urgent message. When he did this it was Cora's sad duty to tell him that his wonderful son Jack was dead.

Getting back home from New Zealand was never going to be a speedy operation, and although Nancy's flight was delayed due to weather I was there to meet her when the plane landed at dusk. She thanked the crew of the Olympic chairman's jet, and after a brief meeting with customs officials we headed back to New Kensington.

I had told Nancy of Cora's invitation to stay with her at Sycamore Hall, but as I expected Nancy wanted to sleep in her own bed. While Nancy spoke with the customs people I called Cora and told her of Nancy's preference.

I knew that Nancy did not want any sort of welcoming committee to greet her at the house but there were a few people who, more for their sake than Nancy's, needed to pay their respects. I explained this to Nancy, although it turned out that the explanation was not necessary; Nancy understood.

Cora, for one, would be there, bringing with her several days' worth of food supplies provided by a catering service. She also wanted to briefly introduce Nancy to the four members of the Kenmore Square Consultants team: The managing partner Al Malone, Alice Birch, Chet Chang, and a woman named Stone; nickname Rocky. Al was to quickly outline how his team would be working to help the Hathaway family and the town deal with the media onslaught. Once that was done they were to leave.

My dear parents couldn't be left out, and naturally Mr. and Mrs. Bain would be bringing Sally there. Both my mother and Mrs. Bain felt compelled to bring casseroles.

Somehow our arrival went unnoticed by the media hordes and we met Cora, the four public relations people, my parents, and the Bains at the Hathaway's house in the early evening. The P.R. people were introduced, Al had his say, and they left.

After all of us spent time hugging, crying, and commiserating, Nancy pulled me aside, put her hands on my temples, gave me that irresistible gray eyed look and said "Carl, I want you to stay here with me tonight; will you? Don't think; just answer."

I quickly said "Yes; of course," although the full implication of this took several seconds to register. Then without moving my head I swung my eyes around the room. Nancy understood my meaning, gave me a kiss and a sexy, as I read it, smile, and said "I'll start with Sally."

Our small group was gathered in the living room at that time, the ladies having finished stowing the food in the pantry and kitchen. Nancy walked to Sally, took her arm, and lead her off into the dining room for some privacy. She started with this: "Sally, I know how deeply in love with Jack you have been and probably always will be."

Sally's response was a nod. Nancy continued: "That's how much I love Carl. I know that you and he have been close friends ever since you met and you wouldn't be human if sooner or later you didn't start thinking about Carl."

Sally shut her eyes briefly, looked down, then back up, and said "I already have and I hate my brain for it."

Nancy smiled weakly and said that she wanted the three of us to always be friends, and then added "Carl is staying here with me tonight."

Sally gave a startled "Oh" and then, comprehendingly, a drawn out "Aaah."

The two girls hugged each other and Nancy told Sally that she was about to tell my parents of our plans to spend the night together, adding that it would be a good time for Sally to have her parents take her home.

Sally, God bless her, bit her lower lip, shook her head once from side to side and with a faint smile said, "That's just what we will do."

Before I had a chance to drag my feet or be embarrassed Nancy put her arm firmly around my side and together we approached my parents, who at that time were apart from Cora and Mr. and Mrs. Bain. Without a preamble Nancy started by saying that she loved me completely and always would. Then, after a very slight pause she told them that I would be staying with her for the night. I don't think my father quite had the picture at that point, but my mother did, and somewhat primly said "I'm not sure–"

I didn't let her finish. Cutting in I said "Mom, don't worry, everything is going to be fine."

Good old Dad, finally on the right page, turned to Mom and said 'Well, there is certainly plenty of food here for them." He then gave me a smile and a handshake, turned to my mother and said "Let's go home honey, I feel like celebrating for some reason."

The Bains, prompted by Sally, had already left, leaving Cora standing erect and alone near the fireplace. With a knowing smile she stepped towards us and said "No need to push; I'm going."

Both Nancy and I had to smile at this, and Cora gave each of us a hug. Before she left she asked for Nancy's permission to have her public relations people arrange a brief press gathering for her at 10:30 the next morning at our town library. This would serve to centralized the media, otherwise they would be widely scattered in their quest for scraps of whatever information they could dig up. Nancy would say a few words, Mr. and Mrs. Hathaway's travel schedule would be reviewed to the extent it was known by then, and the cameras would be able to click away to their heart's content. Miles of film would be run.

Permission received, Cora made for the door. As she went we heard her quietly sing a line from an obscure tune "*c'est la vie* say the old folks, it goes to show you never can tell!"

I walked to the front door and locked it. Nancy, looking thoughtful, said "There goes an amazing woman."

With that she held out a hand towards me, flicked her eyes toward the stairs and simply asked, "Ready?" Was I ever!

Chapter 46

As I went up the stairs hand and hand with Nancy I could not keep myself from thinking that it was strange; almost bizarre, for us to be about to have sex so soon after Jack's death. Looking back after so many years I still do to some extent, but it was intimacy that Nancy needed and I was not going to spoil the mood by raising a philosophical point.

Nancy's bedroom was more girlish than I would have guessed if I had given the matter any thought, which I had not. When we walked into it my heart was pounding, and walking up the stairs wasn't the reason. I put Nancy's hand on the left side of my chest so that she could feel what was going on. That contact developed into a caress and a lingering kiss. As she was unbuttoning my shirt I told her that I was totally inexperienced when it came to sex; a complete rookie. The unbuttoning continued and as she dealt with my belt buckle and zipper she quietly said "Good."

Nancy was wearing a sweater which I then pulled up over her head, helped by some wiggling on Nancy's part. I couldn't help asking if she was also a virgin and she replied "technically, no."

Her skirt had a button and a zipper in the back and as it slid to the floor, where it joined my pants, I asked what 'technically' meant.

As she helped me unhook her bra, a wispy little thing that couldn't have weighed more than an ounce or so, she said that when she was 14 and at the Ski Academy she had heard so much talk among the girls about the joys of sex that she wanted to see about it for herself and seduced a boy she met at a mixer dance. She hadn't liked it one bit, finding it uncomfortable, awkward, embarrassing, and astonishingly brief.

At this point I was standing there in my BVDs, slack jawed at the sight of Nancy, the most beautiful sight I could possibly imagine; barely wearing her peach colored silkies. We came together and out of nowhere I gently bit her neck.

She made a humming sound as she was being fanged, and then said that she was going into the bathroom briefly. When she came back she wanted me to be lying on the bed face up and in my natural state, adding that on her return she would be naked too.

When she came back to the bed to join me she looked so far beyond beautiful that words fell short. The combination of her pale skin, dark hair, perfect figure and wonderful, shyly smiling face was overwhelming. I couldn't lie there and wait. I stood up, joined her, and somehow with a quick adjustment make by Nancy we slipped together.

Afterwards, on the bed we took turns caressing each other. I told Nancy that I was happier that I had ever been in my life, insane though that sounded in view of the circumstances. Nancy told me that she felt the same, adding that I had better not ever even think about not loving her till the end of time, because that was how long she would love me. She then added "I liked it when you bit me."

That was all it took to get us started again. At some point we had a joint freckle hunt; each one to be kissed on discovery. I cheated and kissed some that didn't exist. We both felt that it was wonderful to be able to speak freely about intimate topics.

Once in the night Nancy said that she felt in need of a compliment. When I told her that she was beautiful, she propped herself up on an elbow, and reaching across her chest for a glass of water, said I was sweet to keep saying that, but what else? I quickly said that her butt is a masterpiece.

Nancy was just swallowing some of her water as I came up with this bon mot, and she choked and coughed water over herself. Gasping for breath and giggling she said "That's a terrific compliment but who am I ever going to be able to tell it to?" I replied "Well it is. It should be in the Museum of Natural Wonders." Adding "But I want it to stay put."

Eventually we drifted off to sleep. Nancy launched a frontal attack at daybreak; or it could have been me, who cares? When it reached it's predictable conclusion She said that she was starved, adding "What sort of a breakfast cook is your mother?"

I told her that Mom's Johnny cakes were legendary. I gave my parents a call to alert them, and in less than an hour the four of us were seated in front of a platter of Johnny cakes at our breakfast nook.

My mother seemed to be unusually relaxed and I noticed her giving my father a sly look once or twice. Whatever the celebration was that my father had in mind the night before, it had served it's purpose. Both my parents went out of their way to assure us that they felt that although we were young they knew that we were mature enough to handle a 'complete relationship', as my mother tactfully put it, and that they were behind us all the way.

Chapter 47

After we finished eating it was time to come down to earth and face reality, which on this morning meant that Nancy needed to get ready for her 10:30 press conference. I called Cora and asked if she would arrange for the public relations people to pick us up around then at the Hathaway's house so that they could escort Nancy and me to the library. I planned to lag behind once we arrived, sit in back, and see how the press conference would turn out.

I drove Nancy back to her house so that she would have time to primp and do whatever else she wanted to do in order to prepare for her appearance at the press conference. There were several reporters and camera men hanging around near her driveway when we pulled in, and when we spotted them Nancy said "I'm not surprised; watch this." I thought that she might duck her head and scuttle for the front door but instead she calmly greeted them, and introduced me as a family friend.

She then said that she would not be making any statements or answering any questions until the 10:30 press conference, so she would not be answering the doorbell or re-appearing until she left for that conference. With that she turned and led me into the house, where the telephone was ringing.

I told Nancy that I would stay downstairs and answer the phone so that she could go upstairs and get ready. I answered the call, saying in my most generic tone "Hathaway residence." The call, and several others that followed, were from reporters of one sort or another. They all wanted something, anything, from Nancy. I gave all of them the same answer, which was that she would be at the town library for a press conference at 10:30.

Meanwhile the group that was gathered in front of the house was increasing in size. Apparently word had spread that Nancy, something of a Queen Bee now, had been located. I called Cora, explained what was going on, and asked her to have the public relations people get over to the Hathaway's house for crowd control. A short time later we had reinforcements in the form of Al and Alice. Al was urbane looking, around 40 years old, and straight from central casting; the prototypical P.R. man. Alice Birch was in her mid-20's and looked like she was headed for the Harvard-Yale football game.

They were helpful. Alice went upstairs to talk things over with Nancy, and Al stayed outside making small talk with the media people. I kept myself amused by watching TV coverage of Nancy arriving at her home a short time earlier. There I was also, a bland figure by her side as we entered the house.

Around 10 Nancy and the P.R. lady came downstairs and Al was called in from his defensive position in the front yard. He was cold and asked for coffee. Nancy was wearing light gray slacks, a black, mock turtleneck sweater, with a brown sport coat and looked very serious.

As the coffee was brewing we reviewed how the conference at the library would be handled. The P.R. man and woman would drive us to the back door of the library around ten thirty. The three of them would make their way to the side of the library's small auditorium stage; I was to work my way around to the back of the auditorium and blend into the crowd as an observer. If anyone noticed that I was the one who had escorted Nancy into her home that morning and ask me for some sort of comment I would politely say that I was just a friend of the family, there to provide support. By the time we left the house for the drive to the library most of the media people had already headed there, sensing that prime spots would fill early.

Shortly after 10:30 Al, the urbane P.R. man from Boston walked onto the small stage and once the crowd quieted down expectantly, he briefly introduced himself and explained that he and a few associates were there to assist the Hathaway family as they faced the tragedy that had befallen them.

He then said that he was aware that there was widespread interest in the Hathaways, particularly so because of Nancy's status as a celebrated Olympic hopeful and also due to the uncertainty of the location and travel arrangements of Mr. and Mrs. Hathaway.

He went on to say that he was able to provide some information in that regard. Nancy had arrived in New Kensington the previous night. Mr. and Mrs. Hathaway, who had been vacationing in New Zealand, had been located and informed of Jack's death. They were in the process of making the long trip home, and were expected to arrive late the following night; Sunday. Once the family was together they would be able to make plans for a service for Jack.

He continued; saying that because of the intense national interest in this awful situation Nancy had agreed to address this meeting. However, her remarks would be brief and he asked everyone to remember that Nancy was a 17 year old who had learned only two days ago that her brother had been shot and killed, and that she was grieving. With that he turned to the side and motioned for Nancy. As she walked calmly toward the center of the stage the public relations man stepped to the side and back.

The small auditorium was filled to and beyond capacity. I was among a group who were leaning against the back wall, some of them journalists, easily identified by the notebooks they were scribbling on, and some were townspeople. No one paid any attention to me; all eyes were on the stage.

When Nancy walked onto the stage everyone within the auditorium stood and clapped. In a display of respect for the situation there were no cheers, whistling, or anything like what happens when a TV game show host makes an appearance.

The Urbane man from Boston handed Nancy a microphone and she stood there calmly waiting for the applause to die down. When it didn't, she said thank you two or three times, the last time adding 'Please take your seats." I could see that due to Nancy's skiing success she was used to speaking to the media.

Once the audience was settled the auditorium was totally silent, all attention was focused on Nancy.

She began. "First of all, I want to say that I understand you are all aware of the awful thing that has happened here and that my brother, Jack Hathaway, an eighteen year old high school senior who was loved by everyone who knew him, was shot in the back without the slightest cause and killed by a member of our town's police force. For most of you who are in this room, covering this is part of your job; for my family and the people who live here and knew Jack it is a horrible shock, and a loss that will be with us always.

"As you just heard, my father and his wife; my wonderful step-mother, are expected to be arriving here some time tomorrow night. Once we are all together we will be able to make plans for a suitable service for Jack. When those plans are set you will be kept informed because we know it will also require media coverage. I ask that as you do cover that part of our family tragedy that you remain as respectful as you have been so far. I expect that Jack's services will be within a few days or as soon as possible because as everyone here knows I am part of the United States Olympic ski team, and between now and the start of the Olympics every day is tightly scheduled. It is vital for our team's success that I be with them as soon as possible. Every day is important."

When she finished Nancy took a visibly deep breath, let it out slowly and said "I am willing to answer a few questions."

With that half the audience waived their hands frantically. The other half did not bother with waiving, they simply began shouting their questions. After watching this calmly for a few seconds Nancy, who I suspect had anticipated the uproar, put out her hand and waited. The crowd settled down and Nancy said "That didn't work well did it? If anyone in the third row has a question please raise your hand." Several hands shot up and she pointed at someone. Three people immediately began their questions but Nancy intended to run a tight ship; saying that she had called on the gentleman wearing the plaid jacket. She then heard her first question, which was did she have something she wanted to say about Jack's killer, Vincent DiNardo.

Her answer was terse. "No; his actions speak for themselves."

She chose another questioner who asked if she felt that Chief Hale was guilty to some degree of contributing to her brother's death.

"Not at all. Chief Hale is a good man and a friend of my father's. If he had any way of knowing that one of his officers was going to shoot an innocent citizen he would certainly have prevented it."

There were a few more questions dealing with the shooting and her reaction to it. Nancy then said that she would take one more question. When the question came came it switched from the shooting to her upcoming race. She was asked if Jack's death would have an effect on her performance in the Olympics.

Nancy gave a slight frown, causing two vertical lines to appear between her eyebrows, and replied "I have been skiing since I was four years old and I am good at it. Part of the reason is because I have a gift in that regard but the bigger reason is that I had done everything that I possible can to be the best I can be. I train hard and I concentrate on what I am doing. When I ski I do not think about anything other than the slope I am on and how to get down it as fast as possible." At this point I noticed that the hand that was not holding the microphone was clenched. She continued: "I have never allowed anything to distract me when I am competing and I never will!"

This last was said with such intensity that the gathering was silent. With perfect timing Al, the urbane gentleman from Boston stepped forward, and, smoothly taking the microphone from Nancy, said that would conclude the meeting and that the mayor would remain available during the next few days to answer questions and pass along information. With that he escorted Nancy off the stage and I made fast tracks out and around to the back of the library, as I knew that the P.R. squad wanted to get Nancy back to her house quickly and I did not want to cause them any delay.

The three of them were just entering the car as I trotted around the side of the library. I hopped into the back seat next to Nancy, and we were whisked away; through the town and back towards her house.

As we were driving there the two public relations people assured Nancy that she had done an excellent job on stage; not only had she maintained her composure under stressful conditions and presented herself as an extremely likable young lady, she had also kept the crowded auditorium under control which they both agreed was an unusual achievement. Alice, the P.R. lady, was particularly impressed with the way Nancy had let the media people "Get their 'ya-ya's' out"; whatever that meant. Nancy's response was simple; "Thanks, it took a lot out of me."

Nancy and I were dropped off at her house and the duo from Boston headed for Sycamore Hall to give a report to Cora, seeing as she was pulling their strings as well as being their chancellor of the exchequer. The yard and driveway were mercifully empty. Presumably the out of towners were still in caucus back at the library.

Breakfast seemed to have been totally digested so we rummaged through the freshly stocked refrigerator and made ourselves turkey and stuffing (who has stuffing on hand in January?) sandwiches, along with a side of carrot sticks. After we finished that off Nancy said that she felt like taking a nap, adding with a seductive smile "Want to come along?"

I did.

Chapter 48

Later in the afternoon we decided to pay a courtesy call on Cora so we took a ride to Sycamore Hall. As I drove us there I felt that it was as good a time as any to bring up something that was disturbing me. I opened the topic by saying that there was something bothering me. Were we wrong to be having such a wonderful time being intimate with each other when it was Jack's death that had caused us the opportunity?

Nancy quickly replied, "Isn't that a coincidence? I have been having the same thought. But no matter how badly we feel about Jack, and no matter how much we cry, his murder has brought us together at a time when I, and I think you, needed love desperately. His death just caused us to get into bed sooner than it would have happened if he was still alive."

Nancy had expressed herself clearly and well in just a few words and my feelings were the same. I reached for her hand and told her how relieved I was to know that she felt no guilt about our being together, and that I didn't see how our intimacy could possibly not be proper. With that we both seemed to sense that what was going on between us was right, regardless of the timing and the circumstances.

Nancy jumped to a different topic, saying "Do you know when I first got the hots for you?" Without waiting for an answer, she went on. "It was when Jack first brought you to our house and sprung that walk into the woods on you. Even though you were totally out of your comfort zone you were so funny and such a good sport. That's why I was waiting for you. I was worried that things wouldn't go well out there and that you might not want to come back."

I had to smile at that revelation. In reply I said, "For me it was when we were practicing our dance moves before we went to that

Christmas Dance. I would be putting my hand on the base of your spine and thinking how nice it felt."

"I remember liking that too. Well here we are at Miss Grant's. Who else is here?" The two cars in the car park in front of the house belonged to the public relations people, who were staying there in some of the Hall's many unused bedrooms. No sign of any media presence. Cora had managed to stay off their radar. This was just the way she liked to operate, not that she did not want to be kept informed; she did.

In a quick update we were told that the mayor, with assistance from the woman from Al's team who was called Rocky, was doing a fine job of being available to the press hordes. Our Mayor Billy had recently sold an insurance agency in town that he had owned for years, and was naturally and incurably gregarious.

We were told that Chief Hale was manfully carrying out his duties although visibly crushed by feelings of guilt. Once whatever services Mr. and Mrs. Hathaway arranged were over the chief planed on asking the mayor to activate his letter of resignation.

We were having this conversation in the vast living room of Sycamore Hall. There were seven of us, Five, not including Nancy and I. Al Malone, his preppy looking side kick, Alice Birch, and the two others; the man named Chet Chang and the woman they called Rocky. Cora rounded out the gathering. A fire was blazing in the enormous fireplace, and I thought that for the first time in my experience the living room seemed to be properly utilized. Put enough people in it and it was a wonderful gathering spot. I thought of Cora's request that the ladies who had gathered at the Hathaway's Christmas dinner assist her in coming up with ideas for brightening up Sycamore Hall.

It was late afternoon and Cora had arranged for drinks and appetizers to be served. Cora raised the question of how the arrival of Tom and Kathy Hathaway should be handled. By that she was referring to the logistical side of things. She had no intention of 'handling' them in the sense of telling them what to do.

Al said that he could arrange for the Hathaway's to be met at their gate when they arrived at Logan Airport and then escorted by airport security to a non-public exit. They could be met there by a driver who would bring them home.

Cora listened carefully to this while swirling a small glass of sherry in her left hand. She then said "That would be good. How about this: they will be changing planes in Chicago. I could arrange for them to be met as they get off their plane by an airport representative and escorted to a private jet. That way they would be able to fly directly into our capital's executive airport. It would save them considerable time, avoid the possibility of any contact with the media when they will be most tired and distraught, and the checked luggage could catch up with them later."

Al and his team quickly agreed that cost aside it was a much better plan. With that settled Cora touched on another subject, saying "It's too bad we will be losing Chief Hale."

By this time I knew Cora well enough to be sure that she was not just expressing a passing thought. Nancy and I were sitting side by side on one of the couches that faced each other and I lightly touched her leg with a fingertip; a nonverbal 'watch this'.

The Boston team were by no means slow on the uptake. Chet responded "It is too bad. Jack's death isn't really the chief's fault, although he feels like it is. The town will have a hard time filling his shoes."

Rocky spoke next: "Maybe the mayor could put the resignation at the bottom of his in-box and offer Hale some sort of sabbatical so he has time to get his head back on straight."

Then preppy Alice: "That could work. After all, wherever he goes next he's not going to feel less guilty."

Al was having a scotch on the rocks. He rattled the ice cubes in a ruminating way and then said "Some sign of support from the community could go a long way towards convincing him to stay. How about a sort of special election? Keep Hale, yes or no."

Cora lightly touched the rudder; "Even in our small town, elections take time and cost money."

I stood up and asked if they minded hearing a thought from me. Then, forming an idea as I went along, I said, "It wouldn't have to be an official election if the whole point would be to convince the chief that we want him to stay. Our newspaper could include an informal ballot and run it for one or two editions. Anyone who has access to the newspaper could fill it out and drop it off somewhere."

"Also, how about letting the middle and upper school kids vote? They could do that right in class and they would love to be included. I would bet that they would get their parents to vote too."

I looked around. Everyone was smiling, Cora included. Al said "Carl, that is a hell of a good idea, I see why Miss Grant keeps you around."

Cora, in one of her typical understatements said, "I know the editor of the paper fairly well and I think he will love the idea. It should help sell papers too. Al, why don't you or someone from your team speak to him tomorrow and see what he thinks about Carl's idea. You might want to tell him I said to say hello."

I thought it would be good to leave the gathering on a high note, so Nancy and I headed off to my parent's house where we were expected for dinner. While I was driving there Nancy commented that she thought Cora had been steering the conversation but was so subtle about it was almost impossible to tell. She wouldn't have even noticed it I had not tapped her leg.

"She's like that. Cora has an incredible way of thinking things out ahead of time, I've seen her do it often. Just think; Chief Hale is devastated and intends to quit and leave town, which would mean that New Kensington would have a temporary chief sent in by the governor and who knows how that would turn out."

"Then we would need to find a permanent replacement for the chief. It would be hard to find someone who would do the job as well as Chief Hale."

"But now look. The newspaper is going to get the whole town involved. My guess is that almost no one here blames the chief and the newspaper poll will show that. The school kids will be thrilled to participate. What a civics lesson! Given this show of support I think the chief is likely to agree to stay. Even if he does not we will have tried our best."

Nancy swung around toward me in her seat. "You're always modest Carl. You came up with the best part."

I could not deny that. As we were pulling into my parent's driveway I said "You don't realize how much this town admires and respects you. When you stood up there in the library and told everyone there, and half the world in the process, that Chief Hale was a good man and not at fault, I would bet one of my fingers that millions of people thought that if Nancy Hathaway does not blame Chief Hale then I don't either."

By that time we were walking to our front door. With a sly grin Nancy said "Careful with those fingers, I like all of them."

After dinner Nancy and I headed back to her house. I thought it was borderline amazing how much had changed in 48 hours. Jack murdered, Nancy's speedy return from Europe, she and I (finally) in bed together, Cora's arrangement for emergency public relations help, and, case at hand, my parents taking the news that I would be spending another night alone with Nancy without so much as the blink of an eye. I was reminded of the opening lines of Dickens's 'A Tale of Two Cities' "It was the best of times; it was the worst of times."

Under the heading of 'the best of times', Nancy and I spent another fine night in her bedroom. We had a lot to learn and were proving to be excellent students.

The next day was a Sunday, and finally Mr. Hathaway was able to get a call through to Nancy. He and Kathy had endured very poor connections in the hastily arranged return flights, but they were in Los Angeles, where they were waiting for their flight to Chicago.

Speaking with her father for the first time since Jack's death was another emotional wrench for the girl I loved and it was painful to see her crying as she spoke with her dad and then with Kathy. Towards the end of the call I got on the phone and told Mr. Hathaway that they were going to be met as they got off the plane in Chicago and that Cora had arranged for them to be flown directly here on a private jet, adding that their checked luggage would catch up with them eventually. With a dismissive, humorless laugh Mr. Hathaway told me that their checked suitcases were already lost; somewhere between Wellington and who knew where. Everything they needed was with them in carry-ons.

Chapter 49

The next day, Sunday, for the first time since the shooting we didn't have much to do. Preppy Alice came to the Hathaway's house to ask Nancy if she had an appropriate black dress to wear for Jack's memorial service. It turned out that the closest she could come was a navy suit.

The two of them then went up to the Hathaway's bedroom to see what Kathy had in that regard. She did have a dark cocktail dress which Alice thought might slide by, but after a phone call to her boss she said that Al; with Cora's backing, was going to have twelve black dresses driven up from Boston the next day; six in Nancy's size and six in Kathy's size. They would try them on and pick one to wear. The ones that were not selected would be going back to whatever store they came from. The dresses would be compliments of Cora.

Mr. Hathaway's closet revealed that he did have a black suit. Nancy guessed that it had been worn once at her mother's funeral and then relegated to the far end of the closet. "Just needs a little brushing" was Alice's professional opinion.

I, of course was set. The dark blue suit that Cora had given me for Christmas would be very appropriate.

Then I thought of Sally. Knowing the vast portfolio of clothing she owned I would have guessed that she was covered in regard to mourning garb, but why guess when Sally was a phone call away. Nancy gave her a ring and asked her if she could come over to talk about dresses. The answer was yes; she was on her way.

She arrived looking tired and red-eyed. She and Alice had not met and Alice took one look at Sally, said something like "Oh honey", and they both started crying. Once that show of emotion eased back the three of them started talking about dresses, styles, should there be gloves, (sub-topic, what length), and on and on. I could have put on a war bonnet, grabbed a tomahawk, and run circles around them and they wouldn't have noticed. Eventually it was settled; Another six dresses would make the trip up from Boston; Sally was in on the deal.

We all sat down for a general conversation except that it was mostly girl talk. I drifted into the kitchen and heated up one of the casseroles. When it was done I stuck my head into the living room and said "Come get something to eat, it's chicken casserole with tidbits of stuff in it."

As we were eating we outlined the plans for picking up Nancy's father and Kathy, who we now expected to arrive at the local airport around 6 P.M. Mr. Hathaway had a full-sized station wagon and with them having minimal luggage there would be plenty of room for Nancy and I to take Sally with us to pick them up. Once we were back at the Hathaway's house Sally and I would be leaving. I felt that Mr. Hathaway and Kathy might appreciate being able to be alone with Nancy. Besides, after enduring what must have seemed like an endless trip halfway around the world they were certain to be exhausted.

Alice reported that the P.R. team would be ready to notify the police department and the superintendent of schools as soon as Jack's service was scheduled. There was certain to be a need for traffic control, and it seemed to be probable that school would let out early. All other details would be worked out as they arose.

The dresses were expected to arrive at the Hathaway's house late Monday morning or early afternoon. Alice would be on hand for that, and Sally would be told when they arrived so that she could join in the selection process. As I had come to expect, Al and his team had things under control.

The women had exhausted the rich topic of funeral toggery. Sally went home to freshen up and Alice left to rejoin Al, Chet, and Rocky. As she was leaving she pulled me aside and told me that they thought there was a good chance that Mr. Hathaway would ask me to speak at Jack's service, and also, they felt that in view of Nancy's pressing need to rejoin her team that Mr. Hathaway would want the service to be scheduled as soon as possible, perhaps as early as

Tuesday. With that in mind she asked if I would want her team to create a rough draft for me to consider, should I be asked to say something.

The possibility of being asked to speak at my friend's funeral service had been bouncing in and out of my mind. So far as I knew, family members usually don't do that. Sally might be considered, but she was so close to the Hathaway's that she was almost like family. Besides; she loved Jack so deeply that it would almost be cruel to ask her to express her feelings in front of what I was sure would be a church bursting at the seams.

That left me as a prime candidate. If I was asked it would be a huge honor and of course I would accept, but then what? How could anyone adequately describe Jack in a few minutes and do it in such a way that a church full of both townspeople and media representatives would feel the warmth of his character?

I told Alice that if I was called on then I would need all the help they could give. Giving me nod and a smile Alice said "That's what we expected you to say. We are already working on it, and don't worry, we do this all the time." She then added "But Carl no matter what we write, you will have to be yourself. Don't be concerned about what people might expect you to say, if you simply speak from your heart it will please the only four people who truly count; Tom, Kathy, Nancy, and Sally."

With those words of wisdom, she hopped into her car and drove away. I stood there thinking "Now I have ghost writers; what next?"

Chapter 50

Nancy had been watching my conversation with preppy Alice from the porch and her feminine curiosity was aroused. Speaking directly as she almost always did she asked "What did Alice have to say?" I told her, and added that I didn't want her to bring up the subject with her father. "I won't need to, he is sure to think of you first. If he asks me what I think, I will tell him that you get my vote." Then, with an abrupt change of topic she asked me to add a log to the fire and join her on the couch. It was getting on into the afternoon and she unnecessarily reminded me that we would be sleeping apart for the next two nights.

Once we were settled on the couch Nancy said that she wanted to talk about what our lives would be like without Jack, but that she didn't know how to start or what to say. I did not know either, so I asked her what it was like when her mother passed away.

"It was a terrible time. Mom was so wonderful, she always seemed to know what we needed and she was the happiest person you could imagine. She just loved us all so much."

Nancy was staring into the fire, re-living the time when her mother was there with them.

"Then she started getting headaches, and when they got worse our doctor took some X-rays. Then he had her go to Boston for some more tests. Dad went with her, and when they came back they both looked–I don't know how to describe it, they were changed somehow. They had Jack and I sit down right here and they told us that Mom's headaches were being caused by a tumor; a very serious one. They were going to go back to Boston in 3 days so that Mom could have an operation."

At this point tears were rolling down Nancy's face. I told her that I wished that I hadn't brought up the subject.

"No, I want to talk about it because although the operation wasn't able to remove the tumor and she died a few weeks later somehow we managed to keep going. I was only 9 then and Jack was 10. We missed her something awful but we learned to live a new way. It was hardest for Dad. I don't think he was ever truly happy until he found Kathy. Now he is happier than ever, or he was before this."

We sat quietly, watching the logs burn. I wanted to say something so I started out, not knowing if what I would say would be helpful or not.

"Life can be so tricky. Everything seems perfect and then in an instant; gone. Did you know that I never had a close friend until Jack?"

"No; I didn't know that. But come to think of it I have always been a loner myself. Well those days are over now, I have you."

This was a very poignant moment. I suddenly realized that since Jack's murder we had simply been reacting to events as they happened. Now I knew that although Jack's memory would always be with us eventually it would fade and that together we would be happy. I told her that.

Nancy gave me a small smile. "Yes, we'll pull it together. Do you mind if we just stretch out here on the couch until Sally gets here and we go to pick up Dad and Kathy?"

Of course I was fine with that, and for the next hour or two that is what we did. Some of the time we talked and the rest of the time we just lay side by side lost in our thoughts.

Chapter 51

Sally arrived promptly at five that afternoon and I drove the three of us to the capital airport in Mr. Hathaway's wagon. The Hathaway's private jet was due to arrive at six and we wanted to be sure we were waiting for them when they stepped off the plane.

At our small local airport we were able to drive almost to where the private airplanes parked, and we were able to see the lights of their plane descend and then to see it taxi up. Nancy ran ahead of Sally and me and threw her arms around her dad as soon as he stepped down; Sally and I were not far behind. By then I should have been used to emotional scenes, but I wasn't.

Mr. Hathaway and Kathy looked as if they couldn't have traveled another mile; they were rumpled and hollow-eyed. As they thanked the jet's crew I put their carry-ons into the back of Mr. Hathaway's station wagon. I asked him if he would like me to drive them home and he said, "Thanks." By pre-arrangement Nancy sat in the back with her dad and Kathy. Sally sat in front with me, and before long all the remaining Hathaway's were reunited at their home. Sally and I had our cars there and after seeing them to the front door we left to go to home ourselves.

Sally's car, an eye-catching bright red convertible, was behind mine and I opened her door for her. She leaned into the angle that the door made with the car's body, locked her hands behind my neck, put her hairline against my forehead and said, "I'll be totally lost without Jack; it's as simple as that. I don't know what I'm going to do."

I told her that I did. I told her that she would find a way to be happy again. The only thing I didn't know was exactly how that would happen or when.

Without moving she asked "Is this how I cut your face that day?"

"Almost, your head was just a few inches lower."

She let go of my neck and got into her car. Then she rolled her window down and told me that Nancy was a lucky girl. She didn't wait for me to answer, she just drove off.

I had missed dinner with my parents that night, but Mom had plenty of leftovers and she and Dad sat with me and listened while I told them how Mr. Hathaway and Kathy were holding up. I also told them about Cora's way of making sure that Nancy, Kathy, and Sally would be suitably outfitted for Jack's service. At her direction the versatile team of public relations people she had on hand had made arrangements for Boston's finest dress shops to be scoured. Eighteen dresses were to be driven to the Hathaway residence the next morning for scrutiny and selection; six in each of the lady's sizes.

On hearing this my father shook his head in admiration. My mother wondered out loud if there was ever anything that Cora didn't think of. To this my father replied "In a word, no."

Chapter 52

The next day, Monday was a school day. Superintendent Brown had wisely kept all of the town's schools closed on Friday in view of the high level of turmoil and emotion that had swept our small town in the aftermath of Jack's murder. The plan was for the high school to close again on the afternoon of Jack's service, with the details to be worked out once the memorial arrangements were announced. The Hathaway family had a loose affiliation with an episcopal church in town which, fortunately, was quite large.

As predicted by the P.R. team, Mr. Hathaway decided to hold Jack's memorial service as quickly as possible. It was to take place at the episcopal church on Tuesday, at 2PM. This would be followed by a funeral caravan to the town's main cemetery, where Jack would be laid to rest.

At Cora's request Alice had left a letter for Mr. Hathaway and Kathy at their house when she had visited on Sunday. After expressing condolences, the letter introduced Al and his associates and made clear the fact that they were there to help with whatever details might need to be handled, including funeral plans. The letter explained that the shipment of dress choices was expected to arrive at their house sometime late Monday morning or early that afternoon and that before the dresses arrived she had asked Al to come to the house to introduce himself and to ask how he and his team could be of service. She concluded by saying that she would like to hold a reception at Sycamore Hall directly after the graveside ceremony, provided that they could face the strain of such a thing.

Nancy called me around nine that Monday morning. Once Al had arrived he and Kathy had promptly gone into overdrive. The church would be ready for the Tuesday 2PM service. The upper school would be closing at noon on that day. The police force would be ready to escort what was expected to be a lengthy caravan of vehicles from the church to the graveyard, and the Hathaway family would accept expressions of sympathy at a Sycamore Hall reception immediately following the burial. The minister would conclude the memorial service by extending an invitation to everyone in attendance to the reception.

Rocky was on her way to have a pow- wow with the mayor to iron out details. Chet was headed to the church for a meeting with the minister there. Alice would be at the Hathaway's house for the arrival of the dresses, and Al would be manning the phones at his temporary command post; Sycamore Hall. And would I please come over to her house right away?

As I drove to their house I realized that I had not given school so much as a thought. I was, after all, a senior there, but school would have to wait; I had more important things on my mind, Nancy at the top of the list.

She was waiting by the door when I pulled up and said that her father had something to ask me. She walked me over towards where he and Kathy were talking. When he saw me he came over and said that he had an important question to ask; would I do them the honor of speaking at Jack's service?

Of course I had been expecting to be asked this, but even so I was overwhelmed and suddenly I was crying. When I found my voice I told him that the honor was mine and that I would do my best. He put his arm across my shoulders and said "Thanks, I know you will. The tissues are over there."

Nancy drifted over and when she saw me dabbing at my eyes with a tissue she gave me a light kiss and said "You knew that was coming, right?"

"I know but still–I guess I just don't feel adequate."

She jumped to a different subject. "They know we slept together before they got back."

One thing after another. All I could think of to say was "Okay."

Nancy explained that once Sally and I had left the previous night she had told Kathy about us, said that I was wonderful, and asked that she tell her dad about it when she thought the time was right. Clearly it had not taken long for the right time to show up.

Events were moving so quickly that I hardly cared that our intimacy was household knowledge. I cocked an eyebrow and said "Talk about kiss and tell!"

Nancy was unfazed, saying "I don't care, we waited too long anyway." She then added "Stick around; we may need help unloading all the dresses."

I decided to let that thrill wait, and told her that I was going to stop by Cora's house and see what thoughts the public relations people had come up with as far as helping me deliver a eulogy that would be a modern version of the Gettysburg Address; or at least that short.

At Sycamore Hall the housekeeper opened the door and told me that Miss Grant was in the schoolroom and would like a word with me. I found her seated behind her desk, wearing, of all the improbable things, a North Overshoe sweatshirt. Her first words were "Carl, don't ever play poker, I can read you like a book. You are thinking that this sweatshirt is too frivolous to wear at a time like this."

It would have been useless to deny it, but as I gave it a second thought I changed my mind. Maybe wearing something goofy was not a bad thing to do; there was ample sadness around. No need for armbands.

When I sat down she asked "Has Tom brought up the subject of Jack's service?"

I told her that I had just come from the Hathaway's house and that he had asked me to speak at the church.

In reply she said "That wasn't in doubt. Try not to worry. All you need to do is think what Jack would say if it had been you who DiNardo shot and he was the speaker."

"That won't work, Jack and I are totally different!"

"Only superficially. Jack was bright, funny, kind, loyal, loving, and had wonderful character in many different ways. That's true for you also. The rest is details."

The schoolroom was briefly quiet while I absorbed this. I then said "Thank you, that's a wonderful compliment. Maybe I shouldn't stress about it. After all, only about half the world will hear about it if I make a mess of things." I knew the media would cover Jack's service. Overcover it most likely.

With a smile she stood up, saying: "That's the spirit. Al's team have outlined a few thoughts for you to consider. They are back in the living room." Then she added "Do you think Nancy would like to head back to Europe promptly once she leaves the reception?"

I said that I wouldn't be surprised. I knew she was anxious to get back to her Olympic preparations.

Cora then said "I thought so, I'll arrange for her to have a ride."

I didn't want to seem ungrateful, but I said that I would like to be the one to drive her to Logan airport.

With the faintest of smiles Cora replied "Well unless you can drive her to Europe–"

I knew what that meant; Cora was going to provide Nancy with a private jet. All I could think of to say was "You have already done so much, for the town and for the Hathaway's. I guess you know now that when you do something for Nancy you're doing something for me too."

"Obviously. Tell her she has a ride back. Fortunately, I found some extra money in my piggy bank, so I can afford it."

I gave her a hug and said that someday I would write a book about her. As I headed for the living room I heard her say that she wanted a signed copy.

Al, Chet, and Rocky were ready for me; Alice had already headed to the Hathaway's. She wanted to be sure to be there when the shipment of dresses pulled in. Chet said that Alice was fighting a case of free dress envy and losing the battle.

Al was holding a sheet of paper; one sheet only, doubled spaced and all capitalized. Before he gave it to me he said that they had spent quite a bit of time talking about what I should say and how I should say it. He continued "The more we talked the more convinced we were that we didn't need to put any words in your mouth. Now that we know you, we know that you are very capable of speaking your mind clearly and concisely. You don't need to dazzle anyone and you shouldn't try to. Don't be afraid of saying something funny. This town is awash with grief and sorrow, no one needs more. Everything that we have learned since we arrived tells us that Jack was a happy, light hearted boy; don't be reluctant to say so. Examples work well, and it would be good if you can mention his family here and there as well as his girlfriend. We know the poor girl is devastated. Speak of your friendship and what it has meant to you. When you finish just nod your head, don't say thank you. People don't do that at memorial services."

With that he handed me the sheet of paper, saying that what he just said was summarized on it. He then added this: "If you can, try to do without notes. It won't matter if you forget to say something, just tell about your friend."

The three of them were smiling. "What's so funny?"

Rocky spoke for them: "You look like you are about to walk the plank. Everything you are feeling shows on your face."

"That's the second time I have heard that this morning."

Back to my car and back to the Hathaway's house. I had to admit to myself that Alice wasn't the only person not be picking out a dress who was curious about how it would play out. I might live to be 100 and not see anything like it again!

Chapter 53

The dresses arrived in a full sized van. Two men and a woman had been squeezed into the front seat and they tumbled out just as a light snow began to fall.

One of the men turned to the other, and shaking himself said "You need to lose some weight!"

The other, who actually was considerably overweight, raised his chin in an attempt at dignity, and shot back: "Well at least I brushed my teeth this morning!"

The woman in the group headed towards the front porch, where Mr. Hathaway, Kathy, Nancy, and Sally as well as Alice were coming to meet the van. She greeted them by saying: "Those two have been at this all morning. I'm Caroline Longstreet, I have a shop on Boylston Street; La Couturiere." Alice discreetly rolled her eyes.

The men stopped their bickering and opened the double doors on the back of the van with Kathy, Alice, and the girls craning their necks to see inside. What they saw brought out ooh's and ahh's; there were twin rows of bars running the length of the van, and from each hung nine black dresses, all of them wrapped in plastic and gently swaying, provocatively, on hangers.

The three Bostonians stood proudly aside as the dress beneficiaries feasted their eyes on the plunder. Then Mr. Hathaway broke the spell, saying "Let's get these inside out of the snow so everyone can get a good look at them."

Taking a stab at humor I said, "Sally if this too much for you to handle we understand."

Sally looked at me over her shoulder and replied "I still have a pulse you know." She tried to frown as she said this but a smile broke through.

In a jiffy the eighteen dresses were lovingly transported into the Hathaway's living room, sorted by size, and draped over the back of the couches. Six each for Kathy, Nancy, and Sally to choose from. Each of them promptly started sorting through their swag and all talking at once, with the dress merchants pointing out the salient features of each style.

At this point Alice calmed them all down. Raising her voice, she said "Hold on for a minute, this isn't Filene's basement. We have plenty of time so let's do this one by one. That way when one of you tries out a dress the rest of us can help with the decision."

Everyone in the room agreed. The merchants ceased their fluttering and Mr. Hathaway and I settled into the background to enjoy what turned out to be a fine fashion show.

The running commentary kept me amused. "Is my bra strap showing?" "The hem is too long and the sleeves are too short!" "I like this one, but it's cut too low in front. This is for a funeral, not a Hooters audition!" For the first time in days there was laughter in the Hathaway household. When I say this, naturally I am disregarding what had gone on upstairs between Nancy and I.

What a strange and complex organ the human brain is. The five people who loved Jack more than any other people in the world had only learned of his murder a few days ago and were overcome with grief. And yet we were able to somehow find enjoyment in the selection of dresses for Kathy, Nancy, and Sally to wear at Jack's funeral tomorrow. Apparently some things cannot be fully understood.

The kitchen became the impromptu dressing room and the three of them took turns trying on dresses and displaying them in the living room. Whatever competitive feelings there had been between the three merchants were put aside. Caroline Longstreet at one point brought in a sewing machine and made a quick seam adjustment for Kathy while she was considering a dress that had been provided by one of the other two, only saying over her shoulder "I hope you remember this."

It took the better part of two hours, but in time Kathy, Nancy, and Sally had each selected a dress, and in a kindly roll of fate's dice, each of the providers had one of their dresses chosen; decisions that must have done wonders for the mood inside the van during the return trip.

Kathy and Mr. Hathaway set out an array of cold cuts and other stray items that my parents, the Bains, and the caterer provided by Cora had stuffed into the refrigerator on Friday. Once lunch was finished we helped the Boston threesome place the remaining dresses back into the van and each of them was given a check by Alice.

The checks must have pleased them, as their collective mood, which had been steadily improving once the women began trying on dresses, became almost jovial. The smaller of the two men tried to bend the other man's check so that he could see the amount and his hand was slapped away; but playfully.

The last we heard from them came from Caroline, who exclaimed "This time I'm driving. I don't trust either of you not to put us into a snowbank!"

As we watched the van turn off the driveway and disappear down the road Kathy summarized: "Now THAT was something else!"

Alice and I headed off it different directions. She headed for Sycamore Hall to report on the dress event and I went home. I was invited to have dinner at the Hathaway's, but before that I needed some time alone in my room. I would be delivering the most important speech of my life (and also the first) the next day and I wanted some time to make notes and focus on what I wanted to say.

After an hour at my desk I was not getting anywhere and feeling overwhelmed. I pictured myself being the first person to ever be booed off the stage while delivering a eulogy. I flopped onto my bed defeated.

Then I had an inspiration. Just because my talk would be a big deal; enormous, that didn't mean it had to be complicated. I certainly knew the subject matter; Jack. Why not take the pressure off myself by pretending that Jack was still alive and treat my commentary as if it were some sort of cross between a letter of introduction and a best man's speech at a wedding reception?

The piano that had been balanced on my back vanished and an imaginary shaft of golden sunlight shone through my bedroom window. If I couldn't summarize Jack Hathaway in a few minutes in front of some of his friends and family then my name wasn't Carl Smith.

Back to Nancy's house for dinner. The caterer that Cora had hired to provide the Hathaway family with food for several days had put some small steaks in their freezer, and Mr. Hathaway had decided to grill them. Even though there were still a few snowflakes in the air, by New Kensington standards it was not particularly cold, and I think he was glad to be outside for a while with something to keep him occupied. Kathy was putting the rest of the meal together and the two of them were working their way through a bottle of red wine.

While the dress selection excitement was going on earlier in the day I had totally forgotten to tell Nancy that Cora had found another way to show her generosity; she was providing Nancy with a private jet to transport her back to her front lines–Europe and her Olympic teammates. I thought a good time to pass that information along would be when the three of them were together in the kitchen. The Hathaways could certainly use any and all positive news. I spread the good word the first chance I had.

Nancy was overjoyed; jumping into the air with a loud clap of her hands. "Wowie, that's great! If we leave from our airport after the reception I'll be in Switzerland in the morning and I can sleep on the way. This is going to save me at least a full day and every day is crucial. I love Cora Grant!"

Kathy and Mr. Hathaway clinked glasses. Kathy pronounced that Cora was North Overshoe's guardian angel. Her husband agreed, adding that they would never be able to properly express their appreciation for all she had done for them.

At dinner the four of us spent most of the time reviewing some of the things that Cora had arranged for since the tragedy. Even though I had been aware of what she was doing as she was doing it, her foresight and generosity was impressive.

She had immediately realized that Jack's murder would rapidly become national news, partly because of the pure viciousness of the shooting but more so because Jack's sister was world famous as a gold medal favorite in the upcoming Olympics. Recognizing that the media attention would overwhelm our small town she made arrangements for a team of public relations specialists to be on hand to help. With her guidance the mayor and Chief Hale set a policy of honesty and openness that kept the press coverage as favorable as it could be, given the circumstances. For the most part we had avoided being portrayed as a bunch of rustic incompetents.

Elizabeth Anderson had paid the price for trying to pose as Snow White. The media tore into her like a pack of starving hyenas.

Cora had used her connections to speed up the process of locating Mr. Hathaway and Kathy, and had arranged for them to be met in Chicago and flown by private jet to our local airport, which saved time as well as what little energy they had left after more than a full day of exhausting travel halfway around the world.

Realizing that Chief Hale's resignation would be the loss of a valuable community asset, Cora had arranged the meeting that set in motion our newspaper taking an informal vote of confidence in the chief.

Somehow she had brought in 18 black dresses from Boston for Sally, Nancy, and Kathy to select from, and was opening her house for a catered reception tomorrow at the conclusion of the services for Jack. The latest was the news that she was providing a private jet for Nancy's prompt return to Switzerland and her Olympic team.

I had stayed out of most of this part of the conversation up to that point but I then held up a piece of steak on my fork and added "Don't forget this!" Kathy raised her wine glass and smiled "This too!"

Briefly we were quiet. Then Mr. Hathaway stood up and held our attention. "All four of us have had our hearts broken; we have lost our wonderful Jack. Even so, there are two things that I am grateful for, or I should say two people.

"The first is Cora Grant. She has used her wealth, vision and thoughtfulness to help our family and this town in ways that no one else could have possibly done. Furthermore, she has done all of this without ever giving a thought to calling attention to herself. She does not want credit, she just wants to help. Kathy is right, Cora Grant is a guardian angel." At this point he paused, then turned towards me.

"The second person is you Carl."

Until he said that I had been relaxed; just listening to Nancy's father let his feelings out. When he turned his attention to me I felt myself blush and I sat up a little straighter in my chair.

"Remember when after you and Nancy went to that Christmas Dance you told me that she had pulled your ears?"

At this Nancy turned to me and said "You told him that?" I didn't have to answer, my face said it all. Mr. Hathaway went on: "Later that night I was thinking that the two of you would be perfect for each other. Well, it took you a few years to figure it out for yourselves, but Kathy and I look forward to the day when you are officially part of our family, and so far as we are concerned you already are."

Nancy came over and scrooched on to my chair beside me, giving me an expectant look as she did so. I wiggled my arm around her. My throat was tight with emotion but I managed to say 'She's the only girl in the world for me; I'm here to stay."

Mr. Hathaway then sat down, saying "Good. Now for Pete's sake stop calling me Mr. Hathaway; I'm Tom!

Chapter 54

The weather the next day, Tuesday, was fairly good, mostly overcast but no snow with the temperature in the high twenties; not a lot of wind. I had breakfast with my parents and went upstairs to make sure I had a firm grip on what I wanted to say at the service. After a while I felt that I was doing myself more harm than good.

I gave Nancy a call just to chat and learned that she had talked to her team's manager. He would arrange for a driver to meet her plane when it landed in Geneva. Everyone involved with our Olympic team was anxious to have her back and in training and so was Nancy.

Nancy and her family would be picked up at their house at 1:45 that afternoon by a limousine provided by the funeral parlor. The Hathaways had insisted that Sally be included with the family group, so Mr. and Mrs. Bain would be dropping her off there before they went on to the church. I would be driving my parents to the church from our house.

I wanted to have my car on hand because I would be driving Nancy to our capital airport directly from the reception at Sycamore Hall. My parents could hook a ride home easily enough, and if somehow that didn't work out there was also Al's team as backup.

I was just making myself nervous pacing around our house so I headed over to see what was going on with Cora at Sycamore Hall.

When I pulled in I saw that two catering trucks were already there. Cora had suspected that there would be a large crowd at the reception so she had hired both the town's catering services and told them to work it out between themselves as to which caterer would do what.

Cora was in the living room, along with the Kenmore Square quartet. The P.R. group had been Cora's guests there at Sycamore Hall where there was an ample supply of guest rooms, and also would be spending another night. They wanted to be sure that the reception ran smoothly. They were highly confident that a fair number of the mourners would over indulge and they wanted to be sure that everyone made it home safely.

As usual Cora was not saying much but I knew she was as alert as a Logan Airport air traffic controller.

All of them were casually dressed and seemed relaxed, yet I knew them well enough by that time to know that they had a good handle on what the day would bring.

Between the church's minister, his staff, and the funeral parlor that end of things was well in hand. Traffic around the church would be thick, and the police department was all too aware of the fact. If there was going to be any problem it was likely to be a matter of numbers; it was expected that more people would want to attend the service than the church could hold. The first two rows on the right side would be roped off for family members, with my parents, Cora, and Mr. and Mrs. Bain in the second row. Sally and I would be in the first row along with Nancy, Kathy, and Tom. Both sides of the third and fourth rows were reserved for members of our senior class and jack's teachers. Past there it was open seating.

The media would be a wild card. The ushers were to allow some of them to stand behind the last pews but Al pointed out that as an industry group they were not famous for decorum so time would tell.

All four of Al's people would be keeping an eye on things at and in the church. Al had wanted one of his team to be waiting at the grave site in case any help was needed there, but Chet, Alice, and Rocky all wanted to be at the church and Al relented.

At the conclusion of the church service Cora and Al's team would be returning directly to Sycamore Hall. They assumed (correctly, as things turned out) that more than a few of the townspeople would skip the burial and head directly for the reception. No one was to enter the house before Cora returned and Chief Hale had assigned a member of his force to be there. As backup there would be Cora's housekeeper, in full battle axe mode.

I had to admire everyone's ability to plan things out. I was learning plenty. Then it was time to go home. Show time was drawing near.

Chapter 55

By noon I couldn't stand sitting around the house any longer and got dressed. The dark blue suit that Cora had given me for Christmas was perfect for the occasion and I had a white shirt to go with it. I borrowed one of my dad's many neckties and I had shined a pair of his shoes to wear. I knew they would fit, I had already tried them on. They were serious gunboats; black wingtips, each shoe seemed to weigh approximately seven pounds.

By 1:15 I could not stand another minute of clock watching at home, and for what must have been the one hundredth time I patted each of my suit's inner pockets to be sure that I had what I needed. I knew that my parents prefered to be early for things. We were off for the church.

Even though we were there early the parking lot was filling up. Rocky motioned for me to drive to the front of the church and she parked my car for us so that I could walk in with my parents. They made their way down to their second-row spots but I stayed just inside the front door; I wanted to wait and walk in alongside Nancy. Part of the reason was to be supportive but also, I wanted everyone there, my classmates in particular, to see that we were holding hands. The way I saw it, the more conclusions that were drawn from that the better.

The church quickly filled, standing room in back included, and the ushers were kept busy. A few minutes before 2PM the limo pulled up to the front of the church and as Tom, Kathy, Sally, and Nancy were assisted out and I stepped outside to join them. If they had brought coats with them they were left in the car.

Tom, standing tall, had never reminded me more of Gary Cooper than he did at that moment, but it was the three women who stunned me. Kathy was extremely pretty, more so than I had ever noticed. Sally's black dress and downcast expression couldn't hide her natural beauty. With her blonde hair and blue eyes she was dazzling. Photographers were clicking away feverishly. Publications far and near would be identifying her as Jack's grieving girlfriend.

Nancy was the last to exit the limousine and when I saw her my jaw almost hit my necktie. Her dark hair was absolutely shining, and the combination of her fair skin and perfect posture made her a sight to behold. As she slowly turned her head from one side to the other those clear gray eyes were beyond description. Camera men maneuvered for position. It seemed like a red carpet scene from Oscars night, minus the microphones, smiles, and plunging necklines. I moved next to her, she took my arm, and we followed Sally into the church. As we walked sedately towards the front row she whispered "You look so handsome I wish this was a motel instead of a church."

An even quieter whisper came from Sally: "I heard that."

Eventually the organ ceased playing dirges and the minister started things off. There were 'All rises' and hand motions to be seated. There was singing, there was scripture, prayer, and a talk by the minister about Jack who was described in glowing, almost saintly terms, as well as his beautiful family. He concluded by assuring us that at that very moment Jack was happily ensconced in heaven and looking down on us all. He then called on Jack's dear friend, me, to speak. Nancy gave my hand a squeeze and I walked up a few steps and across to the microphone.

I started by patting the left side of my chest and said: "I have some notes in here and ever since I put this jacket on I have been patting the pocket every few minutes to make sure I still have them. Now that I'm up here I don't think I am going to use them." As I said this I gave what I hoped was a bemused shake of my head and a quiet laugh. The gathering responded with a subdued murmur of laughter. Al was right; they were ready to lighten up. I continued:

"I first met Jack Hathaway when I moved here and started eighth grade. Or I should say I was aware of who he was. Tall, good looking, athletic, popular, certainly I knew who he was. Maybe he noticed me at some point; I don't know. I was also aware of his close friend Sally Bain. All of you have seen her, of COURSE I was aware of Sally; who wouldn't be?"

This got a stronger laugh from the pews. So far so good. I looked toward Sally, who was dabbing her eyes with a tissue and trying to smile.

"Now I am going to tell you how I got to know Jack and Sally. I was waiting for the after-school bus one day. Sally was near me and Jack was a little way away waiting for a different bus. Then a bully came up to Sally and made a very rude comment. Sally told him to get lost, and as she turned away he yanked her ponytail. Sally, naturally yelled 'Ouch'! Then I came to life and got between them, carefully facing away from the bully. I didn't want to start trouble, I just wanted to guide Sally away from the jerk. As I was doing that the guy punched me in the back of my head. This caused me to lurch toward Sally, and Sally, in self-defense lowered her head. As a result, she unintendedly gave me a head-butt that cut me right here."

At this point I pointed to the area below my left eye. The church was quiet; the mourners spellbound.

"As I collapsed at her feet Jack came running to the rescue; fists flying. The bus monitor came and broke up the fight. The bully got in trouble, I got a band-aid from the school nurse, and Jack, Sally and I walked home together. We had a great time! We joked and we laughed. The three of us have been wonderful friends ever since. Did I think getting punched, head butted, and cut was worth it? Best thing that ever happened to me!"

With this I raised both my arms into the air and gave my biggest smile. The church roared with laughter, particularly the class seniors in the third and fourth rows.

The mourners settled down and I continued. "Before long I had the chance to get to know his father Tom, his amazing sister Nancy, and later Tom's wife Kathy. No one ever had a better friend than Jack."

"Now some of you know this about Jack and maybe some of you don't. Jack was a terrific woodsman. Smooth as he was on the football field he was even smoother deep in the forest. He knew the woods around here like Hawkeye. However, he did have one odd quirk (pause for effect) he liked to drag me in there with him!"

Another good laugh as I raised my hands to shoulder height, palms upward and an expression of mock bewilderment on my face.

"And in the woods I learned a lot about Jack Hathaway. I learned that you could trust him; always. I learned that when he was your friend he was going to stick with you, no matter what. I learned that if Jack told you something you could count on it being true. He was totally honest. Except, of course, when he was kidding. Jack had a great sense of humor."

"I learned how much he loved Sally.(I paused briefly) In fact, he may have told me that before Sally pulled it out of him. For those adults here in this gathering who possibly don't remember this, things like that are not easy for boys to say. Most of all I learned how happy he was.

"He told me that once, as an experiment, he told Sally that he didn't want to go somewhere with her. Then as soon as she left without him he felt terrible and ran after her. What a softy!"

At this point I paused and made sure that I was speaking slowly. "When he told me that story he broke into that big wonderful smile he had and laughed and laughed. So I'm going to end by saying to all of you who knew that smile and heard that laugh–" I spoke these last three words very slowly "Weren't we lucky?"

I was blinking back tears and close to choking when I finished this last sentence. I gave a short bob of my head and made for my seat.

As I sat down I was tremendously relieved to have the eulogy finished and behind me. Nancy held both my hands (which were slightly shaking) and Sally stepped across Kathy, Tom, and Nancy to briefly put her arms around my neck. Dad leaned forward and said, "Great job son."

I have no recollection of the remainder of the service other than it was over quickly. The casket, which I had found to be both distracting and grim, was wheeled back up the aisle by employees of the funeral parlor and eased into a hearse. Those of us in the first two rows followed close behind Jack's coffin, and the others who had attended the service worked their way into the center and side aisles and shuffled out of the church.

The next order of business was the formation of a motorcade, lead by a police car with lights flashing, and closely followed by the hearse and the limousine, which slowly made it's way to the graveyard where a few more words were said, more tears were shed, and eventually Jack's casket was lowered.

Then, thankfully, it was over. I recognized that the church service, sad though it was, served a purpose. However, I felt that the graveside ceremony involved more pomp and formalities than I cared for. To me it seemed needless to involve anyone outside the immediate family. It drew out the suffering and, I'm sure in the minds of many, caused the reception to be unnecessarily delayed. I wished I could have skipped the burial entirely. In fact, if I could go back to that day and do things differently I would skip the burial. The family did not need me there and I knew where Jack's body was going; I did not need to see it happen.

When we arrived at Sycamore Hall it was immediately clear that not only had most of the people who attended the church service made a beeline for the reception, bypassing the burial, but a considerable number of people had avoided both formalities to focus on availing themselves of Cora's hospitality. I couldn't blame them; almost no one from the town could remember the last time the doors of Sycamore Hall had been opened wide. Who knew when it might happen again?

Al himself was overseeing the front door. The members of the media were not invited to attend the reception, but Al had asked Cora if he could make a few exceptions to that policy, frankly stating that it would allow his company to build some goodwill that would certainly come in handy for them in the future. Honesty often pays off in dealing with Cora. She asked him how many exceptions he needed, and when he asked for eight she replied with a twinkle that he had a strict limit of eight, but if he found that he needed a few more that he could increase the strict limit. That way if any media representatives asked for an invitation to the reception and he did not care to invite them he could honestly say that he had to adhere to a strict limit. There were well over 300 people milling around, what difference would a few more make?

Sycamore Hall was looking its best for the occasion; all the visible metal surfaces such as door knobs and sconces had been polished as well as the banisters and other wood surfaces. Gallons of Windex had been used on Mirrors and windows, and most of the furniture in the downstairs rooms had been moved to the sides so that people could circulate. The double doors that lead from the back of the dining room were open to the courtyard that occupied the space between the two wings of the Hall, and a large tent had been erected there to handle the overflow. Catering employees were passing appetizers, the dining room table and sideboard were packed with a wide choice of hot and cold items, and; most popular by far, there were bars set up in the school room, the library, the living room (two there, one on each side flanking the fireplace) and also under the tent. Of the downstairs rooms only the gun room was locked and off limits.

Just inside the front door, one on each side, were two large leather-bound guest books, although I could not imagine the Hathaway family ever wanting to recall the day by reviewing the signatures.

Kathy, Tom, and Nancy had formed a receiving line part way down the wide main hallway, and I was pleased to see that they had asked Sally to join them as a part of their family group.

My parents fell into line to sign a guest book. I took a position on the high ground; ducking under a velvet cord and up to the second step of the staircase. From there I had a clear view of the receiving line to my right and also the flow of reception guests moving left towards the goodies in the dining room. From this perch I soon noticed that many of the townspeople were moving from room to room taking in the splendor that was Sycamore Hall. Naturally before doing this they had stopped at one of the bars.

Nancy and I had thought than we would spend about an hour at the reception. Then she would say goodbye to her family and I would drive her to the airport where the jet would be waiting to take her to Geneva, after a stop in Iceland to re-fuel. I had something important that I wanted to say to her and we had cleared this exit plan with Tom and Kathy.

After spending fifteen minutes or so on my second step observation post I could see that this plan was not going to work. The line of people waiting to pay respects to Sally and the Hathaways seemed to be constantly regenerating. Every time the line shortened more people would come to wait their turn. Furthermore, many of those wishing to greet them were not content to say a few words and move along, they wanted to stay for a chat. Our escape plan needed to be modified.

Al and his three cohorts were circulating from room to room, on the lookout for any rough spots that might need some sort of attention, and when Alice passed the foot of the staircase I was able to catch her attention. She ducked under the velvet cord and joined me on the second step saying "The town must be empty, everyone is here."

"I want some professional wisdom. Nancy and I need to get out of here fairly soon so that I can get her to the airport. By the way things look the line of people waiting to say something to them could last for hours."

Preppy Alice's sense of humor was never far beneath the surface. Turning to the throng she said "I think some of them are refreshing their drinks and then going through the line a second time."

"That helps."

"Let's try this. We give it another few minutes and then we can get her to come up the stairs, say a few words explaining that she has a plane to catch and then she can work her way to the door where you will be waiting. In the meantime, I want to tell Al what we are up to. How does that sound to you?"

"Excellent, but how are we going to get everyone to shut up and listen to her? You are standing right next to me and I can barely hear what you are saying."

It was true. The conversational noise level may have been shaking the slate on Sycamore Hall's roof.

Alice saw the point. "We will have Chet call for attention. When he wants to he can be a real foghorn. Have you seen Al lately?"

I had. Al had just passed by the staircase escorting a writer from Sports Illustrated back to the living room, where the mayor was holding court.

Alice headed after him and I worked my way through the crowd and told Nancy, Tom, Kathy, and Sally what we had in mind. Nancy was overjoyed, saying "Brilliant; it was looking like we would be here for hours. Don't wait too long."

Al approved the plan. We located Chet; (who bore a slight resemblance to the character named Oddjob in the James Bond movie 'Goldfinger') in the dining room, and with a grin he picked up a dinner gong and mallet that had been hanging from a mahogany frame towards the back of the sideboard. We took our time easing back to Nancy's spot, and with Chet acting as a human snowplow, several minutes later Chet, Nancy, and I were at the foot of the stairs.

Chet put on a game face, climbed to the third step and pounded the gong several times. This served to diminish, but not extinguish, the noise volume, and when Chet roared "May I have your attention please" and repeated these catch words twice more the school room, hallway, library, living room and dining room fell silent. There were still conversations going on under the tent, but that was merely background noise and unavoidable. Chet gave Nancy the briefest of introductions, saying "Thank you. Nancy Hathaway would like to say a few words."

Nancy had been a very visible figure in the sports world for several years. She was accustomed to being in front of crowds and she was used to speaking in front of groups, so I was confident that she would handle her staircase address with poise and charm. Being beautiful always helps too.

She began by thanking everyone who had come to the reception to pay their respects to her family and the memory of her wonderful brother. She then said that she considered Sally Bain to be a member of their family too, and that she was glad that Sally was able to join the Hathaways in the reception line, as her heart had been broken just as theirs had been by Jack's senseless death. She then continued.

"I don't think there is a person here who is not aware that I am part of our United States Winter Olympic team, and that we are deeply involved in our final preparations for these Winter Games."

"These preparations are crucial if we are to do our best. In other words, I have a race to win, and in order to give myself the best chance to win it I need to get back to Europe and rejoin my team.

"Now I know that it is only natural for people to wonder if this horrible tragedy is going to have an effect on my Olympic performance. Also, I know that there are a few people here who represent newspapers, magazines, radio, and television who may not have heard me say this when I spoke at the town library, so I want to absolutely, positively assure you that when I compete I do not and will not let anything distract me from doing my absolute best on the slope. I hope to win my race, but if I don't it will be because someone beat me, not because I beat myself!"

With that she paused and everyone in the confines of mossy old Sycamore Hall from the mayor to the caterers shouted out their approval.

Then Nancy, who had been very intense, smiled and looked around slowly and added "Before I go I want to thank Miss Cora Grant. First, for opening her lovely home to us for this reception and also for the many other things she has done for my family over the past several days. Miss Grant does not like to have attention called to herself but I have to say that this dress I am wearing is just one example of her thoughtfulness, kindness, and generosity.

"I also want to thank the four public relations people from Kenmore Square Consultants who dropped everything to come here to New Kensington to help. They have been working non-stop under very difficult circumstances. Al, Rocky, Chet, and Alice, we could not have pulled this together without you." As she said this she pointed to each of the four in turn.

"That brings me to my family, Dad and my wonderful step-mother Kathy. Thoughts of Jack will always be with us but your strength will help me see brighter days.

"And last, thanks to a man who has been right by my side through all of this and before. My rock, the guy I love, Carl Smith. Now please excuse me; I have a plane to catch and a race to win!"

With that the rooms exploded again with cheers. Al and his team had adroitly maneuvered Cora as well as Tom, Kathy, and Sally to the cloak room entrance near the front door. This served two purposes; first, they were there to say goodbye to Nancy as she was on her way out, and second, it concluded the painful formality of the receiving line.

There was a final round of hugs and kisses and just before we made it on our way Cora said to me: "Al and his crew will be leaving in the morning. Can you be here by 9?" I quickly agreed and we were out the door.

My car was waiting in the car park and so was the limo, which had Nancy's suitcase and jacket in it which we moved into my car. We were off for the airport and more or less on time. We would be there when expected.

Chapter 56

Once we were on the main road out of town I turned to Nancy and said "Well, you certainly let the cat out of the bag."

With a grin she said "Good; I'm glad. I am in love and I don't care who knows it. If fact with those media people being there, by morning the whole world with know it. Do you mind?"

"Mind? It was perfect timing! There is nothing like having a world-famous beauty get up on a staircase and tell the world she loves you to give a guy a lift."

Nancy slid next to me and kissed my ear. Then she took her shoes off and stretched herself out on the seat as best she could, with her head resting on my thigh and the rest of her curled up on the seat. Because she was still wearing the black dress that she had worn to the funeral it hiked up quite a way, giving me a nice view. She then said "I'm not going to sleep, I'm just going to rest my eyes for a minute or two." Then she was asleep.

My not too well thought out plan was to pull off the road at a spot where there would not be much traffic and propose to her. I had the pretty little box that Shreve, Crump, and Low had given to me in the inside right pocket of my suit and the diamond ring was inside it. I had been thinking that proposing to her before she left to return to Europe and her intense pre-Olympic training would give her spirits a much needed lift and maybe serve to counterbalance the grief she was carrying due to Jack's murder. I was close to positive that she would accept the ring and my proposal; after all, hadn't she just stood on a staircase and told the world that she loved me?

But now that it was time to activate my plan I was having second thoughts. What kind of a proposal would that be? "Here's a ring, I want you to marry me, will you? Okay, good. Now hop back into the car, we don't want to keep your jet waiting."

Shouldn't there be more to it than that? Candles? Music? Some sort of romantic setting? As I was thinking these thoughts we passed a cheesy looking motel. I stole another look at Nancy's lovely hip and leg. I knew that I would never be the most romantic person in the world, or even in North Overshoe, but certainly Nancy deserved something better than what now seemed to me to be little more than the equivalent of a drive-by proposal. Something like "Oh, by the way."

I looked down at Nancy's profile. She put so much faith and trust in me. Suddenly I felt that protecting Nancy and caring for her was both a responsibility and a wonderful gift. I looked down at her face, so relaxed and adorable. I felt a tremendous sense of pride. My girl had managed to handle enormous pressures and sorrow and still show such complete love for me under the worst possible conditions.

I now thought that my quickie proposal idea was as cheesy as the motel we had just passed. With my right hand on the wheel I used my left hand to take the ring's box out of my suit pocket, gave it a kiss and whispered "You are just going to have to wait a while longer pal." Then I placed the box down in the narrow space between my seat and the car door, making sure that it was secure there. I am the sort of guy who hates to lose things; diamond rings in particular. Decision made and feeling greatly relieved, I placed my right hand lightly and protectively onto her wonderful hip.

When we were about ten minutes from the airport I moved my hand up to her shoulder and gave her a light shake. Waking up, Nancy raised her head, looked around, and said "I must have fallen asleep. I hope I didn't drool on your leg."

"I can't tell in this light so you get the benefit of the doubt."

She smiled at that, sat up, straightened her dress, and put her shoes back on. I asked her what would be going on once she re-joined her team.

"Well there Is a fairly important race coming up this weekend but I doubt if the coaches will want me to enter seeing as I have been away. I will be going there with the team of course and getting in some practice runs. The following weekend there is another race, and by then I should be ready to compete. Once that race is finished we will only have a month before the Olympics start. The opening ceremonies should be exciting; I love our uniforms."

"You have them already?"

"I have a whole trunkful. We even have United States Olympic Ski Team pajamas!"

"I will be looking for you when you march into the stadium." As I said this I realized that I would not need to look very hard. The cameras loved Nancy and the network covering these games would be training them on her whenever they could. Nimble Nancy, America's Downhill Rocket, was likely to be the poster girl of our Olympic team.

We were about to pull into the airport and I had one more business sort of question. "After your downhill race, when are you going to announce your retirement?"

"I can't say exactly when that will be. If I don't win the downhill I will definitely enter the giant slalom. That's just two days later. If I do win my downhill then I may go for a second win. It will depend on how I am feeling about things I guess. One thing is certain, the coaches will be pushing me as hard as they can to enter. Medals mean everything to them. I promise that you will be the first to know. Whichever of the two is my last race I will probably make my retirement announcement two days later."

To me this seemed as if she was short changing herself. If she had a reasonable chance of doing well in the Giant Slalom why not enter that race regardless of how the downhill race turns out? I asked her if she was still on bad terms with the head coach.

"No, we get along. He has an abrasive personality but in his own way he is doing everything he can to prepare us to do our best. Overall, although he will never be my favorite person he is working very hard and is a good coach."

"Then I don't understand why you are uncertain about entering the Giant Slalom,"

"I do practice it sometimes and when I enter that race I have done well. Maybe it is because I hesitate to maybe show up the girls on our team who are full time slalom racers."

"Nancy that is so thoughtful and considerate. But how do you think a teammate would feel if they win a medal knowing that they won it only because you didn't compete? How would you feel if you won the downhill only because a better racer didn't enter?"

Nancy was quiet for a few seconds, then replied "I hadn't thought about it that way. Of course I couldn't feel proud if I won because a better skier dropped out. I should definitely enter the Giant Slalom shouldn't I?"

"I think you should. Enter and do your best, just like you always do in every race. There is another reason too. Everyone in America that follows sports at all is so proud of you and wants to see you represent our country and do well. You will be retiring after these Olympics are over and you shouldn't be holding anything back."

"Certainly not! I'm going to jump in with both feet! Carl, this has been so helpful. If I win a medal in the Giant Slalom I'm going to give it to you!"

"Great; I know just the spot for it, hanging around Rocky's neck." Rocky being the carved Cock-of-the-Rock that she had given to me as a Christmas present the Christmas before last and had a permanent perch on my bedroom dresser.

I could tell that Nancy was relieved to have the uncertainty surrounding the second race cleared up; She slid over and rubbed her head on my shoulder. Who wouldn't like that kind of sign language?

There was barely time for one more logistical matter. "I'll be writing often, but can we manage some phone calls?"

Nancy, always the planner, had thought this out ahead of time. "Our days are very tightly scheduled and there is that 6-hour time difference between where you and I will be. We always have some free time around 6 P.M. So that we can clean up before we eat. During the week you will be in school then, but I could call you every Sunday. That would be around noon your time. If you try to call me it would have to be through the security desk and we wouldn't have any privacy. It will be better if I call you. Okay?" It made sense to me and I agreed.

Seeing as I had been to the part of our small airport where the larger private airplanes parked just the past Sunday to pick up Tom and Kathy I knew where to drive to. It was easy to spot Nancy's fancy ride; it was the only jet there and it was a large one at that. Nancy would have plenty of elbow room.

Our drive to the airport had ended sooner than I wanted it to and we arrived right around the time we were expected. It was early evening, the area that was reserved for private planes was quiet, and I was able to drive onto the grounds and park near Nancy's plane. The two pilots and a stewardess came out of a nearby shed and introduced themselves. Although they obviously knew who Nancy was, her good manners caused her to introduce herself as well as me and to thank them for helping her get back to her team. These formalities concluded, one of the pilots carried her suitcase into the plane. It was time for me to do what I did not want to do; say goodbye.

I walked her to the foot of the plane's steps and took her hands in mine. All I could think of to say was "These last few days have changed us forever."

Nancy looked up at me and said "I know, Jack is dead and I finally seduced you. I wish you were coming to Geneva with me."

"I would except I don't have a passport and I hear the Swiss are strict about things like that."

"Picky. Well I will be coming home again in just a few more weeks. Do you want to know what I have learned since I came back?"

She did not wait for an answer "I have learned that most people, almost everyone, are very good. Take Cora for instance. I think that nothing makes her happier than helping others, and this airplane being here for me is a perfect example.

"And all the people from town who came to the church and the reception. Half of them were crying as they came through the receiving line. Did you see that?"

"No, I was standing on the stairs then but I'm not surprised. You and Jack are heroes around here."

"And that Alice Birch. At first I thought she was just around to look good, but she is so warm; smart too."

I saw that the pilot was standing at the top of the steps. I knew he was anxious to get airborne; it was time to say goodbye.

"Nancy darling, I know this sounds crazy, but in a way the last 6 days have been the best part of my life."

"I know what you mean; excluding Jack I feel the same."

"Yes, excluding Jack. The pilot is tapping his foot up there."

Nancy put her arms around my neck and we had a world class kiss. She whispered "No one ever loved anyone as much as I love you." She then scampered up the steps in true Nimble Nancy style. She waved, blew me a kiss, and ducked into the plane. A few seconds later she was waving from a window, then the plane taxied away.

I watched the plane take off and stayed until I couldn't see the tail lights any more. It was still early, I thought that I should swing by the Hathaway's house and tell them that Nancy was safely on her way back to Europe.

Chapter 57

The next morning I showed up at Sycamore Hall a little before nine. Al, Chet, Rocky, and Alice were drinking coffee and relaxing back in the living room, along with Cora, of course, who was sipping tea. All the furniture had been put back where it belonged before the caterers had left and several men were dismantling the tent. The old house seemed to be none the worse because of the reception.

We chatted pleasantly for a few minutes. I asked how the reception had turned out after I left to take Nancy to the airport.

Al replied "I think your fellow citizens of North Overshoe will be talking about it for some time. The receiving line broke up when you and Nancy drove away and that took a burden off Tom, Kathy, and Sally. Tom and Kathy circulated for a while and then headed home. Quite a few of your classmates were here and they had Sally surrounded. I think it gave her some support. Eventually her parents took her home too."

Chet broke in. "But that didn't end things here. The two caterers had brought what they thought would be more than enough beer, wine, and liquor and it's a good thing they did because the bartenders were pouring non-stop. Do you know someone named Mrs. Griffin?" Mrs. Griffin was the old dragon who assigned the students to groups A, B, or C. I replied "Yes, what about her?"

With a smile Chet said that Mrs. Griffin had been standing near the bar out in the tent and was tossing down whiskey sours left and right. After this went on for quite a while she propositioned the bartender. When he blew her off she took a few random steps toward the side of the tent and collapsed; bloto. Several of the townsfolk then rolled her up against the side of the tent and eventually, when Cora and Al thought it was time to end the reception, the bars were closed. Then the catering people loaded Mrs. Griffin onto a cart they had been using to transport cases of beer and soda. She was last seen sprawled in the bed of a pickup truck; to be driven home by a caterer.

I had to smile at this. Mrs. Griffin was a woman of considerable heft. It must have taken several men to get her into the pickup.

Cora then asked me if Nancy's plane had been there on time and how our ride had been. Naturally I made no mention of my aborted plan for a marriage proposal and told her that the ride went smoothly and the plane was waiting for us when we arrived. I went on to say that Nancy and I had talked about the possibility of her entering the Giant Slalom event, which she had been on the fence about. After some discussion she had become definite; she was going to enter both races.

Al said "So you convinced her to do it?"

"No; we talked it over. She made up her own mind."

"You convinced her. She trusts you and relies on you."

I did not bother to continue the subject.

Once we exhausted that topic Al looked at his associates, then Cora, and said "Now our work here is finished and it's time for us to head back to Boston. Before we go; and I am speaking for all of us, we want to say that this has been the best job we have ever had.

"Usually when we get called in on short notice some company has been caught doing something wrong and we are asked to sweep as much dirt under the rug as possible and try to justify what can't be hidden. Here we were told not to hide or sugar-coat anything. We loved being able to be open and honest. The Harvard Business School should do a case study on what has gone on here in the past week.

"We have met some absolutely wonderful people since we arrived here Thursday night, starting with you Cora. This town will never know everything that you have done. We are proud to have worked for you.

"Carl, we don't think you realize what a unique and wonderful person you are. You may feel that you are lucky to have Nancy love you, but we know that she feels just as lucky to have you. If I can find a bookie that will take the bet I am putting my money on her to win the Downhill; maybe the Giant Slalom too. I wonder if bookies would take a skiing daily double bet on her?

"Cora, I have left our invoice on the table near the cloak room. The amount is less than what we agreed on. If we could afford to charge nothing we would. Working for you has been truly a pleasure."

When Al finished Cora reached under a book that was on a nearby table and picked up an envelope. She walked over and handed it to Al, saying as she did so, "I do not need to look at the invoice. Your services have been invaluable, and each of you have earned my respect."

Al looked at the envelope quizzically, and Cora nodded her head and said "Go ahead."

When Al looked at the check inside he said "Good heavens Cora, this is way too much!"

Her reply was classic Cora Grant: "You earned it. Besides, I want to be sure that I can count on you to come back the next time someone up here gets shot. Now get going, it's supposed to start snowing this afternoon."

The suitcases belonging to the Kenmore Square Consultants were already outside the cloak room by the front door. There was a final round of hugs and handshakes. Cora stopped at the school room and I walked them to the door,then out to their cars, and watched them drive away toward Boston.

If I thought that would be the last I saw of Al and his team I would have been wrong. A week later and five weeks before the Olympic opening ceremony I had an unscheduled mid-week call from Nancy; she had a problem. She started by asking if I recalled her telling me that although she had not tipped her hand about retiring from competition she was still being solicited by various advertising and public relations entities trying to persuade her to hire them so that they could steer her to fame and fortune. I certainly remembered that and told her so.

"Then you must remember that although I have not told them anything I had decided to hire a couple from Chicago. They represent a very large full-service organization and they would be my contacts, so that I would not be bothered by lawyers, investment people, and all that fal-de-rol. Now there is a problem with that decision.

"They have a teenaged son who has been diagnosed with some rare form of blood cancer. He will require their full attention and they will not be able to travel. Their company has sent a man who has introduced himself to me as their replacement. He seems to be okay and I still like the company he represents, but I will need someone to travel with me when I am making appearances and giving talks. I am used to travel but it has always been with a team; never alone, and I am not going to do my traveling with some man who I have only met once. Do you have any ideas?"

Actually I had formed the outline of an idea before she was finished explaining the situation. I said "We will have to check to see if this is possible, but maybe that big Chicago company would be willing to hire Al Malone and his Kenmore Square group as sub-contractors. We would need to check with Al first off, but if that is something they would be interested in doing for you then maybe they could handle the travel and ground work along with you, and the people back in Chicago could use their extensive contacts for the rest of it. How does that sound?"

"It sounds great! I would love to travel with Alice, she's beyond cool and super smart."

"Then let me call Al. If this is something they would be interested in, then is it okay for me to tell him to contact Chicago and tell them what you want?"

"You can tell Al this: if he needs to it is fine with me for him to say that if they want my business it will be coming through Kenmore Square or not at all. I have people after me all the time about wanting to grant my every wish. The Chicago bunch have to compete. One man told me yesterday that he could dress me in Ermine. Can you imagine?"

We talked about a few other things and finished the call with me saying that I expected to have an answer by the time she called on Sunday.

Chapter 58

I put the phone down and thought. I expected Al to be eager to help represent Nancy but I also thought that the Midwesterners would not want to share a cut of the pie with some unknowns from Beantown. Thinking that this should be fun, I called Al.

When Al came to the phone he started with "Carl Smith! Don't tell me someone else has been shot up there so soon."

"No, the streets are quiet, but I do have a business matter to discuss with you if you have time. It's about Nancy."

"About Nancy? I just sat up a bit straighter in my chair. What about her?"

I briefly outlined Nancy's situation, carefully avoiding any hint of her impending retirement bombshell. I finished by saying that I thought that it might be a delicate situation, and would he be willing to let me come down to his office so that we could go over whatever details would be involved.

"Carl said Al, "Here is a lesson for you to remember. You, as Nancy's representative, are potentially a whopper (in typical Boston dialect he pronounced the word *whoppah*) of a client. You are not coming down here, I'm coming up to North Overshoe! I'll bring Alice. When can you see us?"

We agreed to meet the next day after school, and with Cora's blessing the meeting was at Sycamore Hall. Apparently I was in the driver's seat for what would likely be millions of dollars' worth of endorsements and public appearances by Nancy, and with Cora listening in I felt that I had the ace of spades up my sleeve if I needed any advice or guidance.

Once we were settled in the next afternoon Al began by saying "I know these Chicago people by reputation. They are good at what they do and they are tough negotiators. I expect that they will take an attitude something like "Whoever you are, we don't need you" when I call them, and in a way they will be right."

I saw Al's point, then said "We can turn that around and say that Nancy does not need them. She will need help, but not necessarily theirs, and that is what they should keep in mind. Nancy wants to have Kenmore Square Consultants be her contact with them so they need to work with you. Otherwise she will hire you to handle the search for lawyers, CPA's, investment advisors and all the rest of the professionals she will be needing, or hire one of their competitors to do that."

From where I was sitting I could see each of the three of them; Al, Alice, and Cora. Cora was wearing her usual look of judicial impartiality. Alice was turned toward Al with an eyebrows-up smile. Al cocked his head and replied "You just told me that we have them by the nuts. I wonder what sort of split we should get?"

I smiled and said, "Well seeing as you said they are tough negotiators maybe you should just accept whatever scraps they are willing to spare and throw yourself to their mercy."

Even Cora laughed at that. Al said, "Don't worry, we will come out just fine in this. Through you we have Nancy. That says it all." He then added "If this goes through you will be getting a very nice finder's fee."

That didn't sound fair to Al's organization or somehow to Nancy. I said "No need for that, all I've done is call you. Besides, I wouldn't want to lose my amateur status."

In reply Al said "Don't worry, it won't be coming out of our pocket or Nancy's. Or even from Chicago. The corporations who are falling all over themselves to pay Nancy to smile in their direction will be footing the bills and they will benefit greatly or they wouldn't be so eager to pay up and be involved."

I finalized the business part of our meeting with this: "I remember a wise woman once telling me that the best business deals are the ones where all the parties benefit. Nancy will want you to be fair."

Chapter 59

By this time things in and around New Kensington had settled down and we were all back into our daily routines. For me this meant school, and even though I missed Jack terribly, had a major case of senioritis, and was very ready to move on with my life I needed to finish my senior year, a fixture of which was the yearly Winter Snowflake Dance.

My interest in attending the Snowflake Dance stood at zero. It had not even crossed my mind for a fraction of a second. Then something odd happened; Faith Barnes asked me if I could find time after school to speak with her for a minute or so; she wanted to ask a favor of me. Faith Barnes was the girl who I had once asked for a Friday night date and she had gotten things so twisted around that we decided to drop the idea entirely. Faith was still a social nonentity at school but certainly not bad in any way. Beside being a brilliant student she was slim, well mannered and quiet, so I agreed to meet her in the senior parking lot when school let out.

Once the last class of the day ended and the final bell had rung I took my time arranging things in my locker. I did not want our classmates buzzing around while Faith and I were talking. By the time I arrived at the senior parking lot it was mostly empty. Faith was sitting on a bench and pretending to be reading a textbook while she waited for me to emerge from the school. As usual she was wearing a drab and shapeless wool overcoat.

Faith began by assuring me that she was not going to ask me for a date — but then she hesitated before continuing. "But I'm going to die an old prune if I don't somehow find a way to socialize," she said, glancing down at her shoe. "I know that you have a girlfriend, but would you possibly be willing to drive me to the Snowflake Dance and then sit with me for a little while? I promise for no more than an hour."

She looked at me earnestly for a moment, then shrugged. "Maybe someone will take pity on me and ask me to dance. If not at least I will know that I made the effort."

As much as I wanted to help Faith, and much as I could relate to her feelings of being left out of things (after all I had been in exactly that situation before I got lucky and became friends with Jack and Sally), I knew without giving it even a minute's thought that I was absolutely NOT going to escort her to the dance, or anyplace else for that matter. Even if Nancy understood — and I thought, but couldn't be sure that she would — I was not prepared to take on the inevitable wave of rumors that would follow.

"Faith," I said, trying to sound sympathetic and not condescending, "I can't. You know what a bunch of gossip mongers we have here. Plus, part of being someone's boyfriend is avoiding things like you are asking."

As the words were coming out, I watched her shoulders droop and her gaze move back to the ground. She looked waiflike and forlorn. The disappointed, lost expression on her face reminded me of someone else and I had a sudden thought. "But–" I said, a little more loudly. I could see her eyes flicker with interest at my tone. I pursed my lips for a second or two, trying to put the idea into words. "What if I could convince Sally Bain to go with you?"

I could feel a plan forming in my mind, despite the way Faith's nose scrunched up skeptically at the mention of Sally's name. She began shaking her head before I could finish.

"No, listen," I said. "Sally is very depressed over Jack's death and hardly leaves the house except to come to school. Even so she is still immensely popular. People love her. If she goes to the dance with you, all sorts of boys will swarm around." I could see a small crafty smile beginning to play on Faith's mouth. "And," I said, tapping her teasingly on the shoulder, "maybe one of them will ask you to dance. Even if that doesn't happen, at least you won't be sitting home alone on dance night."

Faith smiled an elfin smile, something rarely seen. She stayed quiet, though, seeming to consider the idea. "Well," she said after a moment, "I hardly know Sally. Do you think she would think it was a crazy idea?"

I shook my head. "Honestly, I think it would be great for her too. This could be the push she needs to get out of the house — maybe she's more likely to go if she feels like she's doing it for someone else."

Faith looked at me earnestly, as if working out whether I was telling the truth. When she was evidently satisfied, she nodded, then smiled again, this time more broadly. "Okay," she said, "if you think she wouldn't consider it too strange, please do ask her. If you manage to pull it off I will see that you get a cake — your favorite flavor."

"You bake?"

"I can't boil water, but my mother is a whiz in the kitchen. She would bake a hundred cakes if it would get me a date."

I scanned the parking lot, looking for Sally's car. It was nowhere to be seen, so I knew that she had gone home. I extended my hand to Faith. "It's a deal." She pumped my hand as we shook.

A little while later I was knocking on the Bain's door. When Mrs. Bain saw me she smiled and gave me a hug as she said that it was wonderful to see me. She led me to the living room and told me to relax on the couch while she ran upstairs to get her daughter. I found a novel on the side table and managed to get nearly the entire first chapter in before Sally came down the stairs. She looked like she had spruced herself up, but in spite of this she still lacked the air of exuberance she had always carried with her before Jack's death.

Despite the width of the couch, she sat down right next to me, her leg pressed against mine. "I can't imagine why you are here, you always call first, she said softly, taking my nearest hand into hers, but I am so very happy that you came. You have to tell me right now what's up."

As I explained the situation Sally lowered our clasped hands to rest fairly high up on her thigh. When I finished outlining what I was asking her to consider she turned slowly toward me, her breast brushing my arm as she did so.

Sally leaned in, looking intently into my eyes as she spoke. "Carl, I do think helping Faith get in circulation would be a nice thing to do, but I'm still absolutely broken up about Jack," she said. "I do want to help, but I can only manage this if you're part of it. I'll accompany Faith to the dance if you can take both of us there and we stay for no more than an hour." She arched one eyebrow, awaiting my response.

Something seemed vaguely wrong about Sally`s modification of my idea, but I still thought that it would be good for Sally to get out of the house for even a little while. Plus it was hard to say no to my good friend, especially when she was sitting right next to me and holding my hand on her leg. And it would solve several potential issues. Not even the most scandal-minded kid in school could possibly think that there could be anything going on between Faith and me if Sally was along as chaperone. I said I would do it.

On the night of dance, I was to pick Sally up first, then we would get Faith at her house and head for the dance. I was just wearing slacks and a sports coat, I didn't bother with a necktie.

I was a little surprised when I saw Sally. For a girl who I knew was grief stricken her dress was showing quite a bit of skin. Fat chance of any boy noticing Faith with Sally dressed like that!

But much to my surprise Faith came to her door looking almost confident in a short skirt and a loose fitting top that seemed to invite some boy to venture a peek down. Her hair had been cut into a gamine style and her slender arms and legs gave her a sylph-like appearance. Sally slid over next to me while Faith took the window seat. Off we went to the Winter Snowflake Dance.

All our school dances were held in the cafeteria, with some of the tables arranged around the perimeter and the rest folded and moved out of the way. Typically each of the four classes would gather among themselves, so we headed for the tables where the seniors congregated. Once we were settled in, as predicted, our classmates were soon coming around to chat. To my total astonishment one of them was Alves! Also known as That Damn Alves. The same Alves who was reliably self-destructive and frequently disruptive. The Alves who used to run around the track with me when he was banished from P. E. That Alves.

All that said, Alves had settled down, at least to a degree, since I first met him back in eighth grade. Still, so far as I knew he was as socially isolated in his own way as Faith was. To me it seemed highly unusual for him to show up at the Snowflake Dance.

Alves had not been with us for long before Faith stood up and said, "Robert, your tie is crooked, let me fix it for you." With that she moved in directly in front of Alves, gently raised his chin up with a fingertip, and spent what seemed to me to be quite a bit of time fussing with his necktie. Alves stood motionless and blushing as she worked.

Once Faith finished perfecting the relationship between the tie and Alves's shirt, she slipped her hand under Alves's jacket, which was hanging loosely on his skinny frame. With her arm around his waist, Faith turned Alves toward the dance floor and put her mouth near his ear. "Let's try a dance," she said, her voice barely audible above the noise, and they vanished into the crowd.

I opened my eyes as wide as they would go and turned to Sally. She merely shrugged and said, "Cupid covers a lot of ground."

About 20 minutes later Faith and Alves emerged from the throng of dancers, holding hands and hip to hip. Alves wore a stunned, loopy grin as they came to my side. "Thanks for bringing me Carl," Faith said, "but Bobby is going to be taking me home."

On hearing that Sally stood up, took my hand and said, "Well that's settled, we can go now." School dances had never been my style of entertainment, so off we went.

Once in the car Sally again sat close against me, even though the passenger side seat was now empty. I began to feel uncomfortable about the situation. As we turned onto Sally`s street, she said that there was something important she had to say to me and she asked me to pull into a driveway where there was a 'For Sale' sign. I did pull in, but by that time I knew Sally was up to something.

Once the engine stopped I swung my legs around to make a little space between us. Sally asked if I remembered the time she came to my house after her first date with Jack; the time they had trekked out into the woods and she had come by to tell me about it.

"I seem to remember everything Sally, whether or not I want to."

"I was so happy then and you were jealous. I knew that you had a big crush on me," she said, as her left hand moved up into the hair on the back of my head. "That's true isn't it?" Her fingernails began lightly stroking my neck.

"Yes, that's true, me and just about every boy in school. But I am in love with Nancy now so please –" I gently pulled her hand from my head and set it on the seat between us. "– stop tickling my neck."

"I almost loved you then Carl, but I had Jack." With that she pushed my legs down and moved directly against me. "I want you and I don't have time to wait," she whispered in my ear. "The key to this house is under the mat. Please take me inside so we can make love."

There are not enough letters in the word *temptation* to describe my animal instincts at that moment. The thing that saved me from a lifetime of guilt was the image that popped into my head: Nancy`s innocent face as she slept with her head on my leg as I drove her to the airport. I could never betray the girl who meant the world to me.

Much as I desired Sally at that moment I simply could not cheat on the girl I had pledged to love forever. Not even with the girl I had lusted over since eighth grade. "No Sally I can`t," I said as I put both my hands on Sally`s hips and slid her back to her side of the front seat. "I'm a one-girl sort of guy and Nancy's my girl. She always will be. I'm taking you home."

Sally lowered her head and began to cry, I certainly was not going to dump her back on her doorstep in that condition. I took her left hand in my right and said. "This is so terribly unfair to you."

"Oh Carl, Jack and I were so in love." She stopped to blow her nose and sniffle. " How can I ever get over him? I thought that maybe if you and I" She held my hand against her cheek and we stayed that way for a short time. Then she said, "I had to try, do you hate me?"

"No, I could never hate you. I miss Jack too, and every day. I will always be your friend but we can't be alone together, I only have just so much willpower and I just burned through a lot of it. I don't know how much is left."

With a weak smile Sally said, "Well, at least I got a compliment out of you."

Then something dawned on me. "Did you somehow convince Alves to come over to where Faith was?'

"Not exactly," she said. "I did send one of the cheerleaders to tell Alves that Faith thought he was cute. Then I told Faith that I heard one of the boys say that Alves wanted to ask her out but he was too shy to make the first move. It wasn't complicated."

We sat quietly for a minute; I think we were both relieved to shift our focus to the sweet simplicity of Faith and Alves.

After a moment, Sally let out a low, quiet breath and looked at me. "Are you going to tell Nancy that I tried to seduce you?"

"If she somehow gets wind of it and asks me I won't lie about it. Otherwise it will always stay just between the two of us. I want you to be Nancy's friend as well as mine."

Sally nodded earnestly. "Deal. I'll be a good friend too," she said. "you'll see." To that I said "You always have been."

I gave Sally all the time she needed to compose herself and then I took her home.

Chapter 60

Three weeks later we crowded into the Hathaways' living room to watch the Winter Olympics on television. Tom and Kathy, my parents and I, along with Cora, Sally, and her parents sat riveted as my amazing girlfriend, Nimble Nancy, America's Downhill Rocket, demolished the field and won the downhill event. Her competitors seemed to be fighting as hard as they could as they tried to match her times. When Nancy raced it seemed as if a magnet was pulling her down the slope. Her skis hardly kicked up the snow as she flashed downhill. Champagne flowed freely, thanks once again to Cora`s generosity and her father Hammy's farsightedness in stocking Sycamore Hall's wine cellar.

We had watched Nancy zip across the finish line, look up at the giant status board where her time was posted and then throw her arms up above her head. Pulling her goggles down under her chin she turned, smiling, crying, and waving to the thousands of people jammed around the base of the course.

A television announcer briefly interviewed her... when the station switched to commercials, everyone began buzzing again, clinking glasses and stretching legs and marveling over Nancy's victory.

I slipped outside and onto the Hathaway's front porch. I was trying to understand exactly how I felt now that my darling Nancy had achieved her dream of a lifetime, and I was not getting anywhere. I knew I felt relieved that she had won. By then it was accepted within the world of downhill racing that Nancy was the best in the world, but no one wins every race and the pressure on her must have been enormous. With that gold medal around her neck a good result in what would be her last race, the Giant Slalom, would be vastly less important. Now that the race she had been dreaming of for years was over I felt oddly flat. After this huge success would life with me seem boring; hum-drum?

I heard the door behind me open and shut, then her father, Tom, was standing beside me. Neither of us said anything for a minute or so. Then I asked him what he was thinking.

"I was thinking of her mother," he said, putting one foot up on the porch railing and crossing his forearms over that knee, "and how happy she was when Nancy was born. She had wanted a girl to go with Jack. Nancy was a handful when she was a little girl, but I have never known a purer heart."

I smiled to myself. "You must be tremendously proud of her."

"I am always proud of her each and every day. What I am feeling now is happiness because this is what she has wanted. She has worked so very hard for this gold medal and now she has won it. It's truly–"

Just then Kathy stuck her head out the door. "Anyone out here want to talk to Nancy? She's on the phone!"

Three days later the same group gathered at the Hathaways' house and watched as she won a second gold medal in the Giant Slalom — this time in a much tighter race. We watched as Nancy celebrated by throwing handfuls of snow up over her head, then smiling and waving to the crowd.

Tom, Kathy and I were the only ones that knew how Nancy expected the next twenty-four hours to unfold. Her plan was to spend most of the next day relaxing with some of her teammates, avoiding the press entirely and enjoying her surroundings there at the Olympic village — something she had not been able to do before her events. Then, after the evening meal, she intended to ask her team's publicity department to let the press representatives know that she would like to address them the following morning. That was when she would tell the world she had no further plans to ski competitively; she was retiring.

We intended to let Cora in on the secret once my parents and the Bains left the Hathaway's house that night. I would tell my parents what to expect once I got home.

A separate question was when to tell Al and his associates down at Kenmore Square of Nancy`s impending retirement announcement. Nancy wanted her plans to come as a total surprise, but we knew that if Kenmore Square didn't have at least a little advance notice they would be left feeling clueless, as if they were not full-scale members of Nancy`s team. We intended to depend on them in executing our future plans, and we wanted them to feel they could depend on us in return.

A compromise was called for. A few days earlier, Nancy and I had decided I would call Al in the early afternoon the day after the second race and prepare him: At 4 AM the next day our time and 10 AM where Nancy was, she would announce her retirement to the press. We knew in the world of sports news this would be a major bombshell — headline news for certain.

We also knew that it would throw the doors open wide to business opportunities for Nancy. She was frequently solicited by sports agents offering to represent her and pave her path with gold. Instead of being a full time skier who would be hard pressed to find time for photo opportunities and chats with media people, Nancy would be available for modeling clothes, endorsing products, (selectively; she had already decided. No liquor and no snuff were the extreme examples she had humorously mentioned) addressing conventioneers, and in general being a well paid celebrity.

I knew that Al had already reached a preliminary working deal with North Wind, the major sports representative firm in Chicago, the one that Nancy liked. Once North Wind realized that Nancy would hire them through Kenmore Square or not at all (or, as Al had succinctly put it, that he "had them by the nuts"), they had proven to be straight-from-the-shoulder people and easy to work with. I was looking forward to calling Al with what for him would be extremely exciting news.

When I did make that call to Al, he reacted like a firehouse dalmatian that had just heard the alarm bell go off. "SHE'S RETIRING? ARE YOU KIDDING ME? MY GOD, WE JUST GOT CALLED UP INTO THE BIG LEAGUES!" Then, slightly calmer: "Okay, okay, we don't need to rush. What's she have planned for after the announcement?"

I told Al that Nancy intended to spend another day saying goodbye to her Olympic teammates and coaches before flying back to Boston. "I'm meeting her at Logan the day after tomorrow," I told him, "and then nothing. She's going to relax at home for two weeks and do nothing."

Al regained his equilibrium. "That's fine, just about perfect in fact. It will give us time to start lining things up for her," he said. I could hear the sound of him scribbling notes as he talked. "Please tell her this: if she thinks that she has been the center of attention before this, it will go up by a factor of ten. Tell her she needs to tell the press she's agreed to be represented by Kenmore Square Consultants in Boston and North Wind. That will deflect a lot of it toward us and that is just what we want." He scribbled something else. "I'm going to tell Alice, Chet, and Rocky what is coming our way and make them take a blood oath to shut up about it until tomorrow morning."

He paused for a moment, making a tapping sound as he thought. "You know what," he added. "I'm not so sure that North Wind will be able to keep it quiet; they are just too big. If it's alright with you, I'm just going to call my contact there at home early tonight. That way he can call the people he needs to tell without every secretary in the organization knowing they have just landed Nancy Hathaway as a client. We can't have their whole staff calling everyone they know to blab about it."

I gave my permission for Al to do that, thinking as I did it that it was semi-ridiculous for a high school senior to be involved in all this high-level plotting. Then again, Nancy herself would be just a high school junior if she was still actually in school, and she was the reason for all the hubbub.

"After she's had a chance to sleep in her own bed for a night or two, why don't the two of you stop by the office so we can personally thank Nancy for trusting us to represent her? Alice will want to be there, and we might even have some early indications of some opportunities."

"Oh, I–"

The hesitation in my voice was obvious and he cut me off. "I know, I know, nothing for two weeks. I promise we'll keep it short. Let's just touch base, say quick hellos."

I sighed, trying to sound calm though inside my blood was pulsing. "Okay," I said cautiously. "We'll come by later in the week. I'll give you a call." I hung up and took a deep, slow breath. Things were happening.

The next morning, as planned, Nancy turned the ski world upside down by announcing she was retiring from competitive skiing. "I have decided to end my career as a competitive skier. For many years I have centered my life around the goal of winning a gold medal in the Olympic Downhill event and now my dream has come true. However, I never wanted to continue my skiing career indefinitely. This is not a sudden decision, it has been my intention for quite some time to make the team and to do my absolute best to win gold and then to go on to other things.

"In the part of the country where I live a baseball player named Ted Williams is a legend; he hit a home run the last time he came to the plate and then retired. I don't compare myself to Ted Williams, but I am thankful that I have won my last race. Thank you."

She took a few questions and answered vaguely, saying that she was retaining Kenmore Square Consultants and North Wind to represent her and that she anticipated doing some public speaking and that there could possibly be other "opportunities."

After a few minutes, her coach came to her side to bring the questions to a close. The members of the press began lowering their hands as they realized he was indeed ignoring their continued questions. As the room quieted, he turned to Nancy with a look that mixed disappointment with genuine warmth.

"Well," he said into the microphone, "I know I speak for everyone here when I say we can't wait to see what you do next."

Flashing the smile I loved, she leaned into the podium. " Me too! But first I'm going home. There's someone there I'm dying to see."

There was no private jet this time, so I fought the Boston traffic and met Nancy at Logan Airport. Once again she had received the royal treatment; an upgrade to first class. I had obtained a gate pass from her airline so I was there when she stepped off the jetway and into the gate area.

She was wearing navy slacks and a white blouse, with her U.S.A. ski team jacket over her arm, and in spite of the long airplane ride she looked crisp, alert, and beautiful. I was waving to her as soon as she appeared from the jetway, and the second she spotted me she yelled my name; as if *I* had just won two gold medals. We got our arms around each other and I was so overwhelmed with pride and emotion that I was fighting back tears.

There was no hiding from the crowds this time. Nancy was immediately recognized and the people around the gate area were clapping and cheering for her. Nancy was genuinely happy at the reception and was smiling and laughing. She hooked arms with me and whispered, "Don't stop unless I do" and we began working our way to the luggage area. She hadn't traveled light this time, there were two large suitcases to collect, one of which was her trunk full of Olympic team clothing. Her bulkier equipment was being shipped separately.

As we slowly made our way down the concourse she was a one girl sensation; congratulations came from all directions, with the travelers in the open fronted bars being particularly vociferous. People young and old wanted autographs, and from time to time she would stop so that she could be photographed with children. It was a parade of sorts and I was happily invisible.

Eventually we got Nancy's luggage into the car and headed home, where Tom and Kathy were overjoyed to see her. In spite of her perky appearance at the airport I knew that Nancy was thoroughly worn out and needed rest and plenty of it. That night Nancy slept for twelve hours straight, then spent the entire next day in sweatpants and sweatshirt over an old t-shirt. I knew this because I rarely left her side. She wandered restlessly from couch to kitchen to the back yard and to the couch again, nibbling on snacks, sipping water, flipping through magazines and answering questions from Tom, Kathy and me about all the behind the scenes minutia she'd experienced. She drifted aimlessly through the day, talking often about how strange it was to be home — the combination of jet lag and the realization that her life had changed in inconceivable ways was taking time for her to adjust to.

The following morning I picked her up after breakfast and we drove to the office of Kenmore Square Consultants, where we were greeted enthusiastically by Al, Chet, Rocky, Alice, and the entire staff. There were balloons floating around and a large paper banner that read "Welcome Home Champ!" Al spoke briefly, thanking Nancy for placing her trust in them, and promising that they would do everything within their power to deserve that trust.

He explained that later there would be some paperwork for her to review and sign authorizing them to represent her. Because she was still under age 18, Tom would also need to sign.

Alice said she was as excited as was humanly possible to be traveling with Nancy when she would be making appearances, and that very soon they would need to go wardrobe shopping. As she said this she turned toward Al and rubbed her right thumb rapidly over her fingers in the universal sign signifying money. Al shrugged. "Takes money to make money," he said. "We wouldn't want to send you ladies into the field looking shabby."

"I'm having a passport expedited just in case," Alice added, stepping to Nancy's side and putting a reassuring arm around her new client's shoulder. "And the best news of all is that I never snore — just maybe a small popping noise now and then. At least so I have been told."

Nancy laughed. "I'm sure I won't even notice. Once my head hits the pillow I'm dead until morning."

Chapter 61

A few days later Alice called to say that the senior executives at North Wind wanted Nancy to come to their offices so they could introduce themselves and hear directly from her what sort of money making activities she was willing to sign on for — and what she wished to avoid.

"There will be papers for you and your dad to sign, and they already have a few opportunities for you to consider," Alice said. "Let's see — one is a photo for a cereal box, which would require two days in a studio in Los Angeles. They say that one is very time sensitive so it's a rush job"

Nancy wrinkled her nose at the words Los Angeles. "I'm happy to go to Chicago and meet the North Wind people and I want to be on the cereal box," she said, "but I don't want to spend two days for one photograph and I'd rather not go to Los Angeles. There have to be plenty of fine photographers right there in Chicago. Posing for that cover photo for Ski magazine took less than half a day; two days for one photograph? Anyway, I'm not going anywhere until I have spent two full weeks here in New Kensington." She took a breath and looked at me, crossing her eyes humorously. "I have been bouncing around all over the place for the past several years. Right now I need some unscheduled time so I can decompress."

That evening we watched the Olympic closing ceremonies from the comfort of the Hathaway's living room couch, along with Tom and Kathy, my parents, and Cora.

Nancy served as our native guide. "She's one of the nicest ones," she said as the camera panned the American team. Then later: "Oh look, there's my roommate!"

Before the evening ended Cora turned to all the ladies present. "I would be so grateful if all of you would come to my home for lunch on Saturday," she said warmly. "I want to take you up on your Christmas promises to come and advise me on how you think Sycamore Hall could be brought up to date." She turned toward Nancy and added "Especially you." Nancy forced a smile but I could sense her discomfort with being singled out. "Anyway," Cora said, pulling a sage leather handbag over her shoulder, "This will give me a starting point when I hire an interior decorator to come. I really need to yank the old mausoleum into today's world."

Later, when the other guests had left, Nancy and I were alone on the couch reflecting on the evening. "I can't wait to wander around that huge house and look it over," she said, running her hand slowly up and down my arm, "but I wonder why she mentioned me in particular? I don't know diddly-squat about decorating."

I didn't really answer and just made a sound of assent. I had been chewing on that exact question myself. I knew Cora well enough to be certain that she had a reason for wanting Nancy along. Cora always had a reason for everything she did; the trick was figuring out what that reason might be.

The next day was a Monday so I went to school. When I came home my mother told me that Nancy had called, leaving word that she would like me to come to her house. Mother added "She sounded slightly upset." Thinking "What could this be about?" I jumped back into my trusty Buick and drove to Nancy's.

When I arrived Nancy greeted me at the door saying "Well now I've done it, I think I just fired North Wind."

"Good lord, you haven't even met them yet! What happened?"

We went into the living room. Tom and Kathy were at the hardware store so we had the house to ourselves. I plopped down on the couch but Nancy was too upset to sit still and was pacing around as she started to explain.

"The phone rang an hour or so ago and it was the president of North Wind, a guy named Hank Greenwell. He introduced himself, said that he and his staff were delighted to be working with me, and that they could hardly wait to meet me. For a minute or two we had a pleasant chat. Then he said that Alice Birch had passed the word along to them that I was eager to appear on the cereal box, but that I was reluctant to get started on anything until I had two full weeks to relax and unwind. He was very friendly and said that he could understand. The pressure involved in winning the Olympics must have been savage, and so forth.

"Then he went on to tell me that he had just had a call from the president of General Mills, the cereal company. They have found that when they come out with a fresh face on the boxes of their leading brand there is a huge demand and the sales skyrocket. However before too long the excitement dies down somewhat so it is very important that we start this project right away. Then Mr. Greenwell told me that he had stuck his neck out a little and told the General Mills man that he was sure that I would understand and take a short break from my vacation and pose for the photo."

I could see where this conversation would be going from there and said "I don't imagine that sat very well with you."

"Of course not! I have told everyone several times that I need these two weeks to unwind. This isn't some sort of whim, I'm human and I need a break, not more airplane rides."

"And so you said to Mr. Greenwell---"

"I told him that I wished that he had spoken with the people at Kenmore Square about this rush job before he told the General Mills man that he was sure that I would interrupt my vacation and head for the airport. I told him that I was very sorry but I was not available so soon."

"How did he take that news?"

"Not particularly well. He explained again why we needed to get going immediately, and said that if this was about money that he could squeeze an extra 10% out of General Mills to compensate me for the inconvenience."

I thought about cracking a witticism, decided against it, and simply made a sympathetic sound. Nancy concluded by saying this. "I told Mr Greenwell that money was not the point, I needed to recharge my batteries. He got a little huffy and told me that opportunities like this didn't come around often, and that I needed to defer to North Wind's judgement on this or we wouldn't be able to work together. I did not like the sound of his voice and I said that I don't like threats so I would take the 'or'. Then I 'said goodbye Mr. Greenwell' and hung up."

Nancy was like her brother, neither of them liked to be pushed around. She sat down next to me looking deflated and told me that she wished she hadn't been so stubborn, it would not have killed her to take time for the photo shoot. She then said "Now I don't know what to do. Maybe I should call him back, apologize, and say I'll do it"

I told her that I didn't know either but that I knew who WOULD know. I called Cora and asked for an audience.

A short time later we were sitting in Sycamore Hall's school room with Cora, who listened wordlessly as Nancy repeated her conversation with North Wind's president. When she finished she told Cora that she felt as if she had been unreasonable. Should she call Mr. Greenwell back and apologize?

Cora leaned back in her chair, steepled her fingers under her chin, and with the ghost of a smile and a microscopic shake of her head said "I wouldn't. Greenwell has made several mistakes. He shouldn't have assured the General Mills president that you would go along with the rushed schedule. He should have called our friends at Kenmore Square before he called you. It was a poor idea to offer you more money to disrupt what he had to know was a vacation that was important to you. That had to come across as a bribe. Then he compounded the missteps by throwing in that 'either-or' threat. If he isn't sitting at his desk right now with his head in his hands he should be. The world of sports agents is very tight and word travels fast. He has to know that all his competitors will soon be hatching plans to have you affiliate with them. Also, he has a board of directors that he has to answer to. How is he going to explain to them that he managed to lose you as a client so quickly?"

Nancy brightened, and asked if Cora thought she should call the Kenmore Square people to let them know what had happened. To this Cora replied "Say nothing. Let Greenwell make the next move. Go home and relax. By this time tomorrow this matter will be settled one way or another."

Back we went to Nancy's, where we did what everyone does when faced with situations similar to ours; we built a snowman.

The next morning, first thing, Al Malone had a phone call from Mr. Hank Greenwell. The first words out of his mouth were "Al; Hank. I've dug myself into a hole the size of the Grand Canyon and I am desperate. Nancy Hathaway fired my ass yesterday!"

"Am I hearing things? How did you manage that?"

Mr. Greenwell reviewed the conversation that had gone on the previous day between he and Nancy, ending with 'That girl is one cool customer. I pushed her too far about the damn cereal box deal and when I gave her the 'either or' choice she just said she'd take the 'or', said goodbye, and hung up."

Al exhaled loudly and said "Hank, you are a complete idiot. Nancy is a sweetheart and extremely easy to communicate with but she didn't get to be an Olympic champion by letting people push her around."

"So I found out! And to make things even worse I let it slip at the dinner table last night that Nancy Hathaway and I had a disagreement and she fired us. I have a 15 year old daughter who idolizes Nancy. There's a big picture of Nancy on her bedroom wall and she's told her friends that she is going to get to meet Nancy. When she heard me say that Nancy fired us she became hysterical, said I was worse than a murderer, and ran up to her room crying her eyes out. My wife wasn't exactly supportive either. Will you please call her and ask her to give us another chance?"

"Which her do you mean, Nancy, your wife, or your daughter?"

"I'm glad you are enjoying this."

Al laughed and said "Big Hank Greenwell, afraid of a 17 year old girl! You're the one who needs to call her, not me. Just say that you want to apologize for the way that you spoke to her yesterday. Tell her that you were wrong, that the cereal box photo can wait, and if you really want to sound pitiful you can throw in the fact that your daughter now hates you for what you did. She will be gracious and accept your apology. You will keep Nancy as a client and your daughter will stop crying."

"What makes you so sure?"

"If she wanted to replace you she would have called us by now and we have heard nothing. Now give her a call and then let me know how things turn out."

The next day when I got home from school my mother said "Nancy called and said that Cora was right. The North Wind man called back, apologized, and things are fine. She wants you to come over so she can tell you all about it."

When I pulled into the driveway I saw Nancy in the front yard, sitting on a sled and tossing snowballs at a snow shovel that she had stuck upside down into the snow next to our snowman. "Everything is fine!" She exclaimed, giving me a kiss. "Mr. Greenwell apologized and couldn't have been nicer. I told him that I was relieved to be back on his good side and he could tell the General Mills guy that I would come sit for the photograph right away. Boy did that make him happy! He called back in an hour and said they could do it in one day, and in Boston! They are sending a limousine to pick me up tomorrow! How's that for an olive branch?"

With that she fired a snowball at the shovel, scoring a solid hit on it's blade. The shovel fell over backward, and Nancy took me inside for some hot chocolate.

When Saturday rolled around the ladies dutifully headed off to Sycamore Hall for lunch and the decor critique. Tom and I were definitely not invited and we both wanted a first hand report, so we had agreed to meet at the Hathaway's place late that afternoon to get the word. My mom and the Bains had gone directly home from Sycamore Hall, but Kathy and Nancy gave us an earful.

We settled around their kitchen table and Kathy started right in. "She told us that she didn't want dysfunctional politeness, she wanted to get right down to brass tacks, and that is what she got. We started right there in the dining room; it is just too dark. The whole house is, to be blunt, but the main rooms in particular seem like some old fogies smoking club. We loved the furniture in the dining room, it is classic, but the rugs and draperies needed to go and the chairs need to be reupholstered. Cora asked us if we liked the windows; were they the right size? We all thought it would be better if they were much bigger, but the ground floor walls are made of fieldstones and we didn't think the windows could be enlarged." Kathy stopped to sip her coffee and Nancy jumped in.

"You know what Cora said to that?" Nancy's eyes were wide with amusement. "She said of course they can be enlarged. Architects do things like that all the time. We needed to be open minded! You could almost see everyone roll up their sleeves when she said that. We went past the pantry and into the kitchen. It needs to be stripped bare and be totally modernized. Everything is far too old–"

"Except for some of the cast iron cooking gear," Kathy cut in. "You're too young to know this, but cast iron is wonderful. It's timeless."

Nancy glanced at me and smiled before continuing. "None of us had any idea what to do with the servants rooms downstairs or upstairs," she said, "so we doubled back and went right to town. I loved the Cloak Room." She reached out and squeezed my hand. "It seems so romantic to have one."

Kathy laughed and exchanged a look with Tom. "I loved the Cloak Room too, but it doesn't need to be so big. The bathroom in there is small, so our idea–" She began making broad gestures with her arms, attempting the task of showing what she was describing. " — was to move the wall and enlarge the bathroom, taking some space from the Cloak Room."

They kept going. The schoolroom needed new furniture, the pantry needed new paint. Everything needed something. I found my gaze drifting to the kitchen window until I heard the words "Carl's office" and refocused my attention. Apparently none of the women liked the idea of my future office being right in there alongside Cora.

"She said that she wants you to be involved in her business matters," Nancy said, "but we think you should have your own office, and that it should be what is now the Gun Room. The paneling in there is beautiful, some sort of light colored wood that absolutely shines. Of course that awful pig has to go."

Pig? What was she talking about?

Kathy clarified "There's a stuffed wild boar head over the fireplace.

"*And*," Kathy added with a small roll of her eyes, "right now the room is full of guns! Walls of them. I felt like I was back in

Texas! Rifles, shotguns, drawers full of pistols and a little closet for ammunition. There is still some ammunition in there." I didn't like that at all. She's got an armory!"

"*But*," Nancy said, playfully mimicking Kathy, "there is that lovely little fireplace and a window that overlooks a formal garden. If the window could be enlarged it could be the best room in the whole house." Nancy smiled serenely. I wondered if she was imagining me sitting there masterminding some important business deal.

They had all thought the library and it's thousand pound couch seemed about right, and the grandfather clock, with its deep, resonant chimes, added character to the hallway. They also agreed that the living room, huge though it was, was in proportion to the house. The furniture there all needed to be updated and repositioned, probably into smaller groupings to better utilize the beautiful Tiffany lamps, which did not provide sufficient light for the room.

They had approved of the screened in porch beyond the living room, but not the wicker furniture, which was well past its prime. The staircase received rave reviews. "It is perfect," Kathy said. "So wide, and the risers are just the right height. I don't think I have ever loved a staircase as much as I love Cora's."

For some reason her enthusiasm struck me as funny, and when I laughed everyone else joined in.

Apparently all the bedrooms and upstairs bathrooms (there was one adjacent to each bedroom) needed new everything except the bathtubs. Women, I was learning, love bathtubs, and the bigger the better. Conversely, all the closets had to be taken out, lined up against a wall, and shot. They were far too small. Fortunately the bedrooms were all huge, so there was ample room to expand the closets.

A smaller staircase led from the second floor servant's wing up to the third floor; which was unfinished, had a low ceiling, and had always been used for storage. There were a large number of trunks and boxes up there, and Cora had no idea what was in them.

Cora had saved the wine cellar for last. The ladies were surprised at the size of it, and greatly impressed by the number of bottles of wine. There appeared to be more than a thousand, all covered with dust and grime.

"I suggested she have a wine expert come and take an inventory," Kathy said. "I suspect some of the wine might be close to going bad, and it would be a shame to let any of it go to waste. Carl's mom thought a charity wine auction might be interesting."

It was slightly strange to remember that my own mother was part of this entourage of consultants. I imagined her standing in the wine cellar, holding a dusty bottle of red with a contemplative look on her face.

Kathy gestured toward the other side of the kitchen where she'd set a narrow canvas bag. "She gave each of us a bottle as we left," she said. "They were clearly among the most valuable — all shiny and stored in a locked cabinet. She said the lock was to keep Hammy away from the good stuff"

"She sure did," Nancy said nodding. "She also told us our opinions had been very helpful and that we'd be invited back to see the transformation."

The talk of wine prompted Tom to open a bottle from their more modest selection. He handed a glass to Kathy and Nancy topped up both of our waters.

Kathy took a sip and leaned back in her seat, savoring the taste before turning her eyes on me. "Carl, do you know why Cora wanted to be sure that Nancy was with us?"

I glanced at Nancy, realizing we weren't the only ones who had wondered about Cora's pointed comment. Nancy and her father were looking back at me, their expectant expressions almost mirror images of one another.

I decided I might as well be direct and give my best answer. I took a deep breath. "No, I don't know why, but I have formed a guess that I know will stay here in this room." I paused, scanning their faces for reassurance. "Okay. You and my parents are the only people who know that Cora intends to have me eventually take over her business matters, properties, investments, the whole works. It is all very extensive; sort of an empire really, and frankly it scares me half to death.

"One small part of what she owns is Sycamore Hall, and if she wanted Nancy to have a say in how it should be remodeled I think it means that she expects that eventually Nancy and I will be living there."

The room fell silent, but only briefly. Kathy let out a low whistle.

Nancy furrowed her brow as if she was horrified. "Whoa!" She exclaimed. "It would take about twenty kids to fill all those bedrooms. I want to have children at some point but I won't be up for that! We'd have to clean out an orphanage!"

We all laughed and began kicking around the idea of Nancy and me being Lord and Lady of Sycamore Hall, in the process becoming sillier and sillier. Eventually we decided to wait a few years before we worried about it.

There was something much more in the present bothering Nancy and me: privacy. Other than one night when Tom and Kathy went out for dinner and a movie we had not been able to enjoy the benefits of what my mother had tactfully termed 'a complete relationship.' I was starting to think about that house for sale with the key under the mat when my parents solved things for us; they decided to take a week's vacation and go do some shelling on Captiva Island off Florida's west coast.

My mother asked if I thought that I could fend for myself while they were away. I used all my self restraint and merely said that I thought I could manage. While they were shelling Nancy had multiple chances to see her Giant Slalom gold medal as it hung from the neck of Rocky.

Chapter 62

It wasn't long before Alice Birch called, saying that she knew that Nancy wanted to spend two weeks at home, but would she be up for a one day clothes shopping spree in Boston with Alice? When Nancy said yes except that she couldn't come because she didn't have a driver's license and didn't even know how to drive, Alice quickly overcame her shock and said that she would come up and drive the two of them back to Boston. They would clean out a few stores and then drive back. It was going to be a long day, so Nancy insisted that Alice spend the night in their guest room before driving back home the following day.

That spree turned out to be a big success. Nancy later told me that they bought clothes that Alice thought would be appropriate for Nancy's travels and appearances, and also, as expected, the two of them got along great together. They both recognized this was important because North Wind was being flooded with business opportunities for Nancy — it seemed that half the organizations in America wanted to pay Nancy to do something on their behalf — so the two women would be spending a great deal of time together.

Nancy invited me to join them for a late supper back at Nancy's house. As we sat down, Alice revealed that the first of Nancy's corporate appearances was to be a short after-dinner speech where she would address a convention of tool and die manufacturers. "We could work a little on the speech after dessert tonight and a bit more tomorrow morning if you like," Alice had said.

"Thank you, yes, that would be helpful," Nancy said. "But tool and die? What do I have to say to tool and die manufacturers?"

"Ah yes," Alice said, smoothing a napkin over her lap. "You'll find these talks are never about the industry itself, but the ideas behind success within any industry. Hard work, tenacity, overcoming challenges. What made you successful would serve anybody's goals well. And from a practical point of view you will be speaking to them because you are a young, beautiful, world famous Olympic champion. What you say will be less important than how you say it and that it is you who's saying it. Everyone wants to meet you; even tool and die makers."

As we ate, Alice explained that the thinking at Kenmore Square was that Nancy`s speeches should run for about 15 minutes, and that they'd be a summary of her experiences as a skier with emphasis on her ascension from the Mountainside Ski Academy to the Olympic team. She should work in as much of her personal ups and downs as possible, Alice emphasized. Humor would be crucial; Kenmore Square Consultants had found time and time again that business conventions were overwhelmingly technical, serious, often dull, and that the attendees were always starved for laughter and entertainment.

I stopped by the next morning and found that they'd already made tremendous progress. Nancy was used to the spotlight, and after a few practice speeches in front of Alice she felt confident. Her opening line was to be that although her lifetime goal had been to win an Olympic gold medal, her secondary wish had always been to address a room full of tool and die makers. If that didn't get a laugh, then nothing would.

Winter turned to spring; always a sloppy transition in our part of the world, and in June I graduated. Nancy was in constant demand (and was being paid what would have been vastly more money that she had expected if she had started with any specific amounts in mind) to give her entertaining speeches, to model her own line of ski clothing, and, to a much lesser degree, endorse products. She also agreed to a very limited (and highly paid) number of TV talk shows. Before long she cut these out entirely, saying that the formats seemed to be pointless. Furthermore, she also told Alice and me that she did not enjoy the company of the television people. She found them to be shallow and often disagreeable when they were off camera.

Right from the start Nancy had put her foot down and refused to endorse any product that she was not familiar with and liked. Al and his associates had known from the beginning that Nancy was not out to make as much money as possible in the shortest amount of time, but as it turned out her resolve actually made her more valuable. Brands quickly realized that her endorsement carried more credibility, and once the men and women who worked in Chicago for North Wind got used to Nancy's way of doing things she became something of a hero there: the girl who put her principles above profit.

Because Nancy did not want to be on the road constantly she was able to be home in New Kensington about half of the time. While we were together we had a wonderful time. She was starting to think about her idea of running a ski school at some future time. Also, she had beefed up the exercise equipment in the garage and it had become a mini gymnasium. Nancy had no intention of ever returning to the world of competitive skiing, but she was equally determined to stay in peak condition. I became her training partner and with time I found that I enjoyed the routine. That said, I never mastered the vertical situps. Simple crunches were sufficient for me.

True to his word, Al Malone had rewarded me with a finder's fee for guiding Nancy under the wing of Kenmore Square, and the size of the fee was so disproportionate to my time or effort that it was embarrassing. Nancy was becoming much more at ease with her cornucopia-like cash flow. "Don't let it bother you," she reassured me. "Look at me. I just give short talks at meetings and smile for cameras, and before long I'll have more money than Scrooge McDuck!"

In spite of her rapidly increasing net worth Nancy turned out to be naturally frugal. She had plenty of nice clothes, but that was mostly for business reasons; there were no fur coats or fancy jewelry. I had taught her how to drive, (a nerve rattling experience) and she had bought herself a new car once she obtained a driver's license; a modest Subaru wagon. She liked the 4-wheel drive and the fact that she could throw her skis in the back. She still loved to ski.

The day after my high school graduation, I become a full-time employee of Grant Holdings and began collecting a salary. My assignment for the summer was to continue my learning experiences in real estate. Cora was still working to bring more technology companies into New Kensington and her efforts were paying off. Two new companies had come on board, bringing the total to three. Our first twenty-unit apartment building was fully occupied, and we were building two more apartment buildings in the same area. Each of them would have more units than the first, and we already had a sizable list of potential renters. We were in discussions to donate several adjacent acres to the town for use as a recreation area which would make the apartments even more desirable. We were also in negotiations with two custom home builders who were interested in building some higher end homes on some land we owned slightly further outside the town. Cora was transforming the nature of New Kensington.

To me this seemed to be the perfect time to activate the engagement ring. Nancy`s life was turning out exactly as she had hoped it would and I was on a career path that I felt made complete sense. Things could not have been more stable, it was time to propose. The only thing missing was a plan. I needed a how and when.

I have never been a quick thinker. Usually I take my time working things out in my head, but there are always exceptions; my idea as to how and when to pop the question came to me in a sudden flash.

Nancy was telling me about her next corporate appearance. With Alice, as always, she would be going to Detroit to speak at a luncheon meeting of automobile dealers. After the talk, she intended to do what she often did — stick around and chat with anyone who wanted to rub elbows with her. This wasn't part of her commitment, but she enjoyed the interaction and knew it left the corporation that was footing the bill feeling that they got more than they paid for. Along the same line, if she was giving an after dinner talk, she often showed up at corporate breakfasts the next morning. She'd look for an empty chair (she never had to look for long) and do some unscheduled mingling.

Following that meeting, Nancy explained, she was going to visit the cancer ward at a nearby children's hospital to see some youngsters who were in tough shape.

That is when the idea flashed in my head. I knew immediately that I needed Alice's help and gave her a call later that afternoon.

When she heard what I had in mind she was happy to become my co-conspirator.

According to our plan, Alice was to go to the hospital with Nancy, and then make an excuse as to why she needed to return to their hotel. Alice would then hustle back to the hotel and move Nancy`s belongings from their room into a honeymoon suite that I had already reserved and occupied.

Before I arrived, Alice was to tell the head nurse at the children's cancer ward what I was up to. That I was going to arrive there ahead of time, and for her to set up a curtained off bed for me to hide in. Once Nancy showed up, the nurses would show her around and eventually lead her to where my bed would be hidden behind drapes.

All went according to plan and I found myself sitting on a hospital bed blocked off by a beige curtain. The large room held two rows of patients and had the gentle buzz of children in and around their own beds. They knew I was hiding and that the famous Nancy Hathaway was coming soon for a visit. I could hear them shushing each other and giggling, eager for whatever was about to unfold.

Finally a hush fell over the room and I heard the distinctive sound of grownups conversing as they made their way in through the door. Those poor sick children were thrilled to be in on the surprise we had in store for Nancy, and I could hear their high pitched chatter and giggles grow as Nancy went from one child to the next, taking her time as she spoke with them. I began to hope the nurses would bring her more promptly to me, before any of the children let out the secret. Thankfully, before long one of the nurses said loudly, "Now why don't we move down to this end of the room."

That was my cue. I took a breath and settled under the covers, steadying myself against a pounding heart. "And now," the nurse said, her hand appearing around the edge of the curtain, "we want to introduce you to a particularly difficult case."

With that, she flung open the drape. I sat up and said, "Hi."

Nancy screamed, "AARGH; Carl! What in the world?"

The cancer children shrieked with excitement. I got down on one knee and held the opened ring box up to her. "You once told me that no one ever loved anyone as much as you love me," I said. "Now

I`m saying it to you. No one ever loved anyone as much as I love you. Will you marry me?"

Tears streamed down Nancy`s face and she put one hand over her mouth. At first she could only nod, but then she pulled me up. "At last!" she blurt out. "Yes!" Then we were in each other's arms.

The children pranced around us as best they could and the nurses were hugging whoever was closest to them. Everyone wanted a good look at the ring on Nancy's finger, which looked as if it belonged there. Nancy made sure to introduce me to each child before we left. The hospital called a taxi for us and a few minutes later we were getting comfortable in our suite.

We had room service bring dinner to our room that night.

Chapter 63

Meanwhile life in New Kensington moved along. The newspaper opinion poll had shown that over 90% of our population, students included, wanted Chief Hale to remain as our Chief of Police. He requested a one month leave of absence to think about it and headed off to the Florida Keys, but was back in a week to stay.

Things were the opposite for the school board. A new board was elected and Mrs. Anderson was never seen again.

As for Vincent DiNardo, justice was served. Our state is the only state in New England that allows the death penalty and it is an option that our citizens cherish, probably because we never use it. The last time we executed a prisoner was in 1939.

DiNardo avoided a jury trial and the possibility of a lifetime behind bars by pleading guilty to murder in the second degree and was sentenced to 20 years in prison. He actually only served three months of that sentence. A fellow inmate who was serving two consecutive life sentences for murder, acting on his hatred of law enforcement people, plunged a screwdriver into DiNardo`s temple, ending his life.

Shortly after we became engaged, the story broke that before the games a member of the Italian Olympic team, Luigi Vespa, had attempted to rape Nancy and that in the struggle she had bitten off the tip of his nose. Apparently someone had sold the story to a tabloid newspaper.

Nancy had been warned that too many people knew about the incident and that the story was likely to leak out eventually. The press, of course, wanted Nancy to comment, and she would only reply that she had nothing to say.

That might have been the end of it given enough time, but then Mr. Luigi Vespa had the bad judgement to say in front of cameras that it was Nancy who had leaked the story and was lying out of spite. She had been coming on to him for weeks prior to the Olympics despite his insistence that he would always be true to his wife. His nose had been caught in the hinge of a door purely by accident, and that was why he had been forced to miss the Olympic games.

That threw the ball back into Nancy's court and she was ready. We gave Al down in Boston a call, and the next day Nancy and I drove down to Al's office, where he had been delighted to arrange a press conference at which Nancy spoke briefly.

"As you know it has been recently reported that a member of the Italian Ski team, Luigi Vespa, attempted to rape me early this past winter and that I was able to escape him by biting off the tip of his nose. So far I have declined to comment on this.

"But now I have learned that Mr. Vespa is claiming that he never touched me, that I had been coming on to him, that I have made up this story, and that the tip of his nose was somehow pinched off in a door hinge." here Nancy paused, an eyebrow raised cynically, giving the media representatives who were in the room time to consider how wildly improbable this explanation was.

"I was going to let this sordid matter pass without commenting until he decided to insult me with his lies. So now I have this question for Mr. Luigi Vespa: if the tip of your nose was cut off by a door hinge, then how does that tip of your nose happen to be in safe deposit box number 336, which is in my name, at the Alphorn Banque Privee in San Moritz, Switzerland?"

With this Nancy pulled out a safe deposit box key and placed it on a table that was in front of her, saying that she didn't feel like going all the way back there to fish out the nose tip in question, but that she would authorize any responsible party to open the safe deposit box, adding that the piece of nose should still be in fairly good shape, as she had put it in a small jar of formaldehyde.

Nancy's insurance policy, the tip of Vespa's nose, was a perfect squelch.

Naturally the room erupted in shouts and laughter, with no one laughing harder than Al, Chet, Rocky, and Alice, who had not known what Nancy was going to say. Nancy did her best to keep a straight face; I didn't even try to.

Nancy waited for the room to settle down and then added: "I don't blame you for laughing. In a way it is funny. But I can promise you that fighting off a rapist is nothing to laugh at."

Nancy answered questions, signed some autographs, posed for photographs, accepted congratulations, and we were back in New Kensington before dark.

Chapter 64

Ever since Jack's death there had been something on my mind; something that I felt I needed to do. The sort of thing that you feel you should do but don't particularly want to do. Remembering the first time that Jack lured me into the woods behind his house and led me back to the small waterfall and pool, I recalled Jack telling me that someday he would re-blaze the old trail. That someday never came for Jack and I felt an obligation to pinch hit for my best friend and clean up the overgrown blaze marks.

So one clear summer morning when Nancy was in Seattle to speak to a group of Microsoft executives I decided to stop procrastinating and do it. I went to the hardware store, told Tom what I had in mind, and asked for his permission.

Tom gave me a thoughtful look, paused for a second or two, and then simply said said "Yes, you should do that for Jack. Kathy is home, I'll call her and tell her to get out a backpack and a hatchet."

Shortly later I was on the Hathaway's back porch with Kathy adjusting the straps of a backpack for me. Besides a hatchet I had a canteen, two candy bars, a compass,a map, and a whistle. The canteen and hatchet were attached to a webbed utility belt. I figured that once I found the first blaze mark it would all be downhill. Still I was edgy. Plenty of things could go wrong in the forest and my nerves must have been showing because Kathy asked me if I was going to get lost.

"Probably not but I'm capable of it. If I'm not back by dusk send out some Bloodhounds. Will you do that?" Kathy gave my cheek a kiss and I was off; over the old stone wall and into the woods.

Finding the first blaze mark was easier than I had feared and in less than 2 minutes I had freshened up the first tree; both sides.

Taking care not to somehow chop myself with the hatchet I worked my way to the waterfall and pool. I Felt relieved that I had made it successfully and had filled in for Jack. I took off the backpack and utility belt, sat down with my back against one of the rocks, and opened up a candy bar. It didn't feel right to be there without Jack, and I became pensive. My mind seemed to want to reflect on everything that had gone on in my life over the past half year or so.

All in all, going back to the time when I received the mystery letter from Nancy asking me to please pick her up at the Boston airport because she had something important to discuss with me, it seemed that my life gone into overdrive. Nancy had told me that she had fought off a rapist. She had also opened up her heart to me and told me that she loved me. It didn't take long after our first kiss for me to realize that I loved her too, but had hidden my feelings from myself.

Then the awful tragedy of Jack`s murder and the grief and sorrow that it brought. Nancy and I had become intimate, and I had become less a boy and more a man.

My wonderful Nancy had won two gold medals at the Winter Olympics and following her plan had promptly retired from competitive skiing at age 17.Then, with much help from the people at Kenmore Square Consultants, she had become a highly successful motivational speaker and celebrity. And recently, armed with a beautiful diamond ring compliments of Cora, I had asked Nancy to marry me and she had accepted; details to be worked out in the future.

I decided that I should start back towards civilization; blaze marks are much easier to follow during daylight, when they are visible. As I slowly worked my way back toward the Hathaway's house (successfully, as it turned out) I switched my thoughts from the past to the future.

There was just one thing bothering me. One thing that simply did not feel that it would be right for me: college.

Oh I knew that I needed to go to college and I knew that Williams would be a fine place to continue my education. But would I fit in? It wasn't the school, it was the students! Or more specifically the campus lifestyle.

Like Dartmouth and many other colleges and universities that had historically been all male institutions, Williams had become coed, and shortly after taking that action began to phase out its long standing fraternity system. Still, during my two visits to the school, the students had seemed to be much less mature than I felt at that point. Not all of them, naturally, but the scholars were not very visible.

Or to put it another way, many of them were acting like college kids; they liked to party. That had never been me. As a student at New Kensington high school I had avoided the things I wasn't comfortable doing by simply going home. At Williams I would not be able to do that, Williams would BE my home. Unless– Hmmm.

Soon afterwards, one pretty day I asked Nancy if she would take a ride to see Williams with me. I wanted her to see the campus for the first time and, more importantly, I wanted to talk something over with her while we were in the car. The people at Kenmore Square shielded Nancy from almost all the offers that were directed her way, but still, her phone rang frequently. If we were off on a car ride there wouldn't be any interruptions or distractions. We packed a picnic lunch. Nancy would not go near fast food outlets and was making headway in weaning me from most of my worst eating habits.

Once we were underway I presented my 'Life at Williams' plan.

"I need to have a college education and Williams will be a fine place to get it," I said, "but I'm likely to be something of a misfit there. The students are smart and they seem to be good kids, but they want to squeeze in as much fun as they can. They drink, they party, they sing, they yell, they dance. The boys chase the girls and the girls chase the boys.

"I have never been that way, and you certainly know it. I've tried to think of activities I might like to be part of while I am there and all I can think of is maybe acting in a play but that's it. I did have a good time doing "Damn Yankees."

"I want you to be there with me as much as possible, and I expect to come home on weekends often. During the week I can study. Maybe by taking extra courses I could graduate ahead of schedule and get on to graduate school if that is still what I want to do a few years from now."

Nancy looked concerned. "I don't want you to be miserable there. What's the plan; I know you must have one."

"It just so happens that I do have a plan, subject to your approval. Next to Cora you are the best planner I know."

Nancy laughed. "I won't deny that no one appreciates a good plan more than I do. What have you cooked up?"

"For a start I will want to get to know my classmates, and if I can make a few friends when we are starting out that would be good. I`m going to be in a dorm with lots of other freshmen and none of us will know each other. The first few weeks will be chaotic, but so what, it will be a good experience; I hope so anyway.

"But here is where my plan kicks in. I still have that money from the finder's fee sitting around waiting for me to put it to some use. I'd like to buy some land near the school and have a house built for me to live in while I am there at Williams."

"What a sweet idea! Once you get a place of your own you can get away from the dorm and all the screaming and yelling. You will be a Williamstown squire!" She squeezed my leg in excitement. "I want a key to the place, I plan on being there a lot."

We grinned at each other.

"Wait a minute," Nancy said, "why don't you just buy a house and save yourself the bother of building?"

"I thought about that. It would be much simpler. But Williamstown is a small place. There are never too many nice homes for sale and most of them are old places and not modern. There are a few new homes available, but they have been built by builders who want to sell them, make a profit, and move on. That sort of house won't have the quality that I will want.

"Plus," I said, "Cora wants me to learn real estate. Having a house built the way I want it will be an education in itself. I have plenty of cash to buy some land and get a construction loan, and the salary that I am getting every month from Grant Holdings will more than take care of a mortgage and other expenses. When I graduate I can sell the place; or rather we can. We'll probably be married long before I graduate. That's something we still need to figure out. Regardless of when that happens the house will be ours, not mine, and I want you to help with the design. Sound good?"

"Not good, wonderful! A place of our own. I'm giddy!"

I had decided that I wanted our house to have a nice view; maybe an open hillside or possibly near a river. Certainly there were plenty of hills in that corner of Massachusetts. After driving around the campus and its surroundings for a while, on an impulse we walked into a real estate office and met the only person there, a middle aged woman broker. Once she recovered from the shock of having the one and only Nancy Hathaway walk through her door she listened to what we were interested in, and said "I have something in mind that you might like. Do you have time for a short ride?"

Ten minutes later we were looking at an ideal location, a seven-acre parcel on a secondary road. The lot started out level and then ran down a hill to a small river. The opposite side of the river was a thickly wooded hillside. One of the local professors had owned it for the past twelve years, always thinking that someday he would build a house for himself there. Recently he had accepted the fact that he was more interested in retiring and moving to a warmer climate than he was in building and had put it on the market. Nancy and I both loved it. We were looking at the site of what would be my new home before I finished my freshman year. Or, I should say, *our* new home.

Naturally Cora needed to be told what I had planned but I waited until I had a signed purchase contract. Then, the next time she started a discussion of real estate with me I was ready, and interrupted her by saying "Speaking of real estate–"

Acknowledgements

Because this book is entirely fiction I had very little fact checking to do for the simple reason that there are not many facts in this story. However that is not to say that I did not have help; I had plenty.

First, I had constant guidance from my wonderful editor Shari Shallard. Without Shari's knowledge, experience, tolerance, and just plain kindness this book would be much less than it is.

I also had ongoing encouragement from my friend Nancy Hoffmann. Nancy is an experienced writer and there were many times during the year I worked on this story when Nancy's suggestions and encouragement made a difference.

And finally, my wife Cheryl. If she was astonished to learn that I intended to write a book she did a fine job of hiding it, and if she noticed that I spent close to a full year in a state of near constant distraction she never mentioned it. I am almost certain to be a better listener from now on.

Made in the USA
Columbia, SC
24 March 2019

Table of Contents

PART TWO

PART THREE

Preface

We are psychologists who have each spent more than twenty-five years doing pre-marital, marital, and post-marital counseling at the University of Hawaii and in private practice. Although most of the case histories and examples in this book refer to married heterosexual couples, we also counseled unmarried couples and couples in gay, lesbian, committed, and uncommitted relationships. During that time, we saw literally thousands of couples experiencing difficulty or conflict in some aspect of their relationships.

Almost without exception, we used an instrument called the Myers-Briggs Type Indicator® (MBTI®) instrument in our work. And almost without exception, we found this instrument useful. We trained our staff and interns at the University of Hawaii counseling center in the use of the MBTI assessment with faculty and community groups. It has been the most widely used of the psychological measures given at the University of Hawaii campus.

In the late '70s, Ruth used the MBTI personality assessment in an extensive research project using 167 couples to identify the effect of type on satisfaction in marriage. For this piece of research she received the first Isabel Briggs Myers Memorial Research Award.

Jane was one of the earliest users of the MBTI assessment, beginning in 1965 when she was a doctoral student at Auburn University. W. Harold Grant, director of Auburn's counseling center, gave the MBTI assessment to students in his tests and measurements class. Jane studied the first MBTI manual (1962), was impressed with the instrument, and upon graduation brought the MBTI instrument to Hawaii where she introduced it to Ruth. Together, they began to use more answer sheets than anyone else in the country. Isabel Myers asked to meet Ruth and Jane at an American Psychological Association convention as they were so clearly delighted with her work. Thus began a long and wonderful affiliation with one of the MBTI instrument's creators. Isabel Myers was indeed a very special person and truly dedicated to her work.

The MBTI instrument is based on the theory developed by Carl Gustav Jung and explained in his book *Psychological Types*. Many of you are probably familiar with Jung and some of his theories.

It is advantageous, but not necessary, to understand Jung's theories in order to understand the MBTI instrument and this book.

Katharine Cook Briggs and her daughter, Isabel Briggs Myers, devoted much of their lives to the study of Jung's theories and the development of their instrument. Myers' son Peter and her former daughter-in-law Kathy Myers are still deeply involved in the work and carrying on the legacy that Katharine Briggs and Isabel Myers began. Many others, especially Mary McCaulley of the Center for Applications of Psychological Type (CAPT) in Gainesville, Florida, have spent years helping others apply and research theories related to type for the constructive use of differences.

The couples with whom Ruth and Jane worked over the years have indicated that they knew themselves better, understood their partners more fully, and were able to recognize why their conflicts were occurring as a result of understanding their MBTI results. Understanding is only the first step in resolving such conflicts, of course, but it does provide the necessary base for moving ahead to deal effectively with differences and misunderstandings. To extend such foundational awareness to a broad audience, Ruth and Jane collaborated on *Intimacy and Type* (1997), a practical guide for couples seeking to improve and enrich their relationships.

The current revision has been shaped mainly with counselors in mind. Marriage counselors can recommend *Intimacy and Type* to couples or use it as a conceptual framework in their own counseling. The observations and suggestions we make here come from our many years of couples' counseling, supplemented by research on the Myers-Briggs Type Indicator and relationship-satisfaction data from couples in relationships for two years or more. The descriptions of the characteristics of types in relationships offered in this text are based on relatively psychologically healthy individuals whose lives are not clouded by serious mental health issues. Our thanks go to the many people, especially our clients and patients, who contributed so much to our knowledge. Leslie Kathleen Jones, Jane's daughter, contributed valuable insights. The counseling sessions described in this book have been modified and the names of individuals changed to protect their privacy. Nonetheless, the basic dynamics are faithfully represented.

NOTE: Though it is not grammatically popular in modern times, we have chosen to use "they" and "their" in this book even when the antecedent is singular. We have done this to avoid using both "she" and "he" or alternating "he" and "she." We hope this choice will be less distracting for the reader.

Part One

1

Preference in Life and Love

"In spite of all indignant protests to the contrary, the fact remains that love, its problems and its conflicts, is of fundamental importance in human life and, as careful inquiry consistently shows, is of far greater significance than the individual suspects."

C. G. Jung, *Two Essays on Analytical Psychology*

A Preference for Difference

Everyone's different. It is a gift to be unique. Yet there are personal styles that can be characterized in general to aid our understanding of relationships. With enough perspective our clients may even be able to laugh at things about themselves and others that once made them upset or angry. Carl Jung, Katharine Briggs, and Isabel Myers have given us a way to get perspective on ourselves and to offer the same to our clients. They have described natural differences between people in the ways they orient themselves to the world, the ways they prefer to take in information, and how they arrive at decisions. Understanding these natural preferences increases our choices and provides us maximum freedom.

A simple way to understand what we mean when we say "preference" is to think in terms of your two hands. If you're right-handed, the right is your preferred hand. This doesn't mean you don't use your left hand—everyone does every day. You could try this exercise: On a blank piece of paper write your name using your preferred hand. Then write your name using your other hand. Unless you're very different from most of us, the first time you write your name (using your preferred hand) you will be more comfortable than the second (using your other hand), and the product will also be better. Keep this example in mind as we discuss "preferences," because while one style is what each of us will use most often and be most comfortable with, there are often examples of opposite or different types of behavior from the same individual.

We want you to have fun and enjoy the concepts presented in this book. But we also ask you to look deeper, beyond the fun, and hear a message that could change your and your clients' lives. We do not want to minimize anyone's uniqueness by classifying or pigeonholing individuals with general descriptions. On the contrary, we honor our own individuality and yours. We would like you to have a model for enabling the couples you work with to better understand themselves and each other.

Understanding another person's style does not mean putting up with destructive or unacceptable behavior. It means that each partner is clear about what the other is like and what each can reasonably expect in a relationship. It does not mean your clients have permission to act toward each other in the worst ways their mothers or fathers acted or to re-create conflicts from the past. Carl Jung asks that we each become more conscious and through this consciousness become aware of having more choices. In having more choices comes more freedom.

The bottom line is that it's always possible for people to leave relationships; but your clients can also choose to stay and confront some of the very qualities that attracted them to their partners in the first place, qualities that may have acquired a negative side. Clients also get the opportunity to confront their own negative behavior, behavior an intimate relationship inevitably triggers.

Many people don't mind working at their jobs but don't think they should have to work at a relationship. We believe a good relationship with another human being is the most essential ingredient for a satisfying life. This means it is well worth your clients' time and effort to see their relationships realistically and to make choices and take actions that enhance those relationships. This usually demands that each partner grow as a person in the process. Sometimes the outside perspective offered by a counselor helps both partners see the forces between them and allows them to move toward a more rewarding relationship.

Counselor Edition

This edition of *Intimacy and Type* is intended primarily for counselors—professionals such as psychologists, pastors, or social workers involved with couples in a therapeutic capacity. When we first started counseling couples, many of our colleagues warned us not to see both people in a relationship as we would inevitably side with one person (consciously or unconsciously), which would not be fair. We have found this not to be true, and today many counselors now know the value of seeing both people together, as outlined in the following list.

- The counselor is not as easily misquoted and statements are less likely to be used out of context.
- The counselor discovers what each partner is willing to say in front of the other.
- The counselor has an opportunity to rephrase misunderstood or hurtful comments in a more constructive way so the partner can hear the intended message.
- The counselor can establish ground rules to prevent name-calling, cursing, or other negative behaviors from carrying over from the session into a couple's outside life. One of Isabel Myers' most important qualities for a good relationship is mutual respect, which hopefully can be fostered in this context.
- The counselor can use the MBTI® instrument to provide a meaningful explanation of differences in behavior and attitude to each person in the relationship even if the type results are not actually used.
- The counselor can emphasize that changing behavior or attitude is just as difficult for one preference type as another. Behavior or attitude changes that may be easy for one type may not be for another. Each type needs to be asked to do something equally difficult. The burden of change should not be solely on one partner.

Naturally, counselors can still give couples the option of individual sessions as necessary. In such cases, extreme care must be taken not to violate the confidentiality of either partner's session by any means, verbal or nonverbal. For example, if you are asked by one of the partners if the other is having an affair you should assume a poker face and remind the client about confidentiality.

MBTI assessment results can provide you with a unique opportunity to describe and communicate clearly about the real "gifts differing," which can enhance the relationship, but also cause interpersonal conflicts. Some couples have been amazed at how we could describe them so well when we had met only once. Sometimes the very behavior that attracted one person to another can become annoying over time. An appreciation of the different "gifts" is called for, and humor always helps give perspective. Hopefully, you can help clients reach their goals. A good opening question "If you got what you wanted out of this session, what would that be?" Both individuals need to answer for themselves and not talk for or interrupt each other. Sometimes the counselor is like a referee. Good luck managing the dynamics—they can be challenging.

NEEDED: A MODEL FOR EQUALITY WITHOUT SAMENESS

A relationship with an equal partner can be a major challenge. Good models for such partnerships aren't readily available. Business partnerships don't always work well. In families, gender role assumptions may still inform our expectations about how our partner "should" behave, despite claims that patriarchy is dead. Men who want and value an equal partner may still have negative reactions if a female partner doesn't fulfill unexamined stereotypes he may have. He may expect gentle compassionate caregiving from his partner without anger or resentment. On the other side women may have negative reactions if a male partner doesn't fulfill unconscious gender role assumptions she may have and he isn't the main provider of economic necessities, willing and able to do so without complaining. As we shall see in this book, such assumptions about our partner's behavior extend beyond gender and into the domain of personality type as well. In contemporary relationships, more clarity may be needed about expectations of self and others before entering a partnership. We need to meet this challenge and create a model or models flexible enough to fit any couple, yet structured enough so that every decision doesn't have to be debated and discussed at length.

The family, school, and work arenas seldom provide such models. As we grow up, Mom and Dad are older and therefore "in charge." They may have fallen into their role differences but may never actually have addressed the issue. As for siblings, if older, they may be above us, and if younger, below us in the family hierarchy. At work, your boss is authorized to have some power over you. And teachers, whatever their level from kindergarten to university, are elevated above us by virtue of what we agree to be their greater knowledge.

Friendship is really the only arena in which we can find and enjoy equality. Friendship is, however, different from an intimate sexual relationship. The intensity that develops in an intimate relationship is not usually present at the same level in a friendship. It is easier to say no to a friend than to a partner. It is easier to walk away and come back later or never come back at all. There is more freedom and there is more choice. Our neuroses and father and mother complexes aren't as activated in a friendship. But, friendships are a good place to start looking for models of equality.

What if we said never treat a partner worse than a best friend? Is that a criterion to be included in our model? What other parameters might be discussed and adopted or rejected? How are decisions made if someone doesn't have veto power? We will not pretend to answer these questions. At this point, each couple needs to struggle with their own answers. In the process, new concepts will hopefully evolve to clarify intimate relationships.

Relating as equals takes some consciousness. Two independent people may find the compromises or negotiations required are too high a price to pay. Two dependent people may have difficulty leaving each other even if they want to. One independent and one dependent person need to be clear about what each is contributing to the relationship. If one partner is dependent emotionally and one financially, is that okay?

"IT ISN'T EASY FOR PEOPLE IN RELATIONSHIPS TO ALLOW THEMSELVES AND OTHERS—ESPECIALLY A PARTNER, OR LOVER—TO BE DIFFERENT."

It isn't easy for people in relationship to allow themselves and others—especially a partner, or lover—to be different. Seeing the similarities or differences positively enhances a relationship. We will help you find ways to use differences and similarities constructively to counsel couples toward better marriages or relationships. It is your challenge to help them appreciate differences and be glad there is so much human variety from which to choose a partner.

Before we go into detailed descriptions of relationships and the Myers-Briggs Type Indicator® (MBTI®) instrument, here are two examples of how we use MBTI results in our couples' counseling. These examples may help you understand why we find the MBTI personality inventory so valuable. Because most people in relationships struggle with their differences, we use examples in which difference has been a problem.

A Tale of Two Couples

Thinking Man/Feeling Woman David and Betty R. were in their sixties when we started working with them. They had been married over forty years and had three grown children. They are Caucasian, Catholic, and had grown up on the East Coast. The R.'s were referred to us by a church counselor who felt she had not been effective in working with them.

As reported by the church counselor, Betty would spend almost the entire session crying. David would spend the session being defensive. There had never been any major problems between them such as drugs, alcohol, infidelity, or gambling. They both considered themselves moral, ethical people. Betty had reached a point where she was considering either divorce or suicide as an alternative to continuing in a situation where she was so desperately unhappy.

We discovered that the primary difference between the partners in this couple was that David made decisions with his head (Thinking); he believed that if there were a "logical" reason for doing something, that was the thing to do. Betty, on the other hand, listened to her heart (Feeling), and people's feelings were of primary importance to her in reaching a decision.

Strange as it may appear, they had never been aware of that difference between them. Slowly, with much coaching, David was able to stop defending his position as past issues arose in our sessions. Also with much coaching, Betty learned how to present her experiences in the marriage without blaming or attacking.

All of her life, Betty had tried to be a "good" daughter, wife, and mother. This had meant doing what was expected of her without expressing her own needs. Finally, her resentments had grown so great that she was no longer able to control her emotions. David came to therapy hoping Betty could be "fixed."

It took about three months before Betty and David could listen to each other and learn to laugh at themselves and each other. At that point, they were communicating more effectively and really enjoying being with each other. He needed her warmth and feeling responsiveness when she could use them positively. She needed his logical thinking when he wasn't using it to criticize her. They both reported that the MBTI "test" had contributed to their understanding and acceptance of one another's differences.

Extraverted Woman/Introverted Man Sally and Frank O. also reported the MBTI assessment helpful in improving their relationship. Sally, an outgoing Caucasian with strong feelings, had met Frank, a quiet, sensitive Japanese man, in graduate school on the East Coast. Despite parental objections, they married and mutually agreed to move to Hawaii where mixed ethnic marriages are more common and more accepted. They had two children, ages 4 and 6, who were healthy and active.

Overall, both Sally and Frank considered their marriage satisfactory but wanted help understanding the differences in their needs and skills to resolve their conflicts.

Frank worked in human resource development for a large corporation; he had constant and intense interactions with the individuals he supervised. Sally had decided to put her career on the shelf and to devote her time and energy to her family. She was slowly growing resentful, because she had become dependent on Frank for adult interaction. The greater her need became, the more it appeared to her that he withdrew and withheld. Frank, on the other hand, stated that he was a faithful, hard-working husband and Sally was becoming unreasonable in her demands.

In therapy, we used the MBTI instrument to look at the differences between Extraverts (Sally) and Introverts (Frank). Sally learned it was unrealistic to expect Frank to make up for her lack of interaction with others. Frank learned that it was all right for Sally to need more communication with him than he did with her. They each assumed responsibility for improving the situation. Sally joined the League of Women Voters where she found several rewarding friendships. She also felt she was back in her adult world.

Frank discovered that working in his garden replenished and renewed his energy. As soon as he came home, he changed his clothes and gave himself an hour in the yard by himself. Then he felt like going in and sharing his day with Sally.

Both Sally and Frank became less blaming and more understanding of each other's needs. It is very useful to know that some of what we may find annoying in a partner's behavior is usually an expression of his or her natural style and not a deliberate choice to be difficult. We always ask both people to work on the behaviors that are getting in the way of a balanced and healthy relationship. It is rarely one person who needs to change and become more conscious. When no one is to blame, we can move farther faster in resolving the issues.

The Preferences

The MBTI instrument describes people's tendencies in terms of four dichotomies, each composed of a pair of opposite preferences: Extraversion–Introversion, Sensing–Intuition, Thinking–Feeling, and Judging–Perceiving. For each of the dichotomies, we describe typical behaviors and attitudes developed by people tending toward each of the associated preferences. You will probably be able to identify most of your clients' and your own preferences. Remember, the goal is to value the differences and use them positively. If you are right-handed, it will be like identifying the way you use your right hand best. Your left hand represents the four words or letters not chosen and indicates what your less conscious processes have to offer when you are able to tap into them. The best way to know your type and that of your clients is to take the Myers-Briggs Type Indicator assessment. It is available from a wide range of psychologists, counselors, and other consultants. To learn how to take the MBTI instrument and receive personal feedback, go to the CAPT website: www.capt.org. You may also take the MBTI Complete online at www.mbticomplete.com. In the meantime if you are not familiar with the MBTI instrument, you can use your best estimate based on our descriptions, or refer to two publications specifically designed to help newcomers to get oriented to type published by the Center for Applications of Psychological Type—*Looking at Type®: The Fundamentals* by Charles Martin and *Descriptions of the Sixteen Types*, an eight-page booklet by Gordon Lawrence, which is reproduced in appendix A.

If you are qualified and comfortable using the instrument, you can skip this section or use it as a refresher for type behaviors that may affect your couples. See table 1.1 (page 16) for some of the positive and negative aspects of each preference.

Extraversion and Introversion: Directions of Energy

Some people rush out to meet life; others peek at it from around the corner before deciding whether to come out and be seen. These are broad generalizations, and they apply more to some people than others. In children (before they develop their masks of social behavior), these behaviors can be quite pronounced. One child may rush up while you're eating your ice cream cone and demand, "I want a bite," while another may look at you, shyly smile, and hope that you'll offer some.

In America we tend to value outgoing people: we seem to think it's healthier to ask for what you want. We try to train the quiet boy to behave the same way as the outgoing one, while still saying we value individuality. Carl Jung, on the other hand, saw both ways as valuable. He called outgoing energy "extraversion" and ingoing energy "introversion." The MBTI instrument uses E for Extraversion and I for Introversion; the following diagram shows the direction of energy flow associated with each.

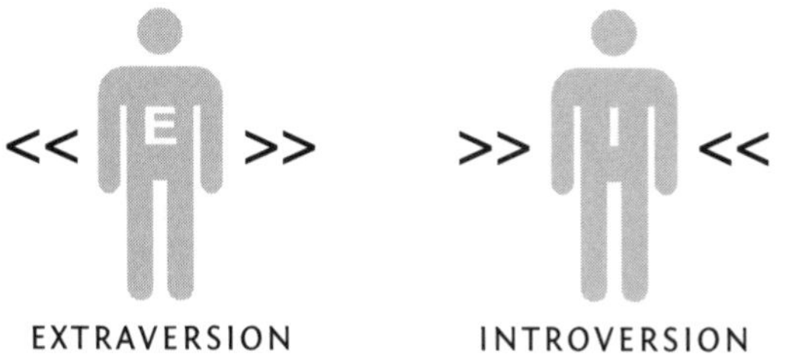

Now, let's get more specific. Extraverts have a different style of interacting than Introverts, as we shall see.

Types Who Extravert (E) Extraverts typically are outgoing and want contact—physical contact, mental contact, emotional contact. They don't want to be out there by themselves if they can help it, and they are energized by talking, working, and playing with a wide variety of people. Extraverts can get bored easily if there's not plenty going on. They are stimulated by a lot of talking and activity. They notice people's body language, but prefer to be told rather than assume they know what it means. While Extraverts can get very angry, once the anger is out they usually get over it quickly. They are typically at ease in their surroundings and like variety, excitement, and stimulation from the outside. They talk easily and like feedback. Talking it out or getting other people's opinions helps Extraverts decide what they think or feel about a situation. Sometimes Extraverts make statements just to see what their effect will be on others. They interact freely with their immediate environment, so any feelings or thoughts they pick up, positive or negative, are likely to be included in their conversations with other people. Since their behavior is highly interactive, Extraverts tend to take in what they need and then move on. They would say, for example, that they don't hold a grudge. At parties, such types are usually good mixers. They can be a big help in breaking long or uncomfortable silences. They tend to look for explanations of problems in the people and events around them.

At their worst, Extraverted types talk continuously, have a difficult time listening or reflecting on feedback, interrupt others, and insist on "having it out," even to the point of following a person who may be trying to get away. At their best, Extraverts are fun and energizing companions, aware of what's going on in the world and able to be a part of it.

Types Who Introvert (I) Introverts typically are quiet and reflective. They take time to answer and make up their minds. They are slow to anger, but sometimes slow in getting over anger. Introverts prefer deep, meaningful conversation with people they consider very special, either in small, select groups or one at a time. Privacy is important to Introverted types: they regenerate their energy when they are alone and usually dislike noisy environments. When they have to make a lot of new contacts in a single day, they are tired and need quiet to regenerate.

On the other hand, when propelled by some deeper meaning, they are tireless. Introverts are cautious in their surroundings and may appear to others to be shy, reserved, or inscrutable. They are generally wary of new contacts and don't like to go to parties where they don't know anyone. If they do find someone they know or enjoy, they tend to get into long intense conversations rather than mingle with the whole group. Apparent stubbornness is often an Introvert's way of resisting external coercion, as they don't want to have to "fight for their rights." In spite of their reserve, they will stand firm if something precious is threatened, often to the surprise of others. They also tend to look for explanations of problems in their own actions and feelings.

At their worst, Introverts withdraw into their private worlds, refusing to come out, maybe for hours or even days and sometimes refusing to say what is bothering them. At their best they are attentive listeners who provide others a different perspective on the outside world and safe harbor from its difficulties.

Sensing and Intuition: Information Source

Some people prefer to experience reality, while others prefer to imagine the possibilities. We all do some of both, even if we have a preference for one over the other. We are each a little more comfortable and confident with our preferred orientation. People who prefer to deal with the so-called "real world" or the practical world, we call Sensing types; people who prefer to deal with the world they can imagine we call Intuitive types. While Jung used "sensation type" rather than Sensing type, he chose his terms in order to differentiate the "sensible ones" from the "imaginative ones." Each preference indicates a way that people take in information—either primarily through their five senses or through intuitive hunches. The Sensing-Intuition and Thinking-Feeling dichotomies are often referred to as the MBTI functions. Both Sensing and Intuition are called irrational functions because they involve how individuals perceive and process information rather than how they evaluate it. Here, the term "irrational" is used as a descriptor rather than as a pejorative.

Sensing Types (S) Along with a preference for Sensing goes a fondness for facts. Sensing types like information that can be seen, heard, touched, smelled, and tasted. They want data to back up the theory. They value things and behaviors that they see as sensible, realistic, factual, concrete, and detailed. Preferring the straightforward to the complex, Sensing types tend to focus on the here and now, not what might be. They are the doers: What good is an idea if it cannot be made into a reality? Their spirituality is likely to be experienced in communion with nature. Sensing types tend to be good with their hands and like a tangible product from their labor. Theories and abstractions interest them much less.

At their worst they think the way it has been is the way it always will be; any possibilities they think of will only make things worse. And they find it difficult to listen to people who ask them to look at the situation another way. At their best they are competent at identifying tangible problems and usually able to know what to do about them.

Intuitive Types (N)* Intuition is perceiving beyond the senses. Intuitive types are quick to see the patterns in details without careful examination of each detail one at a time. They dislike details, except as they pertain to general concepts and patterns. They love to explore possibilities, to play in

**The MBTI instrument uses N instead of I so that Intuition is not confused with Introversion.*

the beyond, to fly in the air psychologically and pretend they don't have to come down. They like complexity and may create it where they don't find it. Intuitive types like abstraction and prefer an abstract that cuts across the board to dealing with a multitude of particulars. They just don't want to "clutter up" their minds with unrelated bits of information. If their intuition is turned on the outer world, they may wish to be all things to all people—a Renaissance person. Or, they may direct their intuition to creating systems, making paradigms, seeing patterns. If it is directed on the inner world, their intuition may furnish a view of how things could be if only their own and others' behavior would accommodate their vision. Their spirituality is likely to come from being in touch with the infinite, with something that transcends time and space. Both are useful for transitions and creative process.

At their worst, Intuitive types ignore the facts, dream on, and spin off into fanciful spaces that may appear strange, remote, and reality-proof. At their best, they have quick insight into available options and what the results of each option would be. When Intuitive types have a hunch or imagine something, they can actually "see it." It is just there. They see it so clearly they just know it is right.

Thinking and Feeling: Decision-Making Modes

Some people prefer to think about things and others prefer to feel about them. You might say this is a way of processing the information they get from their senses or their insights. When a person is making a decision, is the head or the heart more involved? Does the person want to be reasonable or responsive? It's nice to be able to be both, but when a person has to choose, which way does it go? Like Sensing-Intuition, the Thinking-Feeling dichotomy is also referred to as an MBTI function. Both Thinking and Feeling are rational functions, two kinds of reasoning based on an individual's working with, deciding from, or drawing conclusions about information obtained either through the senses or the intuition.

Thinking Types (T) Thinking types use analytical, discriminative, or integrative, reasoning. They are usually somewhat detached from the person or thing being processed in order to get more perspective and see more angles. They want to figure "it" out—to know, if possible, why "it" is or at least what "it" means. Thinking types allow for alternatives and choices and may be able to see logic and make systems. They can tie the past, present, and future together. They love a good argument and can engage in verbal debates or competition for the fun of it. People with a Thinking preference are typically better at troubleshooting than at harmony making.

At their worst such types are detached and critical (sometimes hot and critical). At their best, they are expert strategists and tacticians and can figure out what the next logical move should be to get the results they want.

Feeling Types (F) Feeling types embrace the world. They prefer to "touch" the things they care about with their senses or their intuition. The people they respond to positively can be warmed just by being in their presence. The Feeling function gives a personal dimension to judgment process. The Feeling preference, like the Thinking preference, involves a rational process based on information obtained from the senses or from intuition, but unlike the impersonal stance of Thinking, the Feeling applies personal criteria to the situation. (Feeling judgments are not the same as emotional responses. Emotional responses are in a different category—more equivalent to having your "buttons pushed"—and are not discussed here.) Some values used in Feeling judgment are deeply based in internal or external experience and difficult to change. Others are more fluid and can change rapidly based on what's happening at the moment. When Feeling types' perspectives on an issue or the values related to it alter, it can appear they've changed their minds. Actually, they may have changed their way of looking at the issue and consequently their response to the situation. A thought can be captured in words fairly easily. Words about a feeling are poor translations at best. While Feeling types may be game players, they are less interested in analytical contests that demand logic than in maneuvers to produce an impact, positive or negative, on another person. Neither Thinking nor Feeling types are necessarily conscious of their own games.

At their worst, Feeling types are overly sensitive, reactive, intense, and may get stuck in negative response patterns. At their best, love shines from their eyes to the people they love who experience the love.

Judging and Perceiving: Styles of Responding to Environment

Some people see the world as an open space, a place of possibilities; others look for the underlying structures that comprise it. Individuals with Judging and Perceiving preferences differ in the ways they respond to the external world—to people and situations. For Perceiving types, who hate to give up their options, openness is appealing. For Judging types, who like to know where they stand, various kinds of structures are meaningful. Both preferences, though, involve styles of orientation to concrete, external environments.

Judging Style (J) People with a preference for Judging find structures supportive: if they organize, set priorities, and make decisions, the world somehow has less control over them. Judging types find security in structure, even if they change it tomorrow. They are selective, organize information in manageable ways, and make categories and decisions. Though Judging types often make fast decisions, they are not always "trapped" by them and can re-decide something just as quickly. Because they evaluate objects as soon as they perceive them, the two-step process seems more like a one-step process. In other words, Judging types tend automatically to come to an appraisal of whatever they're dealing with—though sometimes prematurely, of course. Because it's difficult for them to separate perception from evaluation, Judging types must completely reprocess an entity or situation in order to change their view or assessment of it. Such maneuvering may appear to them a waste of time since they tend to be impatient and get anxious if they have to keep things open and undecided.

At their worst, Judging types may tediously repeat "the rules" and not understand why other people don't see how important rules are. In this way, they are a bit like overly responsible parents—full of "shoulds"—and may be perceived by others as controlling. At their best, they get an amazing amount of work done by their ability to plan, organize, and put first things first, whether those tasks are pleasant or not.

Perceiving Style (P) For individuals with a Perceiving preference, the world is full of interesting possibilities. Perceiving types are free-flowing and open. Since something new may always turn up, they don't want to make decisions until there is a real need to do so. After all, decisions can eliminate interesting choices. Perceiving types are often clearer about what they don't want than about what they do want. They prefer to keep available lots of options, all of which may sound interesting. Because perception is receptive, Perceiving types are open to any and all new information. Their orientation to the world is as to a quest without a predetermined goal: they are aware and process information but, unlike Judging types, may not necessarily need to evaluate their discoveries or processes. Judging types are focused on doing, Perceiving types on exploring.

At their worst, Perceiving types can be insecure, indecisive, and resistant—like rebellious "kids" slipping out of their responsibilities, even to themselves. At their best, they are curious explorers and discoverers of the world's secrets and knowledge without necessarily having to do something about their discoveries, except perhaps share them. Which preferences fit you (your partner, your clients) the best?

....	....	....	....
E or I	S or N	T or F	J or P

Interactions of Opposites

Individuals may have preferences not only for the kind of partner they want, but also for the kind of communication or interaction they want at home. Or, more likely they will choose the person they relate to best who meets their other requirements in a partner, and just hope the dynamics at home will live up to their expectations. Here are some ideas about what to expect if the partners you are counseling differ from each other on a preference dimension. If their preferences are the same, other problems can arise, which we will talk about later. We include with these examples several possible exercises that you, as counselor, can give your couples as "homework."

Interactions between Extraverts and Introverts

Extraverts tend to "come forward" and Introverts to "withdraw." The more traumatic the circumstances or discussion, the more pronounced the behaviors on each side. That is, when Extraverts are in a tight spot emotionally, they tend to want to confront their partner and work the problem out or at least to discharge their feelings. Introverts, on the other hand, will go out of their way to avoid a confrontation. Because Introverts tend to absorb rather than discharge energy, bombardment by intense negative energy affects them more deeply than it typically does Extraverts. They may even make concessions they later wish they hadn't. This may be especially true when Introversion is combined with a preference for Feeling. Extraverts have a natural barrier since they are always ready with a comeback. They tend to stay involved in discussions regardless of their content and gain energy from interacting with others. Conversely, Introverts tend to gain energy through quiet time alone.

If Extraverts want to talk about things and Introverts want to be alone, especially if things get intense, what do they do if they're in a relationship together? A research study of couples by one of the authors indicates that while Introverted men tend to marry Extraverted women, both have trouble later on because of differences in interaction style. Remember though that Extraverts do have an Introverted side (like a less-used hand), just as Introverts have an Extraverted side.

TABLE 1.1

Potential Positive/Negative Aspects of Each Preference

POSITIVE		NEGATIVE	
EXTRAVERSION	INTROVERSION	EXTRAVERSION	INTROVERSION
Speak up	Listen attentively	Press the point	Concede the point
Initiate	Respond	Argue	Avoid argument
Socialize	Protect privacy	Intimidate	Retreat
Be active	Be reflective	Blame	Not respond
Energize	Calm	Be "outer" absorbed	Be "self" absorbed
SENSING	INTUITION	SENSING	INTUITION
Do	Know	Be nitty gritty	Be off the wall
Have a method	Have an idea	Oversimplify	Overcomplicate
Be factual	Be imaginative	Tack to the wall	Fly off
Practical solutions	Imaginative solutions	Tinker	Day dream
THINKING	FEELING	THINKING	FEELING
Analyze	Care	Criticize	Smother
Devise	Value	Demand reasons	Demand values
Be fair	Be responsive	Out strategize	Out emotionalize
Keep cool	Show warmth	Be icy	Be gushy
Be objective	Be personal	Be patronizing	Be contemptuous
JUDGING	PERCEIVING	JUDGING	PERCEIVING
Be organized	Be spontaneous	Be a clockwatcher	Be late
Plan fun times	Be fun	Be closeminded	Lose direction
Be on time	Be flexible	Be authoritarian	Be undependable
Be decisive	Be open	Have a lot of "shoulds"	Be disorganized
Hang tough	Hang loose	Lecture	Space out

Example: Extraverts with Introverts In the couples we see, Introverted men are often attracted to and may marry Extraverted women. Such men like the outgoing, social, vivacious style of an Extraverted woman. It is unfortunately true that the very things that people perceive as strengths and that attract them to each other can, over time, become problematic. A couple in this situation fits the stereotype to some extent of the woman who wants to talk a lot and the man who wants her to be quiet. Regardless of gender, Introverts want and need more quiet and alone time than Extraverts. Extraverts need and want more action and interaction than Introverts. If, instead of being annoyed by their dissimilar attitudes toward the outside world, the couple can be guided to use them to handle different necessities of life, apparent problems can be turned into benefits. The Introvert may be more adept at what the Extravert would consider a lonely task, such as writing letters or doing research. The Extravert may be more able and willing to handle situations that would drain the Introvert's energy more, such as disciplining children or handling aggressive people.

Couples' Exercise for E-I Combination If you want an Introvert to talk, you need to set up a comfortable, safe environment. Introverts can talk easily if they don't feel intruded upon, pushed, or commanded. However, because they may have less need to share, they have to be made aware of the Extravert's communication needs without seeming to be required to respond, especially on demand. Take the Introvert out for a quiet dinner (just the two of you), then bring up the topics you'd like to discuss.

Conversely, if you want an Extravert to be quiet, you may need to give them enough information or something enjoyable or interesting to think about that engages their energy. This may involve planning a dinner party, a vacation, or a major purchase together.

Interactions between Sensing Types and Intuitive Types

Sensing types tend to focus on facts, tangibles, and the physical environment. Intuitive types tend to focus on possibilities, creative urges, and their hunches, which often transcend data. The famous lines from Hamlet to Horatio are a beautiful example of an Intuitive type talking to a Sensing type: "There are more things in Heaven and Earth, Horatio, than are dreamt of in thy philosophy." Why concern oneself with facts when possibilities abound for creative change? A Sensing type might reply to this question with much conviction, "Seeing is believing." Sensing types would rather not concern themselves with abstract issues. There is so much to be done in what they regard as the real, physical world.

Misunderstandings between Sensing types and Intuitive types are easy, because what each "sees" is so obvious, they don't expect their partner to see something else. Sensing and Intuition are, as previously described, considered non-rational functions, which are not derived from logic but from the data as it is perceived by the observer. When taking in information from their surroundings, Sensing types tend to bypass the big picture but will naturally describe many details that Intuitive types may overlook; Intuitive types will jump into the middle with creative possibilities that Sensing types may overlook.

"MISUNDERSTANDINGS BETWEEN SENSING TYPES AND INTUITIVE TYPES ARE EASY, BECAUSE WHAT EACH 'SEES' IS SO OBVIOUS, THEY DON'T EXPECT THEIR PARTNER TO SEE SOMETHING ELSE."

So you can see how a meaningful conversation between these two could be difficult; they might even pass each other like ships in the night, without recognizing the full presence of the other. It can be difficult to understand someone who is basically getting information by a means different from one's own and who trusts and believes in his or her own way of perceiving. Remember, though that everyone has access to their opposite functions and attitudes even if it is often in a less conscious way.

EXAMPLE: ***Sensing Types with Intuitive Types*** We have found that those who commit to each other or marry at a young age are often opposite each other in one or more functions or attitudes. Throughout our practice, we have more often seen Intuitive type men with Sensing type women. Intuitive types tend to dislike routine maintenance activities. Regardless of gender, having a partner who is willing to perform such activities and sees the need for them is quite a gift for an Intuitive type. Difficulty may come, however, when communication needs arise. The world of imagination is not always interesting to Sensing types, nor is the concrete world always interesting to Intuitive types. Some give-and-take is again required as it is with E-I interactions. It is easier for Intuitive types to speak the Sensing language than it is for a Sensing type to grasp the abstract nature of the Intuitive framework. Conversations to handle "real world" issues should be held periodically, even if not a turn-on for the Intuitive type. In turn Sensing types need to listen to the creative dreamers in their lives and not discourage Intuitive types even if the "dreams" seem impractical at times.

Couples' Exercise for S-N Combination Encourage the couple to set a task that requires dealing with both facts and possibilities. Perhaps it would be planning a career change, moving to a new place, or deciding whether to have children. Each partner is to listen carefully to the other partner's point of view. Is one partner too afraid of losing possibilities? Is the other's need to be practical cutting out options? Ask the couple to write down the facts and the possibilities and then to analyze and assign values to the items in each list. On the basis of this activity, ask the partners to see if they can agree on a decision that satisfies both of them. If not, you may need to mediate.

Interactions between Thinking Types and Feeling Types

Thinking types mostly use impersonal reasoning and Feeling types mostly reason by way of personal priorities. If you ask a Thinking type a question, you are likely to get an "I think . . ." answer; if you ask a feeling type a question, you are likely to get an "I feel . . ." answer. Thinking types want rationales, analyses, and logic in conversation. Feeling types want understanding, warmth, and appreciation—or at least overt recognition of their values and priorities. Thinking types generally have logic to support their premises, hypotheses, and ideas. Feeling types have values that support their positions; they often use simple statements such as, "I care about this" or "I don't care about that."

In conversation, Thinking types may turn a dialog into a logic contest or sparring match, and in such contests Feeling types are poor competition. A problem may arise when Feeling types get seduced into trying to play the Thinking type's game without being equipped for it. While appearing to lose, all Feeling types know, of course, that they don't give up their values just because a Thinking type tries to reason them away. They usually end up saying something like "Okay, have it your way" and move on, unless they have a lot at stake or perceive that the Thinking type is attacking them personally. (The Thinking type, of course, never means to attack personally, only to speak "The Truth.") In such situations, the Feeling type may be hurt or rally to the defense. Suddenly, Thinking types may find themselves on the receiving end of a statement that gets them "where they live." It is as though the Feeling type has artfully designed the perfect quip to have the greatest impact on the Thinking type and has eloquently managed to impart with only a few words, "Now, we'll play my game." Examples of such statements by Feeling types include, "I really find you boring"; "I never want to see you again"; "If you're so great, how come you aren't better in bed?"

Both Thinking and Feeling are, as previously described, considered rational functions. Both types strive to make rational choices or decisions by processing data either through logic (Thinking types) or values (Feeling types). While Thinking types are tuned into the logic of a situation, Feeling types are tuned into its emotional aspects and quick to pick up on coldness, hostility, detachment, preoccupation, and other features of the "climate" that affect the tone of a relationship. Equally accessible to Feeling types are harmonious, loving, accepting, supportive "vibes." The topic is not the primary focus of the interaction for Feeling types; the relationship is. A Feeling type might say, "I want to talk to you about this because I care about you," and not be interested in an analysis of or solution to the issue being discussed. Thinking types on the other hand can become impatient and critical in a descriptive discussion that doesn't seem to have a point or call for an analysis. They may even provide their best "thinking" on the subject and find it is not what is wanted. It can make them defensive about values-oriented discussions—they are off their own turf in these arenas—and they may try to avoid such interactions.

But all is not negative on the relationship horizon. Feeling types often go to Thinking types for quick analytical processing, and Thinking types often go to Feeling types for warmth and acceptance. Both types have much to give each other. Remember also, that each type has access to the opposite function although it may be at a less conscious level.

The differences between Thinking and Feeling types are fairly easy to see once you are "tuned in" to them. The Feeling type's process, though a rational one, is not usually framed in terms of reasons, so his or her discussions with a Thinking type can sometimes be quite frustrating for both of them. Instead, the Feeling type's reasons are values—what they believe to be important in life, such as human rights. To a third party, such as the counselor, their discussion might sound more like a debate where the

Thinking type advocates justice by presenting reasons and rationales, while the Feeling type advocates mercy by emphasizing values and ideals.

Couples' Exercise for T-F Combination Give the couple a hypothetical situation to consider and ask them to record and compare their views. As an example, they might take the case of a young person in the family who has had too much to drink and gotten into a minor car accident while driving. The police have taken the teenager to jail overnight. The parents are out of town, and the couple has been designated to handle the situation. The partners might consider the following kinds of questions: What action would each of them take based on what they know? How would each of them respond to the young person, who is not injured but afraid and shaken up? Once they've answered questions of this sort, ask the partners to determine whether they would decide to handle the situation separately or agree on a way to do it together. Ask them to assess whether the process of trying to resolve what to do tends to bring them closer or alienate them to some extent. In session, you can review the couple's process and show them how to use it as a model to look back on for assistance in future discussions where disagreement is likely or possible.

Interactions between Judging Types and Perceiving Types

Judging types typically like to create structures and organization and Perceiving types often have an urge to knock them down, go around or under them, and generally prefer to make their own structures as they go along. The Judging–Perceiving dichotomy formulated by Katharine Briggs and Isabel Briggs Myers, using Jungian theory as the base, provides a brilliant but relatively simple explanation for the hundreds of often-perplexing differences that arise between Judging and Perceiving types living together.

On the other side, Perceiving types prefer more flexibility and tend to approach tasks less according to particular, preset patterns and more according to opportunities and moods. They want flexibility and prefer not to be held to the letter of apparent commitments. For instance, they may call a friend to leave a quick message and then get involved in a long and interesting discussion; if they meet someone exciting, they might miss an appointment; they might put off unpleasant tasks in favor of more intriguing ones. Perceiving types tend to feel trapped and confined by structure unless it's of their own making. When Perceiving types set tasks for themselves, they are often very efficient at accomplishing them. But if you try to pin them down, they may elude you.

Perceiving types may appear to Judging types to be irresponsible or lazy, whereas Judging types may appear to Perceiving types to be authoritarian or demanding. Remember, though, both aspects are always present in each of us at different levels of consciousness: the Judging type's inner world may be chaotic, and the Perceiving type's inner world may be ordered. The less conscious aspects often seem to belong to the other person.

Among the couples we see, it is fairly common for one to favor Judging and the other to favor Perceiving. Judging types often pick up more responsibility than they really want to in a relationship because they think they "should." Judging types find attractive the apparent freedom of Perceiving types to do what they please. Perceiving types, more focused on discovery than responsibility, are often attracted to the Judging type's apparent willingness to handle the "shoulds" of life. Nonetheless, each type can see the other as controlling.

Tips for Counselors

- Recognize that we deal with people, not types. Be cautious about your type assessments and their possible ramifications.
- Don't tell clients "how they are" or what they can and can't do on the basis of their types. Help them, first, to understand the strengths and blind spots of each type; second, to relate that understanding to their own situation; and third, to arrive at their own conclusions.
- Keep your own interpretations to a minimum. Let each individual make his or her own interpretations with the information you present.
- In order to give yourself and your clients a deeper understanding of them, consider role-playing how the different types behave.

2
Power in Love Relationships

"Where love reigns, there is no will to power, and where the will to power is paramount, love is lacking."

C. G. Jung, ***Two Essays on Analytical Psychology***

Brief Descriptions of the Types and Power

Freedom to live one's life fully implies having power. Power comes from many different sources: looks, money, high rank or position, fame, charisma, intelligence, knowledge, wisdom, and so on. When we talk about power between intimates, we are dealing with a very complex relationship. In relationships, one person usually has more overt power than the other. In a perverse way, the person who can more easily leave the relationship at any given time—and either partner can be that person at different times—seems to have the power. We say *seems* because the other person often has power he or she chooses not to exercise. If there is a real and basic power difference between partners, one of two things usually happens: the relationship breaks up or becomes more like a parent-child than an equal relationship.

Power and the shifting scale of dependence and independence are closely allied. A careful balance is required. If we handle our dependencies well, we can be close enough to someone we trust to allow ourselves to be vulnerable, cared for, and loving. (It is not possible to trust anyone completely, even ourselves, since the unconscious always has potential to change things.)

Paradoxically, it takes strength or inner power to enter into such a relationship consciously. To avoid intimacy is to be fearful, not strong. To be overly dependent is to be needy and demanding and likewise not strong. On the independence continuum, it is well to be free enough to make independent choices when appropriate and to exert some control over the ways we expend our time and energy. However, if we don't consult our partners on crucial issues or if we don't treat our partners as well as we treat our friends, our relationship has a power problem. There are many other ways power problems can manifest.

"DIFFICULTIES OFTEN ARISE WHEN A COUNSELOR WORKS TO HELP A CLIENT BRING UNCONSCIOUS MATERIAL INTO CONSCIOUSNESS, ESPECIALLY IF THE INDIVIDUAL EXPERIENCES THE INFORMATION AS NEGATIVE."

One person in an intimate partnership can "shut down" or "give up" if they perceive there is little use in continuing to talk. The other partner may not want to hear a different point of view or may be so invested in preserving their own that they don't listen. A person may also shut down or give up when the other person tries to force them to "come around" by talking long and hard enough. Other problems arise when one person thinks he or she already knows what the partner has to say or doesn't really understand what the partner is saying. Overt power is related to psychological type. Extraverts are naturally more demonstrative and often hold more explicit or visible power in relationships and more control over communication. Introverts tend to be more subtle, and their power within intimate relationships is often implicit.

Power interactions between couples can be very much like a dance: Who is following? Who is leading? When do they switch? Do they change partners? In the following discussion, we will focus on power conflicts that are unresolved or unconscious, on what happens when partners negotiate their differences, and on what different "power dances" look like. Some power maneuvers within relationships are not deliberate but result from natural tendencies of type. Because such tendencies are often less conscious, they are also less available for remedial action on a person's part. Once brought into consciousness, trouble-making tendencies and behaviors can be remediated. Difficulties often arise when a counselor works to help a client bring unconscious material into consciousness, especially if the individual experiences the information as negative. Denial and defensiveness abound in these situations. When a strong emotional charge attaches to a client's internal or external experience, something is usually present that needs attention. If the person is ready to become self-aware and especially if the new information is given with love and/or humor or both, positive change can occur.

The power to persuade, the power to intimidate, the power to seduce, the power to involve, the power to influence, the power to change minds and hearts, the power to express love, the power to provide hope, the power to bring serenity, the power to comfort—these are only some examples of how power can consciously or unconsciously inform interactions between partners. To get a sense of how interactions between preference types resemble a dance, look at table 2.1 (pages 30, 31). In the sections that follow, we include exercises you can use with couples in your practice, but we also encourage you to be creative and make up your own!

The Extravert-Introvert Power/Love Dance

Extraverts are usually willing to initiate. Introverts, processing their thoughts internally may not generate enough output to satisfy the Extravert. In love, sex, and communication, balance is desirable. One-sidedness, while sometimes necessary, sets up unconscious energy that can backfire. A couple's effort to assist each other in achieving balance is a challenging dance in itself.

If unresolved or unconscious—The Extravert will come forward (strongly) and the Introvert will back up. The Extravert will get frustrated from lack of contact, and the Introvert will get angry (silently) from so many demands.

If negotiated—The Extravert will back up and not fire such direct energy in the Introvert's direction; when Introverts feel safe, they will come forward and be willing to share more thoughts. When Extraverts have meaningful contact, their energy has an outlet and doesn't turn into frustration or even anger.

The dance—Two steps forward, two steps back: If the Introvert will move forward, the Extravert can move back. Back and forth, to and fro. It can be done.

For assessment, look at party behavior—Extraverts and Introverts tend to behave differently at large parties. An Extravert may enjoy being the center of attention or moving around and making lots of contacts. An Introvert may come in with sufficient interest and energy to enjoy the first hour but then start to find the energy drain debilitating or may seek a quiet conversation.

Prior to coming to counseling, partners have usually started to blame each other for the pain their different styles of socializing can cause. Introverts may see their partner as uncaring, selfish, or insensitive. Extraverts may see their partners as controlling or "socially inept." Even when the couple has already tried to resolve their disagreement (for example, with a plan where the Introvert subtly signals the Extravert that it's time to leave the party), such efforts seldom work because there's too much payoff in the party environment for the Extravert. The Extravert's attempt at seemingly humorous comments, such as "Oh well, here's my jailor again," can escalate hostility and bitterness. In any case, no matter what time the couple leaves the party there can be recriminations on both sides.

It does help for the couple to go into counseling (probably short term), long enough to be aware that it's all right to be different, that one isn't right and the other wrong, one good and the other bad. Having a counselor validate that Extraverts and Introverts are different can be a big help in understanding that behavior from one partner or the other is not meant to be annoying.

One win-win solution to the party problem is for the partners to travel in separate cars. That way, the Introvert can leave when the party becomes unenjoyable, simply saying to the partner with a smile, "I'll see you at home." People do not need to be glued to each other to belong with each other.

Couples' Exercise Ask the couple to consider the following questions for discussion in an upcoming session:

- List three qualities or behaviors you display that helped you to decide whether you're an Extravert or Introvert.
- List three behaviors or qualities that helped you determine whether your partner is an Extravert or Introvert.

- If you and your partner are both Extraverts or both Introverts, what have you experienced as the advantages and disadvantages of being similar in this regard? If one of you is an Extravert and one an Introvert, what have you experienced as the advantages of being different in this regard?

The Sensing-Intuition Power/Love Dance

This is one area in which it is possible to make the opposite type feel inferior. Intuitive types can feel lacking when Sensing types point out facts obvious to them but missed by the Intuitive type. Sensing types can feel deflated when the Intuitive partner points out big, exciting, creative possibilities the Sensing type has overlooked. Dancing well together requires both abilities' complementing not combating each other.

If unresolved or unconscious—The Sensing type will usually take concrete steps in the relationship, while the Intuitive will tend to imagine how it could be "if only." Sensing types may become frustrated by the Intuitive type's need for them to be satisfying on so many levels and in such complex ways. Intuitive types may become frustrated by the Sensing type's daily dance routines.

If negotiated—This is probably the hardest dance of all in which to produce satisfying contact for both partners. Getting the partners to step around each other is one way to handle differences. If the Sensing type is not too bored by the partner's flights of fancy and the Intuitive type not too bored by the partner's everyday routines, some meeting of fact and fancy may occur. Remember that Sensing and Intuitive types each take in and process information differently. It is possible to do and dream, dream and do; in relationships, it's good to have some of each.

The dance—As in a square dance's do-si-dos, both partners tend to work around each other. If they choose to stay in step, they can do so by mixing some difficult, fanciful steps with some simple, basic ones.

For assessment, look at TV-watching behavior—When partners have opposite preferences for Sensing-Intuition dichotomy, their differences readily show up in what they like to watch on television. The Sensing type often prefers to watch news and other fact-based programming, while the Intuitive type prefers to watch TV dramas, fantasies, and other story-based programming. It is probably a good idea for such couples to have two TVs.

If the decision is to watch something together, is one partner accommodating the other's needs or are they genuinely interested in the same show? At what point do facts get burdensome for Intuitive types? For Sensing types when does the creative process seem like avoiding the more immediate concrete issues?

Couples' Exercise Following is an exercise that can help couples sort out and understand their differences regarding Sensing and Intuition preferences.

- Make a list of detectives you've seen on TV, in the movies, or in books. Which ones do you see as relying primarily on their Sensing preference to solve the crime? Which rely primarily on their Intuiting preference to solve the crime?
- Make a list of six individuals you know fairly well (family, friends, coworkers) and hypothesize—on the basis of their attitudes, behaviors, likes and dislikes—which ones are Sensing and which ones are Intuitive types.

"IT'S IMPORTANT FOR EACH PARTNER TO TAKE THE LEAD SOMETIMES AND SHOW THE OTHER SOME NEW STEPS. EACH DEFINITELY HAS SOMETHING TO OFFER."

The Thinking-Feeling Power/Love Dance

Ask a Thinking type what he or she feels and you will almost always get an "I think I feel" response, followed by a word like "confused" or "perplexed"—that is, head words, not heart words. Ask a Feeling type what he or she thinks and you will almost always get an "I feel" response, followed by a values orientation to the subject at hand ("I feel more compassion is needed," for example) rather than a "head" response. Feeling types usually have as much difficulty telling you what they think as Thinking types do telling you how they feel. Because an abundance of feelings can make Thinking types uncomfortable, they often put logic first. Because logic can seem too detached an approach for Feeling types, they often put values first. To people outside the relationship, it may seem as if both people are trying to lead, as if both are insisting, "I have the 'right' way to go about this."

If unresolved or unconscious—The Thinking type tries to maintain some margin of detachment, while the Feeling type keeps trying to get closer and more involved. As dance partners, the two can look pretty clumsy trying to work out their different styles. To the Thinking type's "let's do it right" attitude, the Feeling type is apt to respond, "once more, please, with feeling."

If negotiated—The steps each partner takes to the same tune will be different. One set comes from the head, one from the heart. Since we all need both, it's important for each partner to take the lead sometimes and show the other some new steps. Each definitely has something to offer. So, they need to loosen up and get out on the floor. They can dance together, so long as each is respectful of the other's ability and comfort level.

The dance—Heart to heart and head to head—sounds like a close encounter of the right kind.

For assessment, look at conflict-resolution behavior—The Thinking type usually has the advantage in debates, while the Feeling type usually has the advantage in social exchanges. Rather than envying each other's abilities, the partners can learn to make constructive use of their differences by appreciating and working with the talents each has. Thinking types tend to be more competitive. Let them engage with someone else who enjoys that behavior. Feeling types can seek out a like-minded soul also. Encourage partners to watch each other doing what they do well, which can be useful in each partner's development.

Couples' Exercise Suggest your clients think of a couple with whom both have had some problems. And ask them to do the following:

- Express your points of view about having a dinner party that includes the "problem couple." Are there logical reasons for inviting them? Are there values that would be violated if the problem couple attends?
- Whether you end up agreeing or disagreeing, track how you come to a decision. Does one of you win, while the other gives in, or do you create a process for resolving the issue? Are both of you satisfied at the end of the discussion? In what ways does this exercise show you how to use your differences constructively?

The Judging-Perceiving Power/Love Dance

Perceiving types are usually clear about what they don't want to do. Judging types are usually clear about what they do want to do. If Judging types

TABLE 2.1

Couple Dancing (Communicating) in Type

EXTRAVERT/INTROVERT	**E** comes forward; **I** backs away. The more **E** comes forward, the more **I** backs away.
Solution:	**E** *backs up;* **I** *comes forward (not easy for either one).*
SENSING/INTUITION	**S** describes the here and now; **N** describes the future. **S** says, be realistic; deal with the here and now. **N** says, be creative; change the future.
Solution:	**S** *takes the lead in dealing with the facts now;* **N** *responds and gives balance.* **N** *takes the lead in dealing with a creative future;* **S** *responds and gives balance.* *Both need to be patient; the future is with us longer than the present, but the present can be very demanding.*
THINKING/FEELING	**T** says, give me logical reasons. **F** says, give me what is important (values). **T** may get cool and detached. **F** may get hot and intense (or dramatic). If things get very bad, **T** may get hot and **F** may get cool.
Solution:	**T** *says, my viewpoint is important; I need it taken seriously.* **F** *says, my viewpoint is important; I also need it taken seriously.* *In intimate relationships, a personal request of what one needs is better than taking a position based either on logic or values—unless you both like to fight. If what's important to you is not important to the other person, it's better to work toward solutions that satisfy both needs.*

JUDGING/PERCEIVING	**J** says it's time to decide. **P** says let's be sure we've covered the options first. The more **J** persists, the more **P** delays and vice versa.
Solution:	**J** *takes responsibility to be explicit: that is, unless you tell me otherwise by a specified time, this is the plan.* **P** *takes responsibility for speaking up about what matters early in the decision-making process or for going along with the program.*

make their positions clear, Perceiving types are often able to go along unless they have a strong objection. In the latter case, it is up to the Perceiving type to be clear about not wanting to engage a particular alternative.

If unresolved or unconscious—Judging types have definite, ordered ways of going about things and aren't always comfortable with a free style. Perceiving types, on the other hand, prefer free-style approaches; they like to keep things loose and open. We might think of the Judging type as someone whose steps conform to a plan—either a traditionally established pattern for a specific type of dance, or a plan of one's own—while the Perceiving type's steps ebb and flow according to mood and music. These differences may not make for a smooth, gliding motion, especially if the Judging type is unprepared for or turned off by the Perceiving partner's spontaneous maneuvers.

If negotiated—There are definitely two different sets of steps here; it's really probably two entirely different dances. As a matter of fact, it is very difficult to dance together. It's similar to Sensing-Intuition, except where there was different information, here there is different structure—or rather structure and free-flow. Each can seem equally controlling to the opposite type, although the Judging structure is more visible and explicit. The control of Perceiving free-flow is less visible and implicit. Perhaps today's separate-but-together dancing is a symbolic way of dealing with the problems inherent in being with someone and at the same time being free.

The dance—Though they're out on the floor together, each partner makes up his or her own dance style. The J type partner's dance has a beginning, a middle, and an end, and the steps form a definite pattern. The P type partner moves with the promptings of music and mood in a free-form dance. Both partners do their own thing, and as no one is leading, no one has to follow.

Power and Love Types

How each of us exercises power varies widely. In general though, the different types seem to have natural, characteristic ways of exercising their power in relationships. It is important for partners to find themselves and be themselves in spite of stereotypes and social custom. Power comes in many different forms: influence, intelligence, looks, character, strength in adversity, calmness in crises, to name only a few; which ones do your couple have and which ones do they want?

In this chapter, dancing is used as a metaphor for the many aspects of intimate relationships: how well a couple can stay in step; who follows or who leads; whether toes get stepped on; whether the same music is acceptable to both partners; whether one has to learn new steps or even new dances, to mention only a few. Each type can become annoyed with, or contemptuous of, the other's style. It is important in a relationship for both partners to have in reserve their own power bases, so that one partner's power does not overwhelm or oppress the other's. The relationship agreement should never include a full-on use of all possible power, however. This means, among other things, that no partner should ever hit, curse at, or deliberately demean the other. Partners should have an advance agreement that when tensions escalate, instead of "losing it," one of them can call a "time out," which will be respected. The following profiles—though somewhat overstated to make the point—describe how the different types wield power in relationships. See if they fit any of the couples you are working with. You might also want to look at table 2.2, which outlines how positive and negative power dynamics may be expressed in intimate relationships.

Thinking Types

Extraverted Thinking (ESTJ, ENTJ) Extraverted Thinking types tend to make their power explicit. They'll run as much of the world as you'll let them run. If you disagree, they'll probably argue with you, enjoy it, and maybe even convince you of their point of view. If you're not convinced, you may capitulate anyway, as they can be quite tenacious in their presentations. On the other hand, if you have a good argument, they can be very reasonable. If you don't think fast though, a decision may be made without you, because they're deciders and organizers too. Fait accompli!

Introverted Thinking (ISTP, INTP) Power is more implicit for the Introverted Thinking type. They tend to get their power from having well thought out, reasonable systems that are difficult to challenge unless you're an Introverted Thinking type, too. The fact that they tend to identify with their systems can be problematic, because you may not be able to tell whether they're talking independently or whether their system is talking through them. These systems can be so well developed that they seem to stand over or surround you. But these types don't mean to dominate, merely to find out what they don't know. Some of them may prefer to look at data and figure things out that way. When they get their facts together, everything seems so clear. They hope you'll understand; Introverted Thinking types don't like to explain. But they will tell you once, in concise language, how it is and how it works. Knowledge is power!

Feeling Types

Extraverted Feeling (ESFJ, ENFJ) Extraverted Feeling types get their power from their social facility. How can you get angry with someone who knows your needs before you do? And fills them! Theirs is the power of love and sensitivity. They do like to have a good time while they're taking care of someone, and that person enjoys it too. Of course, all people have times when they don't want to be taken care of. At such moments, this type's power can seem overwhelming or intrusive. Their sensitivity can help them sense when to pull back and give a partner space, and their laughter and love will hopefully loosen things up again, and love can conquer all.

Introverted Feeling (ISFP, INFP) Introverted Feeling types don't relate well to other people's power concepts. As a result, they sometimes find power used against them. The power of Introverted Feeling types is usually internalized as part of their vision, whatever that vision may be. They're so absorbed by their inner quest, that seeing what's going on in the outside world is difficult for them unless it relates to that quest. Introverted Feeling types often couple with someone who handles outer world events for them, so they can be free to pursue their dreams. The perfection of the dream—that's where they want to have impact. They can be so single-minded in this pursuit that others feel left out, unless they also share parts of the dream. Devotion to a dream may seem very constricting, but dreams are important.

Sensing Types

Extraverted Sensing (ESTP, ESFP) Extraverted Sensing types get power from their ability to tune into what's going on "right here, right now" and to bring people together to deal with it. Difficulties may arise, however, if they're one of the people someone else needs to corral. As they are reluctant to let others act or negotiate for them, it may take some time and thought for this type to determine what kind of person would be acceptable to him or her in that role. The Extraverted Sensing type's adventurous spirit and easy acceptance can be intimidating. When they get knocked down, they get right back up again. Circumstances might sometimes slow them down a little, but Extraverted Sensing types won't let anything stop them!

Introverted Sensing (ISTJ, ISFJ) Introverted Sensing types get their power from the fact that they can be counted on. As a result they are typically entrusted with responsibilities. all sorts of things that might never be left with others. They can be counted on. Reliability and consistency sustain their power. They're realistic, and they often have a wry sense of humor.

TABLE 2.2

Positive and Negative Power Dynamics in Love Relationships

	POWER BASE	POSITIVE	NEGATIVE
ETJ	Explicit understanding	Take charge	Take over
ITP	Implicit understanding	Figure out	Be abstruse
EFJ	Expressiveness	Be warm	Be intrusive
IFP	Having a cause	Pursue	Not notice
ESP	Adaptation	Solve	Hold back
ISJ	Responsibility	Be present	Withdraw
ENP	Enthusiasm	Be charming	Be conniving
INJ	Insight	Inspire	Be stubborn

Maybe not now, though. Some things are serious. They'd like to be able to count on others, too, but you can definitely count on them!

Intuitive Types

Extraverted Intuitive (ENTP, ENFP) Extraverted Intuitive types get their power from their contagious enthusiasm. No one can be more energizing than this type in full swing. As for spontaneous humor? They invented it! Come on, when was the last time you had a good laugh that you weren't with one of them? Just their full attention can make someone feel important. They're not trying to con people; they just know what we want to hear. The power of persuasion! The enchantment of the moment! All things to all people!

Introverted Intuitive (INTJ, INFJ) Introverted Intuitive types get their power from what they know. Just ask them; they like to share their knowledge with those on the same wavelength. They are more comfortable in realms of the "known," and what makes sense to them based on their own experiences and knowledge. Partners of these types may find difficulty conversing with Introverted Intuitives as they may adhere strongly to their perspectives. An optimal approach may be to listen first and then find ways to present other information in a form that Introverted Intuitives can appreciate through their insight and task orientation. Those who have preferences for Introverted Intuition have the ability to delve deeply into issues, but may need a gentle nudge to look beyond those internal conclusions and solutions.

Tips for Counselors

- See both people together for most sessions.
- Don't take sides; be on the side of the relationship or the potential in each person.
- Keep confidences given in separate sessions inviolate.
- Hold sacred the vulnerability which often lies right underneath the hurt or anger expressed.
- Develop an ability to speak the language of the different types.
- Make accurate assessments but not judgments (unless some foundational principle or value is being violated such as the ban on violence, name calling, active addiction behaviors, or sexual acting out).

3
Counseling the Types

"THE ATTITUDE OF THE PSYCHOTHERAPIST IS INFINITELY MORE IMPORTANT THAN THE THEORIES AND METHODS OF PSYCHOTHERAPY."

C. G. Jung, ***Modern Man in Search of a Soul***

Counseling and Self-Awareness

Intimacy and Type is written primarily for therapists, social workers, ministers—anyone who works in helpful professional association with couples experiencing problems. Despite a stated focus on couples, however, much of the information in this book also can be useful for working with individuals. This chapter moves the focus from the couple or the individual to the counselor, encouraging additional insights into your own relationships or the relationships of people important to you. Through such insight, you may enhance your professional relationships and effectiveness.

Individuals who are engaged in facilitating the relationships of others need, perhaps more than other people, to have a great deal of self-awareness. In the past, analysts were required to undergo analysis themselves prior to working with others. For the majority of counseling systems, this is no longer true. It is, however, an option you may want to consider.

It is still true, though, that your personal development is important, at least as important as your training and skills. Knowledge of typology is exceptionally useful in enabling you to be aware of your own special gifts and to develop them maximally and to be aware of the limitations of your type and to work through those limitations. Type differences originate in aspects of personality we develop more than others, as well as in our natural tendencies. An understanding of type alerts you to your special skills, gifts, and limitations. It also enables you to understand and communicate with people of all types, not just people like yourself whom you can more easily understand.

One of the blessings that comes with a knowledge of type is that each function and attitude can be developed, made available and useful, if you're willing to put energy and attention into that development. If you're an Introvert, you can learn to develop an Extravert's skills by "stretching" yourself to behave as such—for example, by mingling at large parties, joining a leadership organization, such as Toastmasters, or by learning to be comfortable giving speeches. If you're an Extravert, you can develop an Introvert's skills by doing meditation or by listening to rather than participating in group discussions.

"ONE OF THE BLESSINGS THAT COMES WITH A KNOWLEDGE OF TYPE IS THAT EACH FUNCTION AND ATTITUDE CAN BE DEVELOPED, MADE AVAILABLE AND USEFUL, IF YOU'RE WILLING TO PUT ENERGY AND ATTENTION INTO THAT DEVELOPMENT."

Sensing types can try to stretch their imaginations, and Intuitive types can make themselves notice the facts. If your Feeling function is dominant, you might practice conceptualizing strategic interventions or framing paradoxical intentions. Thinking-dominant types may need to try to get out of their heads and find out what their "heart values" are. Judging types can practice being more flexible and Perceiving types coming to closure sooner. Role-playing and other activities can be useful in developing any of the functions; these will not change who you are but will simply increase your repertoire of behaviors.

We're not suggesting that you need to be fully actualized before attempting to help others, for who among us is? We're suggesting that the more self-awareness you possess and the greater freedom you have in moving from one function to another, the more resources you will have to facilitate understanding and appreciation of differences among the couples with whom you work. Of course, no one can be every type, but we can enhance our effectiveness as counselors by recognizing the gifts that different types bring to counseling.

Using Type Strengths in Counseling

The counselor brings experience, training, and counseling skills to the therapeutic encounter. Type knowledge can add an extra dimension to understanding and communicating with people different from you. It can also facilitate an attitude of openness, nonstereotyped responses, and a general acceptance of diversity and equality. To the best of your ability, draw on these different parts of yourself during your therapeutic sessions, using whatever is most helpful to the individuals with whom you are working.

Use the Skills of the Extraverted Thinking Types (ESTJ/ENTJ)

Stand back and look objectively at the people involved and at their environment. Set clear standards; do not permit evasiveness, and confront clients who find it hard to put energy into working on their problems. Teach both Introverted and Extraverted Feeling types how to strategize when the situation calls for strategy and tactics. Lead your clients into developing their own leadership abilities.

Use the Skills of the Introverted Thinking Types (ISTP/INTP)

Maintain your objectivity by wisely staying out of the traps of sympathy for, or identification with, your clients. Maintain sufficient detachment not to allow your own buttons to be pressed. Help your clients conceptualize and strategize solutions to their problems. Help them examine the rules they've been living by, and encourage them to discard any rules that no longer work or are inappropriate to the situation. Help point out inconsistencies in thought and behavior. Bring concentration and relevance into the counseling sessions.

Use the Skills of the Extraverted Feeling Types (ESFJ/ENFJ)

Create a warm, loving, accepting, responsive environment so that clients will feel willing to engage in looking at themselves. Remember your clients' names. Help them feel at ease. Make them feel important. Be truly tolerant of clients who are different from you in type, style, or values. Teach them how to socialize if they lack those skills. Help them know how to relax and enjoy the socialization process. Use your understanding of others to help them to grow.

Use the Skills of the Introverted Feeling Types (ISFP/INFP)

Teach clients how to get in touch with their own depths. Use your own empathy to help bring out the best in them. Use your own warmth and caring to help them explore their own values and goals. Remain committed to your goal of helping all those with whom you come in contact. Be adaptable and open to new information. Help others get in touch with their feelings.

Use the Skills of the Extraverted Sensing Types (ESFP/ESTP)

Teach clients to live in the here and now. Use your keen awareness of what's going on at every moment in the session to give feedback at the proper time. Help your clients to see the world as the exciting place it can be. Use your negotiating skills to help each couple work out compromises that are satisfying to both, with neither member of the couple feeling they are losing or giving up something important. Be active in the session, not merely a passive listener. Keep the sessions spontaneous, so that they are both fun and useful. Help your clients to remain optimistic, regardless of the outcome.

Use the Skills of the Introverted Sensing Types (ISFJ/ISTJ)

Let your clients know they can count on you to be there for them when they need you. Be punctual for your appointments, conscientious about returning phone calls, and willing to follow the rules of the institution you work for or of the state you work in if you're in private practice. Help your clients learn the positive aspects of loyalty and devotion. Teach them to respect the traditions and rituals of others. Remain calm in the face of chaos.

Use the Skills of the Extraverted Intuitive Types (ENFP/ENTP)

Use your own enthusiasm and excitement about life to move clients out of depression, out of rigid behaviors, and out of situations in which they feel stuck. Use your intuition to brainstorm solutions with and for your clients and to help them learn to deal with life creatively. Open up options and possibilities they may never have considered. Understand the motivations not yet made explicit by your clients and lead them into greater awareness. Help them break out of the molds of rigid conformity. Teach the value of openness to new ideas and situations.

Use the Skills of the Introverted Intuitive Types (INFJ/INTJ)

Use your intuition to know what clients need in order to reach their full potential. Understand your clients in ways that are deep and meaningful to them. Generate alternate outcomes with clarity and depth, and present those outcomes objectively. Understand, value, and relate to the complexity of each of the individuals with whom you come in contact. Teach your clients decisiveness and the value of closure. Help them see the likely consequences of different choices. Use all the positive aspects of the intuition you have available to bring insight and wisdom into their world.

If many of these behaviors are available to you, your clients are fortunate indeed. We hope the foregoing descriptions have helped to make you aware of some of your functions or attitudes that may still need to be developed. Focus some time and attention on those areas. All of us have the potential to become more complete and more whole. Awareness and motivation are places to begin the process.

USING TYPE IN COUNSELING COUPLES: SOME CASE STUDIES

There are, of course, many traditional ways to utilize knowledge of type in working with couples, doing either relationship, premarital, marital, or divorce counseling. One of the most common methods is to administer the MBTI® instrument to each individual and then interpret the results. We find it most effective to interpret the results when both parties are present—as a first step toward understanding that differences between partners are not only okay, but valuable. It is important during this process to watch for signals of one-upmanship, of "my type is better than yours." In our experience, ETJs, particularly ESTJs, seem most likely to express the belief that they're the "best of any possible combination." IFPs seem most likely to express the reaction that the MBTI assessment "understands" them more fully than anyone before ever has.

Another way of using the instrument is to let each partner answer as they believe the other person would and then compare the results with the partner's actual responses. Whether they predict accurately or not can provide a lot of information for the therapist to work with. New awareness opens up new vistas. Still another use for the instrument is to offer it to induce a reluctant partner to come to counseling for the interpretation session. Most such reluctant mates, when they learn valuable information about themselves and their partners, do return for additional sessions and are willing to cooperate in improving the relationship. It is important for the therapist not to make judgments but to give feedback that opens up new options for behavior.

It is, of course, useful to look at each individual's type in assessing the dynamics of the problems the couple is encountering. It is also sometimes useful to focus only on one or two dichotomies, especially at first, to simplify things. At times, differences in Judging-Perceiving attitudes may explain the major causes of a couple's frustrations: "He's never on time"; "She's not flexible about plans"; "He doesn't balance the checkbook"; "She doesn't know how to let go and have fun," et cetera.

For some examples, we'll focus on two dichotomies—Extraversion-Introversion and Thinking-Feeling—to demonstrate possible degrees of comfortable interaction for couples. Any two dichotomies could be used, but these two tend to be fairly easily understood. Keep in mind the probability that Extraverts are likely to desire more social interaction, to be more active. Introverts are likely to require more private time, to enjoy the intimacy of being alone with their partner. Thinking types tend to be objectively critical of themselves (maybe even more so of others) and to take a broad overview of past, present, and future. Feeling types are likely to value harmony, to make decisions according to a set of values developed in the past, and the past may hold more meaning for them than for Thinking types.

Consider with us some of the couples we saw in counseling.

CASE STUDY 1: **Extraverted Feeling Type and Introverted Thinking Type**

Beth is an Extraverted Feeling type and George is an Introverted Thinking type. Their natural preferences are quite different. They are more complementary than similar. Each needs some of what the other has, but they have to exert some effort to understand each other.

Beth didn't like her job and didn't want to go back to school. Since George had a high income, both Beth and George decided she didn't need to work unless she wanted to. Beth expressed a need for interaction with people and a strong preference for harmonious, human relationships. She is comfortable being alone occasionally, but not for very long periods. On occasions when George comes home in the evening, and makes critical comments about her or the people he works with, Beth attempts to harmonize things and move him into an emotional space where she is most comfortable and experiences a state of well-being.

However, George's need for privacy and his preference for objectivity put him in an emotional place quite different from Beth's. As an engineer, he spends one part of his day interacting with clients and the other part supervising the people in his department. He enjoys his work, especially the time he spends designing new projects. He is comfortable interacting with his colleagues, because they have enough in common to make relating easy.

As an Introvert having extraverted most of the day, George comes home in the evening with his energy largely depleted, and he would like to withdraw totally to a private place where he experiences his greatest state of well-being. He wants to be left alone to read his journals, to think creatively, or simply to collapse in front of the television if he has had a difficult day.

He knows he is not making Beth happy because she keeps telling him so, but he wishes she were more independent and didn't need him so much. When he first met her, she appeared much more independent than she does now, and during their courtship she seemed much more interested in adding to his comfort and showing appreciation for the time he spent with her. Now he perceives her as more demanding of his time and attention. He wonders, at times, if marriage—to anyone—is right for him.

Beth, too, is unhappy with the present state of affairs. Before she was married, she had a close circle of friends who met often and did things together. George is adamantly against having people over during the weekday evenings and even on occasional weekends he puts up major blocks to entertaining. Beth is hurt because she knows George would rather be off backpacking by himself than spending a day with her and friends or family.

Being an Extraverted Feeling type, Beth is happiest when she is receiving warm, positive responses from other people, particularly those who mean the most to her. However, she chose to marry an Introverted Thinking type, the type less likely than any other to respond with warm, positive feelings. Expressing appreciation is difficult for George, even when he is feeling the most positive about Beth, and lately he hasn't been feeling all that positive.

Compounding the difficulty is the fact that Beth spends a fair amount of time alone during the day and feels deprived of an interchange of energy (as she actually is) by the end of the day. George gets his interaction needs met during the day and feels deprived (as he actually is) of solitude and privacy in the evening.

There is only a very small area of overlap in which both Beth and George experience a state of well-being. As unlikely as it may appear, it is possible for such a couple to work out a relationship that can satisfy both partners, and this did happen for Beth and George. Their success, however, took a great deal of work, mutual understanding, and compromise. In general, the greater the difference in type, the greater the adjustment each partner will have to make if the relationship is to grow. It is also true that the work and understanding that goes into making such a relationship grow can result in exciting degrees of individual development for each of the two people involved in the relationship.

What we did with Beth was to help her to realize that George would probably never be able or willing to satisfy all her needs. Faced with the choice of finding some satisfaction elsewhere, she decided to get involved with a volunteer agency whose values closely matched hers. She preferred this to returning to her job. As a volunteer, she met many interesting, exciting people, and she came home feeling worthwhile and appreciated, and was more willing to give George the space he needed.

We helped George become aware of Beth's needs while respecting his own. Visualizing himself as an old man living alone helped him to remember why he married Beth in the first place. Although he still takes time when he first gets home to read a journal or watch television, by dinner time he is ready either to share something that happened at work or listen appreciatively to Beth's discussion of her exciting day.

CASE STUDY 2: **Introverted Feeling Types Together**

An Introverted Feeling type, Alicia is an artist who does very sensitive work but has not been publicly recognized yet. Lee, also an Introverted Feeling type, is a psychiatrist, successful in the community, and Alicia often compares her success with his. Lee has recently encouraged her to work with him doing art therapy with a group of youngsters he is seeing professionally. Alicia is considering this proposal but is somewhat concerned about losing her sense of identity in Lee's if she does work with him.

Because of their shared type preferences and values, their relationship is a very comfortable one, and they provide each other a high level of security. Their home serves as a retreat from the world, and they have a small circle of intimate friends they see occasionally. The danger for this couple is that they may encourage each other in a very one-sided view of the world and that neither is likely to learn new skills from the other.

What initially looks like a very satisfying relationship will need work, too, if it is to continue to grow. Since Lee is already out in public to some extent, he may have to be the one to work first on developing Extraverted skills. He may also have to be the one to further develop his Thinking function, a process undoubtedly already begun in medical school. Someone—Lee, Alicia, or both—will have to decide on what investments to make, whether or not to purchase a home, and other decisions which call for the kind of objective analysis associated with the Thinking function. As Lee moves further out into the world, possibly taking more of a leadership role in professional societies or community affairs, Alicia may initially feel some resistance to the process. She may then decide to continue her own growth and develop more of her own skills. If this occurs, Lee, Alicia, and their relationship can develop in meaningful ways.

For this couple, as for all couples, as the partners develop new skills—that is, as they move toward individuation—they bring more choice to their lives and develop greater self-confidence. Although their natural preferences remain intact, movement back and forth into other domains becomes easier, and the movement itself may increase existing levels of energy within each individual or between the partners.

Sharing type information with the couples you are counseling often helps them to look at their interactions more objectively, to understand rather than to exclusively feel or think about their own frustrations or unhappiness. Becoming aware that one can learn to be comfortable in a variety of situations can provide motivation for developing new skills.

Sometimes it is enough to work with the very obvious differences causing problems in a relationship, always being aware, however, of whole-type dynamics as they may play out between partners. Many clients are more comfortable when the counselor describes rather than labels behaviors; labels such as "Thinking" or "Feeling" may make clients feel or think, "this is just jargon." If as a counselor you have some skill in the methods of role-play, you can show what each partner might say in an argument. This gives each partner a real sense that the counselor has genuine understanding of "where they're coming from."

Once you listen carefully to a couple, you'll get a general idea of the main areas of conflict. If you hear the terms "too organized" or "disorganized" a lot, you might focus on the Judging–Perceiving preferences first. If a couple's complaints center on social life or lack of privacy, you might focus on Extraversion–Introversion for a while. If they often disagree and have difficulty understanding one another's points of view, the Sensing–Intuition preferences may need some attention. If one wants things done "right" and the other wants harmony, Thinking–Feeling may need to be the initial focus. From these starting points, you can move into whole type, again using a descriptive and dynamic mode of presentation rather than the specialized language of type.

4

Relating Client Type to Counseling Approaches

"We should try to find, in a change of attitude or in new ways of life, that difference of potential which the pent-up energy requires."

C. G. Jung, *Modern Man in Search of a Soul*

(Whether you work exclusively with couples or mix your practice as we do by also doing individual therapy, you may find the following type-based observations and approaches helpful.)

Extraverted Thinking Clients (ESTJ, ENTJ)

- If they can see the logic in what you're saying, Extraverted Thinking types will put energy into changing their environment.
- Be forceful and direct—a tentative approach will never reach them.
- Extraverted Thinking types will probably challenge and confront you until you prove your authority, perhaps by presenting a perspective, insight, or reality that has never before occurred to them.
- Transactional analysis and rational emotive therapy may appeal more to them, but Rogerian (non-directive) counseling is likely to effect greater change. You can reach them through their heads, but need a more total response for permanent change.

- Extraverted Thinking types may spend time sparring with you instead of hearing what you have to say. Try not to engage them in duels, even if you enjoy duels yourself. Stay aware of what pulls you off course.
- The more objective, "scientific" data you can give these types (test scores, norms, statistics), the less resistant they are likely to be.

EXTRAVERTED FEELING CLIENTS (ESFJ, ENFJ)

- Extraverted Feeling types may be easy to move because they'll probably want to please you. Teach them to work through their feelings before approaching a Thinking partner.
- They may surprise you by moving abruptly between emotional registers. A client who is overwhelmingly in love one day, for example, may assume a mercenary attitude ("let me see what I can get out of this relationship financially") the next.
- When an Extraverted Feeling type client is married to a Thinking type, involve the Thinking type in a schedule of giving their partner strokes or compliments at least once or twice a day.
- Encourage Extraverted Feeling type clients to form support groups. They typically respond well to group therapy.
- Extraverted Feeling types are sensitive to even implied criticism but thrive on appreciation.
- They may have devoted much of their lives to a partner's career, and a divorce, though painful, may force them into growth and the development of their other functions along with a greater sense of their own identity.

EXTRAVERTED SENSING CLIENTS (ESTP, ESFP)

- Extraverted Sensing types are less likely than other types to enter therapy.
- When they do seek therapy, it may be to find practical solutions to practical problems.
- Extraverted Sensing types are likely to be late for appointments or sometimes forget to come.
- Gestalt therapy and dance or music therapy may appeal to their need for action.
- Extraverted Sensing types may respond "off the tops of their heads" to your statements. Encourage them to process before responding.
- Extraverted Sensing types live in the moment. Encourage them to think more of the long term.
- The discipline of homework may be good for them if you can overcome their resistance and make assignments fun!

EXTRAVERTED INTUITIVE CLIENTS (ENTP, ENFP)

- Extraverted Intuitive types are unlikely to appreciate a partner's need for order or structure and may evade or "forget" negotiations in that area.
- With charm and persuasion, this type is generally able to make the environment work so well for them that they may never have learned to conform or adjust to anyone else's needs. Help them see the payoffs of some conformity and the negatives of little or none.
- Extraverted Intuitive types may expect your help in convincing the partner that nothing's really wrong and that his or her requests are unreasonable.
- Remain unpredictable yourself; let therapy take unexpected turns so that Extraverted Intuitive types don't get bored and terminate therapy prematurely.
- Keep one step ahead of them; they'll be intuiting you while you're intuiting them.

- The discipline of homework assignments may be good for them if you can overcome their resistance or engage their enthusiasm.
- Extraverted Intuitive types seek new challenges; help them make personal growth one of them.
- They can be outrageous; help them use that quality to help themselves.

Introverted Feeling Clients (ISFP, INFP)

- Introverted Feeling types tend to personalize statements that could possibly be interpreted as negative and be sure they are in the wrong.
- When their values are supported, Introverted Feeling types thrive.
- They can learn to be assertive with their partner or other people through role playing.
- Introverted Feeling types respond well to MBTI® assessment and interpretation, to Rogerian (non-directive) techniques, and to art therapy.
- This type asks perfection of a partner, as well as of themselves; appeal to them through their sense of humor to tone down their perfectionism.
- In addition to affection, offer Introverted Feeling types techniques for dealing with their environment.

Introverted Thinking Clients (ISTP, INTP)

- Introverted Thinking types create systems to live by that aren't easily adaptable. Try to form bridges between your system and theirs, or you'll have no impact. You can't just pull them into an unfamiliar system.
- This type may need to be taught the logical benefits of giving positive strokes to others, especially their partners.

- Encourage Introverted Thinking types to pay more attention to what matters to others.
- Rational emotive therapy and transactional analysis may appeal to their logic; you can start there and slowly move them to access more feeling.
- Just because they're often skillful in professional areas, don't assume Introverted Thinking types know much about making relationships work.
- Therapists who prefer Intuition, Feeling, and Perceiving may experience difficulty in motivating these clients unless they or their relationships are in a state of crisis.

INTROVERTED SENSING CLIENTS (ISTJ, ISFJ)

- Introverted Sensing types will listen carefully as long as you don't get too theoretical.
- They may be difficult to move out of traditional concepts and roles.
- Transactional analysis and behavior modification techniques usually make "sense" to Introverted Sensing types.
- Allow sufficient time for Introverted Sensing clients to process and respond; don't fill in the silences.
- If you give them enough data and they have confidence in your ability, they'll put energy into changing themselves.
- When this type discovers that an adaptation is really important to a partner, they'll put energy into changing themselves.
- Introverted Sensing types often look calm even when they're upset.
- You may need to help Introverted Sensing types find the words to express their special reactions.

INTROVERTED INTUITIVE CLIENTS (INTJ, INFJ)

- Introverted Intuitive types are very individualistic, so you had better be patient while anticipating change. Once they commit to change, however, they typically follow through.
- If you can "hit" one of their deep places, they will respond in depth.
- There are relatively few Introverted Intuitive types among all the types, so they can really have trouble finding kindred spirits.
- If what is important to their partner is consistent with their own value system, Introverted Intuitive types will put a great deal of energy into changing themselves.
- These types respond well to Jungian analysis, dream interpretation, eclectic therapy, exploration of psychic or spiritual matters (especially Feeling types), or types of therapy that capture their imagination.
- Don't bore this type with facts or details; if they buy your concept, they will follow through on the necessary facts and details themselves.
- Introverted Intuitive types are unlikely to become dependent on you.
- Be creative; Intuitive types hate to be bored.
- Of all the types, Introverted Intuitive types generally have more access to and draw on the unconscious mind. So helping them do conscious reality testing can be important for them if it can be made palatable.
- Higher education in the humanities, arts, or sciences can lead them to find the meaning they seek in their lives.

A Note of Caution

Just one final note of caution: Monitor yourself as well as your clients. Have you worked through the limitations that come with being the type you are? If you cannot accept some of your own limitations, are you also unable to accept them in your clients? If you're working with a couple, do you tend to identify with the individual who shares your preferences, becoming biased in his or her favor? Or do you strive to see how each type has unique gifts to contribute to a relationship?

5
The Types in the World and in Love

"Understanding, appreciation, and respect make a lifelong marriage possible and good. Similarity of type is not important, except as it leads to these three. Without them people fall in love and out of love again; with them a man and a woman will become increasingly valuable to each other and know that they are contributing to each other's lives. They consciously in the world value each other more and know they are valued in return. Each walks taller in the world than would be thinkable alone."

Isabel Briggs Myers, *Gifts Differing*

Know Your Client's Life and Love Types

It is helpful to know the personality types of your clients. Then you have a handle on what their relationship is and what it can be. We may be asking for a little more awareness than is comfortable for you right now, but after a while discerning clients' types will be a habit and you won't have to think about it. Paying attention to the types in a relationship will pay off in more rewarding sessions.

Now we want to go further on our journey with Carl Jung, Isabel Myers, and Katharine Briggs. Recall for a moment that the Myers-Briggs

Type Indicator® personality inventory describes four dichotomies, each made up of a pair of opposite preferences: Extraversion-Introversion, Sensing-Intuition, Thinking-Feeling, and Judging-Perceiving. Altogether these preferences can be combined in sixteen possible ways. A list of the Jungian dominant types and the corresponding MBTI type codes are provided in table 5.1. In this chapter, we are going to present preference pairs, so that we wind up with eight combinations for each of the attitudes, Introversion and Extraversion (sixteen combinations in total).

TABLE 5.1

Type Designations

JUNGIAN TYPES	MBTI TYPES
Extraverted Thinking	(ESTJ, ENTJ)
Extraverted Sensing	(ESTP, ESFP)
Extraverted Feeling	(ESFJ, ENFJ)
Extraverted Intuition	(ENTP, ENFP)
Introverted Sensing	(ISTJ, ISFJ)
Introverted Feeling	(ISFP, INFP)
Introverted Intuition	(INTJ, INFJ)
Introverted Thinking	(ISTP, INTP)

Now let's proceed on our journey of the types. We'll start with the Extraverted Thinking types.

EXTRAVERTED THINKING TYPE

ESTJ

EXTRAVERTED – SENSING – THINKING – JUDGING

Being or living with an ESTJ

ESTJs tend to

- want to be in charge of the relationship
- be practical and realistic in making decisions
- be more authoritative and possibly less sensitive to a partner's needs
- want to be responsible and provide stability in the relationship
- see a need for romance as unrealistic (though they will give gifts—usually practical ones: a plant rather than a bouquet of flowers)
- believe sexual fantasies are unimportant and take the sexual act seriously, as an important experience
- be faithful to their partners and the commitment of marriage
- expect sex as a way of making peace, regarding it as separate from and unconnected to an argument
- see it as their duty to tell their partner or children what to do
- know what is right for their children and expect children to live up to their standards
- expect their partner and children to participate in community affairs
- unfairly place their anger on those most dear to them

In their partner or children, ESTJs value

- conformity
- demonstrations of respect
- cooperation
- lack of emotionality
- punctuality
- warmth
- appreciation for who they are

EXTRAVERTED THINKING TYPE

ENTJ

EXTRAVERTED – INTUITIVE – THINKING – JUDGING

Being or Living with an ENTJ

ENTJs tend to

- express most of the overt power in the relationship
- display a great deal of self-confidence
- articulate about what they want from their partner
- provide excitement in the relationship
- distrust compliments and seldom pay them
- believe sexuality is important—either as an expression of love or as a release from tension
- see discord over intellectual or philosophical issues as enjoyable mental games
- remain committed and loyal in a long-term relationship
- expect children to comply and to show self-discipline and motivation
- be surprised to learn that some of their statements have deeply wounded their partner or children (they intend to be just, honest, and logical—not cruel)
- strongly dislike what they consider inefficiency in a partner and children and are vocal in their attempts to reshape such behavior

In their partner or children, ENTJs value

- intelligent behavior
- cooperation
- competency
- demonstrations of respect
- warmth
- self-esteem
- appreciation for who they are

Extraverted Sensing Type

ESTP

Extraverted – Sensing – Thinking – Perceiving

Being or Living with an ESTP

ESTPs tend to

- love the excitement of risk-taking—physically, financially, emotionally
- be confident of being able to charm others
- be socially sophisticated (party-goers)
- can be skilled in manipulating a partner and getting their own way
- dislike being bored or locked into routines
- start projects but leave them for a partner to finish
- like and collect "toys"
- dislike being "fenced in" by a partner
- have a difficult time apologizing
- live in the "here and now"
- make a lot of money or possibly lose a lot of money (finances may be on a see-saw)
- be realistic, not idealistic
- enjoy sexual experimentation (sex in itself is very important)
- may be sexually impulsive and then have to be creative to get uninvolved
- bring unexpected guests home for dinner (fine if the partner is also an ESP type)
- generally treat children as equals and are not unduly worried about their upbringing

In their partner or children, ESTPs value

- experimentation
- follow-through
- playfulness
- a willingness to stay out of, or at least share, the limelight
- self-reliance
- appreciation for who they are

EXTRAVERTED SENSING TYPE

ESFP

EXTRAVERTED – SENSING – FEELING – PERCEIVING

Being or Living with an ESFP

ESFPs tend to

- make any party a successful party
- have no difficulty attracting lots of dates and probably do the choosing in selection of a partner
- be stimulated by food, wine, clothes, travel, et cetera
- be both realistic and spontaneous
- need positive feedback from their significant others
- be warm and loving without expecting much in return
- are sexually responsive and playful
- expend a lot of energy to avoid being bored
- be sensuous in addition to being sexual
- enjoy sharing the limelight–as well as being in it
- want romance to have an immediate concrete payoff (Romeo and Juliet were not this type)
- have a home that will look "lived in" but tasteful
- delight in allowing each member of the household to do whatever he or she feels like doing

In their partner or children, ESFPs value

- sociability
- nonjudgment
- emotionality
- optimism
- spontaneity
- appreciation for who they are

Extraverted Feeling Type

ESFJ

Extraverted – Sensing – Feeling – Judging

Being or Living with an ESFJ

ESFJs tend to

- be loving and warm-hearted
- clearly articulate their own values and what they believe is best for the family
- put a great deal of effort into maintaining harmony in the home
- want a home that is well furnished and well maintained
- dislike being criticized or given negative feedback
- care about the rituals and traditions associated with holidays
- be concerned about community affairs and want their partner to be similarly interested
- want a lot of interaction with a lot of people
- maintain stable relationships, especially with a partner
- want praise and appreciation, returning both freely
- be uninterested in experimenting sexually
- desire and love children, who will be given a sense of family history and taught the "right way" to do things

In their partner or children, ESFJs value

- conformity
- loyalty
- predictability
- responsibility
- warm communication
- appreciation for who they are

Extraverted Feeling Type

ENFJ

Extraverted – Intuitive – Feeling – Judging

Being or Living with an ENFJ

ENFJs tend to

- be considerate and loving
- communicate easily and well
- be natural leaders of people
- believe love is more important than power
- be charming and have a wide circle of friends
- be easily hurt by lack of appreciation or feeling ignored
- show enthusiasm and inspire their partner and children into experimenting with new ideas or ways of doing things
- be turned off by sex if it doesn't include romance
- show sensitivity, support, and understanding with family members
- be affectionate and expressive with words and gestures
- move out of a relationship with remarkable facility once they've decided it's over
- give freely but resist emotional demands
- vigorously support their children, sometimes to the detriment of the child's growth
- have difficulty disciplining children or feel terribly guilty afterwards (e.g., they may overreact to the notion of injuring a child's self-esteem)

In their partner or children, ENFJs value

- harmony
- closeness
- authenticity
- imagination
- happiness
- appreciation for who they are

Extraverted Intuitive Type

ENTP

Extraverted – Intuitive – Thinking – Perceiving

Being or Living with an ENTP

ENTPs tend to

- be stimulating and ingenious
- dislike dull routine and manage to delegate it to others—a partner if he or she is willing to pick it up
- take any side of an argument for the joy of debating (this can dismay the partner who deeply values harmony)
- need lots of appreciation and admiration from a partner and children
- focus on the future rather than the here and now (and because the future appears to stretch on so endlessly, ENTPs may take on more than they can handle)
- choose relationships with the head more than the heart, moving out of them fairly easily (or so it seems to other types) when they don't work
- set their own standards for sexual behavior
- be willing to study means and methods of arousing a partner sexually
- be willing to use sex occasionally as a release from tension, though generally preferring that it hold more meaning
- want a partner to be at their own level intellectually
- care more about acquiring knowledge than money
- show inconsistency in giving time, energy, discipline, and attention to their children

In their partner or children, ENTPs value

- independence
- adaptability
- competence
- success
- quickness of wit
- appreciation for who they are

Extraverted Intuitive Type

ENFP

Extraverted – Intuitive – Feeling – Perceiving

Being or Living with an ENFP

ENFPs tend to

- be excellent at communicating and require communication from their partner
- be emotional
- have enough energy for themselves and a partner
- enjoy romance—in every sense of the word
- truly appreciate a partner's accomplishments and communicate that appreciation warmly, with all the right words
- search constantly for the meaning in life
- seem like mind readers to a partner, who will feel unable to hide anything
- feel it important that everyone in the family take care of everyone else in the family
- make a partner the center of attention during the courtship process
- may feel deeply disappointed if the real partner doesn't match their fantasy
- search for the perfect relationship
- show affection both verbally and physically to their partner and children
- include romance and sexual fantasies in the sexual act
- be overprotective of children
- be unpredictable in disciplining children, shifting from threatened punishment to loving understanding

In their partner or children, ENFPs value

- motivation
- originality
- imagination
- communication
- follow-through
- appreciation for who they are

Introverted Sensing Type

ISTJ

Introverted – Sensing – Thinking – Judging

Being or Living with an ISTJ

ISTJs tend to

- take responsibility for a task they undertake and expect a partner to do the same
- believe it's their duty to tell a partner and children what to do and how to do it
- make decisions based on practicality
- prefer recreation when it has a practical purpose (such as maintaining a healthy body or learning something)
- want to be secure financially, but may never feel secure enough
- keep a tight rein on children and expect to be obeyed and respected
- participate actively in community affairs
- be faithful to their marriage vows
- want their home and furnishings to be practical and conventional
- be attracted to an opposite type whom they may try to "reform"
- willingly shoulder a larger share of tasks, obligations, and projects
- forgive a partner if the partner is sufficiently repentant
- pay more attention to work than to a partner
- view sex as one of the rituals of marriage, take it seriously, and be appreciative of a partner's cooperation
- be conservative rather than experimental about how, where, and when sex is to happen
- take comfort in familiar patterns (keeping the same friends, eating at the same restaurants) and may find it difficult to relate to a partner's observation that such patterns can become boring

In their partner or children, ISTJs value

- community mindedness
- morality
- punctuality
- productivity
- thriftiness
- decisiveness
- appreciation for who they are

Introverted Sensing Type

ISFJ

Introverted – Sensing – Feeling – Judging

Being or Living with an ISFJ

ISFJs tend to

- cooperate to the utmost
- have less need to be in control of a relationship
- have a wry sense of humor that pops out unexpectedly
- desire a church affiliation or some kind of traditional religious values
- be the worrier in the family
- expect respect from children and may be dismayed by a child who doesn't want to conform
- maintain a well-ordered home with everything in place
- be devoted and loyal to a partner
- be agreeable to undertaking the chores related to house and yard: cooking, cleaning, decorating, gardening, mowing the lawn, maintaining the car
- feel unappreciated
- see sex as a necessary part of a love relationship
- be unlikely to do much sexual experimentation as to where, how, or when
- foster family rituals and traditions and create a sense of family history for partner and children
- find life interesting and are typically not easily bored
- be slow to speak up about things that bother them

In their partner or children, ISFJs value

- thoughtfulness
- adherence to tradition
- religiosity
- responsibility
- practicality
- appreciation for who they are

Introverted Feeling Type

ISFP

Introverted – Sensing – Feeling – Perceiving

Being or Living with an ISFP

ISFPs tend to

- be "private" people
- like nature, sports, and animals
- have a great degree of sympathy for others
- want to please a partner and children
- be pleasure oriented in an idealistic kind of way—never at the expense of others
- dislike routine except those that are self-imposed
- have the five senses well developed and be sensitive to sound, touch, taste, color, and form
- resist conforming to rules and regulations and may be unlikely to impose them on a partner or children
- have special affinity for and ability to understand animals and small children
- have difficulty communicating verbally
- have some difficulty choosing a career
- be very responsive to different forms of sexual stimulation that appeal to the five senses
- demonstrate a love of nature by filling home with plants and animals
- be impulsive and live in the moment

In their partner or children, ISFPs value

- social skills
- loyalty
- love of nature
- ability to be happy now
- sensuality
- appreciation for who they are

Introverted Feeling Type

INFP

Introverted – Intuitive – Feeling – Perceiving

Being or Living with an INFP

INFPs tend to

- be among the most romantic of all the types and expect high levels of intimacy in a relationship
- desire harmony, dislike conflict, and try to avoid disagreements unless basic values are at stake
- be responsive in a relationship and delight in pleasing
- have a tendency to live more in the world of imagination than in the practical world
- search all their lives for the meaning in life
- become very cynical if they harbor too many disappointments and resentments
- be articulate and want to communicate with a partner at deep, meaningful levels
- need a room of their own into which to retreat and regroup their energies
- find romance and anticipation of the sexual act important
- be naturally elusive in a relationship, which may keep a partner pursuing them
- extend charm and graciousness to those they choose to invite into their home
- have a tendency to support children against everyone else

In their partner or children, INFPs value

- creativity
- honor and ethics
- real-world skills
- a need for harmony
- self-esteem
- appreciation for who they are

Introverted Thinking Type

ISTP

Introverted – Sensing – Thinking – Perceiving

Being or Living with an ISTP

ISTPs tend to

- be adventurous in their choice of sports and hobbies
- observe life coolly, privately
- react spontaneously to present-day situations
- have a wry, unusual sense of humor
- show skill at how mechanical things work and how to fix them
- appear uncommunicative to a partner
- want to be right more than they want to please
- be unlikely to change for a relationship, but may try to convince a partner to change
- respond to overt sexual stimulation rather than abstractions or romance
- dislike feeling trapped or bound by a partner's emotional responses
- have plenty of activities going on, some of which may carry risk
- be generous with their partner and children
- have difficulty choosing appropriate relationships

In their partner or children, ISTPs value

- flexibility
- lack of emotionality
- love of adventure
- self-sufficiency
- appreciation for who they are

INTROVERTED THINKING TYPE

INTP

INTROVERTED – INTUITIVE – THINKING – PERCEIVING

Being or Living with an INTP

INTPs tend to

- be unlikely to use frequent or profuse terms of endearment
- be dogmatic, so strong is their faith in their own view
- want to be seen as competent and want to be respected for their competence
- approach all issues intellectually
- feel that nobody understands them–and this may be true
- appear cold or uncaring
- be private people, even within relationships
- expect children to accept the consequences of their behavior and choices
- not follow through on a project once they've intellectually solved its problems
- limit participation in community activities and projects
- show caution in managing finances
- find sexual contact more meaningful than recreational, though this may not be apparent to a partner
- not enjoy sex preceded by emotional conflict
- have little tolerance for their own mistakes

In their partner or children, INTPs value

- ingenuity
- competence
- independence
- intelligence
- complexity
- logic
- appreciation for who they are

Introverted Intuitive Type

INTJ

Introverted – Intuitive – Thinking – Judging

Being or Living with an INTJ

INTJs tend to

- be quietly stubborn or persistent
- show a high degree of self-confidence
- want to get things decided quickly and make decisions easily
- enjoy challenges and respond to them creatively
- be seen as a "general" by those in intimate relationships with them
- drive their partner and children as hard as they drive themselves
- appear difficult to satisfy to a partner and children
- be difficult to read
- be sensitive to rejection, though no one may know that
- show genuine devotion to a partner and children
- be independent and value independence in a partner and children
- expect perfection from themselves at work or at play
- want to be asked for advice rather than impose it on others
- insist on logic and reason as the basis for accepting a partner's point of view
- show fairness and expect it in return (but if they feel unfairly treated by a partner, INTJs may be angry for long periods of time)
- help their partner and children develop their full capabilities
- be skillful and competent lovers
- appear cold and demanding at times

In their partner or children, INTJs value

- intelligence
- competence
- achievement
- ingenuity
- complexity
- appreciation for who they are

Introverted Intuitive Type

INFJ

Introverted – Intuitive – Feeling – Judging

Being or Living with an INFJ

INFJs tend to

- want to please others and enjoy and need harmony, but not at the expense of their own integrity
- value achievement as part of their lifestyle—as students, employees, partners, or parents
- need closure so badly that they may push for premature decisions, without seeing the discomfort this can cause a partner
- show affection in their own way and at their own time
- be among the most stubborn of all types—they will keep the door open a long time, be forgiving and compassionate, but when the door closes, that's it
- want the atmosphere to be warm and loving before responding sexually—they enjoy romantic fantasy
- be deeply bonded to their children, even to the point of prioritizing them over the partner
- do everything they do intensely and to the maximum
- need support and recognition from a partner (criticism closes them up, turns them off, and even makes them ill)
- highly prize variety and freedom and may feel confined by standard chores
- dislike being overburdened by too many details and may ignore written instructions
- have a deeply spiritual inner life, which they share with few others and only those they totally trust
- be difficult to challenge when they say they "know"

In their partner or children, INFJs value

- achievement
- intelligence
- complexity
- "real-world" skills
- imagination
- loyalty, spiritual, moral, ethical values
- appreciation for who they are

Closing Thoughts

Most of the qualities we value or desire in a partner are qualities we already possess. Often however, at least when we are young, it is not unusual to fall in love with and marry our opposites, that is, individuals different in two or three preferences and, therefore, possessing qualities quite different from our own. Then, when the honeymoon glow is over, we experience disappointment or resentment and may even attempt to redo our partners in our own images.

All of the types have valuable perspectives and strengths. Understanding and accepting a partner's and one's own needs and contributions to a relationship—especially when those needs and contributions differ—enriches each partner's life and helps them develop the undeveloped facets of their own personalities. Having a partner who is supportive of one's professional and personal growth is far more valuable than a relationship with a replica of oneself.

Part Two

6

The Types in Interaction: Extraverts with Extraverts

"Whether people first hear about the two kinds of perception and two kinds of judgment as children, high school students, parents, or grandparents, the richer development of their own type can be a rewarding adventure for the rest of their lives."

- Isabel Myers -

What Type Is the Best Type for Me?

Clients often ask us, "What type should I be looking for?" or "What type should I have married?" or "Who would be my ideal partner?" We generally respond to such questions by letting clients know that there is no "best" type for anyone. Regardless of the kinds of excitement, comfort, joy, and/or problems we may encounter with whatever "type" of person we choose, every relationship has the potential to be deeply satisfying.

We now would like to provide you with some perspectives on the possible interactions, briefly describing the kinds of interactions that ensue when a relationship is working and when it isn't. You can help clients who are married or involved in serious relationships to use this information to find the type combination that best represents the relationship and to assess whether or not they are constructively using their differences and similarities to make their relationship as satisfying as possible. Remember, too, that each of your clients brings his or her personal history to the relationship—including interactions with parents, siblings, and friends—and that this and other factors will contribute to the uniqueness of each and every relationship.

In this chapter and the next two, we indicate some of the advantages and disadvantages associated with any pairing of types. It is very important that clients be aware that through their self-awareness, mutual respect, and acceptance of differences, any pairing can create a satisfying and mutually rewarding relationship.

In deference to the greater number of Extraverts in the United States, we begin with Extraverted pairings in this chapter, continue with Introverted pairings in chapter 7, and end with Extraverted-Introverted pairings in chapter 8. Please also note that the publisher, Center for Applications of Psychological Type, has available electronic reports for couples based on the content of this book. Visit www.capt.org for more information.

Extraverted Thinking Types (ESTJ/ENTJ) Together

When it's working: Both individuals are likely to be achievers, with high standards for themselves and each other, and are likely to respect each other's accomplishments. They typically will meet each other's needs for punctuality, organization, and a sense of order; desire and be involved with social contacts; and enjoy intellectual discussions, though their points of view may differ. The partners may even view each other as allies confronting life on separate battlefields. If either or both are ESTJs, they are especially likely to be conservative, community-oriented, and stable members of society.

In lieu of evidence to the contrary, it is our impression that this pairing is more rare. There were no such pairings in our research study, and neither of us has encountered them in either of our personal or professional lives. Possibly one reason for this is that opposite types are often attracted to each other: Extraverted Thinking types are perhaps looking for Introverted mates who will listen to them or for Feeling types who will provide the warmth, encouragement, and appreciation that they may have not yet learned to express for either themselves or others.

When it's not working: When two Extraverted Thinking types disagree on either a perception or a decision, there is the potential for explosions (usually verbal) with neither party being willing to concede or mediate. Both individuals are likely to crave the limelight, and resentments may grow if they can't share it equally.

An Extraverted Thinking type woman may be more interested in her career than in her home and children (though both would tend to be well organized). A man who has fixed ideas of how a woman "should" act, may grow angry and resentful over what he regards as her competition with his role and may express himself both freely and frequently with pointed jibes and criticisms.

If the children born to this couple are also Thinking-Judging (TJ) types, they may cope quite well with the standards and expectations of their parents. However, children who prefer Introverted Feeling (INFP or ISFP), may require more encouragement, warmth, support, and understanding than either parent is easily able to provide.

Some Helpful Hints

Any relationship can work if both people want it to and are willing to make the necessary effort. Encourage your clients to remember what attracted them to each other in the first place, and urge them to discover if it is still there. This won't work, however, if only one person wants the relationship to continue and the other does not. The constructive use of the same personality style for two ETJs might involve their appreciating each other's logical and organizational abilities—how smoothly they plan and accomplish their goals. They should set a time and place for expressing positive evaluations of each other and their accomplishments. Although it's hard for ETJs to express appreciation, they do need to receive it. Neither is naturally good at applying the emotional glue in a relationship.

The most helpful thing outside of work for ETJs is to have a source for tenderness, warmth, and appreciation, as feeling is their least accessible function. They can handle a lot of other things very well, but without this resource, they may get stuck in a pattern of negative evaluations and emotions. ETJs' learning to make a mental note to focus on the positive aspects of the relationship and to express them will be a gift to each partner. The partners can achieve more balance and harmony this way. Statements such as "It was great to see you pull off that business deal" or "You have such a flair for high-level performance"—statements like these convey warmth and appreciation, even if it's difficult for either ETJ to say "I love you."

Extraverted Thinking Types (ESTJ/ENTJ) with Extraverted Feeling Types (ESFJ/ENFJ)

When it's working: In this fairly common pairing, both individuals tend to be communicative and enjoy interactions with others, community minded, and somewhat traditional and conservative (the SJs perhaps more than the NJs). If the man is the Feeling type and the woman the Thinking type, traditional parenting roles with the children may be reversed.

When it's not working: If the woman is the Extraverted Feeling type (and this is likely to be the case considering the lower percentage of males to females who prefer Feeling), she is likely to desire and, at times, even demand a great deal of interaction with and attention from her partner. If most of his energy is going into his career, he may be unlikely to respond to her needs; consider them inappropriate and unessential; and respond to her tears, anger, or overtures with logical reasoning or anger. Neither response will satisfy her and may result in an emotional separation within the relationship. The woman may then pour a lot of her energy into the children, her own career, community efforts, or perhaps into a relationship with another man (or men in a series of relationships). The man may seek solace with another "more understanding" woman while still maintaining the formal marriage contract or relationship.

If the man is the Extraverted Feeling type, the woman's career and success may instigate jealousy and competition if he is not as successful or secure in his own life path. Extraverted Thinking types benefit by developing the ability to show sensitivity in relationships. Since direct knowledge of feelings is difficult for Thinking types, information gathered through the opposite functions of Sensing or Intuition can enhance ETJs' sensitivity. Thinking type women may have a more difficult time in relationships than Thinking type men because of the cultural expectation that women are naturally warm and empathic. If this marriage results in divorce, relatives and friends are apt to be more supportive of and sympathetic toward the husband, who may feel that his wife "put her career first."

Some Helpful Hints

Difficulties in an ETJ-EFJ relationship may be overcome if the partners can appreciate why they may have gotten together in the first place: to benefit from the combination of logical thinking, sensitivity, and responsiveness. Once mutual appreciation is re-established, each partner may eventually learn, through the other's example and support, how to be both logical and sensitive—for their own and their partner's sake. Ultimately, the partners can complement each other through their opposite Thinking and Feeling functions. At first, though, since the least accessible function for a Feeling type is Thinking and for a Thinking type, Feeling, the partners can easily misunderstand each other's needs and ways of communicating. Thinking types usually need to understand issues, while Feeling types need heartfelt responses when problems arise. If each can learn to ask for what he or she needs in a way that doesn't alienate the other, the partners will have come a long way toward resolving their conflicts. Encourage the partners to use positive "I need" statements rather than negative "You didn't" statements. For example: "I need a hug" (EFJ) and an ETJ's, "I really appreciate your being there for me," can help the couple get through some hard times.

EXTRAVERTED THINKING TYPES (ESTJ/ENTJ) WITH EXTRAVERTED SENSING TYPES (ESTP/ESFP)

When it's working: If ETJ and ESP types happen to get together and if they can cultivate a great deal of mutual respect, each partner will learn from the other and experience significant personal growth. Since both types tend to be verbal and outgoing, both will express opinions freely. The Extraverted Thinking type will espouse discipline and commitment; the Extraverted Sensing type will espouse tolerance and fun. Both will benefit from a balance of these two sets of values, as will children brought up in the ETJ-ESP household.

When it's not working: If mutual respect is lacking, frequent battles may erupt as a result of Extraverted Thinking types' need to control and shape up what they may regard as an "immature, acting-out, unpredictable" partner. Extraverted Sensing types, in turn, will not be controlled or shaped up and will find in such a partner's reformism more reason for staying away from home, for indulging in risk-taking behavior, and for not following through on "assigned" chores and responsibilities. Mutual frustrations will increase and–if in addition to this basic ETJ-ESP conflict, a couple of rebellious teenage children are added to the picture–alliances will form between them and the Extraverted Sensing type parent. The Extraverted Thinking type parent may even come to be seen as "the enemy."

Some Helpful Hints

Such difficulties can be overcome if the Extraverted Sensing type can learn to appreciate the ETJ partner's logic and if the Extraverted Thinking type can learn to appreciate the ESP partner's practical approach to solving problems. Extraverted Thinking types can benefit from more humor; Extraverted Sensing types can benefit from greater recognition that actions have consequences. Each can add to the other's repertoire of behaviors. Growth for both partners can be achieved by complementing the other's style and at the same time learning from it. ESP types can learn to be more organized, and ETJ types can learn to loosen up. An ESP's, "Come on, let's drop everything and go away for the weekend" or an ETJ's, "I read about this great restaurant, let's make a reservation for Saturday" exemplify a couple of the ways these types can take care of each other. If one partner is an ENTJ, the Intuitive preference will influence that type's inclination toward open options and possibilities rather than the facts preferred by Sensing types. Factual people may seem mundane to Intuitive types; creative people may seem to fly around too much to Sensing types. But each has something valuable to offer the other.

Extraverted Thinking Types (ESTJ/ENTJ) with Extraverted Intuitive Types (ENTP/ENFP)

When it's working: Communication and understanding between an Extraverted Thinking type and an Extraverted Intuitive type will doubtless be easier when the ETJ type also has a preference for Intuition because they may be more likely to follow each other's thought patterns. When the Extraverted Thinking type also has a Sensing preference, communication may be more difficult, although the Sensing function of an ESTJ may help balance the relationship by enabling that partner to follow through with details and practical matters that might otherwise fall through the cracks.

Relationships between Extraverted Thinking and Extraverted Intuitive types often hold a great deal of excitement. Like ESP types, the ENP types tend to keep things stirred up and moving, and the Extraverted Thinking type will not be averse to lively debates, interactions, and involvements. If anyone can "handle" an Extraverted Thinking type, it's probably the Extraverted Intuitive type, who can influence, charm, and persuade with the greatest of ease. In return, the Extraverted Intuitive type is likely to benefit from the stability, organization, and discipline that the Extraverted Thinking type is apt to contribute to the relationship.

When it's not working: Both Extraverted Thinking types and Extraverted Intuitive types, regardless of gender, tend to be "power types" and are used to getting their own way (although the Extraverted Intuitive may be somewhat more subtle about it). Moreover, Extraverted Thinking types often exhibit a strong need to organize people and things in their environment. Extraverted Intuitive types (or any NPs) have a strong need for freedom and are likely to push back, rebel, or escape from attempts at controlling them.

An Extraverted Thinking type is apt to be highly critical of projects left uncompleted, a lack of punctuality, and procrastination, all of which the Extraverted Intuitive type is likely to exhibit and shrug off as unimportant. The home scene may be turbulent. Extraverted Intuitive types may teach children how to get what they want from the Extraverted Thinking type parent, promoting evasion and strategy rather than discipline.

If the Extraverted Intuitive type is an ENFP, the Feeling aspect may modify the conflict to some degree, because of the preference for Feeling types to value harmony. On the other hand, the Extraverted Thinking type may devalue such harmony and see the ENFP as warm hearted but fuzzy headed. If the Extraverted Thinking type is an ESTJ, communication may prove especially difficult, unless the ENP can overcome the tendency to dismiss facts and details brought by the ESTJ to support the logic of a position different from theirs.

It would probably be wise for any type partnering with an Extraverted Thinking type to have his or her personal authority problems already worked out. If such issues are not resolved, the partner of an ETJ may land in the middle of a power struggle that may demand fairly immediate resolution if the relationship is to work. Extraverted Thinkers tend to sound like authorities on whatever topic they espouse.

Some Helpful Hints

Most people with Extraverted Intuition have a strong proclivity for creativity and novelty. In contrast, Extraverted Thinking types specialize in organization. If the Extraverted Thinking type can be creative about organization and the Extraverted Intuitive type more organized about creative solutions, both will be happier in the relationship. The Extraverted Intuitive type can help the Extraverted Thinking type to lighten up. The Extraverted Thinking type can help the Extraverted Intuitive to focus and follow through. Extraverted Thinking types should not make the mistake of thinking they can "shape up" the Extraverted Intuitive. Appreciation of the latter's flair for novelty will get the Extraverted Thinking type a lot further than any structured reform program they might try to implement. For example, ETJs who want a budget will probably need to manage it themselves, with the ENP having some discretionary spending money. An organized approach to recreational or free time—"Let's take every Friday night and go to a different restaurant"—can please both types of partners by combining the order an ETJ can count with freedom of choice and variety of experience an ENP loves.

Extraverted Feeling Types (ESFJ/ENFJ) Together

When it's working: This pairing should result in a loving home atmosphere, with both partners responsive to each other's needs, cherishing harmony and cooperation, enjoying social interaction, and being somewhat traditional in their values. If both are Intuitive types, there will probably be long and frequent conversations about the meaning of life. If both are ESFJs, the focus will probably be more on day-to-day activities and possibly the accumulation of material possessions. In either case, this couple will probably be the center of a social group with similar values, interests, and goals. Their children, no matter what type, will be earnestly cared for, both emotionally and physically.

When it's not working: The paramount challenge for this couple is the inclination to sweep problems under the rug for the sake of harmony. Issues may smolder there until they become explosive. One specific area in which this couple may experience problems is in bed. Sexual attraction is often greater when there are differences, because differences create tension and excitement. This couple may find they are loving companions, but neither has much desire to respond to or to initiate sex.

Other difficulties may arise if the partners have not developed flexibility. For inflexible Feeling type partners locked into differing ideas, values, or goals, their differences can seem to be irreconcilable because neither will be looking for a logical solution. Extraverted Feeling types, when their emotional assessment of a relationship changes, are sometimes able to walk away from a difficult situation with apparently no concern at all for the partner to whom they once had been totally committed.

Some Helpful Hints

Extraverted Feeling types can overcome their difficulties by appreciating what they have in common and by working toward developing their less preferred Thinking function to achieve more balance or find a respected Thinking type who can help. When Feeling types gain the perspective the Thinking function enables, the desired harmony can be achieved and excitement can be kept alive. Conflict can actually enhance a relationship between Extraverted Feeling types, as long as the partners can maintain an underlying respect and appreciation for each other. However, if the partners find themselves fighting all the time, you may need to provide the needed perspective through counseling, guiding them toward new and constructive ways of solving their problems. Help the couple develop a routine that allows for the relaxation and warmth necessary to each partner's being more responsive and responsible. A regular pattern of "together time"—for example, a movie every weekend with time for a snack afterward while someone else takes care of the children—can provide the time and space both need to feel freer and more loving.

Extraverted Feeling Types (ESFJ/ENFJ) with Extraverted Sensing Types (ESTP/ESFP)

When it's working: In this combination, the Extraverted Feeling type will probably bend over backwards to please and accommodate the Extraverted Sensing type partner, for the needs of these two types will probably be very different. The Extraverted Sensing type's tendency to live on the edge may provide just the touch of excitement an Extraverted Feeling type may enjoy. The Extraverted Sensing type will probably also tolerate and accept the Extraverted Feeling type's needs for stability and structure, even though such needs may seem unfathomable to the Extraverted Sensing type.

When it's not working: The risk-taking proclivities of the Extraverted Sensing type will be admired by the Extraverted Feeling type if the risks end in success. If they fail, the Extraverted Feeling type's need for security may be threatened. "Oughts," "shoulds," and "musts" will permeate the discussion, with the Extraverted Sensing type probably turning a deaf ear to all the admonishments. The Extraverted Sensing partner may also feel the need to make frequent moves, disrupting the Extraverted Feeling type's development of a sense of community.

Extraverted Sensing types are less likely than other types to put up with boredom, judgments, or heavy disapproval. If this is all they get at home, they could drift into another relationship. Since they tend to be charming and comfortable with people, Extraverted Sensing types easily can allow themselves to get involved in extramarital affairs.

Some Helpful Hints

These partners can resolve difficulties if their appreciation of each other's gifts can be rekindled. The fun and excitement of the Extraverted Sensing type and the loving responsiveness of the Extraverted Feeling type can add a great deal to a relationship as long as their inner and outer judgments are focused on the positive. Extraverted Feeling types, especially ESFJs, can be great salespeople. Extraverted Sensing types relish experience and are "hands-on" people. Both types love social situations, and the potential for fun in their relationship is great. When the FJ organizes and the SP participates, life can be very enjoyable.

EXTRAVERTED FEELING TYPES (ESFJ/ENFJ) WITH EXTRAVERTED INTUITIVE TYPES (ENTP/ENFP)

When it's working: Excitement, warmth, and enthusiasm may permeate the home of such couples. Friends will probably drift in and out, always feeling welcomed, always finding something interesting going on. The charm, the surprise, the unexpected gifts of the Extraverted Intuitive type may make the Extraverted Feeling type feel loved, which is generally a primary need of this type. In return, there will be expressions of admiration and appreciation, and the Extraverted Intuitive will respond to and bask in these expressions. The Extraverted Feeling type can provide stability for the children; the Extraverted Intuitive type can encourage the curiosity and exploration that stimulates their growth.

When it's not working: Unless the Extraverted Intuitive type has developed some self-discipline, a lack of follow-through may create a great deal of anxiety for the Extraverted Feeling type. The very qualities that originally attracted the Extraverted Feeling type (such as spontaneity and excitement) will pale in the face of what seems like the Extraverted Intuitive's lack of responsibility, e.g., inattention to punctuality; leaving chores unfinished; avoiding discipline of the children; neglecting to adequately consider financing the future; or shrugging off commitments to relatives and friends. Each of these can seriously disrupt a Feeling type's sense of security and well-being. On the other hand, the Extraverted Intuitive's spirit of freedom can possibly be incorporated by the responsible and responsive Extraverted Feeling type into a model of balance, but only if the Extraverted Feeling type partner isn't overly upset by these differences. The Extraverted Intuitive type will come through, but only on his or her own time, not that of the partner's. Whether male or female, an impatient EFJ partner may turn into an emotional, demanding, critical "parent," withholding from the ENP the warmth and support they are capable of supplying.

Some Helpful Hints

Such difficulties can be resolved if each partner brings his or her best qualities to the task: for the Extraverted Feeling type, feeling responsiveness; for the Extraverted Intuitive type, creative energy. To facilitate interaction, EFJ types with a Judging preference may need to work on becoming more flexible, while ENP types with a Perceiving preference will probably need to work toward recognizing how to mesh their interests with the schedules and commitments demanded by the Judging type world most of us live in. Extraverted Intuitive types need variety of experience, and Extraverted Feeling types need a lot of appreciation. If the Extraverted Intuitive will tune in to their partner's world, they are capable of making wonderfully appreciative comments: "Your eyes are like stars. I can see my soul reflected in them." Such compliments can make an EFJ's day. Similarly, an EFJ's planning a safari trip to Africa might be just the thing to delight the ENP partner. Relationships work best when each partner sees the other clearly enough to give the other what he or she wants.

EXTRAVERTED SENSING TYPES (ESTP/ESFP) TOGETHER

When it's working: Extraverted Sensing type partners tend to understand each other's craving for excitement and variety, will tolerate many of the differences that arise between them, may be involved in a great many activities, and may share interests in sports and the great outdoors. There may be a continual turnover in friends, jobs, and homes, but this will be pleasing rather than distressing to both partners. This couple will probably also like to live well, with respect to their own financial status. They can easily move on to the next adventure.

In our experience, ESP type couples rarely come for counseling. Perhaps as an extension of their aversion to sitting still for long periods of time, the idea of regularly sitting down for an hour of introspection in a therapist's office may appear distasteful, even boring. Perhaps, too, they would prefer not to be examined, but rather to be experienced.

When it's not working: The variety and excitement that both enjoy might lead them in opposite directions. Extraverted Sensing types may be more likely than other types to participate in recreational sex and, in general, to do whatever appears available and exciting in the moment. If both partners are out "doing their own things," there will be no one providing a stable home base. Sometimes, what's "sauce for the goose" is not necessarily "sauce for the gander," and feelings of resentment and jealousy may create an atmosphere of tension and anxiety. Moreover, Extraverted Sensing types usually prefer to leave rather than deal with anxiety and tension at home.

For children of the same type as the parents, life can be exciting. But if the children differ in type from their parents, they may need more quiet time, stability, and privacy than is normally available. Such children may not fare as well in the home environment, especially as ESP type parents may not deal well with what they perceive to be maladaptive behavior.

Some Helpful Hints

An ESP couple can get through many of their difficulties as they both have a solid grounding of common sense. If they can focus on living life with a spirit of fun and not mind too much that some priorities aren't always handled on time, they can laugh and love and enjoy. Division of responsibilities with a minimum of structure can also help. An open attitude and willingness to be somewhat spontaneous when one of the partners needs to get away will add to the sense of adventure that makes both feel more alive and vibrant. They may also be able to work on projects separately or together and bring their excitement about handling tangible reality to the benefit of their conversation and relationship. Such efforts can give them energy to live through the more mundane aspects of their life together while enabling them to maximize the effectiveness of their natural abilities and inclinations.

Extraverted Sensing Types (ESTP/ESFP) with Extraverted Intuitive Types (ENTP/ENFP)

When it's working: A relationship with this pairing is likely to sparkle with excitement, although the Extraverted Sensing type is more apt to look for excitement in the moment and the Extraverted Intuitive type for excitement in the future. Both will want to be in the limelight and may play off well against each other, leaving other couples slightly envious of the fun and activities this couple seems to share. If at least one partner has the Feeling function developed, there will be warmth as well as excitement in the home, and both mates and children will feel loved even if expressions of love are sporadic.

When it's not working: ESP and ENP types may actually enjoy order and neatness in their environment, but typically don't want to put the effort or energy into creating that order themselves. Neither partner is likely to want to take care of nitty-gritty details, follow through on chores, balance checkbooks, make reservations, or make decisions. So life at times may be chaotic for this couple, with each partner blaming the other for the chaos.

Some one-upmanship will probably occur, for both types are accustomed to being able to get what they want. The friction will increase if either one comes across sounding like a parent, for neither is likely to respond well to authority figures. Each may attempt to find ways to sidestep issues or manipulate the other to get things done his or her way. Neither partner will have much tolerance for being "shaped up" to suit the other's needs. In fact, both individuals are more likely to go their own ways rather than undergo what they would see as subjugation.

Children in this pairing may find their parents are not consistent in delivering discipline. Ultimately, because mom and dad may try to be friends or pals, their children may also lack structured parenting. When things are going well, however, children will enjoy the spontaneity and fun that ESP and ENP parents tend to naturally generate.

Some Helpful Hints

If they each use their best function to help the relationship, ESP/ENP couples have the benefit of being able to combine both factual and creative approaches to life. Finding ways to appreciate each other while sharing the mundane aspects of domestic life can bring the partners closer together, especially as both would rather have fun than be serious much of the time. Even minimal structure can help the couple manage necessary chores and details and leave more time for freedom to enjoy and experience life. ENPs can dream up ideas that ESPs can help bring to fruition if they don't get bogged down in how to organize the effort. Where ESP and ENP types are concerned, it is much more effective for each partner to contribute when he or she is in the right frame of mind to do so than to impose a schedule on either one.

EXTRAVERTED INTUITIVE TYPES (ENTP/ENFP) TOGETHER

When it's working: All that enthusiasm, innovation, and activity under one roof? This relationship will probably work best if one partner is an ENTP and the other an ENFP. Nevertheless, no matter whether the couple is comprised of two ENTPs, two ENFPs, or one of each type, conversations typically sparkle, energy should abound for new undertakings–and no one is likely to throw cold water on anyone else's inspirations. Opportunities for each partner to build on the other's creativity will always be present. Spontaneity and creativity will be valued and nourished by both.

When it's not working: Here, as with two Extraverted Thinking types, we have the potential problem of two leaders and no followers. If a good idea should surface (and many will), neither partner may want to bother with the details of putting it into practice or seeing it through to completion. Until maturity has led the partners to develop their other functions, many a good idea may remain in limbo.

There is the danger, too, of each partner's seeing through the other's charm and becoming increasingly disillusioned if promises are broken and commitments forgotten–even if both partners are guilty of the same thing!

Other relationships may also be a problem. The excitement of a new encounter, the fun of learning all about someone new–physically, emotionally, and intellectually–can be a very strong stimulant to someone as curious about life as an Extraverted Intuitive. Neither partner will experience much difficulty forming new and varied relationships, and this may be a threat to a primary relationship if it is not grounded.

For children who require a stable home base or who need to master self-discipline, such a couple may provide little security or helpful role models. For children who are flexible and adapt to new challenges, this couple can provide them with a wealth of challenges and opportunities.

Some Helpful Hints

To make this relationship work and to use similarities constructively, EN partners should divide undesirable tasks equitably, look for innovative ways to enjoy each other, and appreciate each other's creativity. Among all the types, this pairing has the chance to have the most fun and innovative conversations. ENs' wit and spontaneity can keep things moving fast, and their wordplay and punning abilities can be exceptional. The relationship will be more satisfying to both partners if, rather than resisting routine matters, they use their lively approaches to dispose of them quickly. This approach is generally more successful than hoping the other person will pick up the responsibility and much more effective than hoping those responsibilities will go away if ignored long enough.

7 The Types in Interaction: Introverts with Introverts

"Whatever the circumstances of your life, understanding of type can make your perceptions clearer, your judgments sounder, and your life closer to your heart's desire."

- Isabel Myers -

Expressing the Inner Self

All Introverts must learn to find ways and times to share what is going on in their inner world. Without an Extravert to push for interaction and initiate external conversation, Introverts can go for a long time without communicating in depth with anyone. Although they may not always seek interaction, they need at least one person in their lives they can trust at a deep level in order to connect to the world outside themselves. The less safe and the more vulnerable they feel, the less they tend to share.

Another thing to be aware of with Introverts is that their best and main function (whether Sensing, Intuition, Thinking, or Feeling) is directed inward for use in their inner worlds. Negotiating public domains with a less well-developed function tends to make Introverts less facile than Extraverted types in the outside world. It may also make them less direct in their dealings with people. Introverts are always receiving and processing information from two different sources: the outside world and their inner world. Whereas you might say that with an Extravert, "what you see is what you get," with an Introvert, you have only a partial view. Introverts typically attend to the outer world after attending to their inner world in what amounts to a dual processing system. Extraverts may find the Introvert's pause needed for this dual processing annoying or frustrating. In a similar way, Introverts may feel annoyed or frustrated when talking to an Extravert, who gets distracted by someone interesting entering the room. Neither is intentionally offending the other, but each may need to give the other a little space for behavior that comes naturally with their different ways of being in the world.

Introverted Sensing Types (ISTJ/ISFJ) Together

When it's working: These couples are often seen by friends and relatives as "salt of the earth" people. They tend to be consistent with each other and with those around them, participate to some degree in community affairs, be circumspect in their political and economic views, and enjoy the predictability of family and/or religious customs and traditions. They also tend to be consistent both in making and applying rules and regulations for their children and provide them with a stable home base. Whether similar or different in type from their parents, the children will always know where their parents stand and what they expect.

In our research, we learned that SJs partnered with SJs reported themselves more content with their relationships than other type combinations. The fact that ISTJs and ISFJs tend to avoid ambiguity in their rules and standards may result in decreased stress and, ultimately, more comfortable relationships.

When it's not working: When disagreements arise between Introverted Sensing partners (as they do in all relationships), both individuals are likely to silently withdraw and stubbornly withhold affection, cooperation, and communication until one of them breaks the ice. We have known couples who were able to maintain a formal frigid silence with each other for several weeks.

Problems may also arise when children become teenagers, particularly if they are quite different in type from their parents. Rebellious, acting-out adolescents may confuse their parents. Parents who feel powerless to control formerly obedient children may blame each other for not being strict enough, for being too strict, for driving a child from their home, or for allowing things to get out of control. Angry, wounding accusations are not easily forgiven by Introverts and, while the relationship may be maintained, there may be a permanent rift.

Some Helpful Hints

Because ISJ types value a disciplined life based on facts, this couple can get through a lot. If allowed to balance each other, the partners can share handling the practical world effectively and still have time for play. Without the development of Intuition to help reframe the picture, there may be a danger of getting stuck and thinking things are hopeless. The partners need to share, especially when there are difficulties. Getting a new perspective from an Intuitive type friend may help. The sense of humor often expressed by ESP types may help ISJ types loosen up.

INTROVERTED SENSING TYPES (ISTJ/ISFJ) WITH INTROVERTED FEELING TYPES (ISFP/INFP)

When it's working: Isabel Briggs Myers, author of the MBTI® instrument, and her husband Chief, represent this type combination. She would speak often of the necessity of valuing differences in styles and of partners allowing each other room for being different. Chief was an ISTJ; Isabel an INFP. Introversion was all they shared in common. His attention to detail and ability to deal with the practical world (Sensing function) allowed her the freedom over the course of her lifetime to use her creativity (Intuition function) to craft an instrument that would prove useful for thousands upon thousands of individuals, groups, and organizations throughout the world. An Introverted Sensing type can handle many of the details of the sensory world effectively. While Introverted Feeling types can also pay attention to details, their preference is to do so only as related to their goals and ideals. When partners understand this about each other, the relationship can be satisfying to both.

When it's not working: Strains and stresses typically occur in these relationships when the Judging type in the pair gets locked into "shoulds," "oughts," and "musts," and the Perceiving type in the pair gets locked into "wants" and "desires." The ISJ may become self-righteous and accusatory about apparently neglected commitments, chores, or obligations, which may hold no meaning for the Introverted Feeling type. In reaction, the Introverted Feeling type may become evasive or rebellious and respond and feel as if the ISJ is an overbearing parent.

Unless both partners hold similar parenting principles, discipline for children may prove erratic and inconsistent. In addition, children may develop the knack for knowing which parent to approach to get what they want depending on the situation. For instance, if it's important to get to baseball practice on time, they'll probably ask the ISJ. If they want permission to drop a class and replace it with art, they'll probably approach the parent with a Perceiving preference. Both parents are apt to resent being left out of a decision-making process where the children are concerned. And because both are Introverts, they may sit on feelings of resentment, which may build a barrier between the couple.

Some Helpful Hints

By sharing and exploring differences, these partners can come to understand each other. Because Sensing types value facts and Intuitive types value possibilities, some kind of bridge is needed to bring them closer together. If each contributes to the relationship what they do best, all can go well. When one relies on the Sensing function and the other on Intuition, as with Isabel and Chief Myers, the partners' appreciation of their differences and realization of how each contributes to the other's well-being are invaluable. Introverts with an Intuition preference almost always prefer that someone else take care of practical obligations, such as taxes, car repair, and yard work. Introverts with a Sensing preference can enjoy the visions and possibilities an Intuitive partner provides, such as creating a home atmosphere and bringing fresh perspectives to daily life.

INTROVERTED SENSING TYPES (ISTJ/ISFJ) WITH INTROVERTED INTUITIVE TYPES (INTJ/INFJ)

When it's working: Depth and sincerity, a sense of responsibility, and dedication are likely to provide strong bonds for pairings of these types. While the

Introverted Sensing type may perceive the Introverted Intuitive type as too fanciful at times, a sense of loyalty and a desire to make things work help the IS partner appreciate and sympathize with needs that may not make rational sense to him or her. The Introverted Intuitive type is likely to value the Introverted Sensing type's willingness to handle the more concrete routines of life such as filling out tax forms, balancing checkbooks, or taking the car in for servicing. The Introverted Sensing type is likely to value the excitement that accompanies the Introverted Intuitive type's ability to access a variety of possibilities in planning events.

Children are likely to be brought up with consistency and trained in the values that the couple holds. If either or both members of the pair have a well-developed Feeling function, warmth, caring, and intimacy, which may be expressed in subtle, undramatic ways, will nonetheless be felt by both partners and their children.

When it's not working: A danger for this pairing is an Introverted Intuitive's desire for novelty—which may lead to that partner's exploring possibilities outside the relationship that may exclude the partner. The INFJ's desire for romance may lead to unhappiness if things become too routine at home. Similarly, ISJ types may become bored or impatient with the INJ type's apparent lack of respect for the obvious. The Sensing type may be frustrated by the Intuitive type's constant focus on dreams and on changing things rather than accepting them.

A quiet stubbornness, too, may create problems for this pair. Both may become locked into their own perceptions (which can be very different) and judgments about these perceptions. Since silence is easy for Introverts to live with, communication may be shut off for days. In such cases, the children may be used to keep some communication open: "Tell your mother she left the light on in the kitchen"; "Ask your father to pass the salt."

Some Helpful Hints

Self-exploration and personal development are keys to maintaining this relationship as with most couples. Both types need to introspect but not get stuck in their own ways of seeing things. Each needs to stay open to the other's goals and support them, even when those goals are considerably different from their own. It would be well for the couple to develop a negotiated way of ending silences. Intuitive types can bring flexibility to ending deadlocks, as they can often see the many possible choices. Sensing types are generally more accepting of the way things are. Combining mutual acceptance with attention to new options may help these partners resolve impasses.

INTROVERTED SENSING TYPES (ISTJ/ISFJ) WITH INTROVERTED THINKING TYPES (ISTP/INTP)

When it's working: Introspective and analytical, the Introverted Thinking type is likely to maintain logical, precise communications with an Introverted Sensing partner. And if that partner is also a Thinking type (ISTJ), communication may be easy and two way. If one partner is a Feeling type (ISFJ), the desire to help and care for the Introverted Thinking partner may make up for any difficulties in communication. Often absorbed in their own thoughts and cognitive systems, the Introverted Thinking type is not always an easy partner to live with. But the ISJ partner can highlight the priorities in the relationship and keep things grounded.

The Introverted Sensing type's dedication to family and community may not always be understandable for the Introverted Thinking type. However when the Introverted Thinking type sees that the motivation is altruistic and not for attention or applause, respect and understanding will follow. Introverted Sensing types typically focus on home and job, express patience, and value the Introverted Thinking type for different but nevertheless valuable contributions to the family and to the world.

When it's not working: When Introverted Thinking types (ISTP, INTP) are coupled with Introverted Sensing types with a Thinking preference (ISTJ), the partners are likely to have difficulty communicating (or even getting in touch with) their emotions. Introverted Sensing types with a Feeling preference (ISFJ) are likely to recognize their emotions about a given issue, but they may lack the willingness or the skill to actually communicate their feelings. When asked how they feel, Thinking types usually preface responses with "I think I feel—." Relationships in which the partners struggle to access and express emotions may be in trouble, because emotional ingredients are what bind many relationships together. INTPs can become bored with the more down-to-earth Sensing types but may be so comfortable in the relationship that they stay put. The Introverted Sensing type may become disenchanted if the Introverted Thinking type does not value some visible success in the outer world.

Once problems arise in the relationship, one or both partners may pull inward, feel misunderstood (which may be true), and become resentful and alienated. Discussions may be brief and to the point, and the partners may spend an entire lifetime together with neither one willing to risk being vulnerable by revealing sensitive, hurt feelings. Children growing up under these circumstances may have no role model for creating intimacy in relationships. They may wonder why their parents stay together in what seems to be a relationship with few rewards.

Some Helpful Hints

The practical approach of the Introverted Sensing type can complement the internalized and thoughtful approach of the Introverted Thinking type. The ITP type may be quite satisfied in the relationship if the ISJ partner also has a Feeling preference. Having access to feeling, even through someone else, can be helpful to Thinking types. Moreover, ISJ types who are also Feeling types can bring liveliness to the ITP's more detached world. The Introverted Thinking type will probably need to exert some effort to respond to the couple's more mundane domestic responsibilities, so that the Introverted Sensing type isn't overburdened in those areas.

Introverted Thinking types are often good at writing programs for changing their behavior. If they can get a model program in their heads, it may make changing a behavior easier. Sometimes it has worked for us to suggest, especially to male Introverted Thinking types, that they try to behave like a certain movie star. In one case, an INTP's efforts to be like an actor he admired proved helpful in changing his wife's anger toward him. This client became more practical in dealing with some of his ISFJ wife's concerns by emulating this actor, who, in dramatic roles tended to be blunt, to the point and to not avoid issues. When the husband was more willing to stand there, to be present and not retreat into theoretical positions vis-à-vis the problem, he and his wife were able to resolve some of their household and relationship issues.

It is often helpful, especially with Thinking type men, to talk in terms of specific behaviors. A husband's "What am I supposed to do?" will not be adequately answered by a wife's somewhat vague answer, such as "I need you to be more responsible." A statement such as "I need you to take the garbage cans to the sidewalk every Tuesday night" is more specific and will likely achieve better results. Once Introverted Thinking types have a concept and the pattern, they can usually implement a program more easily. If each partner can express what they specifically need from the other, communication can be considerably improved.

INTROVERTED FEELING TYPES (ISFP/INFP) TOGETHER

When it's working: Shared values, belief in similar causes, sensitivity, and striving for perfection can create a beautifully harmonious relationship when two IFs get together, particularly if both have worked through their personal insecurities and are achieving goals they value. When IFP couples have come to us for premarital or marital counseling, it has not been because of serious problems, but because they wanted their relationships to be as perfect as possible! The partners' care for each other was evident, and the level of intimacy and sharing was very beautiful.

Parents of this type, possibly because of their own pain growing up and feeling different, strive to provide their children with a sense of acceptance no matter what each child's type may be. The creativity and the deep expressions of care that they contribute as parents can provide a very stable base from which a child can operate.

When it's not working: Real or imagined hurts for these sensitive types can create barriers between partners. A feeling of having been betrayed once they have committed to someone (and commitment is not always easy for IFPs) results in a loss of trust that is hard to regain. And no matter what the partner may say or do to try to make amends, forgiving and forgetting for IFP types may be difficult. In the face of conflicts, Introverted Feeling types are likely to withdraw or flee the situation. And if both mates withdraw, issues will neither be confronted nor resolved. Suppressed problems are likely to create a pressure-cooker atmosphere of tensions and stress. Then each partner may turn to someone outside the relationship for understanding and intimacy, or they may search for new partners altogether.

Some Helpful Hints

If they can keep feelings and creativity flowing, IFP type partners can maintain a high level of intimacy. Few other types have the creativity or capacity for depth that Introverted Feeling types have. They will sometimes need to talk things out, which is not always easy for them. Although their styles are similar, they should not assume their feelings are the same and should make a practice of checking things out with each other. A partner with a preference for Intuition (INFP) can help bring fresh approaches to the relationship, keeping it lively and interesting for both. The partner with a Sensing preference (ISFP) can enrich the couple's reality by bringing sensitivity to it. The partners can also strengthen their relationship by actively supporting each other's ideals.

Introverted Feeling Types (ISFP/INFP) with Introverted Intuitive Types (INTJ/INFJ)

When it's working: This is not a common pairing: Introverted Feeling types and Introverted Intuitive types are underrepresented in the general population. It can be a very satisfying pairing, however, as the partners tend to possess and value creativity in themselves and in each other. Family will be important to both, and there will probably be a mutual desire for close, intimate friendships and a lack of interest in partying or having a large circle of casual social contacts.

While Introverted Intuitive types do not like to be bored, an ISFP partner will also resist boredom. INJ and IFP type couples generally find ways to bring excitement into their lives—excitement different in tone and texture from that sought by Extraverted Intuitive or Extraverted Sensing types. Dedication to lofty ideals, involvement with humanitarian causes, mutual delight in discovering favorite new authors or artists, finding new ways of sharing or playing together are examples of what may be energizing for these types.

In most cases, children of IFP and INJ parents feel loved and supported. (If one of the parents is an INTJ, however, children may experience significant pressure to perform. INTJs tend to have very high standards and can be critical if those standards aren't met). The Introverted Intuitive will probably be the disciplinarian of the pair, but the discipline will be fair. The Introverted Feeling type is likely to be the more flexible partner in small matters and will probably do more of the accommodating. But when a really important issue surfaces, IF types stand their ground and are generally able to work out a satisfying compromise with the Introverted Intuitive partner.

When it's not working: The Introverted Feeling types' (particularly INFPs') lack of interest in everyday routines may irritate the Introverted Intuitive. Tasks such as household chores, checkbook balancing, filing deadlines, stocking pantry shelves—the myriad details and routines of everyday life—are generally unpleasant to both types. The Introverted Intuitive type's internalized standards of achievement will motivate them to do their share, but they are apt to resent a partner who isn't equally motivated. If these resentments aren't verbalized, it may take a long time for IFP types to become aware that their partner has become disenchanted with them. By that time, damage already may have been done to the relationship. Once an INJ type has become convinced that a partner is irresponsible, uncaring, or untrustworthy, that perception may be hard to change. Moreover, it may be difficult for Introverted Feeling types to live with a partner's disapproval, and they may look to someone new for approval and appreciation.

Some Helpful Hints

Once problems begin to surface, both INJ and IFP type partners readily benefit from sessions with a relationship counselor. Both types are willing to listen to constructive feedback and to work out compromises. They are not likely to come to sessions merely to have the counselor shape the other one up. However, if the partners each use the sensitivity inherent in their type, counseling may not be necessary. The desire both have to make the world a better place through creative change can lead each to admire and respect the other's views and choices. INJs are typically gifted with insight and IFPs with high ideals. If respect and sensitivity don't get bogged down in mundane demands, such a relationship has great potential for depth and mutual satisfaction.

Introverted Feeling Types (ISFP/INFP) with Introverted Thinking Types (ISTP/INTP)

When it's working: This pairing often results in a very comfortable relationship. IFP and ITP types share enough similarities to find mutual understanding and have enough differences to provide each other with different ways of perceiving and making decisions about the world. Neither one may want much to do with the structured world, however. The Introverted Thinking type is more likely to be the one to do the financial planning and to make long-range economic decisions. The Introverted Feeling type will probably be more concerned with the home's emotional climate—as it affects every family member—and be interested in creating an attractive home environment. Because the Introverted Feeling type so desires harmony and because the Introverted Thinking type spends so much time living in his or her own thoughts, there should be few arguments. Those arguments that do occur will probably relate to very important values or issues on which both should be able and willing to compromise.

When it's not working: One roadblock IFP and ITP couples may meet is related to the Introverted Feeling type's strong need for approval, security, and feeling loved. And while ITP partners can love and approve of their mates, they aren't disposed to give many verbal reassurances of that fact. An Introverted Thinking type's, "Of course, I love you—I married you, didn't I," is not the kind of tender response that helps an IFP type partner feel adored. Another danger for this couple may arise from a lack of communication and a tendency for each partner to assume that they know what the other is thinking, feeling, or wanting. Since these partners do tend to see life differently and to have different needs, assumptions about the other are often off base.

Some Helpful Hints

Learning to be more demonstrative—with flowers or cards or funny little gifts if words are hard to come by—can be an important task for the Introverted Thinking type in this relationship. This is true no matter what type an ITP is involved with, but especially so in pairings with Introverted Feeling types. Although their perceptions differ, both partners very much want to be understood by the other and can work to make this happen. The introspection and depth each is capable of—one in a Feeling mode and one in a Thinking mode—can provide a study in contrasts that enhances the total relationship if the partners don't allow their differences to become alienating.

Introverted Intuitive Types (INTJ/INFJ) Together

When it's working: This can be an almost ideal relationship; the partners intuitively understand each other, value each other's goals and accomplishments, and appreciate the need each has to achieve. They can meet each other's needs for punctuality and performance. If they are secure in themselves, there will probably be little jealousy between them. As parents, Introverted Intuitive types form strong bonds with their children and are typically able to give them deep understanding. In matters of discipline, INJ parents strive to be fair, just, and loving and, as they probably have similar ideas about child rearing, are unlikely to accuse each other of spoiling the children or of being too harsh. These partners are typically well aligned.

This pairing is rare, for there are few INTJs and INFJs in the general population. Moreover, those few INJs who seek counseling in the early stages of dating or marriage are more often paired with their opposites. In such cases, the Introverted Intuitive has generally sought out someone who enjoys and is more comfortable in the extraverted world, who easily navigates large groups of people, and who handles practical affairs with facility.

When Introverted Intuitive types partner later in life or choose a second partner after losing the first to death or divorce, they often have already developed experience dealing with the practical world. They may even enjoy doing so and may then search out another Introverted Intuitive with whom to share life. Introverted Intuitive types attempt to be fair, just, and loving with children. When secure in themselves, INJ types experience little jealousy in their relationships.

When it's not working: Introverted Intuitive types tend to find each other later in life. As a result, they may already be pretty set in their ways, and adjustment to another person, despite the love, may prove difficult. Introverted Intuitive types can be "picky"; they want things done their way, because they know their way is right (in this idea, they're hard to budge). Put two rather immovable objects together, and a very artful mediator may be necessary to get them interacting again.

Of all the types, the Introverted Intuitive type is unusually self-sufficient, and such self-sufficiency can prove both a blessing and a curse in a relationship. Two self-sufficient individuals sharing a life may sound ideal—a couple united primarily because they love each other rather than need each other. But all relationships require adjustments. Both partners need to risk being honest about any negative reactions they have toward each other. Simply avoiding unpleasantness over the long term could eventually drive the partners to avoid each other.

Some Helpful Hints

If the INJ partners can be persuaded to be clear with each other about individual needs, they may be able to increase their emotional flexibility, which can lead in turn to overall psychological development. Because they tend to have the same strengths and blind spots—unless one partner has a Thinking preference and the other a Feeling preference—they can use their Intuitive powers to find the best balance between them.

It is also important that the partners readily address resentments that occur—not, perhaps, in the heat of the moment, but at the earliest time possible that still shows regard for each person's needs. If resentments build up and are not taken care of, there may be an erosion of the relationship that may be difficult to repair. An agreed-upon time to express complaints and discuss problems can be very valuable to this pair. Both have long memories for the very worst moments but also for the very happiest times. Because IJ types have a difficult time in general letting go of bad feelings, they need to practice doing so on a regular basis. INFJs approach the world through their Feeling, which is not their best-developed function. This less-developed Feeling function can distort the value of events for INFJs, causing them to have disproportionately intense reactions when they need to consciously seek balance. Disproportion also effects INTJs, whose less-developed Thinking function influences their overly cool reactions; in intimate relationships where feelings are important, too much or poorly timed detachment can be hurtful.

Because IN couples have Sensing as their least developed mental function, they are likely to neglect concrete details and blame each other for the neglect.

INTROVERTED INTUITIVE TYPES (INTJ/INFJ) WITH INTROVERTED THINKING TYPES (ISTP/INTP)

When it's working: This is also an unusual combination because of the smaller numbers of INJ and ITP types in the general population. Yet if the pairing occurs, it can be satisfying. Both partners will be very much inner-directed. They will value their personal standards of integrity above the opinions of others, and they will highly value such standards in each other. Devotion to primary family members tends to predominate. Friends and business associates take second place. Discussions, when they occur, tend to be stimulating. Both partners are likely to work outside the home, for neither is likely to cherish what they consider routine household tasks. Both will ask for private time, and private space, and both will be happy to provide it for each other. INJs and ITPs can make fine traveling companions, anticipating and exploring the new with great enthusiasm. The Introverted Intuitive may end up being the one to make plans and handle reservations, even though neither of them may enjoy handling such details.

Probabilities are high that both partners did well in school. Standards set for children tend to be high, but there is likely little disagreement between the parents about such standards. If the Introverted Intuitive type in the pair also has a Feeling preference, he or she can bring warmth to the emotional climate of the family. The responsiveness, appreciation, and sensitivity shown by Feeling types is always welcomed by Thinking types despite their own difficulty expressing tender and loving emotion.

When it's not working: When disagreements occur, as they do in all relationships, both partners have a tendency to withdraw and maintain their own positions. The one who makes the first concession toward reconciliation may feel resentful over having to say "I'm sorry," because this is not easy for either an Introverted Intuitive or an Introverted Thinking type. Both types show a tendency to "know" they are "right," whether they are or not. Moreover, they are invested in their positions, whether they involve politics, an abstract concept, a philosophical issue, or how to organize household tasks. If any children of this pair happen to be Extraverts, their need for interaction and parental involvement may be experienced as an energy drain by both parents. If the couple can afford child care or have relatives to help out, such support may lessen the stress. At the least, Extraverted children of these couples should be encouraged in activities that engage their Extraversion such as after school programs and group sports. In the event that this couple cannot agree on major issues, a split may leave them wary of entering into other relationships.

Some Helpful Hints

Having others take care of the more routine tasks (housekeeping, lawn maintenance, taxes) may relieve stress in the relationship. Each partner's emotional needs, as well as those of the children, need to be made explicit. While the Intuitive function may be useful for self-exploration, INJs and INTPs should not rely on it for accurate information about each other; they should seek direct, first-hand feedback instead. Clarity about and willingness to express their needs can go a long way toward helping such a couple avoid serious problems. The Introverted Intuitive partner may have to take the lead in these discussions, as the Introverted Thinking type may prefer to stay in more technical realms (the ISTP partner) or more theoretical realms (the INTP partner).

INTROVERTED THINKING TYPES (ISTP/INTP) TOGETHER

We have never counseled a couple made of two Introverted Thinking types, nor have we found this combination among the many couples we've known socially. Therefore, our description of their interactions is more hypothetical than our descriptions of the other pairings.

When it's working: Conceivably, two Introverted Thinking types might meet as colleagues in a work environment. Each might then develop sufficient respect for the other's values and systems of thought that they would decide that a life together as mates would work out well. Their needs for perfection in articulating whatever they wished to communicate would be met with understanding from their partner. This would be experienced as especially satisfying after what may have been countless experiences of feeling like a "stranger in a strange land" in interactions with other types. Social life would be selective for this couple; neither partner would much care to mingle with large or diverse groups of people. Instead, they would cultivate solid friendships with people whom they could respect—people with good minds and interesting or challenging ideas. The couple's occasional small and intimate dinner parties would be well orchestrated and stimulating. If one or both of these mates were ISTPs, involvement in sports and hobbies—hands-on activities—would probably punctuate purely intellectual interests. This variety would likely bring more liveliness, more earthiness, and a greater sense of joy into the relationship.

When it's not working: In our experience, few types can be more surprisingly dogmatic, more sure of their position, than Introverted Thinking types—albeit often in a quiet way. If both partners were to move simultaneously into strong positions on opposite sides of an issue, it is difficult to imagine what might ease so tense a situation. With both partners focused on matters of the mind, many daily tasks—keeping the refrigerator stocked, remembering medical appointments, taking out the garbage, maintaining social contacts (even desired ones), managing children's schedules, and so on—might easily fall by the wayside.

Some Helpful Hints

Sharing intellectual interests can be a strong point in this relationship. Since feelings are not readily expressed by either person, having a group of friends, a spiritual life, or some musical or artistic expression that can help balance out all the thinking would be helpful. Later in life, each partner needs to make an effort to discover some of the more unconscious aspects of self. For these types, studying dreams can be a very good way since they enjoy introspection. These types can also benefit from having a good Feeling type friend who can help them keep things in perspective. Introverted Thinking types tend to spend so much time figuring out things that they are heavily invested in their own point of view. If they can come up with a model or paradigm that includes sensitivity to others' points of view, they can be more effective in their personal relationships.

8

The Types in Interaction: Extraverts with Introverts

"We cannot safely assume that other people's minds work on the same principles as our own. All too often, others with whom we come in contact do not reason as we reason, or do not value the things we value, or are not interested in what interests us."

- Isabel Myers -

Negotiating Extraversion and Introversion

Often when people observe couples and comment that it does seem to be true that opposites attract, it is because one is Extraverted and the other Introverted. Differences on this preference are more easily discerned, and more people are aware of the concept of Extraversion-Introversion than of the other three preferences pairs. Nevertheless, there does appear to be a strong attraction between opposites on this particular preference. Sometimes this attraction is helpful in keeping a relationship intact; sometimes it is not.

Nearly always the Extraverted partner needs more overt interactions than the Introverted partner. Introverts are less likely to wish to interact after a hard day at work. They may have their socializing needs met on the job and prefer to have more introspective time following work. As for Extraverts, the solo commute home may provide all the time needed for quiet processing, and he or she is ready for a social evening. What's needed by an E-I couple is an honest negotiation about times and circumstances for privacy and introspection as well as for socializing and engagement.

EXTRAVERTED THINKING TYPES (ESTJ/ENTJ) WITH INTROVERTED SENSING TYPES (ISTJ/ISFJ)

When it's working: This can prove to be an exceptionally satisfying combination of types. The Introverted Sensing type is unlikely to challenge the Extraverted Thinking type's desire to take the lead on most issues. The Introvert's sense of responsibility and ability to follow through will please the Extravert and bring about little need for criticism or complaint. The household is likely to function like a well-oiled unit: plans will be made and followed, checkbooks will balance, dinner will be served on time, and savings will be invested after adequate research. Between them, the partners will typically show a great deal of consistency in raising children. Rules will be clear, and discipline for infractions is likely to be firm but fair. Children are likely to know what is expected of them and where they stand at all times.

The Extraverted Thinking type is likely to bring the most excitement to the relationship and will probably lead the Introverted Sensing type into more horizon-expanding experiences than he or she may have engaged in independently. The Introverted Sensing types typically enjoy the responsibility and focus of taking care of details in a relationship, which provides a balance for the Extraverted Thinking types, who tend to want to explore and solve challenges and actively organize work and play.

When it's not working: If the Introverted Sensing type in this pairing is an ISTJ, he or she may present more challenges to the ETJ's desire to maintain leadership. In addition, ISTJs and Extraverted Thinking types are prone to express explosive tempers, which can be set off by perceived irrationality or irresponsibility (to mention only two triggers). Where there is a lack of agreement on basic premises, battles may be long and stormy until logic finally prevails.

If both partners prefer Thinking judgment, neither is likely to offer compliments or express much in the way of appreciation for a partner.

The Extraverted Thinking type is likely to distrust anything that smacks of "flattery," and the Introverted Sensing type is apt to be reserved and not typically expressive. By focusing on what is working between them and by becoming more willing to express the positive, this couple will be better able to get through some of the rough times. Children of ISJ and ETJ parents may find their home base secure but lacking in warmth. If the children are either insecure or rebellious, they may see their parents as bosses rather than as loving guardians.

Some Helpful Hints

This pair will probably have an easier time if the ISJ also has a Feeling preference. While Thinking types are adept at good discussions, both ETJs and ITJs tend to want to be in charge. If both the Introverted and Extraverted partners are Thinking types, it would be well to divide the domestic work so that each knows exactly who is in charge of what. Couples of these types in relationships do well to develop sensitivity to each other's needs and to put time and energy into balancing critical comments with appreciative ones. By using their cognitive abilities to reframe constructive criticism of their children into supportive comments, Thinking types can enhance the home life. Natural tacticians, Thinking types excel at strategizing. If they bring this talent to planning ways to improve the relationship, things can work very well. For example, the "time out" strategy can be used to defuse heated arguments. Setting a regular, specified time to suspend pursuit of goals in favor of relaxation and togetherness is another strategic approach to relationship improvement.

EXTRAVERTED THINKING TYPES (ESTJ/ENTJ) WITH INTROVERTED FEELING TYPES (ISFP/INFP)

When it's working: Such couples are truly pairings of opposites: the goal-oriented, decisive, and planful Extraverted Thinking type with the flexible, creative, and emotionally aware Introverted Feeling type. We have seen countless ETJ and IFP pairings among our counseling clients, our friends, and couples (especially military couples) at workshops.

The Extraverted Thinking type is generally comfortable in the world and can be adept at providing a stable, secure environment for a relationship. The Introverted Feeling type can provide spontaneity, creativity, and harmony to the relationship. In our research, couples of this combination often reported themselves very satisfied with their relationships. Roles were well defined, and there were very few power struggles. Both partners in this pairing also typically report the Extraverted Thinking type to be "the competent one," the person who may be the most authoritative outside and inside the home. Often, the Introverted Feeling partner is unaware of how much power he or she actually has and how much the ETJ partner needs them for their warmth and sensitivity.

Children of this couple will be expected to follow rules, typically established by the Extraverted Thinking type, but will be comforted by the Introverted Feeling type after being disciplined for infractions. If the IFP type strongly favors molding children through positive reinforcement rather than punishment, the couple may strive valiantly to maintain such practice at home. This might take the form of praising desirable behavior while ignoring less desirable behavior or of a general fostering of children's self-esteem while avoiding criticism. However, should the Extraverted Thinking partner decide to mete out punishment, the Introverted Feeling partner may withdraw and suffer silently, especially if he or she disagrees but is reluctant to interfere.

When it's not working: When an Introverted Feeling type, who has relied on or submitted to an Extraverted Thinking type's authority, evolves and develops a sense of personal competency, the ETJ and IFP marriage may change and along with that change experience difficulties. Whether or not partners surmount these issues often depends heavily on the flexibility of the Extraverted Thinking type to adapt to change. When the Introverted Feeling partner insists on being heard and questions the authority that previously was lovingly accepted, the Extraverted Thinking type may experience a threat to his or her self-esteem. If the ETJ partner responds by putting down the Introverted Feeling type with sharp criticism (which they are generally adept at doing), they may end up maintaining the relationship's status quo at the expense of each partner's personal growth.

Because it is almost impossible for Introverted Feeling types not to be aware of how they feel at any given moment, the fact that the partner may be unaware of their feelings is difficult for an IF to understand because it seems so obvious. In responding to a partner, IF types may give the kinds of responses they would prefer to receive—those that take account of emotions. On the other hand, rather than speak up, they may go along with the Extraverted Thinking partner's program but quietly withdraw feelings and emotional involvement. This is the last thing the Extraverted Thinking type wants, but ETJ types don't always realize how to demonstrate and honor feelings while getting a point across. For Extraverted Thinking types, recognizing and accessing emotion requires slowing down and looking deeper within themselves. To recognize emotions in others, they can learn to pay close attention to nonverbal cues.

Some Helpful Hints

If the Extraverted Thinking type offers logical support and strives to support the self-esteem of the partner, initial conflicts may resolve themselves. When both partners are on an equal and satisfying footing, the Introverted Feeling type can be caring and insightful and the Extraverted Thinking type, active and achieving. Both can respect and value each other's gifts. The Introverted Feeling partner may need to learn how to protect themselves (without shutting down) from the intensity of the Extraverted Thinking type's language and presentation style. The Extraverted Thinking type may need to use his or her analytical skill to assess what's going on in the relationship and to decide on a strategy to handle it well.

EXTRAVERTED THINKING TYPES (ESTJ/ENTJ) WITH INTROVERTED INTUITIVE TYPES (INTJ/INFJ)

When it's working: This can be a satisfying relationship: both partners are likely to be achievement oriented and to respect each other for their mutual accomplishments. A good match in strength, there will probably be more parity in this relationship than in relationships between Extraverted Thinking types and Introverted Feeling or Introverted Sensing types. If the Introverted Intuitive is an INFJ, there will be more warmth in the home for both partner and children; if the Introverted Intuitive is an INTJ, there will be easier communication, particularly around decision making.

To outside observers, it might appear to be a typical Extravert-Introvert pairing, with the Extravert in charge and in the limelight at social functions. Most Introverts have less of a need to be that visible. If you spend a great deal of time with these couples, however, you will come to realize the respect the Extraverted Thinking type holds for the Introverted Intuitive partner. Often the Extraverted Thinking type relies on the perceptions and perspectives of the Introverted Intuitive, which are usually given in more private settings.

When it's not working: An Extraverted Thinking type prefers to be in control and in charge, which may come in conflict with the INJ type's need for independence, and may be more pronounced when the partner is an INTJ, as those who prefer Introverted Intuition can be the most quietly stubborn. Although the INFJ (like most individuals with a Feeling function) will value harmony, it will not be valued at any cost. Their convictions will keep them from buckling in a controversy, no matter how loud or angry the Extraverted Thinking type becomes. The INTJ, who may not place as high a value on harmony, is even less likely to buckle if a difference of opinion arises.

Many problems may arise for this couple over child rearing. INFJs, in particular, tend to be especially bonded to their children, and the Extraverted Thinking type may at times feel left out of the intimacy between partner and children. The Introverted Intuitive type is also likely to come to the defense of the children if the Extraverted Thinking type appears too stern a disciplinarian; in such a case, it is another circumstance where the ETJ type partner may feel like the outsider.

In ETJ and INJ pairings, it is especially important for Extraverted Thinking types to learn to curb their tempers. Comments made in anger that sting or wound the Introverted Intuitive type (particularly an INFJ) are not easily forgotten or forgiven: the ETJ partner may hear twenty years later of the hurt they once inflicted in a stressful moment. Most Introverts tend to take longer than Extraverts to get over hurt or angry feelings. Extraverts are more likely to ventilate and forget. This seems to be especially true in pairings of Extraverted Thinking and Introverted Intuitive types.

Some Helpful Hints

Introverts tend to internalize information, hold it, mull it over, and reflect on it; Extraverts tend to collect information from everyone they meet and share it. The difficulty of "letting go" for an Introvert is a real one; for an Extravert, it is a more natural, and easier process. An ETJ and INFJ pair need to pay careful attention to the kinds of energy and information they put out and kinds they take in. FJs tend to want harmony; TJs tend to want resolution. If both can be achieved by discussion and implementation, this pairing has great potential. Extraverted Thinking types tend to get Introverted types moving and more involved in the world around them; Introverted Intuitive types are good at providing Extraverted types with insightful alternatives to their own ideas.

Extraverted Thinking Types (ESTJ/ENTJ) with Introverted Thinking Types (ISTP/INTP)

If you have difficulty imagining this pairing, think of a person highly driven and successfully married to a person who is logic-driven and an analytical individualist. Of course, if one of the couples you are working with does embody this combination of types, you will have little difficulty conceptualizing an Extraverted Thinking type living with an Introverted Thinking type.

When it's working: For both individuals in this relationship, job or career may take priority over family. Success in their chosen professions will enable each to develop self-confidence and become sufficiently secure to admire and respect the partner's achievements, even in a totally different field. Two incomes allow the partners to fulfill many of their personal dreams whatever these are. If their dreams differ, the partners should be able to use logic to work out mutually satisfying options, even separate vacations.

When it's not working: Introverted Thinking types are sometimes dreamers or "crank" geniuses, never quite able to make it in the practical world. In such cases, their Extraverted Thinking type partner may lose respect for them. Even when both partners are successful, difficulties can arise. The Extravert will undoubtedly want to socialize more, especially with professional associates. The Introvert may resent being "dragged out" to functions where he or she shares little in common with the other guests. Because ITP types dislike "small talk," they will consider such gatherings a waste of their time—and will wish that they could use it more productively in their own pursuits. Further, when Introverted Thinking types express resentment, it usually involves some form of withdrawal: using "silent treatments," for example, or possibly withholding sex.

The children of ETJ and ITP parents will probably receive all the material and cultural advantages the parents are able to afford. Often arriving late in the course of the marriage, the children are also likely to be doted on by parents and grandparents. If the parents have different views about child rearing, they may have out-and-out battles, and a child may hear mixed messages. If they perceive their child as an underachiever, the parents may consciously or unconsciously heap criticism and disapproval on the child.

Some Helpful Hints

The relationship of two people with primary Thinking functions can be very stimulating. Because Thinking types enjoy debate, often regardless of which side they take, they can effectively use this capacity to explore many aspects of life and thereby clarify for themselves what they actually believe. Harmony is not often a prerequisite for this pairing of types but mental stimulation is.

EXTRAVERTED FEELING TYPES (ESFJ/ENFJ) WITH INTROVERTED SENSING TYPES (ISTJ/ISFJ)

When it's working: This pairing can produce a comfortable relationship, especially if both partners are at ease with organization and structure. Any of the four possible combinations will have a Judging preference in common, so each one's needs for order and planning should easily be satisfied within such relationships. Extraverted Feeling types tend to favor professions that involve daily human interaction: teaching, counseling, and ministering. As a result, quiet evenings at home with an Introverted partner can become attractive, even for an Extravert. The Introverted Sensing type partner will definitely want quiet time, especially if she or he has a job that calls for Extraverted behaviors. In fact, this partner may want "alone time" even before "together time." The ISJ type will appreciate a partner's warmth, demonstrations of affection, and involvement with the children. The EFJ will appreciate the security, stability, and follow-through provided by the

ISJ partner. The partners typically experience mutual respect and can count on each other to follow through on responsibilities. Stability and security are typically important values for both.

When it's not working: Extraverted Feeling types tend to need affection and feedback, and compliments do not flow easily from Introverted Sensing types, particularly ISTJs. Without frequent praise, the EFJ feels unhappy and undervalued. As a result, he or she may decide to put time and energy into a job or volunteer work where appreciation is more readily available. Other problems may arise if the EFJ is either in a career that permits minimal interaction with others or has chosen to stay at home with small children. In any case, the EFJ is apt to need more social activity than the ISJ cares for, and resentments between the partners related to this disparity may escalate.

Some Helpful Hints

Partners with Judging preferences need to focus their desire for an orderly physical environment on making things work smoothly between them. They may need to ease up on their natural tendencies to make "judgments," substituting instead the work of accurate evaluation and acceptance. It's not always easy for individuals with a Judging preference to understand that their opinions about the outside world may be "right" for them, but not necessarily for others. Feelings should be dealt with as they arise, with the Extravert avoiding pushiness and the Introvert resisting reticence. Both EFJ and ISJ types need to build some fun into their normally responsible styles. These types can handle the burdens of daily life, but also need to take care of each other.

EXTRAVERTED FEELING TYPES (ESFJ/ENFJ) WITH INTROVERTED FEELING TYPES (ISFP/INFP)

When it's working: As any pairing within these four types will contain two feeling types, there should always be substantial warmth in the household, which the partners will express toward each other and especially toward the children. Sensitivity to hurt feelings and desire to make amends will especially benefit the Introverted Feeling type, who generally needs to be treated with tender loving care. Extraverted Feeling types are especially well suited to help the Introverted Feeling type feel sufficiently secure to pursue and attain their goals. In turn, the IFP type will provide the EFJ partner with a sympathetic, listening ear. The Introvert may also help the Extravert balance social needs with broader and more humanitarian perspectives. Even if the children are Thinking types, EFJ and IFP parents will provide sufficient love and allowance for differences to permit the children to develop in healthy ways.

When it's not working: Jung indicated that the greatest misunderstandings may occur between two individuals with the same primary function (Feeling in this case) when it is Extraverted in one but Introverted in the other. Conflicts occur in every relationship, of course, and when they arise for this couple, the Extravert will want to "talk it out" now! Extraverted Feeling types need to get their reactions out—they can't sleep until they do. Introverted Feeling types, on the other hand, have a tendency to withdraw. Trying to manage their own reactions along with listening to a partner's is sometimes more than they can handle—without sleeping on it first.

Money problems can sometimes sabotage this couple's relationship. Extraverted Feeling types tend to have more material desires and needs that require the maintenance of an adequate income. In contrast, when Introverted Feeling types identify and pursue their goals, they are apt to be more interested in personal fulfillment than income. Discussing each person's needs and desires and striking a balance is a way to resolve these potential financial differences.

Some Helpful Hints

Since harmony is so important to both types, this area requires a good deal of attention. Extraverted Feeling types need to be sure to ask for and listen to the Introverted Feeling type's responses. Introverted Feeling types need to be willing to share their values and reactions with the Extraverted partner. When IFP type partners keep reactions to themselves in an effort to avoid unpleasantness, they may unconsciously build up a reservoir of negativity which, by prompting them to gradually withdraw, can seriously erode the relationship. The partners' willingness to air grievances and work them out is necessary to the well-being of the relationship. If the Introvert is willing to talk, the Extravert needs to be willing to listen attentively. Introverts who are not heard may stop talking altogether and eventually leave the relationship.

Extraverted Feeling Types (ESFJ/ENFJ) with Introverted Intuitive Types (INTJ/INFJ)

When it's working: This combination works best when the pair is made up of an ENFJ and an INFJ. The couple's values, goals, and modes of action will be similar, and the difference created by one partner's Extraversion and the other's Introversion can add sparkle to the relationship. Children will be raised with love and discipline. Each partner's appreciation of the other's integrity can add depth to the relationship. In any of these pairings, each partner's Judging preference can help ease many of the minor problems couples tend to encounter. Plans will be followed; chores will be done; no one will be kept waiting without very good reason. The Extraverted Feeling type's desire to please and maintain harmony in the home will go far to defuse potentially divisive situations. Once aware that their partner is an ally who has their best interests at heart, INJs' stubbornness usually melts away.

When it's not working: Though it's not an unusual combination, the pairing of an ESFJ with an INTJ can be difficult. On one hand, the social skills and humor of the Extraverted Feeling type can enhance the goal-directed behavior of the Introverted Intuitive type, who tends to be more serious and persistent. Moreover, the partners are apt to respect and admire each other for the part each is playing in attaining a satisfying lifestyle. On the other hand, an INTJ can be very undemonstrative, and an ESFJ usually requires more interaction and appreciation than an INTJ naturally provides.

Should the Extraverted Feeling type focus attention on career or community, the Introverted Intuitive partner may look outside the relationship for someone who shares their interests and "understands" them. When Extraverted Feeling types cannot get their needs met constructively in a relationship, they may overindulge in food or drink, pursue a series of flirtations, or engage in impulsive buying sprees. If the EFJ is male, his caring qualities and ease in expressing feelings will make him very attractive to members of the opposite sex. Many women appreciate interaction with a man who can speak the language of feeling, and they may be attracted to their ministers, doctors, or therapists—men often assumed, by profession, to be proficient in the language of feeling. And while an INJ female tends to be independent and self-sufficient, her jealousy of women attracted to her EFJ partner can lead to misunderstanding, hurt, and resentment.

Some Helpful Hints

If both partners are Intuitive types, each will have considerable knowledge of the other's needs and wants. These partners, however, will be wise to check out their hunches, avoiding assumptions and possible misunderstandings. If one is an ESFJ, he or she can bridge the gap created by the Intuitive type's lack of interest in practical matters by creating time and space (often with humor) to deal with necessary tasks. The INJ type can meet his or her Extraverted partner half way by offering creative suggestions for making such tasks easier or more entertaining. Both types tend to be responsive and responsible, so a division of labor is usually easily attainable.

EXTRAVERTED FEELING TYPES (ESFJ/ENFJ) WITH INTROVERTED THINKING TYPES (ISTP/INTP)

When it's working: Although Introverted Thinking types may not express emotions verbally, Extraverted Feeling types who can read between the lines can be aware of their Introverted Thinking partner's concerns and help them negotiate relationship issues. Perhaps because of their difficulty being understood by others, those relationships that Introverted Thinking types do form are of special importance to them—particularly the relationship with their spouse.

While the EFJ partner may carry the lion's share of interaction with the children, the ITP partner is more apt to appreciate than sabotage such intimacy. The successful EFJ and ITP relationship has appreciation flowing both ways. Having time to devote to personal pursuits—whether that means developing a new theory or refining a technique—is of primary importance to Introverted Thinking types. If the Extraverted Feeling type can allow the ITP partner personal space and function without the kind or amount of attention he or she might desire, the relationship can endure and thrive.

When it's not working: The following interchange exemplifies the kind of miscommunication that can occur between Extraverted Feeling and Introverted Thinking types.

EFJ: "Do you still love me? You never tell me you love me anymore."

ITP: "Why do I have to tell you I love you? I married you, didn't I?"

If the Extraverted Feeling type is in any way insecure about his or her desirability as a partner, the Introverted Thinking type partner isn't apt to add much in the way of self-confidence. ITPs aren't being cruel, but they tend to be out of touch with their own emotions and even more with those of others. The world of feelings is one they neither want to live in nor comprehend. The more the Extraverted Feeling type pursues a partner for an expression of feeling, the more the Introverted Thinking type is apt to withdraw—into books or other pursuits. This may leave the EFJ partner frustrated and resentful, wondering if any of their needs are being met in this marriage to an alien creature. In fact, both individuals in this pairing are often likely to wonder what attracted them to each other in the first place. The sexual attraction may be the only bond that persists between them.

Some Helpful Hints

If couples of EFJ and ITP pairing are sufficiently mature to appreciate their differences and help each other in developing the distinctive aspects of themselves, their relationship can work. The Extraverted Feeling type can offer his or her partner a model for dealing with social environments, skill in relating to people, and awareness of feelings. In return, the Introverted Thinking type can teach the Extraverted Feeling type the value of introspection, the art of concentration, and the benefits of being self-directed.

EXTRAVERTED SENSING TYPES (ESTP/ESFP) WITH INTROVERTED SENSING TYPES (ISTJ/ISFJ)

When it's working: If a couple of this pairing utilizes their individual strengths in a balanced, cooperative manner, the partners will learn from each other, appreciate each other's differences, and value what each has to offer in the relationship. ESP and ISJ couples need to be especially careful in the handling of financial matters. The Introverted Sensing type likes the security of a bank account with savings sufficient to cover emergencies. The Extraverted Sensing type likes to be able to satisfy his or her risk-taking proclivities. The partners' understanding and appreciation of each other's choices can help them develop a system—whether it's separate accounts, allotted income percentages, safe and high-risk investing, or some other system—that works for both them.

ESP types can encourage ISJ partners to resist settling into a rut, which, no matter how comfortable, can end up boring and depressing the Extraverted Sensing type. Introverted Sensing types can keep their ESP partners from jumping off some cliff without looking to see if there's a safe landing place below. That is, if the partners understand and value their differences.

When it's not working: A marriage between an Extraverted Sensing type and an Introverted Sensing type can be a disaster if the partners don't appreciate each other's gifts. Each will feel deliberately thwarted in pursuit of their goals. Anger, bitterness, and resentment can mount on both sides. If you can imagine marriage between a grasshopper and an ant, you may gain some understanding of the dynamics. The ant knows what it has to do, how busy it has to be, how hard it has to work, and wants its partner to pull its share of the load. The grasshopper knows how much fun it is to leap from leaf to blossom to tree trunk to rain barrel, trusting the future to take care of itself and wanting a partner to play along and not worry over everything.

Of course, if the relationship gets too heavy or uncomfortable, the grasshopper (or ESP) is very likely to hop right out of it. Extraverted Sensing types, if they are unable to effect compromises, are not likely to remain too long in situations that don't please them. Introverted Sensing types, no matter how unhappy, are much less likely to initiate a separation once they've entered a relationship. They'll often keep trying to make it work.

Extraverted Sensing types seem less likely than other types to enter therapy. Most do not enjoy introspection and would simply rather escape into another environment. If any partner does seek counseling, it will probably be the Introverted Sensing type. Counseling can be effective in helping Introverted Sensing types release pent-up emotions and gain a broader perspective on their situation.

Some Helpful Hints

Extraverted Sensing types can add the sparkle, zest, and excitement to life that steady, reliable Introverted Sensing types often prefer but don't typically generate. Introverted Sensing types can provide the stability that may sporadically exist in the lives of many Extraverted Sensing types. The children of this couple can benefit from having one parent who is more focused on providing structure and one who more often finds ways to offer fun and unexpected surprises.

EXTRAVERTED SENSING TYPES (ESTP/ESFP) WITH INTROVERTED FEELING TYPES (ISFP/INFP)

When it's working: When these two types become involved, the attraction, especially the sexual attraction, can be very strong. Each partner's style puzzles and intrigues the other. The depth and mystique of the Introverted Feeling partner's inner world often stirs and challenges the Extraverted Sensing type. The flair and ease with which the Extraverted Sensing type handles the outside world often amazes the Introverted Feeling type.

The Extraverted Sensing type is likely to create fun and excitement for children in the family. Play time is highly valued by the ESP parent, who will probably encourage active recreation. If there are problems, however, with a child being ill or unhappy, it is more likely to be the Introverted Feeling parent who comes through and provides the support the child in crisis needs.

If the Extraverted Sensing partner decides to "experiment" with the family's financial resources, the Introverted Feeling type is apt to feel less anxious and annoyed than most other Introverts would. Money and material possessions generally hold less value for Introverted Feeling types than for other types. When Extraverted Sensing partners are successful financially, Introverted Feeling partners are happily freed from having to make ends meet and can pursue their interests wherever their creativity leads them.

When it's not working: Sometimes, the differences between Extraverted Sensing and Introverted Feeling partners will lead to intense clashes over the values each one lives by. Expediency and idealism make strange bedfellows, and when mutual respect disappears from the relationship, there isn't much left to keep it glued together. Despite the fact that more couples today choose a partnership of equals, there can often be more problems in ESP and IFP relationships where the male is the IF type. The traditional cultural role model for males remains imprinted on our society and, spoken or unspoken, the male is often expected to be the primary financial provider. Couples would do well to examine and discuss their expectations and even consider taking turns being the "provider," thus freeing the other up to pursue interests regardless of financial status.

Problems involving the children can also be severe for ESP and IFP parents. The Extraverted Sensing type is more likely than other types to disappear when problems arise because in an Extraverted Sensing type's perspective, life is supposed to be fun and exciting. Similarly, if the Extraverted Sensing parent withdraws physically, the Introverted Feeling type may withdraw into an inner world to avoid wrangling with problems that seem beyond control. In such cases, children may feel both physically and emotionally abandoned at the very time they need their parents most. It might be wise for ESP and IFP types to postpone parenting until they have resolved some of their own relationship dynamics.

Some Helpful Hints

If the nitty-gritty details of everyday life don't interfere in the process, these two have a great deal to learn from each other. The Introverted Feeling partner can help the Extraverted Sensing type become more self-aware and develop a richness of character instead of coasting on the surface of life. The Extraverted Sensing partner can encourage the Introverted Feeling type to experience the outer world more often, to develop more effective social skills, and to recognize his or her strengths.

EXTRAVERTED SENSING TYPES (ESTP/ESFP) WITH INTROVERTED INTUITIVE TYPES (INTJ/INFJ)

When it's working: If you want to observe yet another attraction of opposites, you'll find it in this pairing. Extraverted Sensing types are very much "outer" directed. They are always aware of who wants what and why, and their actions tend to be governed by these perceptions. Introverted Intuitive types are very much "inner" directed and are likely to miss what is going on around them because of the intensity with which they focus on their goals. Extraverted Sensing and Introverted Intuitive styles may prove complementary, and indeed each partner has a lot to learn from the other. This pairing is highly unusual, however, and there may be, according to our experiences, little to hold such couples together past the initial dating period. If the individuals do commit to long-term relationships, each partner will need to make adjustments. More often than not, though, the Extraverted Sensing type will be the partner to make the most and the biggest adjustments. While an INFJ may "accommodate" a partner to some extent, an INTJ is less likely to do so.

If he or she misinterprets the INJ type's reserve as weakness or compliance, the ESP partner is probably in for a rude awakening. If each partner can learn to understand and value the other partner's strengths, the couple can work to develop a satisfying relationship.

Where child rearing is concerned, the Introverted Intuitive parent may provide the necessary stability and resourcefulness. The emotional and physical bonds between an INFJ parent and his or her children are likely to be especially strong. While the Extraverted Sensing type parent may provide the children with fun and stimulation, the Introverted Intuitive partner will probably function as the steady caregiver.

When it's not working: When the romantic glow of a fresh relationship is gone, the ESP and INJ partners are apt to step back and see each other in the cold, hard glare of reality (or what each perceives as reality). The Introverted Intuitive type, who values integrity above all else, may appear to the Extraverted Sensing partner as rigid, impractical, eccentric, almost like a creature from another planet. The Extraverted Sensing type, who values practical ability to make things work, may appear to the Introverted Intuitive partner as manipulative, flighty, bereft of values—the kind of person who believes the ends justify the means. The disapproval, disrespect, and mutual scorn each partner may show for the other will certainly threaten the survival of this relationship.

The Introverted Intuitive partner's long-range goals and future vision provide little immediate satisfaction for the Extraverted Sensing type, who is much more likely to live in the here and now and want what they want today. The expensive gifts and exciting toys purchased by the Extraverted Sensing type may seem like sabotage to the INJ partner, whose dreams and plans often include more sensible purchases, such as a new home or a child's college education. Battles over finances and who is to control the checkbook will undoubtedly play a large part in this couple's life—until they learn to capitalize on each other's strengths.

Some Helpful Hints

By talking things out and seeking resolutions that bring each partner at least moderate satisfaction, the couple can prevent the accumulation of resentments and hostilities. In the long run, finances are best handled by the Introverted Intuitive type, recreation and entertainment by the Extraverted Sensing type. Each partner's willingness to let the other do what he or she does best will help resolve differences. The Introverted Intuitive partner would be wise to encourage the Extraverted Sensing partner to plan that hot air balloon trip, for instance, and be willing to go along, even if it seems like a waste of time. Similarly, the ESP partner needs to check in with the INJ partner before making large, luxury purchases, and both partners should negotiate an agreement on the big-ticket items.

EXTRAVERTED SENSING TYPES (ESTP/ESFP) WITH INTROVERTED THINKING TYPES (ISTP/INTP)

When it's working: This combination of types works best when the Introverted Thinking type is an ISTP rather than an INTP. The Extraverted Sensing type's engagement in the here-and-now world is not matched by the INTPs detached cerebral interests. And, from the INTP's logical standpoint, a relationship with someone of such radically different perceptions, styles, and values wouldn't make much sense anyway. Common interests unrelated to type may be the glue that holds them together.

The ISTP type will be more appealing to Extraverted Sensing types than the INTP. Extraverted Sensing types and ISTPs approach life as an adventure, and excitement is a high priority for both. As partners the two are apt to congratulate themselves and each other for not being "stuck" with someone too conventional or traditional. ESP and ISTP parents will encourage their children to take risks and to be fully present in the physical world.

When it's not working: When things go awry for ESP and ITP couples, the partners will find fault with and blame the other and not understand why "someone" isn't picking up the pieces and bringing order out of chaos. Structuring and continuity in family life are not assets for these types. Both partners may withdraw physically or emotionally when problems arise, and their children will have little stability as a result.

Some Helpful Hints

If the Introverted Thinking type shows willingness to step forward and grasp the adventure that ESP types prefer, the Extraverted Sensing partner may be willing to set aside time for the quieter pursuits the ITP type enjoys. In other words, the partners need to find ways to share each other's worlds. Extraverted Sensing types are acutely aware of and stimulated by everything that happens around them. The Extraverted Sensing type can learn to appreciate the more introspective focus of the Introverted Thinking type regardless of the interest, and the ITP type can discover joy in participating in the ESP type's suggestion of active expression of those interests.

EXTRAVERTED INTUITIVE TYPES (ENTP/ENFP) WITH INTROVERTED SENSING TYPES (ISTJ/ISFJ)

When it's working: If ENP and ISJ partners can find ways to complement each other, this relationship has good potential. The Extraverted Intuitive partner can bring excitement and flexibility into the relationship, and the Introverted Sensing partner can provide stability and structure. Few types can rival the Introverted Sensing type for dependability and a sensible approach to life. Few types can rival the Extraverted Intuitive type for ease of manner and lively discourse. If one partner happens to have a Feeling preference and the other a Thinking preference, the couple will embody opposite preference pairs on each of the four dichotomies. While this can present challenges, it also offers each partner the rare opportunity to discover unconscious aspects of his or her own psyche mirrored in the partner. Such an opportunity for psychological self-discovery and growth is seldom so readily available at home.

When it's not working: Chances are the Introverted Sensing type will want a predictable, traditional lifestyle—a good steady job for one or both partners, dinners at home, enough money to be able to plan and budget—values that Extraverted Intuitive types may find confining. ENP partners, who tend to get caught up in the moment, may forget to extend their mates certain relationship courtesies (like calling home when they're going to be late), and such behaviors can become a source of friction.

Introverted Sensing types tend to expect that certain routines will be followed; Extraverted Intuitive types tend to go with the flow. When an ENP partner disrupts the established routine, the ISJ partner is apt to misinterpret that action as an expression of disregard. The Extraverted Intuitive partner, on the other hand, is apt to find the Introverted Sensing partner unreasonably controlling and can't understand why dinnertime has to be set in stone.

Some Helpful Hints

Introverted Sensing types prefer order. In marriages or intimate partnerships they tend to impose order through schedules and rituals of various kinds. Extraverted Intuitive types, on the other hand, want to be open to life's possibilities and don't want to be bound by artificial structures. Both partners' wishes must be taken care of if this relationship is to work well. Introverted Sensing types need to be careful not to make so many and such rigid demands that they fuel the ENP's natural resistance to customs or patterns they haven't agreed to. Extraverted Intuitive types need to be careful not to be too elusive or random. ENPs can learn to participate in some of the more mundane duties that are part of any relationship. Extraverted Intuitive types will respond better if chores can be made fun. Encourage the partners to put the music on, laugh, and talk as they work around the house or do errands. Life doesn't always have to be serious!

Extraverted Intuitive Types (ENTP/ENFP) with Introverted Feeling Types (ISFP/INFP)

When it's working: The quality of sensitivity that ENP and IFP type partners offer each other can be truly remarkable. Both partners are apt to cherish a dream of self-fulfillment, and because both may be creative and unbound by convention or tradition, realization of this dream is possible. When both partners are Feeling types, their love can rival that of a romantic movie's hero and heroine; when both are Feeling types, their sharing of emotional values can keep the relationship alive and well. Even though ENTP types may not share a partner's Feeling preference, they still need to receive warm, open expression from a partner, as they don't often allow themselves to be vulnerable in other situations. A rich and animated social milieu and meaningful personal lives will characterize ENP and IFP type relationships when they're working.

When it's not working: If the Extraverted Intuitive partner's moods are unpredictable and volatile (as they sometimes are), the Introverted Feeling partner may eventually give up trying to significantly interact with the EN partner. In turn, the ENP partner may feel misunderstood and unappreciated if they get little or no response from the Introverted Feeling partner. What's more, the Extraverted Intuitive type may be shocked to discover that, under pressure, the IF partner can explode and rant, too. Because Introverted Feeling types typically want harmony, ENFP and INFP partners may try to avoid unpleasantness until their repressed resentment gets almost too big to handle. The ENTP, by contrast, is more likely to confront problems earlier and more directly, which can also be alienating if it is not done in a manner sensitive enough for the Introverted Feeling type. Emotional distance, silence, and resentment broken by emotional outbursts can characterize this relationship when it's not working.

Some Helpful Hints

Both partners need to pay enough attention each other. When the Extraverted Intuitive type gets caught up in the outside world and the Introverted Feeling type is immersed in his or her own pursuits, the partners tend to lose sight of each other. Both partners do best when their relationship is a stage for enacting their dreams; the partners need only manage the workaday world well enough to avoid serious disarray. Mundane tasks should be equitably divided and the partners free to do their chores on their own timetables. Criticism needs to be constructive and kept to a minimum. Because the creative potential in this relationship is substantial, realizing that potential is perhaps the most important goal the couple can pursue. IFP types sometimes have trouble finding ways to tangibly express their ideals in a public domain. The Extraverted Intuitive type can help the Introverted Feeling partner translate his or her ideas and ideals into action and accomplishment. The Introverted Feeling type can help the Extraverted Intuitive partner, who tends to try to be all things to all people, find center and act from it. Such forms of mutual support can be quite profound, and through them each partner may find his or her own way to psychic wholeness.

Extraverted Intuitive Types (ENTP/ENFP) with Introverted Intuitive Types (INTJ/INFJ)

When it's working: A host of knowledge and possibilities are available to these couples because in all the combinations Intuition is the dominant function in each partner. Intuition allows them to see opportunities and explore ideas with more facility than other types. Because Extraverted Intuitive types focus on the outside world and Introverted Intuitive types on their inner worlds, the partners' combination of insights can be astonishing. While the partners may be puzzled about practical applications for their insights, the depth and excitement they bring to the relationship may be expressed in high romance. Mutual sensitivity is crucial to the success of this relationship. Intuitive types can be acutely aware of the "atmosphere," and if Introverted Intuitive types get too caught up in being responsible, a sensitive partner can monitor this tendency, help out, and alert the INJ partner when it's time to take it easy. Extraverted Intuitive types can spread themselves too thin, taking on too many projects for too many people. Again, a sensitive partner can help the ENP gauge limitations, prioritize, and rest from labors.

When it's not working: If both types get caught up and busy in handling the world, the sensitivity they normally express for each other may be diminished. The Introverted Intuitive partner may resent the time and energy the Extraverted Intuitive partner expends outside the relationship, especially if home responsibilities get neglected. In turn, the more hostility, frostiness, and resentment the ENP partner picks up at home, the more he or she is apt to avoid the INJ partner, thus aggravating the whole syndrome. If the Extraverted Intuitive partner shares the couple's problems with a friend, the Introverted Intuitive partner is apt to experience such disclosure as a violation or betrayal. A partner's positive energy is essential to keeping the ENP partner's engine running; deep, loving involvement from one special person is crucial to the INJ partner's contentment.

Some Helpful Hints

Both partners can use their considerable insight to discern one another's needs and meet them in the particular ways each one prefers. Introverted Intuitive partners may need extra help handling some of the responsibilities that tend to weigh so heavily on them and that they find so difficult to put down. Extraverted Intuitive partners may need more of the positive interaction that energizes them to respond to the routine requirements of the relationship. If both partners can remember that people in relationships tend to give the kind of attention and responses they want back (and not necessarily what would come naturally from a partner), they can gain helpful insight into one another's longings.

An Introverted Intuitive type will occasionally need the partner to take more responsibility—a role Extraverted Intuitive types may find hard to fulfill unless it is in their own time and in their own way. An Extraverted Intuitive type needs a good experience of the relationship, which the Introverted Intuitive may have trouble providing if they feel resentful about shouldering too many responsibilities. Both partners must learn how to use their creativity and goodwill to end stalemates. Otherwise, the ENP partner may flee the scene, while the INJ partner remains behind to sulk alone.

EXTRAVERTED INTUITIVE TYPES (ENTP/ENFP) WITH INTROVERTED THINKING TYPES (ISTP/INTP)

When it's working: When both partners have a Thinking preference in common, there can be a great deal of understanding between them. While maintaining the relationship, each partner will be similarly engaged in active pursuit of their unique interests. If one partner has a Feeling preference (the ENFP), the relationship can be enhanced by two differing perspectives: one colored by the Feeling type's values and the other by the Thinking type's logic. In our experience, individuals with a Feeling preference and those with a Thinking preference do tend to pair up. The partners' sharing of singular insights and ideas gleaned from their distinct interests can add sparkle to the relationship. At times though, Extraverted Intuitive types can be too wordy, while Introverted Thinking types can be too terse. The partners can still enjoy stimulating conversation if each cultivates patience for the other's rhetorical style.

When it's not working: Because of their desire to be all things to all people, Extraverted Intuitive types may seek more variety, excitement, and fun than the contemplative and intellectually self-reliant ITP type can provide.

In such cases, communication can become frustrating or break down entirely. The Extravert's need for social activity and the Introvert's need for solitude can drive the partners to argue about how they spend their time and energy. Many ISTPs and INTPs, for example, want to spend a lot of time in virtual realities, reading, or online. If sustained over time, however, this kind of withdrawal can drain energy from a relationship. Although ENP and ITP types (especially INTPs) both tend to be creative and original, when their relationship is under stress they are apt to criticize rather than appreciate one another's gifts in vain efforts to remake their partners in their own images.

Some Helpful Hints

New and creative ideas and innovative ways of saying things will always intrigue the Extraverted Intuitive type. Thus, if he or she is willing to share it, the Introverted Thinking partner's inner world can become a point of common ground for the couple. ENP and ITP types prefer to pursue their own interests in their own ways, rather than follow someone else's lead. Either partner's interference in or criticism of the other's creative route or independence can prove not only hurtful but crippling. It is important for each partner to give the other ample room to be themselves, appreciating their particular style and gifts for what they are. The Extraverted Intuitive type can escort the Introverted Thinking partner toward more outwardly interactive involvement in life; the Introverted Thinking type can find ways to systematize domestic details in order to free both partners to pursue their separate and mutual interests. The ITP partner prefers to devise ingenious systems; the ENP partner prefers to generate lively enthusiasm: this combination of gifts can make great things happen.

Part Three

9
A Closer Look at Conflict Areas

"THE ARTFUL DENIAL OF A PROBLEM WILL NOT PRODUCE CONVICTION; ON THE CONTRARY, A WIDER AND HIGHER CONSCIOUSNESS IS CALLED FOR TO GIVE US THE CERTAINTY AND CLARITY WE NEED."

C. G. Jung, *Modern Man in Search of a Soul*

The Subtleties of Conflict

Our clinical population is from Hawaii, where we have been in practice for more than thirty years. Hawaii is both liberal and conservative. On one side, it was the first state to pass the Equal Rights Amendment. On the other side, many residents maintain traditional values even though most women in the state work. Because Hawaii has many immigrants from Asia, the Pacific Islands, and the Philippines, we frequently see men who expect, with regard to their cultural traditions, to be absolute "heads of household." Some expect to continue defining women's roles as they were defined in their native countries. Transition from traditional to more modern gender roles is currently in progress, however.

Many psychologists, sociologists, and anthropologists have studied both successful and unsuccessful relationships in an attempt to predict the possibility of two people living "happily ever after." But while similarities of cultural variables such as age, race, religion, ethnic origin, and socioeconomic class provide a less stressful context in which partners can interact, such similarities provide no guarantee that a relationship will last. Most research looks at partners' similarities or differences in terms of the marriage relationship, but this paradigm is pertinent to intimate relationships in general—both heterosexual and homosexual. Though in this book we give examples of male-female relationships, our experience indicates that type concepts apply to same-sex couples as well.

We have found that it's possible to look at even relatively good relationships and still identify areas where conflicts are likely to occur. Partners in such relationships may share similar cultural and socioeconomic backgrounds. There may be no indications of spouse or child abuse, no problems of alcohol or drug addiction, no incest, and no involvement of either partner in criminal activities. Even so, these apparent and fundamentally important similarities and behaviors are not always enough to keep a relationship intact.

We have also learned through our practice that for every couple there are certain key areas of potential conflict that can make or break a relationship. These fall into the following twelve categories: (1) communication; (2) money; (3) sex and affection; (4) values; (5) interests; (6) recreation; (7) decision making; (8) time and responsibility; (9) chores; (10) children; (11) in-laws; and (12) friends.

As we take a closer look at these areas, consider how they relate to interactions between your clients as partners on the basis of their types. In this chapter we offer do's and don'ts that your couples may find useful as guidelines for resolving problems. Tables 9.1 and 9.2 will give you a quick overview of how type figures into general areas of conflict in relationships. Other tables in this chapter address specific areas of conflict.

POWER FACTORS IN CONFLICTS

The first three areas of potential conflict in relationships—communication, money, and sex—are often the arenas in which needs for power and control are played out. Struggles may be overt or subtle, conscious or unconscious. Almost every other kind of relationship problem will also manifest in these areas. In other words, how we spend our money, when and how we "make

TABLE 9.1

How Some Preference Combination Viewpoints May Lead to Relationship Conflict

The following examples are expressions of ways in which various preferences or combinations of preferences may view experiences. Consider each viewpoint and become familiar with how these can lead to conflict among couples.

PREFERENCE(S)	VIEWPOINT
ISJs	If you take a long time to do something, you're slow and compulsive; if I take a long time, I'm thorough.
EJs	When you go ahead and do something without consulting me, you're testing my limits; when I go ahead and do something on my own, I'm showing initiative.
Ps	If you don't follow through, you're lazy; when I don't follow through, I'm busy.
Js	When you state your side strongly, you're being bullheaded; when I state my side strongly, I'm being firm.
SJs	When you take on extra work at your job, you're ignoring the family's needs; when I do, I'm planning for the family's security.
Ns	When you do something unexpected, you're inconsiderate; when I do something you weren't expecting, I'm original and creative.
ETJs	If you get your chores done and have time to relax, you probably could have done a better job; if I finish my chores early, I'm an effective organizer and planner.

TABLE 9.2

The Types and How They Fight

EXTRAVERTED THINKING TYPES

ESTJs and ENTJs prefer to strategize. If that doesn't work, they may speed up verbalization, overpower the partner with a specific tone of voice, and/or use explosions of anger to win a point. The competition is fierce, even when the going gets rough.

INTROVERTED THINKING TYPES

ISTPs and INTPs may become so theoretical and abstract that partners get lost following the mazes they construct. Partners may finally give up just to get their minds "unboggled." Partners may understand but not agree.

EXTRAVERTED FEELING TYPES

ESFJs and ENFJs may become emotional, cry, and then become angry. However, because they prefer harmony, their hearts aren't really in the fight. They'll concede fairly quickly if they can find a reason for conceding. Unity will win over logic.

INTROVERTED FEELING TYPES

ISFPs and INFPs are likely to withdraw very quickly (either emotionally or physically) from any battle unless their primary values are at risk. If partners think their Introverted Feeling type partners are pushovers, they're in for a surprise. There can be no compromise: ideals are ideals to many Introverted Feeling types.

EXTRAVERTED SENSING TYPES

ESTPs and ESFPs typically use their ability to see details and to tolerate another's point of view to gather all available information in the effort to effect a compromise. Coming to a workable solution quickly is more appealing than the fight.

INTROVERTED SENSING TYPES

ISTJs and ISFJs may believe that they know all the facts, all the rules and regulations that may pertain to the situation, and quote them—perhaps more than once. Organization and facts lead to solutions.

Extraverted Intuitive Types

ENTPs and ENFPs may take the wind out of partners' sails by seeming to be agreeable. But subsequently the partner finds him or herself doing exactly what the Extraverted Intuitive type wanted in the first place. Use finesse to gain accord.

Introverted Intuitive Types

INTJs and INFJs tend to simply "out-stubborn" partners. Those who think they can win a fight with an Introverted Intuitive type by shouting, manipulating, or coercing will find that none of these tactics work. The Introverted Intuitive type quietly but persistently holds onto his or her own point of view, while the partner's energy runs out. Such conflicts need to be resolved at a deeper level because there may be underlying issues.

love," and whose ideas prevail in a discussion are all important indices for establishing equity and balance in a relationship. When one partner feels she or he must go along with the other partner, and there is no real choice, anger and resentment—expressed or not—build up. On the other hand, when each individual can trust that decisions in the relationship are joint and mutual, supporting both partners' best interests, then the relationship is strengthened and enhanced.

Communication

Communication—the interchange of thoughts and feelings—can be verbal or nonverbal. Sometimes a look or gesture will have more meaning than spoken words. A gentle hand on the shoulder, a look that says, "I'm really glad to see you," a wink and a smile—each of these can brighten a dull day for either partner. Nowadays, as in the past, women tend to voice a greater degree of dissatisfaction with the quality and quantity of communication in their relationships than do men. Relationship counseling is often initiated by the woman in an attempt to get her needs in this area met.

Satisfying communication is essential to a relationship. Almost everyone who enters couples' counseling starts by defining their problems in terms of communication. Details of clients' communication patterns are important and often intersect type-based behavior. While some clients may resist being specific, precision is crucial to outlining exactly where and how types differ. Questions from a counselor such as "*What* does she say that makes you angry?" or "*How* do you feel controlled by his moods?" can help clients filter out real issues from the haze of negative feeling.

Extraversion and Introversion seem to have more impact on communication than do the other preferences. As you'll recall, Extraverts need to interact with others in order to clarify their thoughts and feelings while Introverts need to process information internally before entering into dialogue. It is clear how such needs might be in conflict. Added to this is the fact that Extraverts are energized by interaction while Introverts are often drained by it. When an Introverted partner is out spending most of his or her energy in on-the-job interactions and an Extraverted partner is at home with the children (and therefore bursting with energy and starved for adult conversation), their encounter at the front door in the evening is apt to be less than satisfying for both.

One of our Extraverted clients, thoroughly frustrated with an Introverted Thinking man, reported the following:

> *"He doesn't say things that need to be said, how he feels about the situation, how he feels about me. As an example, we have talked quite a bit recently—or I have—about my having too much of the burden of housework, child care, et cetera. In your office he said that he felt bad about this. He never said that to me. His response to things that upset me is often so blah that sometimes I find myself yelling just to get through to him. If I try to bring up problems he either gets preoccupied with TV or a book, or interrupts with superficial solutions."*

Another Extraverted woman reported:

> *"He doesn't want to hear anything bad, sad, or upsetting if it concerns me. So I have not been relating my innermost thoughts and fears to him—and this is not how I expected marriage to be."*

Introverts also voice complaints, as one woman reported:

> *"I always felt I did 90 percent of the listening and that what I had to say was of marginal importance. He just gets frustrated when I have difficulty articulating what's bothering me and walks away."*

Men also voice complaints.

> *"I've told her many times how tight our budget is, but when she gets unhappy, she just buys things we don't need. It's as though she doesn't hear me."*

Perhaps an incident from Ruth's marriage will demonstrate what happens when needs are in conflict. Ruth and her husband were awakened by the police telling them that their daughter had been in an accident and that she was being taken to a hospital. On the drive to the hospital, Ruth's Extraverted husband needed to talk to handle his anxiety. She could not talk. As an Introvert, she needed her energy to handle her feelings and get them under control so she could be calm and supportive for her daughter when she arrived at the hospital.

Neither Ruth nor her husband was bad or wrong—but she recalled being unable to give him the conversation he needed to handle his feelings; and he was unable to give Ruth the quiet she needed to handle her feelings.

Where communication problems are concerned, Sensing (S) and Intuitive (N) type partners tend to talk past each other. When partner N wants to talk about "what could be" and partner S want to confront "the facts," they may both get extremely frustrated. "Why discuss buying a house if we have no money?" This is the kind of fairly typical reproach with which a Sensing type partner challenges an Intuitive type partner. Sensing types may bore Intuitive types with details. Intuitive types may begin discussing a subject at a narrative midpoint, an approach that is often unclear to Sensing types, who want a frame of reference or a topic sentence.

Interestingly, differences in the ways Thinking and Feeling types make judgments can be mutually beneficial or create conflict, depending on context and specific variables. A Thinking type man, for example, expressed dissatisfaction about communications with his Feeling type wife: "She's impossible to reason with. Her logic is nonexistent on most topics, regardless of the critical nature of the topic." The woman in this situation was equally frustrated: "He makes me feel backed up against the wall—like we're playing some game and I don't know the rules. He makes me feel inadequate and then I get furious with him."

Feeling type women really can infuriate Thinking type men, especially Intuitive Feeling type women who often make the time-worn complaint, "If you really loved me, you would know how I feel." NF women aren't always willing to tell a boyfriend or husband how they feel, because in their view "he should already know." Even when he makes the effort, a Thinking type man has enough difficulty unlocking his own feelings let alone those of his partner. An ENTP man, discouraged with his Introverted Feeling partner, stated: "If I say something my partner disagrees with, she turns away completely and will not speak to me at all—about anything—sometimes for days. So we almost never get anything important resolved."

Communication between Judging and Perceiving partners holds just as many challenges as it does for other types. Judging types can seem pushy and demanding in their need for closure. Perceiving types tend to revisit decisions after a partner thought they were settled. Partner J's, "I thought we decided we were vacationing at the beach this year," is apt to be met by partner P's, "I know, but I think I'd really rather go camping or hiking."

If these kinds of problems sound similar to some of those your clients have described, here's a list of practical solutions we've found to be effective in keeping communication open and healthy.

 ***Don'ts to share with your couple clients:***

- Don't bring up controversial issues at a busy time. Save them for weekend or after-dinner discussions when you can devote time and attention to issues without being pressured.
- Don't use information that's been shared earlier against your partner in an argument. It's a sure way to destroy trust.
- Don't rush to fill in conversational gaps if you're waiting for a response from an Introverted partner. A few moments of silence provides Introverted types room to answer.
- Don't talk over or louder than the other person, especially when you disagree. Wait your turn, or say, "I need my turn now."
- Don't make judgments until you have heard your partner. It's easy to assume incorrectly that you know what they're going to say.

 ***Do's to share with your couple clients:***

- When an Introverted partner comes home after a day at work, wait awhile to initiate communication. Introverts need time and space to regroup energies in some way, for example soaking in a tub, reading the newspaper, having a drink, watching TV, or whatever else gives them an opportunity to go "inside" and process the day. Depending on the stress of the day, this can be from twenty minutes to an hour before an Introvert is ready to share. But it will be better quality sharing!

- Introverts need to learn to share with their mates. In a partnership, both people need to stay informed, at the very least, about important events; they also need to periodically update one another about personal information.
- Schedule time for sharing if you can. A long, leisurely walk after dinner (the dishes can wait) without interruptions from telephone, TV, or children can provide the structure and atmosphere for continuing dialogues.
- Extraverts, who love to talk, need to remember to create a safe space in which an Introvert can respond. Introverts will usually talk when they feel comfortable. If they sense they've entered a conflict zone, however, they may say nothing or leave it as soon as possible.
- Learn to speak the other person's language—just a little—to appreciate your partner's point of view better and to learn how to be more patient.

Tips for Client Communication

Encourage your clients, before they engage in a serious conversation with a partner, to take a moment to facilitate the process by using one of the following communication strategies.

When you want to communicate with—

Extraverts, *because of all the competing outer-world things they attend to,*

Say, *"I have something to talk about. Is this a good time? If not, when?"*

Introverts, *because of all the competing inner-world things they attend to,*

Say, *"Are you available? I want to talk about something."*

Sensing types, *because they prefer to focus on tangibles,*
Say, *"Can we be creative about this?"*

Intuitive types, *because they prefer to focus on intangibles,*
Say, *"Can we focus on the factual basis for what we're talking about?"*

Thinking types, *because they prefer to stay somewhat detached,*
Say, *"This is something very important to me. I need you to understand, not solve."*

Feeling types, *because they prefer to get quite involved,*
Say, *"Take a moment to consider this point of view before you respond."*

Judging types, *because they want to know what the plan is,*
Say, *"Please keep an open mind while I explore options with you."*

Perceiving types, *because they want to have it all,*
Say, *"Tell me what's most important to you."*

Finances

The power conflicts that crop up in this area generally relate to the earning, management, and distribution of income. Nowadays, we know it is typical for both partners in a relationship to work and earn money. In fact, economic necessity often requires that both partners work outside the home, even if one partner only works part time. Both partners typically have to weave child rearing around their careers, and it isn't unusual for a woman to get only six weeks' leave for childbirth, recovery, and bonding with her infant before having to return to work. Women today know their freedom is tied to economic independence; relationships don't always last "till death do us part," even though we still may say those words.

Self-supporting women in relationships are typically more assertive and demand more equity in economic decision making than their female predecessors of earlier times. This economic power shift has brought with it more open conflicts regarding money and partners need to be careful in their division of economic responsibilities. Some partners believe they are better money managers and, reluctant to pick up household responsibilities, stake out finances as their principal domain. Other partners, who are apt to feel responsible for the home despite their day jobs, often resent the others thinking their responsibilities end as soon as they enter the house at the end of a workday. At this juncture, we might recall Carl Jung's words: "Where love rules, there is no will to power." All of us will be wise to negotiate what we want in a relationship in a spirit of love; acting out of power or control can be destructive. We need to continually check our own motivations.

Type differences also contribute to power struggles over family finances. Sensing Judging type partners are likely to hold conservative values where money is concerned. They are more than likely to invest carefully, want to save for a home, have some sort of retirement plan, and maintain college funds for their children. Sensing Perceiving type partners may be more willing to take financial risks than other types and are less likely to want to be tied down to a job or community through home ownership. One ESFP woman reported in a counseling session that her ESTJ partner invariably tried to talk her out of spending: "I often agree that what I want isn't necessary, but then I feel angry and resentful." Another ESFP woman attributed her wild spending sprees to her resistance to being controlled by her Judging type partner: "He treats me like a child—why not act like one?" Attitudes about how money should be spent are also influenced by type differences. Speaking of her ISTJ partner, an Introverted Feeling type (INFP) wistfully reported: "I'd much rather have had a romantic vacation—even a weekend—than the dishwasher my partner bought me!"

Where money is concerned, particular types have particular and very real needs. Because Judging types prefer to have a security about money, they might want to keep a personal savings account in addition to a joint account. Perceiving types, on the other hand, prefer to have a certain freedom to spend money. They might want to maintain a vacation account or a luxuries account. Extraverted Perceiving types may take the kinds of financial risks that make Introverted Judging types anxious. They may gamble occasionally or make high-risk investments. Each type should be free to have as many needs met as possible without jeopardizing a partner's mental health or the financial stability of the household. Some types can pull off a big gamble; others are better savers. Clients need to know their own and their partners' capacities and limitations in money matters and set up their finances accordingly.

If your clients are arguing about money, it's likely that one partner is a Sensing and the other an Intuitive type or that one is a Judging and the other a Perceiving type. To these couples you can recommend the following do's and don'ts.

Don'ts to tell your couple:

- Don't make each other account for every penny.
- Don't expect to continue to use your money any way you choose. In a relationship, how you spend money has an impact on your partner.
- Don't use credit cards (except for gas) if one of you is a compulsive or impulsive spender.
- Don't plan only for the present or the future; both need to be considered.

Do's to tell your couple:

- Set up triple checking accounts (yours, mine, and ours) with either a small percentage of each salary (if salaries are fairly similar) or matched amounts going into the individual accounts. Neither partner should have to account to the other for expenditures out of his or her individual account, so make sure you're comfortable with the arrangement from the outset.
- As an alternative to the triple accounts approach, pool your funds, but consult each other to reach an agreement before making expensive purchases when shopping alone. Use your financial situation to decide the cutoff point: $200, $500, $1000, and so on.
- If one of you is not a wage earner, discuss what you are or will be contributing until both of you are satisfied that this is a valuable contribution. Without sufficient exploration, discussion, and agreement in advance, both of you may feel used and resentful later on. Statements such as "You never contributed anything—it was all my hard work and money" or "I gave up my career to have your baby" are the kinds of accusations we hear when equity isn't established between partners.
- If one of you has a Judging preference and the other a Perceiving preference, consider letting the Judging type partner keep the joint checkbook as the Judging partner may be more willing to deal with the structure involved in maintaining the checkbook while the Perceiving partner may not have the need for precision bookkeeping.
- While honoring the need for careful bookkeeping, allow each other the occasional fun of spontaneous spending for special things.

Coping with Stress

Stress isn't always a bad thing. It can be a great motivator, driving people to survive accidents and misfortunes and to accomplish things they wouldn't otherwise accomplish in a relaxed or passive state. On the other hand, certain of life's events, both expected and unexpected, impose particularly intense coping demands on individuals, with the death of a spouse or close family member, separation and divorce, major personal illness, or losing a job ranking among the top ten most significant stressors.

We tend to forget that stress is an actual physical response of the body to a variety of internal and external pressures and that internal, as much as external, pressure can cause physical and mental pain. Personality type impacts the experience of and ability to cope with such pain. The perfectionism of an Introverted Feeling type, for example, can in itself be a source of stress as an individual of this type strives to avoid error, to excel in all pursuits, to please others and, in expecting the same of others and the world, struggles with anger and disappointment.

When one partner experiences prolonged or extreme stress, it puts a strain on the relationship; when both people are needy at the same time, the relationship may be in serious trouble. If one partner loses a parent and the other a job, for example, neither will have much mental or physical energy left over to give the other. By becoming aware of the nature and extent of their own and each other's struggles, the partners will be better equipped to give a partner healthy support at critical moments. In table 9.3 (page 146) are some examples of the type-based support you can encourage your clients to offer each other.

Sex and Affection

Researchers have probably paid more attention to the sexual aspect of relationships than to any other source of marital difficulties. From the extensive research of Kinsey (1948, 1953) and Masters and Johnson (1970) as well as the Hite reports (1987, 2004) to the popular how-to-do-it books of the present era, our primary relationship focus, at least in America, has been on the pleasures of sex. The principal assumption underlying this focus seems to be that, among all other causal factors, sex can make or break a relationship.

Power issues often affect sexual attitudes and behaviors. In traditional power dynamics between men and women, men want to be "the pursu-

TABLE 9.3

Types and Stress

Extraverted Thinking Types (ESTJ, ENTJ) can offer their partners . . .	A rational look at the overall picture. A description of strategies to help reduce stress.
Introverted Thinking Types (ISTP, INTP) can offer their partners . . .	A deep, perceptive analysis of the situation causing the stress and solutions for dealing with it.
Extraverted Feeling Types (ESFJ, ENFJ) can offer their partners . . .	Sincere caring and support and suggestions for how to deal with some of the people involved in the situation.
Introverted Feeling Types (ISFP, INFP) can offer their partners . . .	Awareness of the partner's depth of feeling. Creativity to help a partner see their situation in different, and possibly lighter, ways.
Extraverted Sensing Types (ESTP, ESFP) can offer their partners . . .	Fresh views of the situation which may help develop productive insights. Examples of how not to stay caught in a stressful, nonproductive situation.
Introverted Sensing Types (ISTJ, ISFJ) can offer their partners . . .	Certainty that their mate is going to stand by them through this stressful time.
Extraverted Intuitive Types (ENTP, ENFP) can offer their partners . . .	Imaginative, creative problem-solving. Wisdom and insight that make "letting go" easier.
Introverted Intuitive Types (INTJ, INFJ) can offer their partners . . .	An insightful look at the problem and how it came about. A variety of options for resolving the problem.

ers," aggressively seeking affection and sex. Increasing social intolerance of sexual harassment has mitigated this attitude to some extent, even while it has made some men more cautious about how they seek relationships. At present, the sex roles of men and women are no longer as clearly or rigidly defined as they were at least through the first three quarters of the twentieth century. Women are more likely to initiate relationships as well as sex, and men are more likely to appreciate this traditional role reversal. The threat of sexually transmitted diseases, particularly HIV and AIDS has increased the caution of both sexes where casual coupling is concerned. As compared with attitudes that persisted even through the 1970s, when virginity was still considered if not a necessity then at least an asset, current research indicates that men and women nowadays prefer to partner with someone experienced and talented in lovemaking.

Most of us know the old joke that people stop having sex after marriage. This "joke" has a basis in reality, borne out by medical research indicating that body chemistries and brain wave patterns of people during courtship differ from those of people in stable, settled relationships. Sex is an important element in the initial bonding of individuals, but once they enter and establish committed relationships, juggling and maintaining the multiple responsibilities that come with them, sex may take a back seat to other more pressing concerns. In our clinical practice, we hear both women and men complain that their partner is "just not interested" in sex. One EFJ wife, concerned about her relationship with her ITP husband, stated, "I would be willing to settle for just twenty to thirty minutes a week for being intimate in bed." Her husband responded, "If I gave you that, pretty soon you'll want an hour, then two or three hours a week. You're just insatiable."

Type similarities and differences also influence a couple's sexual dynamics. Sensing types are generally likely to be in touch with their sensuality; Intuitive types are likely to have romantic fantasies and to experience greater arousal when an atmosphere of romance surrounds the sex act. Types with a preference for Intuition and Feeling (NFs)—whether Introverted or Extraverted and regardless of Judging or Perceiving preference—tend to make love a priority in the sexual experience. For NFs, the interchange of good feelings prior to sexual contact is more important than it is for other types. One SJ man we met in therapy continually complained that his wife was "never interested." After learning that a gift of fresh-cut flowers was almost guaranteed to romance her, we encouraged the wife to communicate this information to her husband. Unfortunately, this very practical man saw bouquets as "impractical" and continued to bring her potted plants as an expression of his affection.

Sexual relationships that occur outside the primary relationship can of course elicit major emotional reactions from partners. Such reactions often differ according to type and appear to be particularly related to the Judging and Perceiving preference in individuals. One young Judging type husband reported that he didn't feel right about extramarital affairs: "It seems to me that pursuing affairs indicates a lack of commitment which two people make with each other. I would like to see us make an honest effort to fulfill each other's needs."

One newly married ESTP woman expressed a different point of view: "My husband and I have a difference of opinion in that extramarital affairs are okay with me as long as they don't interfere with our relationship. Sexual intimacy has greater significance for him. Of course, even if he decided extramarital relationships were okay for both of us, we're not sure we'd act on it. We realize if we did, a lot of working things out would be necessary."

Both Judging and Perceiving types may, however, get involved in sexual relationships outside of their principal relationship, albeit for different "reasons." One of our ESTJ clients thought he was "entitled" to extra sex as a reward for having "made it" in the professional world. An ENTJ client suffered no significant pangs of conscience for finding an additional sex partner to make up for everything she wasn't getting from a late-working spouse. In spite of such examples, however, most partners *want* monogamy whether they are willing to maintain it or not. Fear of contracting or transmitting a potentially deadly virus, like HIV, has made monogamy more attractive than ever before and has resulted in more couples frankly discussing sex, both to avoid sexual acting-out, and to work on strengthening their relationships.

To partners experiencing conflict or dissatisfaction in the sexual domain of their relationship, you can offer the following recommendations. You will notice that the recommendations are not type specific. They apply regardless of type pairings. Our suggestions that are type-related appear in table 9.4 (page 151).

Don'ts to tell your couple:

- If your partner isn't responding to you sexually because of stress, illness, or anxiety, don't rush into another relationship for confirmation that you're still desirable. Give your partner time.
- Don't expect your partner to feel loving and sexually responsive after you've been angry or critical. You may feel better, but in all likelihood, your partner won't.
- Don't be in a hurry; some of a couple's most intimate moments occur with the sharing of thoughts and feelings before, during, and after sexual contact.
- Don't act out your partner's fantasies unless they are also your fantasies. Rather than strengthening the bond with your partner, playing a role unnatural to you can cause alienation and repressed anger.
- Don't make too many explicit demands about performance. Where trust, love, and goodwill prevail, intimacy will be meaningful, even if it's not "just like in the movies" or in fairy tales.

Do's to tell your couple:

- Once a month if you can afford it—every three months even if you can't—get away alone to a place you both really enjoy: a luxury hotel, a cabin in the mountains, a seaside bed-and-breakfast, whatever works for you. Get reacquainted with the person you chose to marry. Go dancing if that's what you used to like. Have a bottle of champagne and order room service. Relax and enjoy each other.
- Be aware that difficulties in other aspects of your relationship are likely to show up in the bedroom as well. Take a hard look at your relationship; be honest with your counselor.
- The fact that sexual needs differ means that one partner isn't necessarily right and the other necessarily wrong. Look for mutually satisfying solutions, even trade-offs if these work for you. For example, if a foot massage relaxes and helps your partner open up sexually, do it! If staying in shape makes you more sexually appealing to your mate, consider some exercise!
- Remember that passion doesn't maintain a peak even in the most ideal relationships. Stress, illness, anxiety, and the responsibilities of daily life all affect the frequency and quality of sexual contact. Some

types want sex as a comfort or to reduce tension. Decide for yourselves if this is okay for you too. But communicate about it!

- Attitudes about the purpose of sex abound. It is for procreation, for closeness, for fun, for relaxation, and so on. Try to locate your common attitudes about sex, satisfying each individual's needs, if possible, in the process.

Love Preferences

An understanding of how type intersects intimacy may help your clients avoid some of the pitfalls couples typically encounter. It may also enable them to develop greater sensitivity to their own and each other's sexual needs and desires. The following table provides some of the guidelines to help answer the question "How do I love thee?" as it applies to couples and type.

INTERNAL FACTORS IN CONFLICTS

The next three conflict areas that often bring couples into counseling involve values, interests, and recreation. Since each of these originates with the individual, we call them "internal" factors." In the long run, partners' mutual respect for and accommodation of each other in these areas is more useful to the health of relationships and individuals than each partner's trying to have it their way.

Values

Differences in values are often due to differences in type, but values also are greatly influenced by education and by experiences as one grows up. Unfortunately, some couples don't get around to making their values explicit until after the marriage ceremony or sometimes not until after children are born. In addition, remember that values may change as people grow and age, so keeping open a clear line of communication can help forestall arguments or misunderstandings as differences crop up. Following are just some of the questions it is wise for partners to discuss before committing to a long-term relationship (or as an ongoing dialogue as the relationship matures).

TABLE 9.4

Preference Pairs in Love Situations

EXTRAVERTS	INTROVERTS
Want to be active	Want to be relaxed
Are energized by the unknown	Are comfortable with the known
Are willing to initiate	Prefer not to initiate
Prefer variety	Prefer depth
May move too close to another's space	May withdraw too far away
May have difficulty holding back	May have difficulty engaging
Are typically active	Are typically focused
Enjoy the excitement of a group	Enjoy being alone with a loved one

SENSING TYPES	INTUITIVE TYPES
Want sensual pleasure	Want the right atmosphere
Seek new experiences	Have implicit expectations
Look for different methods	Look for new possibilities
Provide sensory stimulation	Are imaginative
Want sexual contact, then maybe spiritual	Want spiritual contact, then maybe sexual

THINKING TYPES	FEELING TYPES
Want to touch intellectually	Want to touch emotionally
Look for successful lovemaking strategies	Want romantic interactions
Want respect	Want expressions of love
Tend to analyze the situation	Tend to be responsive to the partner
Prefer partners to be rational in a crisis	Prefer partners to be understanding in a crisis

JUDGING TYPES	PERCEIVING TYPES
Prefer commitment	Prefer various freedoms
Prefer continuity and acceptance	Prefer to go with the flow
May not respond when certain boundaries are violated	May not respond when feeling trapped
Typically enjoy sex in ways they have had it before	May enjoy experimenting with sexual interactions

Fighting Styles of the Types

When conflicts turn into hostility, the path to resolution may be soothed by an understanding of how type plays into fighting styles.

What are our political affiliations? Do we both support community-based or other forms of social involvement? Do we believe in charity? Will we observe religious practice, and if so, must our religions be the same? Is a well-educated partner important to each of us? Do we want to have children? What are our purposes in having children? How important is career to each of us in relation to family? Do we want to cultivate a stable home environment or have varied experiences in various places? How important is it for both partners to work full time? How much money do we need; how much do we want; how much does each of us have to make to maintain economic balance in the relationship? How important is sex to each of us? What are our attitudes about smoking, drinking, and drug use? Values related to eating, smoking, and using alcohol and drugs will also impact a relationship positively or negatively. Some individuals would never partner with a smoker; others would find it difficult to endure life with a teetotaler.

The more partners' values differ, the more difficult it is likely to be for them to negotiate successful resolutions to their problems. Negotiating values takes mutual respect, and partners need to dispense with the notion that there is one right way and one wrong way of looking at issues.

Individuals who prefer Feeling to Thinking often have strong values about people and relationships and want to act in ways that make others happy. Conflicting values about how money should be spent, for example, brought one young couple into therapy with us. The IFP partner wanted to set aside funds in a very tight budget for buying gifts for family and friends. Her partner, an ISTJ, believed every available penny should go toward the house they were planning to build and thought that friends and family could "go on hold" for several years.

Extraverts' values tend to be shaped and altered, perhaps unconsciously, by current trends. In order to change their values, Introverts need to be satisfied that a new idea is a better idea, as they tend to believe some trends are fads. Because they are grounded in the present, Sensing types value common sense and methodical, incremental change, rather than leaping at new concepts as Intuitive types tend to do. The value of common sense may appear overrated to a forward-looking Intuitive type partner, who is apt to value vision, creativity, and imagination. Thinking types often value objectivity and fairness, while Feeling types tend to value caring for people and the environment. Judging types usually value order, planning, and predictability, while Perceiving types tend to value discovery, openness, and flexibility. Descriptions of the Sixteen Types (appendix A) is a valuable source for comparing and contrasting basic values of the types. The descriptions there can be the basis for productive dialogue in counseling sessions.

The following do's and don'ts may help your clients who are having problems because of conflicting values.

 ***Don'ts to tell your couple:***

- Don't ask your friends or relatives for opinions. Friends and family will probably have similar experiences and attitudes to yours and will not be able to bring perspective to the situation.
- Don't be closed and judgmental. Try to see the world through your partner's eyes, and try to find something valuable in his or her position.
- Don't marry someone who holds values radically different from yours and expect them to change after marriage. For example, we have seen relationships break up because one partner wanted children and the other didn't.

 ***Do's to tell your couple:***

- Discuss values conflicts early on in therapy. Values are so close to each person's core that it's very difficult to be objective about them. Until values conflicts are resolved, it may be hard to make progress in other areas.
- See if you can identify the origin of your own values. Sometimes learning more about yourself will better enable you to accept differences in others.
- Test yourself to see if you can be open to a different point of view or at least to negotiating certain values.
- If you hold one or more values that you cannot change without compromising your personal integrity, be honest and direct about it with your partner.

Interests

While individuals with radically different values aren't likely to find much common ground, partners with different interests can often create very satisfying relationships. This will be particularly true of partners who both subscribe to the belief that people don't have to be "glued to each other" to have a fulfilling relationship. When we work with couples who have disparate interests (he loves tennis and fishing, she enjoys the theater and bridge), we often query them about the activities they enjoyed together during their courtship. Unless they both maintained substantial pretense during that time, it is generally possible to recover and revive some common interests. (Of course, if to please him, she pretended to enjoy golf, while he pinched himself awake at operas just to be with her, you will have to help your clients look for new areas of common interest.)

All of us, of course, have preferences, both conscious and unconscious. A partner with opposite preferences can open doors to experiences we wouldn't have sought out ourselves. The person who normally shuns physical exercise in favor of reading a book, for example, is apt to be pleasantly surprised that walking can be a joy when it is done in a certain place, at a certain time, with a certain person. The college football coach may be astonished to find the ballet his wife enjoys almost as enchanting and beautiful as she does; he will almost certainly appreciate the talent and physical training it requires. Discovering new interests through a partner can make for a richer life and enable us to stretch in ways we never imagined possible.

Extraverted types particularly like activity and feel most alive when they are "doing something." Introverts, on the other hand, often don't want to always be "doing;" they like time to reflect and meditate. Partners who share a Sensing function tend to have similar interests—perhaps in nature or sports—and to maintain those interests over time. They especially enjoy a great range of sensory experiences, from canoeing and dancing to gourmet cooking and carpentry. Intuitive types tend to enjoy entertaining possibilities; they may imaginatively place themselves and others in different future scenarios and enjoy activities that involve similar kinds of "projection." Thinking types may enjoy activities that involve intellectual exercise and strategizing, such as a good game of chess or bridge or a fencing match—literally or figuratively, a "battle of wits." Without having to think about or do any one thing in particular, Feeling types often enjoy sharing close and comfortable moments with the people they love. Judging types' interests are likely to involve planning, arranging, and prioritizing—on a small scale, doing or creating some kind of puzzle or, on a large scale, tackling a complex building project. Perceiving types may prefer spontaneous responses to the environment and people who leave them maximally free to pursue whatever is of interest at the moment.

To couples who need help aligning their interests, you can make the following recommendations.

Don'ts to tell your couple:

- Don't insist that your partner give up a strong, long-standing interest for the sake of the relationship. You will only breed resentment and make the relationship a prison. If a partner's interest is dangerous, share your concerns and ask them to be careful. (If you can't live with the worry, this might not be the right partner for you.) If the activity is time-consuming, ask your partner to monitor themselves and provide equal quality time for the relationship.
- Don't complain during the hours you have together. Use that energy instead to make yourself a more interesting individual.
- Don't go too far pursuing an expensive interest that can add to or cause financial problems. Where a costly hobby is concerned, make sure you both agree that it will be worth the investment.
- Don't be so conservative that you avoid all interests that might not "pay off." Both partners should be free to take risks.

Do's to tell your couple:

- Put some energy into finding out more about your partner's interests. Sometimes just having more information—like understanding the rules of a football game or keeping up with what performances will be at the local theater—will please your partner and inspire an interest for you.
- Cultivate a new interest for both of you such as taking a photography class; joining a little theater group; taking up golf; volunteering to help with a political campaign. If you live in a college town, you should be able to find a wide variety of continuing education classes, credit and noncredit, that can help both of you grow. Partnering to do volunteer work with hospitals, environmental groups, or other such organizations can add a new dimension to your relationship.

- If you have young children, consider taking a parent-effectiveness training class, joining the PTA, or the like. Children may already be a shared mutual interest, and discussions with other parents can be helpful.

Recreation

A third internal factor that can cause disagreements in relationships is recreation. Interests and recreational activities overlap, of course, because most people take part in recreational pursuits that satisfy their interests. If your clients are having problems in this area, they might want to examine their preferences for either Introversion or Extraversion to see whether attitude differences are contributing to their difficulties.

Extraverts, in general, will want to be out and about, usually with one or more people, doing many activities. Introverts on the other hand, while apt to be very social and have many interests, may find too much socializing draining and may enjoy smaller groups and more individualized activities.

If both partners happen to be Extraverts, the recreational component of their relationship is likely to be dynamic and very satisfying. If both partners are Introverts, they are apt to be similarly satisfied by spending quiet time, together or apart, enjoying the recreations of solitude: reading, taking long walks, gardening, watching movies, meditating, and so on. One complaint we often hear from Introverted partners, however, is that neither tends to initiate new activities; at the end of a long weekend both are apt to be restless and believe that their time was "wasted" reading the newspapers, watching TV, or lounging around in pajamas.

When one partner is Extraverted and the other Introverted, more adjustment and compromise is likely to be required than it would be for partners who share the same preference. Such difference, however, can also be an asset: Extraverts can pull Introverts into fascinating experiences they might otherwise dismiss, and Introverts can encourage Extraverts to explore the riches of solitude. Sharing and using differences constructively helps build good relationships.

Sensing types are likely to favor recreation that involves new experiences; Intuitive types are likely to prefer recreation that has a creative edge or involves experimentation. An Intuitive type partner might attend a poetry reading, while the Sensing type partner opts for a tennis match.

By occasionally crossing recreational lines to participate in activities favored by the other person, both partners can grow. Ask your clients to stretch themselves by considering and defining the value of recreations they wouldn't normally choose.

A battle of wits is almost always recreational for Thinking types. Feeling types, on the other hand, prefer recreations that will please others and invite their appreciation. In competitive activities, Thinking types like to win and may get huffy if they don't. Feeling types may participate in activities their partners principally enjoy simply to feel included and appreciated. Thinking types also want to be appreciated, but they're apt to seek out performance-based recreations where participants have to meet certain standards. This can cause problems between partners if, instead of offering "constructive" pointers for success, Thinking types take an offensive or negative approach. You may need to coach Thinking partners to frame remarks positively: "It might work better if you . . . ," instead of "You're not doing it right." Help your clients pay attention to the effect of their words.

Judging types may prefer a regular or scheduled time to do something recreational so that they can enjoy looking forward to it. Perceiving types may want to decide on the spur of the moment what to do.

To couples who need help aligning their preferred recreations, you can make the following recommendations.

Don'ts to tell your couple:

- Don't set up too busy a recreation schedule for workdays. If one of you is tired or has had a bad day, you won't be much fun to be with. If the chosen recreation is relaxing, however, it can help turn a bad day around.
- If you choose to participate in one of your partner's recreations that you aren't crazy about, don't spoil it by complaining. If you were involved in the same activity with a stranger, you'd probably at least be polite and pretend to be having a good time. Give the person you're committed to at least as much consideration.
- Don't make the mistake of insisting that all recreation be joint recreation. Partners need to have things they do together and things they do alone or with others.

Do's to tell your couple:

- Share the responsibility for planning recreational activities. Decide together during the week what you're going to do over the weekend, or alternate planning the weekend's activities. If it's your turn to do the planning, try to think of something you'll both enjoy.
- Even if you both have hectic schedules, make sure that you spend at least one weekend a month playing or relaxing. If you forget how to have fun together, you'll miss out on one of the primary joys of being a couple.
- Allow time for quiet if you're an Extravert and time for activity if you're an Introvert. Once your initial resistance is gone, you may be surprised by how much you enjoy the "other side."

PRIORITY FACTORS IN CONFLICTS

Three areas of potential conflict for couples—decision making, responsibilities, and chores—are closely related to type differences, particularly differences between Judging and Perceiving preferences. The priorities each partner establishes in order to make choices or respond to domestic and social responsibilities can create conflict. Expectations need to be discussed and negotiated.

Decision Making

If you look back at the descriptions of Judging and Perceiving types in chapter 1 or in appendix A, you will get a clearer sense of why trouble may erupt when it's time for J and P type partners to make a decision. Whatever the decision relates to—where to vacation, which house to buy, even what movie to see—the partner with a preference for Judging is apt to feel uncomfortable while a decision is in process. A Perceiving partner, on the other hand, may be more comfortable while the decision is pending but less comfortable once the decision is made.

It's not unusual for us to hear the following kind of exasperated declaration during a couples' session: "I've made all our vacation plans for the last ten times. Now I want you to do it!" If this individual is a Judging type and the partner is a Perceiving type, we tend to discourage any alteration of this arrangement. Instead, we try to help the Judging type partner understand that the Perceiving type has made a contribution through willingness to go along with preplanning. It is comfortable and pleasant for Judging types to have things decided. The Perceiving type partner contributes to the decision-making process by providing multiple options within the context of working toward a conclusion.

Judging types are happiest when plans are set well in advance: reservations made, tickets purchased and checked for accuracy. Then, they can relax. Perceiving types often prefer to get close to a deadline before deciding what they want to do or where they want to go. After all, they might hear of someplace new and exciting just before they lock into the planned destination. If tickets are already purchased, they've lost the option of making a different decision.

If both partners are Perceiving types, the pitch of the conflict may intensify. During a conversation, Isabel Myers shared with us the opinion that two Perceiving type partners will be particularly challenged by the decision-making process. She pointed out that because neither one enjoys the necessity of making a decision in the first place, whichever partner ends up in the role of "decider" will resent the other. Even though Judging types may not want the whole burden of decision making, at least they are getting their own needs met in the process. Where couples' interactions are concerned, perhaps some duties are best delegated to the partner who dislikes a particular task least.

When two Judging types are involved, there is always the danger that they will arrive at different decisions. If neither can muster the flexibility to compromise or make a change, deadlock can occur. Resolution may have to come about through some kind of pre-established system for determining how decisions are made or compromised when partners disagree. Sometimes this basis may involve degree of importance to each individual or simply the fact that some things naturally fall within the scope of one partner's expertise and some within the other's.

Type differences can improve family decision making, but in our experience they also figure into conflicts surrounding the process. Extraverts can be impatient; Introverts can be slow. Sensing types tend to base decisions on short-term goals and common sense; Intuitive types base theirs on the big picture and long-term goals. Thinking types want to decide with logic; Feeling types want to decide with other people's interests and sensibilities in mind. The Judging and Perceiving functions may show up most vividly in decision-making processes, but the other functions and attitudes have their impact as well. Every couple needs to work out a process that works for them.

The recommended model for decision making includes all four functions: Sensing and Intuition; Thinking and Feeling. Start with the facts, add the possibilities, process with logic and analysis, and finish up with people values. This method of decision making is often called the zigzag model and was developed by Isabel Myers and applied and written about by Gordon Lawrence, Ph.D.

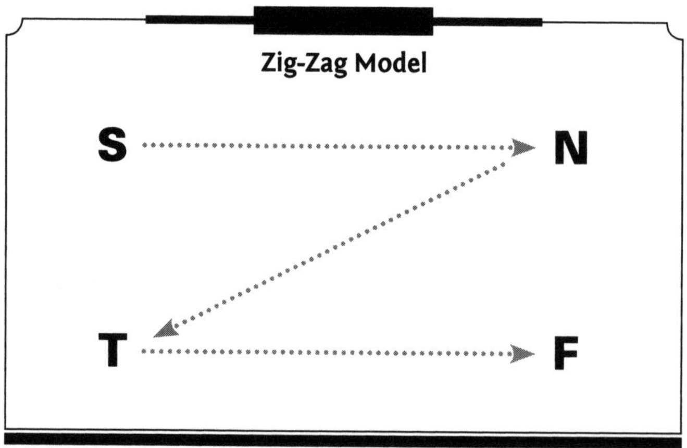

The following do's and don'ts may help couples embroiled in disputes over decision making.

 ***Don'ts to tell your couple:***

- Don't put down your partner for being different from you or devalue yourself for being different from your partner.
- Don't let winning become more important than solving the problem.
- Don't ask outsiders to support your decision against your partner.

 ***Do's to tell your couple:***

- Examine your types and see how they may be affecting your process.

- If you're both Perceiving types, alternate responsibility for making decisions: "I'll decide this week which movie or restaurant to go to; then you choose next week."
- If you're a Feeling type and your partner is a Thinking type, present your decision in a logical form to garner a better reception. Be confident that you can find some objective rationale for the decision you've made.
- If you're a Thinking type with a Feeling type partner, try to understand the effect of your decision on your partner's feelings. The actual decision is less important than how you present it and your recognition of its possible impact and your sensitivity to its possible results.

Responsibilities

Type differences intersect the division of family responsibilities and can lead to constructive action or conflict depending on the kinds of adjustments partners are willing to make. Judging types are quick to shoulder responsibilities, but are apt later to resent being overburdened if their partner fails to share the load. Some partners truly may not notice an imbalance. Other times, though, the "not noticing" is deliberate. One partner can manipulate the other through inaction, as one of our clients admitted: "If I wait long enough I know my partner will do it." Division of labor on the basis of talents and competencies rather than gender is the best way to go. We also recommend that partners distribute areas of responsibility so that the time expenditure required of each person will be basically the same regardless of how many tasks each person is doing. This is especially effective when responsibilities are assigned according to who is good at what.

Because they enjoy social interaction, Extraverts are often suited to responsibilities that involve liaising with the public, such as negotiating with salespeople, meeting with insurance agents, representing the family at parent-teacher events, and so on. Introverts, on the other hand, may be better suited to responsibilities that require solitude, such as doing the family bookkeeping, dealing with paperwork, or other at-house projects. Sensing types tend to excel at meeting concrete responsibilities, while Intuitive types excel at abstract ones. Concrete responsibilities are generally those that carry with them immediate consequences or rewards: regular home maintenance, for example, or running a small, on-the-side business to bring in extra family income. Abstract responsibilities are generally those that don't have a definite or immediate reward, such as promoting the family's cultural awareness or researching genealogy as a way to maintain family history and tradition. Thinking types excel at handling responsibilities that require objective reasoning, while Feeling types excel at those that promote harmonious family relations. However, the Thinking type partner might be the best person to assume the role of family mediator, for example, weighing complaints and finding fair solutions. The Feeling type partner might be the best person to assume the role of values instruction, modeling important principles such as kindness, compassion, honesty, goodness, sensitivity.

Chores versus Responsibilities Chores, of course, are related to responsibilities and the terms may be used interchangeably. If we're being very precise, the term "chore" denotes a single, repeated activity, whereas the term "responsibility" tends to denote a broad domain of accountability. The responsibility to educate one's children, for example, can involve many discrete tasks, just as the responsibility to maintain the repair of one's home involves multiple separate chores. In general, partners share responsibilities even while they do so by handling different kinds of chores. Though their activities are different, the parent who teaches their son to play baseball and the parent who teaches the same son how to cook are both sharing responsibility for nurturing and educating children.

Most people resist (and postpone) home maintenance and related responsibilities, which almost always entail a host of routine chores: cleaning the gutters; washing windows, painting the house; changing the fluids in the car. The list goes on. It is therefore preferable to delegate duties so that each partner is responsible for some routine items and some creative items. Negotiations can be tricky and are probably best handled in a counseling session where there is a witness to the parties' agreements. Alternatively, the couple can draw up a short-term "contract" of duties that is open to revision on an established, periodic basis.

Where particularly tedious or dreaded chores are concerned, it's not a bad idea for a couple to hire service professionals to handle those that neither partner wants to do–as long as they can afford it. For many couples, filing income tax returns–a task that can be postponed but not ignored without serious penalty–fits into the "dreaded chore" category. Thankfully, tax accounting services have become quite affordable, and for partners who enjoy working on computers, doing taxes with any one of several good accounting software packages may reduce the dread factor. If a couple can't or doesn't want to hire outside help, it's always best to divvy up the "bad chores" in some way both partners clearly agree on. If it takes one partner six hours to do the income tax, then what one or two equally difficult jobs can the other partner do to counterbalance the mate's efforts? The main thing is that the tasks be matched by time and degree of odium. It isn't fair, for example, for one partner to try to counterbalance a six-hour tax preparation job with a six-hour crafts or home carpentry project. No one partner should have to shoulder all the distasteful jobs.

Time Troubles Of course, domestic responsibility doesn't end with household duties, but extends to the courtesies we owe our partners (and all people) as people. Few of us like to come home to an empty house; even less do we like to worry about a partner gone AWOL. One ISF woman we saw in counseling actually filed for divorce because her husband, an ENP, rarely showed up for dinner on time.

ISFJs, like Chris, naturally expect people to be on time. But Greg was seldom just half an hour late; he'd be two or three hours late. Greg adored Chris and considered himself a good husband, and he genuinely could not understand why she would contemplate divorcing him for what he regarded as a minor infraction. "I'm not out with other women," he would say, "and I'm not gambling, or doing other things I know she would be justified in objecting to. It's just that after work a few of us guys talk over our accounts over a couple of beers and I hate to keep watching the clock."

In Greg's and Chris's case, we needed to address the responsibility issue as it overlapped time management. People with a Perceiving preference, like Greg, don't necessarily mean to be discourteous; but because they tend to be spontaneous, they don't always have the best concept of time or its passage. To help Greg meet his responsibility to keep Chris from worrying, we got him a wallet and had "Call Chris" engraved in large letters on the inside flap. Whenever he opened it to pay a bar bill, he had an instant reminder in front of him. Chris also agreed that when Greg called, she would not demand that he come home. More upsetting to Chris than Greg's absence was the uncertainty as to his whereabouts and a lack of clarity as to his plans. She also agreed that if he were more than fifteen minutes late, she would go ahead and eat with the children rather than keep dinner waiting. He agreed that if she had already eaten, he would fix his own dinner (mostly warming leftovers) when he got home.

While this may not appear to be an ideal solution, it worked for Chris and Greg. Their children were old enough to be aware that if Chris knew Greg was going to be late, she had options. Instead of gathering anxiety as she waited for his car to pull into the garage, she could visit a neighbor, go to a movie, or pick up a book.

As the preceding case illustrates, the ways that different types understand and manage time can cause lots of minor annoyances, along with attendant accusations: "You're always late" or "You always have to get there early." Conflicts about time most often involve partners with opposed Judging and Perceiving preferences. Judging types prefer an orderly world, where things run smoothly and according to schedule. Perceiving types regard time constraints as imprisoning and are often uncomfortable with, and sometimes resistant to, timeframes and deadlines. If these types are partners, each will need to give a little so that neither is overwhelmingly or frequently uncomfortable. Judging types are wise not to take a Perceiving type literally when he or she says, "I'll be there by 8:00 p.m." If, in a partner's experience, the Perceiving type tends to run late, the Judging type partner might do well to tag on some additional time based on previous experiences. Otherwise, the Judging type is apt to greet the tardy partner with hostility; the Perceiving partner is apt to feel unwelcome; and next time, the Perceiving type may be less punctual, much to the Judging type's ongoing chagrin.

Perceiving types, on the other hand, need to realize that Judging types are in most instances not trying to control them. They simply want sound information so they can make their own plans. The core problem lies in the fact that a Perceiving type's agenda is flexible, while a Judging type's agenda is fairly fixed. When Perceiving types do something other than what they said they would do, Judging types are apt to misinterpret their flexibility as dishonesty. For this reason, Perceiving types probably need to avoid making statements that Judging types will take literally. Instead of assuring a partner that they'll be home at a certain time, for example, the Perceiving type partner might make a somewhat more open-ended statement: "I'll be home sometime between 8:00 and 9:30 p.m., unless something big comes up; I'll let you know." The Judging type partner mainly needs to know that the Perceiving type partner can still be trusted even if he or she will always need a certain amount of room to move around in. With cell phones being ubiquitous, staying in touch about timing is an easy task. Judging types not only tend to prioritize early, but do so with a partner primarily in mind. In turn, they tend to expect more or less the same consideration from a partner, not realizing that priorities for Perceiving types are not so predictable and may easily shift.

Changing from one to another mode of meeting responsibilities or managing time isn't easy, but trying to do so to accommodate a partner's needs can be a gift of love. To help couples who are struggling to negotiate responsibilities, you can present the following guidelines.

Don'ts to tell your couple:

- Don't judge your partner's motives without talking about them first.
- Don't rebel without first understanding or telling your partner what it is that bothers you.
- Don't always put your own agenda first; sometimes nurturing a relationship requires negotiation. Be open to discussion.

Do's to tell your couple:

- Try to be at least as courteous and attentive to your partner as you would to a client, customer, or coworker.
- Try to remember that your partner's behavior is often a reflection of their type and not necessarily an indication of how much or how little they love you.
- Aim to strike a balance between structure and freedom. Allow time for fun as well as for meeting your responsibilities.

Chores

Just as type differences enter into the handling of responsibilities, they also enter into the ways partners manage routine chores. Chores, as we discussed earlier, are necessary activities cyclically repeated—daily, weekly, monthly, annually, and so on. Some chores stand alone, while others are related in groups that constellate a particular realm of responsibility. (Think of preparing income tax returns—a stand-alone chore—as opposed to the multiple tasks involved in keeping the family car well serviced and safe.) If it isn't equitable, chore distribution can be a source of conflict between partners.

In both our research and counseling experience we find that among the various type pairings, Extraverts paired with Introverts are particularly likely to report conflict as partners over chore management. Introverts may expend a lot of energy at work, especially if their occupations call for considerable human interaction, and they prefer to use their time at home to replenish their strength, not to use it up further on chores. Extraverts who are often involved in outside activities have less time at home for doing chores. Extraverts are also likely to voice their complaints and demands, which rarely helps an Introvert get moving.

If both partners are Intuitive types, neither is likely to derive much satisfaction from the performance of routine chores. Intuitive type partners need to share their views and negotiate chore priorities: which chores absolutely have to be done; which can wait; and which can be dispensed with altogether. Once their priorities and expectations are clearly enunciated, the partners can formulate an equitable division of labor. Both partners have to be on the same page, though; if one N partner doesn't mind going for a month without cleaning the bathroom and the other N partner recoils at the thought, this difference needs to be factored into the negotiations.

Sensing types usually see what needs to be done and can even be comfortable doing routine tasks in the interest of having things look nice, be clean, and function well. Intuitive types are less likely to notice the tea stains in the sink, the dust tumbleweeds under the bed, or the blinking "check engine" light in the car, but they often like the results of a completed chore if they can "just do it" and not spend overly long processing or resisting. Stretching ourselves to take care of less interesting but necessary tasks can contribute to our personal growth. Some of the energy we expend resisting a chore or disagreeing over "who it belongs to" can be saved by just doing it.

Regardless of type, certain organizational strategies can lighten the household chore load. For example, making bridges or connectors among "to do" items in different categories can help facilitate and expedite accomplishment of two or more items. For example, exercising, picking up groceries, and spending more time with one's son can be combined into taking the son swimming and stopping for groceries on the way home. Strategic combinations of this kind not only help assure that each necessary chore is accomplished but create the potential for enjoyment and companionship, as well.

Managing chores seems to be less problematic for couples where both partners have a Judging or a Perceiving preference than for those where these preferences are opposed. When two Judging type partners agree on getting chores done according to schedule or when two Perceiving type partners agree to be relaxed and spontaneous about the completion of chores, things run more smoothly. When priorities differ, however, when partner J insists the dishes be washed immediately after dinner every night and partner P asks, "What's the big deal about when the dishes get done," the partners will have to work out some trade-offs to achieve a fair division of labor.

If your couple is having difficulty delegating chores, you can offer the following do's and don'ts.

 ***Don'ts to tell your couple:***

- Don't get caught in the trap of thinking "If my partner loved me, I'd have a clean shirt to wear" or "If my partner cared about my safety, the car would be fixed." Dislike for doing laundry (or any other kind of chore) has nothing to do with love and not all people are mechanically skilled.
- Don't get caught up in gender stereotypes that prescribe "women's work" and "men's work." Negotiate for each partner to do the chores he or she prefers (or dislikes least). If she loves to mow the lawn and he loves to cook, then that's how these chores should be delegated.
- Don't allow control or power issues make big deals out of little chores.

 ***Do's to tell your couple:***

- Make several detailed lists: one of daily chores; one of weekly chores; one of monthly chores; and one of chores that need to be done only once or twice a year. As you review the lists, initial the chores you enjoy doing most or least mind doing. (Having signed up to take on a chore makes us less likely to dispute it later.) If you both sign up for some of the same chores or can't decide who is to do those left untaken, draw lots to decide. Sound fair?
- If you both work—even if you don't but can afford it—hire service professionals to do the chores you hate most. One couple we saw in counseling, both of them professionals earning very decent salaries,

almost broke up because neither wanted to do the laundry. (In this case, finding a good laundry service would be well worth the cost.)

- Implicit expectations can lead to problems. Be clear about your own wants and needs and compare them against those of your partner. Where you discover a discrepancy, negotiations can begin.

Other People as a Factor in Conflicts

The last area of potential conflict between partners involves interactions with other people: children, in-laws, and friends. The positions other people take, the opinions they express, the support they give or withhold, and the judgments they make—all impact a couple's interactions.

Children

Children are necessarily one of the primary focuses in a relationship. If they become the sole focus, however, or when parents fundamentally disagree about how children should be raised, the partners are apt to neglect their own relationship. Moreover, quick to pick up on their parents' tendencies, even those that are unspoken or unconscious, children can soon learn to get what they want by playing their parents off against each other. When partners are aware of their own and their children's types, they are better prepared to meet and resolve the problems they will surely face as parents.

A child's type preferences may become apparent early in life or over time as he or she matures. As one might expect, different types of children thrive under different styles of parenting. There are a number of resources available that can help individuals identify and modify parenting styles, including parent-effectiveness workshops, secular and faith-based parent support groups, parenting magazines, and Web sites to name just a few. The different type preferences indicated on the MBTI assessment do, of course, intersect child-rearing values and can enter into the problems that arise because of them.

In our counseling sessions, child raising issues often come up between Thinking and Feeling type partners. Because this pairing is fairly common, you will not only almost certainly encounter it in your own practice, but many of your Thinking and Feeling type clients are apt to be struggling with parenthood. Feeling type parents tend to be very emotionally invested in their children. As a result, they are likely to put harmony in the home ahead of other child-related concerns, such as discipline and competency. If a child is hurt or upset by a Thinking type parent's criticism or performance demands, the Feeling type partner will probably be hurt or upset as well.

Because partners' child-rearing values may differ greatly, they're not easy to negotiate. Partners can balance each other in this area by avoiding complete opposition to one another's approaches in exclusive favor of their own. Children require support and confidence building in addition to discipline and competency, and the parent best suited to supply these different needs can be determined by various means including type preferences. A Feeling type partner, for example, is probably better suited to build children's confidence and enrich their range of values than, say, the Thinking type partner, who is probably better suited to nurture their competencies and self-discipline. If they can give up being overly attached to their own perceptions, both parents can find much merit in one another's child-rearing values. Thinking types tend to be firm, setting requisite boundaries; Feeling types tend to be demonstrative, providing warmth and love: children, of course, need both.

Extraverted parents usually encourage their children to be active and enjoy playing and interacting with them. Introverted parents enjoy quiet times with their children and find it easier to leave them alone to play by themselves. Children can learn valuable skills from both types of parents.

Intuitive type parents may have more challenges than Sensing types with some of the confining routines involved in parenting. Intuitive type parents may focus on cultivating children's imaginations, encouraging them in creative and innovative games and activities. Sensing type parents may prefer to concentrate on supplying their children's day-to-day needs, providing comfort and security.

Judging type parents are generally better than Perceiving type parents at providing the structures children need, while P type parents are better than J type parents at giving children the space they need to explore and make discoveries. These different styles can complement each other.

For couples having difficulty with parenting issues, the following do's and don'ts may be helpful.

Don'ts to tell your couple:

- Don't repeat the same parenting style your own parents used, unless you believe it was truly beneficial. It's easy to unconsciously follow old patterns even when they aren't functional. Try to stay aware of parenting options and make good choices.
- Don't think of discipline as punishment. Related to education and knowledge, a "discipline" is something useful that can be learned. If your children don't learn from you, they will learn later from the world—and it can be a much more difficult teacher. Think of discipline as part of your responsibility to your children's education until they have learned to discipline themselves.
- Don't let the children become a divisive force in your relationship, especially if one child is your type and another one is your partner's type. Don't allow your home to become a boxing arena with, for example, Intuitive Feeling types pitted against Sensing Thinking types or males pitted against females.
- No matter how much you love them, don't let your children become the ruling passion in your life. Even if you can't afford it, find ways to occasionally get away with your partner to renew your relationship. The children will be gone someday, and you won't want to discover that there's nothing left between you.
- Don't leave the raising of the children totally in your partner's hands, no matter how capable he or she is. Children need both parents.

Do's to tell your couple:

- Model the many behaviors that comprise a good human being, so your children can learn by observing you and your partner.
- If Feeling is your dominant function and Thinking the dominant function of both your partner and children, leave the room or the house when they begin to argue or shoot barbs back and forth. They often do enjoy the dueling, and you will be the one to get hurt if you stay there. Don't attempt to be a peacemaker between individuals who are enjoying a strong debate or argument.
- If you and your partner have very different parenting values, workshops in parent effectiveness (including "tough love") can help you

see the value in each of your approaches while at the same time helping to unite you as a team.

- Teach love and respect by the way you treat your children and each other. Fathers and mothers can help children of both sexes navigate identity-formation processes by understanding and appreciating differences. Keep communication lines open to gain a better understanding of your children and each other.

In-laws

Particularly because of its Pacific Island and Asian populations, extended families are common in Hawaii. Even a "small" Hawaiian wedding can involve as many as 200 people—or more, when all family members and "calabash" aunties and uncles are included. Family is a similarly important priority for Asian individuals, who often have to manage intricate in-law dynamics. Because Hawaii is relatively small geographically, second-, third-, and fourth-generation local residents may find it almost impossible to avoid being influenced by family members, who are apt to live close by.

In-laws often exert significant influence over couples and their relationships. How an individual presents his or her partner to family members frequently determines how they will relate to that person in the future. When a son or daughter, grandson or granddaughter appears happy with a partner, the family is apt to share the joy. On the other hand, some family members may become angry if the time, attention, or money they've come to expect from a child, grandchild, niece, or nephew diminishes because of his or her intimate relationship. Some in-laws give a couple too much advice, while others decide to avoid the couple altogether. In-law attitudes and responses are as varied as the individuals concerned.

While family members normally look to their "kin" for cues about relating to the new in-law, type variables will influence how they treat and how readily they accept that person. Once Judging types make decisions about people, they typically work from that hypothesis, basing upon it all subsequent judgments and opinions unless they receive explicit contradictory data. If a Judging type in-law makes a positive evaluation, it will not be easily dislodged. But neither will a negative one. Perceiving types appear to be more tolerant as in-laws, largely because their open-ended and spontaneous style makes it less likely that they will form hard-and-fast opinions about anyone. They are comfortable maintaining their views "in process."

As important as they can be to a couple's relationship, perhaps more important than in-laws' views of one mate or the other are the partners' attitudes about their in-laws. Where such attitudes are concerned, our research indicates a varied and sometimes disjointed array of type-based responses across a range of interactions. These include partners' openness to family social events and their general attitudes toward in-law expectations and inclinations.

As we might expect, Introverts may be reluctant participants in large family gatherings; their partners may need to be willing to attend functions alone sometimes, especially if they occur often. Extraverts typically welcome family get-togethers and enjoy many and varied events of this kind; Introverted partners need to be willing to participate in the important gatherings at least. Perceiving types in particular may need to push themselves to stay longer than they would like at family gatherings. Their restlessness and spontaneity may prompt them to want to bound into and just as quickly out of family social events—an action natural to Perceiving types, but which family members may misinterpret as rudeness or dislike.

Disagreements with in-laws can create conflicts for couples. In the interest of maintaining good family relations, partners will be wise to be aware of and sometimes work against their type-based attitudes toward others. Extraverted Feeling and Introverted Sensing partners (both Judging types) are more likely than other types to want to meet in-laws' expectations. Thinking types probably won't object to in-laws' expectations, as long as family members treat both partners with respect.

Sensing types are apt to be impatient with in-laws who seem to be dreamers and lack common sense. Intuitive types are apt to be frustrated by in-laws who seem rigid and reality bound. Both S and N types may need to cultivate greater tolerance of family members with opposite types if in-law relations are to remain satisfying. Judging types who have formed harsh opinions of certain in-laws may need to temporarily suspend such assessments in the interest of civility; they might need to consciously push themselves to identify in these people characteristics they can value or appreciate.

Feeling types may need to protect themselves in family situations where their values might be offended. Not all people are either sensitive or conscious, and Feeling types may negatively misinterpret these "lacks" in their in-laws as deliberate assaults against their own values and sensibilities. Thinking types probably need to stay away from religion, politics, and other "loaded" topics with their in-laws, especially if any of them—the T type partner or the family members—has a need to be right.

What family members collectively expect of their interactions depends not only upon ethnic and cultural background but upon the relationship of a son or daughter with his or her parents. When one partner has a close, warm relationship with parents, he or she will naturally want the other partner to share that closeness by attending family dinners, picnics, reunions, and so on. If one partner's relations with family are characterized by anger or rebellion, those emotions are apt to spill off onto the mate, even if the couple only sees in-laws infrequently. If one partner is extremely close to and involved with family, the other partner may wind up feeling subordinate to the in-laws. When one partner is distant or detached from family members, there is some indication that he or she will find it difficult to share intimacy with a mate as well.

If your clients are having difficulty resolving in-law issues and relationships, you can offer the following suggestions.

Don'ts to tell your couple:

- Don't put your partner in the position of having to choose sides between you and their parents.
- Don't go into business with, borrow money from, or live with in-laws if you can avoid it.
- Don't let yourself get away with showing your negative side if you choose to attend in-law functions. Go to family gatherings only when you know you can take part willingly.
- Unless it's comfortable for your partner, don't expect him or her to stay all day with the in-laws.

Do's to tell your couple:

- Try to put some physical distance between your home and your parents' home. Minimize potential expectations that your relationship values will correspond with those of parents on either side.
- Help your partner understand the family system and traditions; introduce them in ways that facilitate acceptance on both sides.
- If it's *your* parents, take on the task of turning down an invitation, of reminding them how you want the children disciplined, and so

on. Don't let parents come between you and your partner any more that you would allow children to do so.

- Remember that each type potentially has skills associated with their preferences that can make relations with in-laws better: the social ease of the Extravert and the depth of the Introvert; the common sense of the Sensing type and the creativity of the Intuitive type; the wit of the Thinking type and the loving diplomacy of the Feeling type; the flexibility of the Perceiving type and the commitment of the Judging type.

Friends

Friends are the third group of people who may influence relationships. Friends can impact a relationship in many ways. They often tend to be supportive rather than objective. Referring to the fact that opposite types often marry and friends tend to be similar types, Joe Wheelwright, a Jungian therapist in San Francisco, once said, "So you can wind up being married to someone you wouldn't even have for a friend." He was noting how challenging a marital relationship can be as well as pointing out that something less conscious occurs when you choose a partner that does not occur when you choose a friend. Society and relationships, though, have changed and we believe that our life partners can also be our best friends.

We do choose friends who are more similar to ourselves, and then we don't have to work as hard at relating. As therapists, we recommend both partners have friends of their own as well as friends in common. Each needs to take care that the separate friendships do not detract from, but rather enhance, the primary relationship. This means choosing the time wisely to be with the separate friends and not slipping over into a romantic or sexual involvement with them.

Extraverts tend to have more friends and want to socialize with many of them; Introverts tend to have fewer and deeper friendships and enjoy socializing in smaller groups.

Sensing types tend to look for an experience and activities along with their friendships and the conversation; Intuitive types also often want experiences but those experiences may be more abstract.

Thinking types like to verbally spar and may look for friends who enjoy a good debate or friendly argument; Feeling types may look for friends with whom they experience harmony and good "vibrations" without any verbal battles.

Perceiving types are likely to move fluidly from friend to friend, while Judging types are more likely to want to be with their "best friend" more of the time.

Extraversion and Introversion among couples bear a closer look. The Extraverted qualities of being outgoing and socially at ease that attracted a more Introverted partner in the first place may prove an irritant once they are living together. Women, in general, Extravert or Introvert, tend to have close friendships with other women, and this, too, can be an irritant to males who may think that they are being discussed and criticized with "strangers." Women may also worry and wonder about how men talk about them, or about women in general, when the men get together.

According to a Hite report (1987), women turn to female friends because they often have some difficulty in sharing emotional intimacy with their male partners. In our experience, Thinking type males, especially men who also prefer Introversion, often experience powerful emotions of anger, tenderness, or sadness that they do not express for fear of being vulnerable or out of control. We have also seen hundreds of men learn to appreciate and participate in emotional intimacy, although it does seem to come more easily for Feeling males than for Thinking males. A man certainly can learn to share feelings and emotions to the point where a spouse feels a close "friendship," although perhaps not to the extent she may feel with her female friends. Regardless of which partner is more emotionally available, both partners should practice sharing friendship with each other as part of a healthy relationship.

Couple should also respect each other's solitary pursuits as well as the friendships each shares outside the marriage.

Consider offering the following tips to help your clients with their friendships.

 ***Don'ts to tell your couple:***

- Don't be critical of your partner's friends so that your partner is driven to defend them. If you think the friend is getting more attention than you are, ask for what you need from your partner. Discern whether you really don't like the person or whether you're feeling left out.
- Don't sulk or make scenes at parties. If you really don't want to be there, you have options. Don't go, find a way to leave early (take

two cars, if this is likely to happen), or "put on a happy face." You can help create a pleasant experience for the individual you loved enough to live with or marry. You may even find you enjoy the party yourself.

Do's to tell your couple:

- Work out a time with each other for mutual social engagements, engagements in which you participate with your own friends, and time to be alone with each other. The balance you develop will of course depend on your own types (especially the Extravert-Introvert and Thinking-Feeling preferences) and your own work patterns.
- If one of you is a Judging type and the other a Perceiving type, take advantage of this difference. Let the Judging type schedule activities with friends; let the Perceiving type create spontaneous, fun happenings with friends.
- If you're an Introvert, let your Extraverted friends help pull you out into the world and its activities.
- If you're an Extravert, let your Introverted friends teach you how to meditate or stop the action for awhile and be at peace.

What we have presented in this chapter is by no means an exhaustive list of problems that couples bring into therapy to resolve. But an understanding of type, along with mutual respect and a sense of humor, can help couples work out differences.

10
Individuation and Type Development

"... AS SOON AS PSYCHOTHERAPY REQUIRES THE SELF-PERFECTING OF THE DOCTOR, IT IS FREED FROM ITS CLINICAL ORIGINS AND CEASES TO BE A MERE METHOD FOR TREATING THE SICK. IT IS NOW SERVICE TO THE HEALTHY AS WELL ..."

C. G. Jung, ***Modern Man in Search of a Soul***

How Families of Origin Affect Intimate Relationships

One's family of origin can have a potent effect on how type preferences develop. Jung believed neurosis could be caused by an individual being pushed to behave in ways alien to their natural inclinations. Most therapists and counseling professionals are aware of the popular psychotherapeutic formula that "everyone marries their mother." We're among a group of therapists who believes instead that individuals tend to marry someone similar in type to the parent with whom they still have unresolved issues. This tendency makes marriage a crucible in which the volatile components of an individual's psyche either resolve or continue to erupt.

By now, you are probably able to identify the types of the individuals closest to you: your parents, siblings, mate, children. Some of you may have determined your own type using the MBTI® instrument; others of you may have trained to use the Indicator for administration to clients. For those of you in the early stages of learning about type, it's probably easiest to first identify someone in terms of one of the preference pairs on the Extraversion–Introversion and Judging–Perceiving dichotomies. Start from there and move on to the preference pairs on the other dichotomies, using the descriptive information provided in this and other books on type.

As you become more confident in your ability to identify type preferences, explore with your clients their assessments of their parents' types. Your goals are (1) to determine whether your clients and their parents share similar type preferences; (2) to identify what impact those similarities or differences have had on their relationship; and (3) to consider whether their interactions with parents are echoed in their interactions with partners. We have guided clients through similar explorations. As the following illustrations from our own practice indicate, clients can gain fruitful insights into how their type-based relationships with their parents have poured over into their intimate relationships.

Example one. Paul an INFP (Introverted Feeling type) was a creative, successful architect. His personal relationships, however, left something to be desired. He was now on his third marriage and seriously considering asking for a divorce. As we examined his relationship with his parents during counseling, it became apparent that he identified with his father and had never resolved his relationship with his mother. His mother appeared (at least to Paul) as critical, cold, and demanding. After studying the type descriptions, Paul said that she was probably an Extraverted Thinking type. Extraverted Thinking types (ESTJ/ENTJ) show preferences almost opposite those of an INFP and might appear cold and critical to a sensitive Feeling type, like Paul.

Seeking warmth and acceptance from women, Paul appeared invariably drawn to those who aggressively pursued relationships with him. Once he committed to or married one of these women, they immediately set about attempting to remodel him in their own image. As we studied these relationships, Paul was able to identify elements in them reminiscent of his interactions with his mother.

It was too late to do anything about his first two marriages except to learn from them. But Paul's third wife, Gloria, was amenable to counseling to see if their marriage could be saved. Gloria, a very successful business executive (an ENTJ), was willing to look in depth at the dynamics of their relationship. Nonetheless, she often became exasperated by Paul's withdrawal from confrontation. Gloria's own mother seemed similar to an ISFP. She was a homemaker whose only enthusiasm was her garden. Gloria claimed to have little respect for her mother and reported that there was very little communication between them.

In our sessions, Gloria learned gentler ways of approaching Paul with her perceptions and needs. She also learned to verbalize her love for him prior to asking for some change in his behavior. At first, Paul experienced Gloria as manipulative and saw no real change in her acceptance of him. But after a few sessions in which he was really able to "feel" her love, he became more accessible, no longer confusing her with his mother. A year after starting counseling, during their annual check-in, both Paul and Gloria indicated that their relationship was more satisfying. They said they believed they could continue to work things out.

Example two. Like Paul, Eunice also had unresolved issues with a parent that seemed to be impeding her ability to form intimate relationships. As an Extraverted Feeling type (ESFJ), Eunice tended to thrive on affection and approval. From her descriptions of him, Eunice's father appeared to be an INTJ, an Introverted Intuitive type. Successful as a university professor in engineering, he left the raising of his children to his wife (probably an ENFJ) to whom Eunice related easily. She was definitely a "Mommy's girl" but was also hungry for more interaction with her father whom she respected and admired.

At 29, Eunice was a social worker and had never been married. She was an attractive, articulate woman who was confused by what she perceived as "a failure in the personal area" (as she labeled it). Despite the fact that she had been in a series of relationships since she was 18, none of them had culminated in marriage. In most cases, the men had retreated and ended the relationship.

By examining these relationships with her, it became evident that Eunice was attracted to men similar to her father in a number of ways. She sought men whose interests evince depth (Introversion) rather than breadth (Extraversion) and men who were ambitious, achievement-oriented, and rather reserved socially. Eunice, who reported having initiated most of the social contacts, believed she had contributed a great deal to each of her relationships only to be unappreciated and abandoned.

Early on during her therapy, we asked Eunice to bring her father in for a session. With a little bit of prodding, he was able to express his affection for Eunice and felt genuinely distressed that he might have deprived her in any way. He also described some of the difficulties he had experienced early in his relationship with Eunice's mother and how they had set about resolving their differences.

Following this session, Eunice was able to look more objectively at her previous relationships. She realized that she had probably tried to remake her INJ partners as Extraverted Feeling types, despite having been drawn to them in the first place because of their Introverted Intuitive qualities. Eunice also consciously decided that a relationship with a man more similar to her would probably be easier and more satisfying. After making that decision, Eunice explored several relationships with men different in type from her father and ended up being seriously involved with a fellow social worker, an Extraverted Sensing type (ESFP).

Relationships: Tips for Working with Couples

The kinds of explorations illustrated above often help clients recognize the extent to which we all tend to see ourselves in our partners. The initially self-reflexive nature of attraction accounts for the very common pitfall of trying to remake our partners in our own images. Part of the goal of relationship counseling is to help individuals distinguish others from their own projections, to come to a sense of their own and a partner's unique personhood. With this goal in mind, we offer the following tips.

1. It is only with others that we can test out our behavior and see how effective it is.
2. It is only in committed relationships that we are involved enough not to leave when things get difficult, when our own and our partners' primal or undifferentiated personality functions emerge to create havoc.
3. What we "hate" in others is often an unconscious dimension of our own personality that we have unwittingly projected onto someone else. As we follow our "projections" and work to consciously integrate them, we work toward individuation.
4. Old gender-role stereotypes have changed, as has the concept and reality of marriage. Whether or not they involve civil marriage, all relationships in these modern times need to be equal partnerships.

5. Civil marriage may be the best form for a relationship that results in children. Otherwise, children may have to bear the social brunt of their parents' choice if their parents aren't married.
6. The twenty-first century stresses both individuality and social responsibility. Finding some comfortable balance between these two demands is a challenge for all of us.

Personal Growth as Individuation

The challenge of helping couples achieve meaningful and lasting relationships provides us with an opportunity to enrich our practices by expanding into a domain that is simultaneously theoretical and practical. The depth psychology of Carl Jung and the applications brought to it by Isabel Myers and Katharine Briggs offer us fresh perspectives and creative methods to help us meet our counseling challenges more sensitively and effectively.

A distinction needs to be made here between counseling and therapy. In our model, counseling works with the practical, "real world" issues of daily life: career concerns, relationship and parenting issues, financial problems, long- and short-range goals, decision making. The list goes on. While there is considerable overlap with counseling, therapy focuses on bringing to light the attitudes, behaviors, insights, and perspectives that enable

" . . . INDIVIDUATION INVOLVES BRINGING INTO CONSCIOUSNESS THE UNCONSCIOUS DIMENSIONS OF OUR PERSONALITIES IN ORDER TO ACHIEVE PSYCHOLOGICAL MATURITY OR WHOLENESS."

clients to become more fully realized as individuals and, often, more effective in the world. Counseling is focused on external concerns or the social world; therapy is typically focused on internal concerns or the inner world. For the purposes of this book, we use the umbrella term "counselors" to refer both to professionals who do counseling and to those who do therapy.

Ideally, counselors will gain the education, training, and experience necessary to develop competency in both modes.

In Jungian terms, individuation is the goal of life, particularly the second half of life when the approach to death makes the discovery of meaning more important to us. Individuation is also the goal of "counseling" as Jung defined it. Comprising several complex and ongoing processes, individuation involves bringing into consciousness the unconscious dimensions of our personalities in order to achieve psychological maturity or wholeness. Individuation is also an ethical model; as a process that enables us to confront and integrate our inferior and destructive aspects, it also enables us to act truly for the benefit of others (and ourselves). The individuation process does not promise to remove our defects; rather, by guiding us to confront and consciously integrate our dark or "shadow" aspects on an ongoing basis, it helps us to minimize their destructive impact on others and to use their negative energy creatively toward positive ends.

Returning to the issue of type for a moment, in the earlier chapters of this book we asked you to try to determine which primary function (Sensing, Intuition, Thinking, or Feeling) you and your clients prefer to use in daily interactions. This primary or "dominant" function is analogous to the captain of a ship. In turn, what we call the "auxiliary" function and liken to the ship's "first mate" (the auxiliary function supports or balances the dominant function) is sometimes described as different "in every way" from the dominant function. That is, if the dominant function is S or N, then the auxiliary function will be T or F. The reverse is also true. These two functions, the dominant and the auxiliary, along with direction of energy (Extraverted or Introverted) and the preferred way of relating to the outside world (Judging or Perceiving) form the "type" that describes how the personality manifests itself.

While it is comfortable and natural for human beings to act from their dominant and auxiliary functions, the process of individuation described by Jung—a process specifically aligned with psychological development during the second half of life—involves accessing and learning to work with our opposite or least comfortable functions, attitudes, and preferences. (Think of the analogy of a right-handed person learning to use his or her left hand.) Reliance on the dominant and auxiliary functions is necessary during the first half of life when we are defining our social selves and goals. As we go through life, however, if we are to mature and become more whole as human beings, we need to learn how to use all of our functions. To this end, we recommend that individuals identify one of their nonpreferred functions and work with it fairly exclusively for awhile. Taking on too much can seem overwhelming, and resistance to psychological overload is natural. Delving into the unexplored regions of the psyche will hopefully be an exciting journey for you and your clients. We once heard "personal therapy" defined as "graduate education of the self." We concur.

Jungian psychology and the Myers Briggs Type Indicator® assessment are the theoretical foundation upon which much of our therapeutic method is based. We use other models, of course, but the meaning, depth, and complexity offered by Jungian analysis and the MBTI assessment provide us with the tools we find most effective. Even though we don't always articulate our methods for our clients, our primary aim is to help them search for wholeness, for meaning, for higher consciousness—that is, to seek the depths where true healing can take place. We prefer not to medicate but to understand suffering when it occurs and to make conscious the choices that devolve around it.

For Jung, our concerns during the first half of life are necessarily outwardly directed, centered as they are on establishing a place in the world, on establishing a family and a career, however we define them. And because they are outer-directed, these tasks require conscious modes of action driven by our most readily accessible personality preferences. The concerns of the second half of life, on the other hand, are, or should be in Jung's view, internal, centered on finding meaning in our life and in our death. This inner-directed second life-stage requires exploratory, excavatory, and recuperative modes of action to make conscious the unconscious components of our personalities so that we may become more integrated and whole. These unconscious aspects are often communicated metaphorically through images of the opposite sex or images involving gender ambiguity. The contrasexual—and typically unconscious—aspect of one's psyche is referred to as the anima in men and the animus in women.

Unconscious contents are also revealed in waking life in the form of what Jungians would call "projections." Projection often accompanies arguments between partners and involves one person's projecting upon another the unconscious, undervalued, or rejected contents of his or her own psyche. These contents are frequently gendered, carrying negative or ambiguous characteristics associated with the sex opposite our own. For example, a man who unknowingly badgers his children all the time but accuses his partner of being "a nag," is projecting upon his mate the traits typically associated with the "nagging wife" stereotype. The woman who bullies others while accusing her husband of being a tyrant is projecting upon her mate the characteristics associated with a tyrannical man. In each case, the projected contents aren't those of the person who receives them but of the person who projects them; and that person isn't really aware of their projection. In fact, "the projector" in each of these examples would probably vigorously deny having even a tendency to nag or bully others. In any case, as you can see, the way our unconscious reveals itself to us often overlaps relationship to the opposite sex, both actually and metaphorically.

Revisiting Type

In the following sections, we outline the basics of type as we have used it. This section is meant as a refresher for those who use type in their counseling practices. If you are new to using the MBTI assessment with clients, we encourage you to seek out books and seminars that can give you greater and more in-depth information about the Myers-Briggs Type Indicator instrument.

The Four Functions Sensing and Intuition are called "perceiving functions," because they characterize how individuals receive information. Because the process of receiving information is one over which we have little control, the perceiving functions are sometimes called "irrational" functions. They are non-rational in that no reasoning is involved in their use. People with a preference for Sensing favor receiving concrete, tangible information through the five senses. People with a preference for Intuition favor receiving abstract or theoretical information, especially information that fits into broader or related contexts. One of the two perceiving functions (either Sensing or Intuition) is represented by the second letter in the four-letter type acronym: the S in ESTJ for example.

Thinking and Feeling are called "judging functions," because they characterize how individuals make rational choices on the basis of the information they receive. People with a preference for Thinking like to make choices on the basis of logical analysis. People with a preference for Feeling like to reason on the basis of values, ethics, and ideals rather than logic. One of the two Judging functions (either Thinking or Feeling) is represented by the third letter in the four-letter type acronym: the T in ESTJ, for example.

Together, one of the two perceiving functions (either Sensing or Intuition) and one of the two judging functions (either Thinking or Feeling) make up the core of an individual's type framework description and are represented by the middle two letters in the four-letter type acronym. The dominant function is the most important function (the "captain," so to speak) whether it appears in the second position (S or N) or in the third position (T or F) of the four-letter acronym.

The Two Attitudes or Orientations The terms "Introversion" and "Extraversion" refer to attitudes determined on the basis of which way an individual's energy is oriented—either externally toward the outside world or internally toward an inner world. One of these two attitudes is represented by the first letter in the four-letter type acronym: the I in ISTJ, for example.

The terms "Judging" and "Perceiving" point to the function an individual prefers to use in relating to the outside world. As you will recall, Sensing and Intuition are Perceiving functions; Thinking and Feeling are Judging functions. One of these two preferences (either Judging or Perceiving) is represented by the last letter in the four-letter type acronym: the J in ISTJ—in this case meaning that the Judging preference is used outwardly.

MBTI Theory Review

- The preferred or dominant function is the "captain of the ship."
- The balancing or auxiliary function is the "first mate."
- Only Sensing, Intuition, Thinking, and Feeling are functions; the other letters are attitudes or orientations to life.
- The four functions together can be thought of as a family within each individual. The first and second functions (also called dominant and auxiliary) are like adults leading the way, while the third and fourth functions (also called tertiary and inferior) are like children that need the adults' support and assistance to develop.
- The fourth or inferior (that is, "youngest") function can cause problems for an individual while it remains unconscious, but once integrated can assist in the quest for wholeness.
- Once we reach midlife, and from there to life's end, attention to our less developed functions helps us to avoid or to work through crises.
- A partner's type differences can provide us with valuable information for learning how to develop tolerance for paradox and ambiguity.

Type Dynamics

Jung hypothesizes that we may have more difficulty with people whose dominant function is couched in an attitude different from the one we bring to our own than we do with people who are of completely opposite type. In other words, we, the authors, as Introverted Intuitive types, may have more difficulty with Extraverted Intuitive types than with Extraverted Sensing types.

The opposite of our preferred or dominant function is the function least accessible to us. For Thinking types it is Feeling; for Feeling types, Thinking; for Sensing types, Intuition; and for Intuitive types, Sensing. This opposite of the dominant is called the "inferior" function. In this context, the word "inferior" doesn't carry a value judgment but simply refers to the function that is "least developed" and least conscious in an individual. Marie-Louise von Franz (Boa 1988, von Franz and Hillman 1971) states that while the devils come in with the inferior function, so do the angels. In other words, because our inferior function is also the aspect of our personalities most aligned with the unconscious, it is a doorway to that domain of metaphoric devils and angels, of forces that can hurt and destroy but also heal and create. Awareness of clients' type dynamics and differences in terms of typological development (table 10.1) will not only allow you to

TABLE 10.1

Dominant and Inferior Functions

DOMINANT FUNCTION		INFERIOR FUNCTION
What's easy ›	**For these types**	**‹ What's difficult**
THINKING *(Head stuff)*	ESTJ, ENTJ, ISTP, INTP	FEELING *(Heart stuff)*
FEELING *(Heart stuff)*	ESFJ, ENFJ, ISFP, INFP	THINKING *(Head stuff)*
SENSING *(Tangible stuff)*	ESTP, ESFP, ISTJ, ISFJ	INTUITION *(Intangible stuff)*
INTUITION *(Intangible stuff)*	ENTP, ENFP, INTJ, INFJ	SENSING *(Tangible stuff)*

help them mitigate or avoid problems with others but will also enable you to find the opening to each one's unconscious, that deep well that waters the individuation process.

Type Dynamics in Relationships

The attitudes of Extraversion and Introversion profoundly impact how individuals behave in the world. These attitudes also shape the ways that different types prefer to make decisions and reenergize themselves. Extraverts readily use their dominant function in the social world, the outside world. Introverts, who save their dominant function for use by themselves (or for less visible use), interact with others using their auxiliary function. This means, for example, that an Extraverted Intuitive type will direct his or her dominant Intuition toward you while interacting with you. Introverted Intuitive types, on the other hand, will interact with you using their auxiliary or less preferred Judging function (either Thinking or Feeling), while reserving their dominant function, Intuition, for internal or "behind the scenes" use. Because most of us prefer to use our preferred function in the preferred way, the Extravert tends to be more comfortable with other people, alone or in groups, than the Introvert, who is more comfortable being alone.

Both Extraverts and Introverts are aware of pressures exerted by the opposite attitude. To use a very concrete example, Introverts feel a pressure to interact, more than they want to, with others at work. In many cases, though, individuals experience oppositional pressures less literally, perhaps as an odd or anxious sense of something pulling at them, of something not quite right. When we are young, some of these pressures and demands may be consciously avoided, but at midlife they often become more demanding. Jungian theory, borne out in our own experience, holds that it is constructive for people to use their preferred attitudes and functions when they are young, but that at midlife and beyond, they need to develop their less preferred attitudes and functions in order to become more complete and realized human beings, in order to become whole.

What are the implications of this development for the couple that stays together ten, twenty, thirty years or longer? The impact of the midlife shift in consciousness can be quite a wake-up call. We see more people between the ages of 35 and 55 for relationship work than for any other kind of counseling.

Some Concepts in Individuation

- Jung's term for personal psychological development is "individuation."
- Tension between opposites (opposites of all kinds) is necessary to becoming conscious; individuation requires conscious integration of paradox and, ultimately, transcendence of opposites.
- Masculine energy complements feminine energy in much the same way that other paired opposites complement each other. Differences cause tension, but also enable us to become complete both in ourselves and in relation to others.
- Transcending the tension between the dichotomous pairs that comprise the four functions, integrating opposites in paradoxical union—both of these are milestones on the path to individuation.
- Things that are unconscious in us, we often project onto others.
- Making friends with our shadow or dark side reduces its power over us and allows for greater personal freedom and choice.
- The inferior function is the least conscious and darkest, but it can also be where "our angels come in."
- If you find someone backing away from you, don't chase them. Give them room, but indicate clearly that you care, if you really do care.
- Reactions are often places where we are stuck and have little choice. When you have a bad reaction, try to catch it before you act or speak, and find a way to give yourself a choice.

Counseling Couples: Tips for Counselors

- Extraverts need to learn to introvert occasionally, and Introverts need to learn to extravert occasionally.
- Intuitive types must know the facts to be effective; Sensing types must not disregard the possibilities.
- Thinking types need to get out of their heads to be effective in some situations; Feeling types need to balance heart with head to be effective.
- Judging types need to loosen up and put "the evaluator" on hold sometimes; Perceiving types sometimes need to close down other options to make the best decisions they can.

- Take a stand against behaviors destructive to self, other, or the relationship.
- Use humor whenever possible to point up repetitive patterns that need attention.
- Give clients explanations of how their partners' types work, helping them understand that those behaviors are true to type and not directed "against them."
- Suggest that both partners be cautious of interpreting each other's behavior or in assuming they know what the other will say or do in a given situation.
- Use the MBTI assessment descriptions to assist the partners in understanding each other; caution them against using such descriptions to blame or stereotype.
- Use the MBTI assessment constructively to help partners appreciate their differences, to enable each person to "individuate" or grow in their own way.

Type Development and Individuation

The complexity of Jungian theory is both a gift and a challenge. This part of chapter 10 makes an effort to delve deeper into the complexity of the theory. We have explored the dominant and auxiliary (or "parent") functions as they inform type theory and relationships, and we generally understand what they are and how they work. It remains to explore the tertiary and inferior functions, those only partially developed (or "child") functions that are less available to consciousness. Even further remote are those other and shadowy functions—the ones not manifest in our conscious personalities—that exist somewhere in our psyches in varied attitudes of Extraversion or Introversion.

Good type development requires a differentiated dominant function and a differentiated auxiliary function. This means using our Judging function (either Thinking or Feeling) and our Perceiving function (either Sensing or Intuition) in ways that serve us effectively. It means keeping some balance between them, as one will be Extraverted and the other, Introverted. Isabel Myers tells us that a Perceiving function deficit will produce decisions based on faulty or poor information. A Judging function deficit will produce indecision or decisions based on misinterpreted information. In the first case, poor decisions come from poor information; in the second, good information is put to poor use.

The dominant function is usually the first to become conscious and often appears quite early in our lives. The auxiliary function, which balances the dominant one, usually develops second, often during adolescence. On

"While it is natural and normal for human beings to busily concentrate on developing their dominant and auxiliary functions during the first half of life, ignoring the other two functions will not work."

the other hand, type development does not necessarily follow a linear sequence but may depend on situational and environmental factors that require of us certain orientations. The less conscious function-attitudes may appear as needed or even at random.

After we have developed and learned to use our dominant and auxiliary functions effectively—a process that usually extends from childhood into middle adulthood—further type development involves accessing our less conscious functions to whatever extent possible and thereby gaining some control over their manifestations and expressions. This second phase begins around midlife and, as part of the individuation process, extends through our maturity. Once we begin the process, we can usually access the third or tertiary function with some conscious effort. The fourth or inferior function, however, can be more problematic and may pop up in unpredictable or even embarrassing ways. Thinking types, for example, may fall into sullen moods, prey to an inferior Feeling function. Feeling types may display rabidly emotional opinions, victims of an inferior Thinking function. Sensing types may fear negative possibilities, haunted by an inferior Intuitive function, while Intuitive types may be drawn to negative realities, impelled by an inferior Sensing function.

While it is natural and normal for human beings to busily concentrate on developing their dominant and auxiliary functions during the first half of life, ignoring the other two functions will not work. The proverbial midlife crisis is generally an eruption of these less developed functions (a sleight of the left hand, if you will)—a wake-up call to consciousness, warning us to become aware of our unconscious aspects so as to minimize their potentially harmful impact. If we keep trying to use the strengths that worked for us in the past, we're apt to find that they no longer work as well. We need to explore all our options to lead satisfying lives.

Depth Therapy

At this point in the chapter, we offer you a way to contact clients on a deeper level. This may not be something you're interested in as a counselor, nor will every client be open to this kind of treatment. Some clients may not understand, others will be bored, and some may be "anti-" anything spiritual or self-appraising. Rather than changing themselves, some clients will want the world to change. Others may believe their personality is fixed and that behavior is subject to conditions or moods beyond their control. For still other clients, the prospect of depth therapy will be intriguing, even fascinating: delving into the unconscious' strata to see what comes up—jewels to embrace or junk to work on. Depth therapy, the approach to individuation, is something Jungian theory has to offer those in search of a more meaningful, a more involved, and an inspired life.

In our experience, Sensing types are less likely than other types to seek therapy, and when they do, they tend to ask for help with the "real world," soliciting advice and practical solutions to relieve their stress. Some may request medication as a solution if they believe it will alleviate their symptoms. As counselors, we have our own biases about the treatment of choice, but we need to allow each individual to search and find his or her own way. Because Sensing types are often better at maintaining a "Be here now" attitude than Intuitive types, it stretches those of us who are Intuitive types to work with their differences and ours.

Intuitive types like deep, complex explorations and can get excited by the process while working for results. In fact, where Intuitive types are concerned, client and counselor can so enjoy the exploratory process that they neglect to focus enough on the goal. Whereas Sensing types often want quick results, definite solutions, and even advice, Intuitive types engaged at a meaningful level can talk at great length about their symptoms and insights without making any significant changes. It behooves the counselor in both cases to find a way to work with whatever material the client presents, distinguish real issues from superficial or counterfeit ones, and facilitate a healing process.

One way to open a session is to ask, "If you get from this session what you would like to get, what would that be?" This seems to help client and counselor focus right away on where they want to go instead of "talking story."

The good news is that while we are all stuck with our basic inclinations, we are not stuck with our responses and can change them with some effort. One way to change is by shifting our outlooks (how we perceive information); another is by changing our behavior (what we decide to do about that information). If we can reframe our outlooks, the therapeutic results come much faster. If we go for behavior change, the process can often be as difficult as altering an ingrained habit. Sometimes as counselors we encounter people who have been on "automatic pilot" for so long, they no longer see that they have choices. One of the best things we can do for these and all clients is to open up new vistas for them to explore. Table 10.2 describes some of the intervention or "opening up" strategies we have found effective in our own practice.

Seven Qualities that Facilitate Individuation

In addition to Jungian psychology, constructive use of type differences was a motivating concept in Katharine Briggs' and Isabel Myers' development of the MBTI instrument. Type development can take place internally as we integrate various facets of our personalities by ourselves, in solitude. It can also take place in the outside world where, by observing our impact on people and events, we can bring unconscious functions into consciousness and there develop them among our repertoire of other behaviors and attitudes. Jung stressed the need to follow our projections and find ways to integrate them.

In Jungian psychology, integration can be achieved in relation to specific archetypes—ancient and semi-autonomous constellations of meaning that often take concrete form in the motifs and metaphors of myth, art, literature, and other creative forms of human expression. Archetypes can be models of action, and Jungian depth therapy indicates three individuation archetypes we must experience in our quest for wholeness: the shadow, the anima or animus, and the Self. The ultimate goal of individuation is discovery of the Self. (So as not to confuse them, the ego is the personal "I" and the center of one's consciousness, while the Self, more domain than entity, is both the center and totality of the psyche, that place where unconscious and conscious aspects—as well as other opposites—unite as an integrated whole.) Edward Edinger in *Ego and Archetype* (1972) devotes an entire chapter to Christ as the paradigm of the individuating ego—a process in which the ego is gradually more and more subsumed into the Self. (The capital "S" distinguishes this archetype of divinity and wholeness from the personal self.)

In their applications from Jung's work on psychological type, Myers and Briggs also identified approaches that contribute to our living satisfying, even inspired lives. The ongoing process of psychological growth first requires that we become aware and active participants in our own behavioral and attitudinal development. It also requires us to evolve response patterns that enhance rather than inhibit our life-coping skills and strategies. When available, these approaches enrich our lives; when absent, they need to be developed.

Our conscious pursuit of these approaches along with our work to develop the function-attitudes to whatever extent possible comprise by analogy major steps in the individuation process. (The phrase "comprise by analogy" points to the fact that ongoing type development and experience of the individuation archetypes aren't identical but analogous steps.) Jung postulated that world peace would be possible if each of us worked to attain a higher level of consciousness and peace within ourselves. World peace is a long way off, but by coming to terms with our own demons and striving for wholeness, we have at least made a contribution toward that goal. For Jung, the key to the world's salvation is the conscious individual. While manifestations of the "dark side" of human nature presently abound (and appear likely to continue to do so), our individual efforts at consciousness—that is, at bringing to light and confronting the evil in our own natures—can impel us to act to alleviate suffering in our midst. We can never eradicate our dark side (the "shadow" in Jungian terminology and first of the individuation archetypes), and it would be unwise to do so as it is a source of vital energy. Instead, our goal is to become conscious of the shadow and to convert its energy for individual and creative use. Look back for a moment at table 1.1 and the negative characteristics associated with

TABLE 10.2

Strategic Intervention for Counselors to Use with Clients

REFRAMING

To promote alternate and healthier responses, help clients see a situation in different ways, much in the way that putting a different frame on a picture can change its appearance and the viewer's response. For example, ask the clients to see a situation as a "challenge" or an "opportunity" rather than a "problem."

METAPHOR

Drawing an analogy between a "stuck" place and a comparable place where your client has been successful and energized. As a formal paradigm, metaphor allows individuals to see patterns without getting tangled in emotion. A person who needs to break through a decision-making impasse might use metaphoric terms to describe "a time when I had my feet on the ground and went forward" with "a time when I'm flying in all directions and going nowhere." In this case, the client might see that a particular kind of locomotion—one that is measured and incremental (walking as opposed to flying)—produced successful results and try to use that kind of approach to bring about positive change.

AS IF

Setting up scenarios in which the client is able to imagine themselves behaving in different ways, for example:

- as if they were successful;
- as if they can accomplish what they want to accomplish;
- as if they look the way they would like to look; or
- as if they were clear about their goals.

DREAMS

Using everything and everyone in the dream to identify destructive and creative energies at work within an individual's psyche. While a dream's imagery may seem negative, the fact that unconscious material and energy have been "constellated" in the dream will bring a troubled individual some relief. Because dreams bridge the conscious and the unconscious, their language (or imagery) is usually metaphoric and can be decoded.

PARADOX

Teaching clients to recognize the unity in disparity in order to help them deal with their own conflicting energies and impulses, and to tolerate ambiguity. Reconciliation of opposites is one of the principal tasks of individuation. To illustrate you can use a yin and yang symbol, which is a whole circle divided into two apostrophes—one black and one white—nested within each other. In the fat end of the white apostrophe is a black dot, and in the fat end of the black apostrophe is a white dot, thus demonstrating the black within the white, and the white within the black.

Clarity

Helping clients distinguish among available options in order to discover new, alternative choices. Many clients tend to think about decision making in dualistic terms as a choice between two options only, when in fact hundreds of options may exist. Helping people see various perspectives and options is a gift.

Meditation

Showing clients how to replace doing with being by giving them techniques for "getting out of their heads" or for detaching from thoughts. By emptying stale rice from a bowl, one makes it ready to receive the fresh rice.

Reflection

Helping clients to see, first, the value of slowing down; second, of taking time to interpret the meaning of experiences and statements; and third, to formulate what response, if any, they need to make.

Avoiding labels

Discouraging your own and your clients' use of terms that diminish others or that both discharge and provoke negative emotion. This means avoiding descriptors (adjectives), such as "stupid," "arrogant," et cetera, as well as names (nouns), such as "bitch," "bastard," and the like.

Dichotomy

Helping clients identify the opposite or complementary aspects of a situation by thinking in terms of dichotomous pairings, such as good-bad, male-female, and so on. If a client describes something as bad, ask him what might be good about it. If a client describes something as good, ask her what might be bad about it. Ask clients whether good and bad dimensions are simultaneously present in a given situation (see also Paradox).

different type preferences. This information could be a good place to start in terms of helping clients explore their negative or shadow dimensions.

You might now want to return briefly to chapter 5 to remind yourself of the most effective behaviors associated with each type. Play with how you might integrate these into your own psychological repertoire and how you might help clients do the same. Constructive use of differences is the underlying message in all applications of the MBTI instrument. By pursuing our own individuation quests and by helping our clients realize their fullest potential, their capacity for wholeness, we are hopefully contributing to a better world by becoming and nurturing better "selves." As integrated and well-developed individuals, we are capable of a wondrous variety of creative, compassionate, and humanitarian achievements.

The following list of qualities that facilitate the individuation process may be useful to you and your clients as a kind of behavioral roadmap. We also hope you will pursue Jung's collected works to get a richer understanding of the archetypes of individuation and their meaning in the individual's life journey.

- *Open-mindedness*—The ability to take in information and relate to it without immediately rejecting or reacting to it in a predetermined way; allowing and acquiring new perspectives or awareness; getting past a "made-up" mind; being open to new ideas, not closed to new input.
- *Confidence*—Trusting oneself to know what to do to achieve desired results; the ability to enjoy being oneself; the capacity to be calm, independent, expressive when desirable, decisive when necessary.
- *Compensation*—Keeping a balance; not overreacting to environmental input or conditions; reacting positively or neutrally to differing ways of viewing the world and responding to situations; avoiding defensiveness, cynicism, resistance.
- *Stamina*—The ability to "hang tough" when the going gets rough; perseverance in the face of difficulty; the capacity to recover quickly and come up with alternative approaches that may change situations; the ability to implement alternatives, without giving up.
- *Enjoyment*—Being able to have a good time, to laugh, and be joyful; taking pleasure in simple as well as special things; experiencing life in positive ways.

- *Appreciation*—Being able to be easy on oneself and others; to be enthusiastic about life and to value relationships, nature, new experiences, new ideas; to be thankful for one's gifts and the ability to make a difference, anticipate bad things, and appreciate goodness.
- *Acceptance*—Not hanging on to the past but living in the present; not grieving about losses or hurts; not carrying past injuries; not regretting events or choices; making the most of the current situation; letting go and moving on.

Transcending Type

Beyond the dichotomies of male and female, black and white, singular and plural lies wholeness and unity, a unity to be recognized, approached, and integrated. To become fully who we are entails our ability to integrate paradox and tolerate ambiguity (among other things) as we work toward clarity. Clarity allows us to achieve the objectives we set out for ourselves. Ambiguity is useful to any process that requires weighing information and alternatives, because it is a state wherein multiple associated and dissociated perceptions and possibilities are available to us. On the other hand, a state of ambiguity can be overwhelming when we are trying to decide upon a specific course of action, unless we can relate to its individual elements and synthesize them.

Earlier in this chapter, we touched upon the concept of anima or animus projections (see Jung's *Two Essays on Analytical Psychology*). Often represented in myth as the marriage of a king and queen, the "marriage within" of conflicting psychic elements can begin with an understanding and transformation of anima/animus projections. These typically consist in a range of barely conscious or unconscious (and gendered) desires unknowingly projected onto other people. The woman who cherishes a vague ideal of the perfect man may unconsciously seek "celebrity types" in the real world. A man whose sensitivities remain immature may unconsciously seek as a partner a woman he can "rescue." In both instances, unconscious projections may draw individuals into risky, even harmful situations. Individuals who have had bad experiences with the opposite sex tend to project negative associations upon all members of that group: the man who regards all women as "babes" or "whores" or "bitches"; the woman who regards all men as "bastards" or "rapists" or "bullies." The journey toward individuation requires recognizing and getting past such projections in order to see ourselves and other individuals as they really are, with all their beauties, flaws, and complexities.

Central to the individuation process is our ongoing recognition of the many facets and manifestations of self and our accompanying effort to take responsibility for the behaviors that emanate from them. The more we integrate these disparate facets, the further along on the individuation journey we progress. Psychological wholeness (the archetype of the Self, often represented by a circular symbol called a "mandala") can be understood in typological terms as a union of all of the attitudes, functions, and preferences. To be complete and fully realized we need all four functions—Sensing, Intuition, Thinking, and Feeling. Being able at will to access our most-needed function (or function-attitude) requires an integration and possible transcendence of the opposites: in the case of type, of typological opposites. (A figure for one pair of opposites might be a see-saw; for two pairs of opposites, a cross.) In other words, we want to come as close as we can to achieving "wholeness," a state we can imagine in spatial terms as a circle rather than as a see-saw or a cross.

"CENTRAL TO THE INDIVIDUATION PROCESS IS OUR ONGOING RECOGNITION OF THE MANY FACETS AND MANIFESTATIONS OF SELF AND OUR ACCOMPANYING EFFORT TO TAKE RESPONSIBILITY FOR THE BEHAVIORS THAT EMANATE FROM THEM."

The see-saw provides a metaphor of the need for balance. If you stand in the middle of the see-saw and keep shifting carefully from one foot to the other, you can keep your balance. If you move too far to one end without something to counterbalance you, you will be out of balance and may fall off. If you try to run quickly from one end of the see-saw to the other, you will stir up a lot of energy but still be out of balance. You may also fall off if you try to stay still in the middle without moving at all. In addition to serving as a metaphor of balance, the see-saw—particularly that image of someone's running rapidly from one to its other end—serves as a metaphor of compensation. As a human example, we might consider the kind of person who generally follows all the rules, who would feel guilty disobeying them, but who nonetheless at some point unpredictably "flips" over into a rebellious mode.

In Jung's *Function-Attitudes Explained* (1996), Dick Thompson brings clarity to a discussion of the four functions by showing that each has the possibility of being either Extraverted or Introverted. In other words, each function has two possible attitudes, giving us eight "function-attitudes" altogether. Incorporating these, Jungian analyst John Beebe in his recent article "Evolving the Eight-Function Model" (2005) proposes eight archetypal complexes carrying the eight functions. Theoretically, we can use each function in both attitudes, Extraverted and Introverted, if we can make them available to consciousness. While this is unlikely in reality, it is nonetheless an enticing prospect for the individuation opus. While Thompson offers multiple examples of the function-attitudes in his book, Beebe's model has the benefit of incorporating symbolic dimensions based on Jung's archetypes of individuation. For example, the cross diagram he uses to represent the "compensatory personality" with its "less conscious" function-attitudes he also associates with the shadow, the first of the individuation archetypes.

The Jungian concept of compensation has important implications for client treatment. If an individual strives to be too good or wonderful, for example, the unconscious is on call and ready to adjust an unbalanced self-perception, often undermining an individual's best efforts to appear and actually be good in embarrassing or upsetting ways. One example might be found in the person whose heartfelt vow and observance of chastity ends in a drunken one-night stand. Thus, having clients "make friends" with their shadow in order to make conscious and balance the energy attached to each of the compensatory personality's function-attitudes can help them achieve a more centered personality. It also minimizes the prospect of being stuck in a persona (the mask we wear in our social interactions) at the expense of the Self. The shadow is adept at bringing the ego down.

The following diagram shows one example of type development based on Beebe's model and Thompson's function-attitudes. The numbers represent the relative conscious standing these functions have in the psyche, with "1" being more conscious (and typically earlier developed), and "8" being the least conscious. In this diagram, shadow and ego are integrated into the circle of the Self.

Example of Beebe's Model of Type Development

INFJ

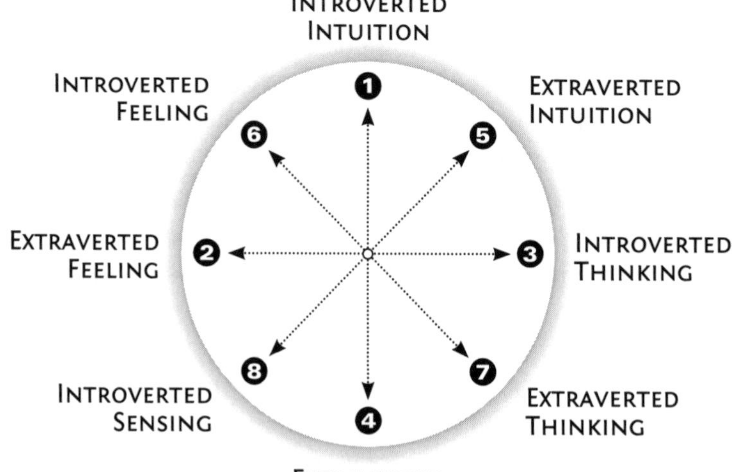

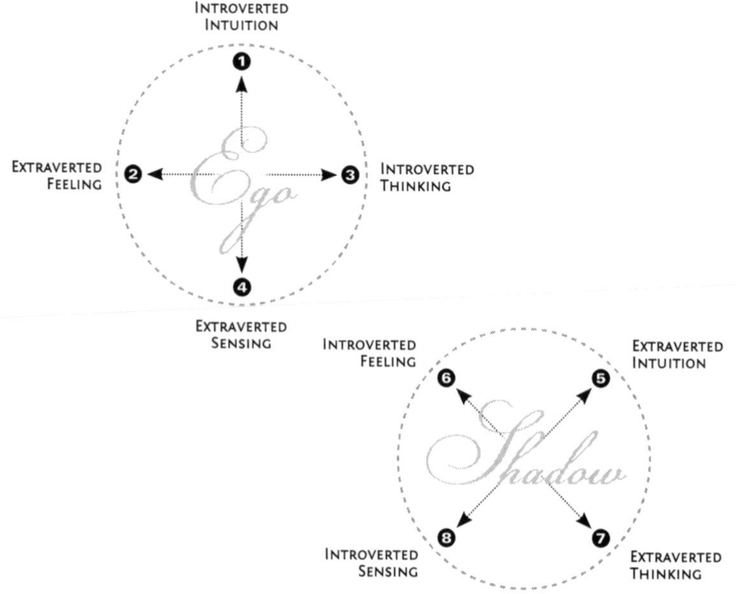

To Sum Up

Individuation is the process of achieving psychic wholeness by bringing to light and consciousness our unconscious aspects. It is the process of enduring the tension between opposites to at length unite and transcend them. It means dragging the mud of the shadowlands for jewels. It means embracing suffering in order to travel beyond it to freedom. It means mining dreams for the symbolic passwords that will open doors to new horizons and perspectives. Above all, individuation means being on a spiritual journey. This is what it meant for Jung, for Katharine Briggs and Isabel Myers, and what it means for us and our clients, for you and your clients. Vaya con Dios!

REFERENCES

Beebe, J. 2005. Evolving the eight-function model. *Bulletin of Psychological Type* 28.4: 34-39.

Bernard, J. S. 1972. *The future of marriage.* New York: World Publishing.

Boa, F. 1988. *The way of the dream: Conversations on Jungian dream interpretation with Marie-Louise von Franz.* Film documentary. Toronto: Windrose Films.

Bradway, K. 1964. Jung's psychological types. *Journal of Analytical Psychology* 9: 129-34.

Campbell, J., ed. 1976. *The portable Jung.* New York: Penguin.

Comfort, A. 2002. *The joy of sex.* 1st American ed. New York: Crown.

Edinger, E. 1972. *Ego and archetype: Individuation and the religious function of the psyche.* New York: Putnam.

Elston, L. 1984. *Square pegs and round holes: How to match the personality to the job.* San Diego: First Step Enterprises.

Grant, W. H., M. Thompson, and T. Clarke. 1983. *From image to likeness: A Jungian path in the gospel journey.* New York: Paulist Press.

Hill, G. S. 1992. *Masculine and feminine: The natural flow of opposites in the psyche.* Boston: Shambhala.

Hirsh, S. K., and J. M. Kummerow. 1989. *Life types.* New York: Warner Books.

Hite, S. 1987. *The Hite report on male sexuality.* New York: Ballantine.

Hite, S. 2003. *The Hite report: A nationwide study on female sexuality.* New York: Seven Stories Press.

Isachsen, O., and L. V. Berens. 1991. *Working together: A personality-centered approach to management.* 2nd ed. Coronado, CA: Neworld Management Press.

Jung, C. G. 1923. *Psychological types.* Trans. H. G. Baynes. Rev. R.F.C. Hull. Princeton, NJ: Princeton University Press, 1976.

———. 1928. *Two essays on analytical psychology.* 2nd ed. Trans. R.F.C. Hull. Princeton, NJ: Princeton University Press, 1972.

———. 1933. *Modern man in search of a soul.* Trans. W. S. Dell and C. F. Baynes. New York: Harcourt, 1950.

———. 1963. *Memories, dreams, reflections.* Rev. ed. Rec. and ed. A. Jaffe. Trans. R. and C. Winston. New York: Vintage, 1989.

———. 2000. *Collected works of C. G. Jung.* 21 vols. Ed. G. Adler, M. Fordham, and H. Read. Trans. R.F.C. Hull. Princeton, NJ: Princeton University Press.

Jung, E. 1957. *Animus and anima.* Dallas, TX: Spring Publications, 1985.

Keirsey, D., and M. Bates. 1984. *Please understand me: Character and temperament types.* 4th ed. Del Mar, CA: Prometheus Nemesis.

Kinsey, A. C., W. B. Pomeroy, and C. E. Martin. 1948. *Sexual behavior in the human male.* Bloomington: Indiana University Press, 1998.

Kinsey, A. C., W. B. Pomeroy, C. E. Martin, and P. H. Gibhard. 1953. *Sexual behavior in the human female.* Introd. John Bancroft. Bloomington: Indiana University Press, 1998.

Kroeger, O., and J. M. Thuesen. 1988. *Type talk: 16 personality types that determine how we live, love, and work.* New York: Delacorte.

———. 1994. *16 ways to love your lover: Understanding the 16 personality types so you can create a love that lasts forever.* New York: Delacorte.

Kummerow, J. M. 1985. *Talking in type.* Training handout. Gainesville, FL: Center for Applications of Psychological Type.

———. 1986. *Verifying your type preferences.* Gainesville, FL: Center for Applications of Psychological Type.

Larkin, C. 1989. *Headlines of my life.* Del Mar, CA: Human Perspectives.

Lawrence, G. D. 1985. *Communication patterns.* Training handout. Gainesville, FL: Center for Applications of Psychological Type.

———. 1993. *People types and tiger stripes.* 3rd ed. Gainesville, FL: Center for Applications of Psychological Type.

Masters, W. H. and V. E. Johnson. 1966. *Human sexual response.* New York: Bantam Books.

Masters, W. H. and V. E. Johnson. 1970. *Human sexual inadequacy.* New York: Bantam Books.

Meier, C. A. 1990. *Personality: The individuation process in the light of C. G. Jung's typology.* Boston: Sigo.

Murphy, E. 1992. *The developing child: Using Jungian type to understand children.* Palo Alto, CA: Davies-Black.

Myers, I. B., 1998. *Introduction to type: A guide to understanding your results on the Myers-Briggs Type Indicator.* 6th ed. Palo Alto, CA: Consulting Psychologists Press.

Myers, I. B., M. H. McCaulley, N. L. Quenk, and A. L. Hammer. 1998. *Manual for the Myers-Briggs type indicator: A guide to the development and use of the MBTI.* 3rd ed. Palo Alto, CA: Consulting Psychologists Press.

Myers, I. B., with P. B. Myers. 1995. *Gifts differing: Understanding personality type.* Palo Alto, CA: Davies-Black.

Myers, K. D. 1985. *Decision-making and type.* Training handout. Gainesville, FL: Center for Applications of Psychological Type.

Page, E. C. 2005. *Looking at type: A description of the preferences reported by the Myers-Briggs Type Indicator.* Updated ed. Gainesville, FL: Center for Applications of Psychological Type.

Quenk, N. L. 1993. *Beside ourselves: Our hidden personality in everyday life.* Palo Alto, CA: Consulting Psychologists Press.

Sherman, R. G. 1981. Psychological typology and satisfaction in intimate relationships. Doctoral dissertation. Saybrook Institute.

———. 1981. Typology and problems in intimate relationships. *Research in Psychological Type* 4: 4-23.

Smith, J. C. 1990. *The neurotic foundations of social order: Psychoanalytic roots of patriarchy.* New York: New York University Press.

Thompson, H. L. 1996. *Jung's function-attitudes explained.* Watkinsville, GA: Wormhole.

Von Franz, M. L., and J. Hillman. 1971. *Lectures on Jung's typology.* Dallas, TX: Spring Publications, 1986.

Wheelwright, J. 1971. *Psychological types.* Book and sound recording. San Francisco: C. G. Jung Institute.

Wickes, F. G. 1966. *The inner world of childhood.* Introd. C. G. Jung. Englewood Cliffs, NJ: Prentice-Hall, 1978.

Wyse, L. 1967. *Poems for the very married.* Colorado Springs: Garret Press.

FURTHER READING

Bernard, J. S. 1972. *The future of marriage.* New York: World Publishing.

Bradway, K. 1964. Jung's psychological types. *Journal of Analytical Psychology* 9: 129-34.

Jung, C. G. 1928. *Two essays on analytical psychology.* 2nd ed. Trans. R.F.C. Hull. Princeton, NJ: Princeton University Press, 1972.

———. 1933. *Modern man in search of a soul.* Trans. W. S. Dell and C. F. Baynes. New York: Harcourt, 1950.

———. 1963. *Memories, dreams, reflections.* Rev. ed. Rec. and ed. A. Jaffe. Trans. R. and C. Winston. New York: Vintage, 1989.

———. 2000. *Collected works of C. G. Jung.* 21 vols. Ed. G. Adler, M. Fordham, and H. Read. Trans. R.F.C. Hull. Princeton, NJ: Princeton University Press.

Keirsey, D. 1995. *Portraits of temperament.* 3rd ed. Del Mar, CA: Prometheus Nemesis.

Keyserling, C. H. 1926. *The book of marriage: A new interpretation by twenty-four leaders of contemporary thought.* New York: Harcourt, Brace.

Martin, C. R. 1997. *Looking at type: The fundamentals.* Gainesville, FL: CAPT.

Quenk, N. L. 2002. *Was that really me?* Palo Alto, CA: Davies-Black Publishing.

Rogers, C. R. 1972. *Becoming partners: Marriage and its alternatives.* New York: Delacorte.

VanSant, S. 2003. *Wired for conflict.* Gainesville, FL: CAPT.

Zeisset, C. 2006. *The art of dialogue.* Gainesville, FL: CAPT.

Other Resources

Association for Psychological Type
9650 Rockville Pike
Bethesda, Maryland 20814-3998
301-634-7450
www.aptinternational.org

Center for Applications of Psychological Type
2815 NW 13th Street, Suite 401
Gainesville, Florida 32609
352-375-0160
www.capt.org

CPP, Inc. (formerly Consulting Psychologists Press)
1055 Joaquin Road, 2nd Floor
Mountain View, CA 94043
650-969-8901
www.cpp.com

APPENDIX A

THE DESCRIPTIONS OF THE SIXTEEN TYPES

The descriptions are grouped in two ways. The types who prefer Extraversion are on the left side of each page, and the types who prefer Introversion are on the right. The types with Thinking as the strongest mental process are grouped together and across from those with Feeling as the strongest mental process (pages 210-213). The Sensing types are across from the Intuitive types (pages 214-217). The strongest mental process in each case is indicated by the larger letter in the four letter type designation, such as ISFP.

The descriptions are arranged with opposite types across from each other on the same page. For example, ENTJ is across from ISFP, the type that is opposite in all four dimensions. As you read the phrases listed for each type, you should not assume that a positive value listed for one type implies a negative trait for the opposite type. For example, when we read that ENTJs value efficiency, we must not infer that ISFPs are inefficient. Similarly, because ISFPs value compassion does not mean that ENTJs are cold-hearted. Opposite types are across from each other to help you decide your best fit type. The contrasts shown by the opposites help to clarify what is given priority in our mental processing. What has high priority for ISFP is not given high priority by ENTJ, and vice versa

The descriptions emphasize the values and priorities of the types more than they tell what behaviors are associated with each of the types. The values are emphasized because they are the motivational energy behind the behaviors.

ENTJ

Intuitive, innovative ORGANIZERS; analytical, systematic, confident; push to get action on new ideas and challenges. Having Extraverted THINKING as their strongest mental process, ENTJs are at their best when they can take charge and set things in logical order. They value:

- Analyzing abstract problems, complex situations
- Foresight; pursuing a vision
- Changing, organizing things to fit their vision
- Putting theory into practice, ideas into action
- Working to a plan and schedule
- Initiating, then delegating
- Efficiency; removing obstacles and confusion
- Probing new possibilities
- Holding self and others to high standards
- Having things settled and closed
- Tough-mindedness, directness, task-focused behavior
- Objective principles; fairness, justice
- Assertive, direct action
- Intellectual resourcefulness
- Driving toward broad goals along a logical path
- Designing structures and strategies
- Seeking out logical flaws

ESTJ

Fact-minded practical ORGANIZERS; assertive, analytical, systematic; push to get things done, working smoothly and efficiently. Having Extraverted THINKING as their strongest mental process, they are at their best when they can take charge and set things in logical order. They value:

- Results; doing, acting
- Planned, organized work and play
- Common sense practicality
- Consistency; standard procedures
- Concrete, present-day usefulness
- Deciding quickly and logically
- Having things settled and closed
- Rules, objective standards, fairness by the rules
- Task-focused behavior
- Directness, tough-mindedness
- Orderliness; no loose ends
- Systematic structure; efficiency
- Categorizing aspects of their life
- Scheduling and monitoring
- Protecting what works

ISFP

Observant, loyal HELPERS; reflective, realistic, empathic, patient with details. Shunning disagreements, they are gentle, reserved and modest. Having Introverted FEELING as their strongest mental process, they are at their best when responding to the needs of others. They value:

- Personal loyalty; a close, loyal friend
- Finding delight in the moment
- Seeing what needs doing to improve the moment
- Freedom from organizational constraints
- Working individually
- Peacemaking behind the scenes
- Attentiveness to feelings
- Harmonious, cooperative work settings
- Spontaneous, hands-on exploration
- Gentle, respectful interactions
- Deeply held personal beliefs
- Reserved, reflective behavior
- Practical, useful skills and know-how
- Having their work life be fully consistent with deeply held values
- Showing and receiving appreciation

INFP

Imaginative, independent HELPERS; reflective, inquisitive, empathic, loyal to ideals: more tuned to possibilities than practicalities. Having Introverted FEELING as their strongest mental process, they are at their best when their inner ideals find expression in their helping of people. They value:

- Harmony in the inner life of ideas
- Harmonious work settings; working individually
- Seeing the big picture possibilities
- Creativity; curiosity, exploring
- Helping people find their potential
- Giving ample time to reflect on decisions
- Adaptability and openness
- Compassion and caring; attention to feelings
- Work that lets them express their idealism
- Gentle, respectful interactions
- An inner compass; being unique
- Showing appreciation and being appreciated
- Ideas, language and writing
- A close, loyal friend
- Perfecting what is important

ESFJ

Practical HARMONIZERS, workers with people; sociable, orderly, opinioned; conscientious, realistic and well tuned to the here and now. Having Extraverted FEELING as their strongest mental process, they are at their best when responsible for winning people's cooperation with personal caring and practical help. They value:

- An active, sociable life, with many relationships
- A concrete, present-day view of life
- Making daily routines into gracious living
- Staying closely tuned to people they care about so as to avoid interpersonal troubles
- Talking out problems cooperatively, caringly
- Approaching problems through rules, authority, standard procedures
- Caring, compassion, and tactfulness
- Helping organizations serve their members well
- Responsiveness to others and to traditions
- Being prepared, reliability in tangible, daily work
- Loyalty and faithfulness
- Practical skillfulness grounded in experience
- Structured learning in a humane setting
- Appreciation

ENFJ

Imaginative HARMONIZERS, workers with people; expressive, orderly, opinioned, conscientious; curious about new ideas and possibilities. Having Extraverted FEELING as their strongest mental process, they are at their best when responsible for winning people's cooperation with caring insight into their needs. They value:

- Having a wide circle of relationships
- Having a positive, enthusiastic view of life
- Seeing subtleties in people and interactions
- Understanding others' needs and concerns
- An active, energizing social life
- Seeing possibilities in people
- Thorough follow-through on important projects
- Working on several projects at once
- Caring and imaginative problem solving
- Maintaining relationships to make things work
- Shaping organizations to better serve members
- Sociability and responsiveness
- Structured learning in a humane setting
- Caring, compassion, and tactfulness
- Appreciation as the natural means of encouraging improvements

INTP

Inquisitive ANALYZERS; reflective, independent, curious; more interested in organizing ideas than situations or people. Having Introverted THINKING as their strongest mental process, they are at their best when following their intellectual curiosity, analyzing complexities to find the underlying logical principles. They value:

- A reserved outer life; an inner life of logical inquiry
- Pursuing interests in depth, with concentration
- Work and play that is intriguing, not routine
- Being free of emotional issues when working
- Working on problems that respond to detached intuitive analysis and theorizing
- Approaching problems by reframing the obvious
- Complex intellectual mysteries
- Being absorbed in abstract, mental work
- Freedom from organizational constraints
- Independence and nonconformance
- Intellectual quickness, ingenuity, invention
- Competence in the world of ideas
- Spontaneous learning by following curiosity and inspirations

ISTP

Practical ANALYZERS; value exactness; more interested in organizing data than situations or people; reflective, cool and curious observers of life. Having Introverted THINKING as their strongest mental process, they are at their best when analyzing experience to find the logical order and underlying properties of things. They value:

- A reserved outer life
- Having a concrete, present-day view of life
- Clear, exact facts (a large storehouse of them)
- Looking for efficient, least-effort solutions based on experience
- Knowing how mechanical things work
- Pursuing interests in depth, such as hobbies
- Collecting things of interest
- Working on problems that respond to detached, sequential analysis and adaptability
- Freedom from organizational constraints
- Independence and self-management
- Spontaneous hands-on learning experience
- Having useful technical expertise
- Critical analysis as a means to improving things

ESTP

REALISTIC ADAPTERS in the world of material things; good-natured, easygoing; oriented to practical, firsthand experience; highly observant of details of things. Having Extraverted SENSING as their strongest mental process, they are at their best when free to act on impulses, or responding to concrete problems that need solving. They value:

- A life of outward, playful action in the moment
- Being a troubleshooter
- Finding ways to use the existing system
- Clear, concrete, exact facts
- Knowing the way mechanical things work
- Being direct, to the point
- Learning through spontaneous, hands-on action
- Practical action, more than words
- Plunging into new adventures
- Responding to practical needs as they arise
- Seeing the expedient thing and acting on it
- Pursuing immediately useful skills
- Finding fun in their work and sparking others to have fun
- Looking for efficient, least-effort solutions
- Being caught up in enthusiasms

ESFP

REALISTIC ADAPTERS in human relationships; friendly and easy with people, highly observant of their feelings and needs; oriented to practical, firsthand experience. Extraverted SENSING being their strongest mental process, they are at their best when free to act on impulses, responding to needs of the here and now. They value:

- An energetic, sociable life, full of friends and fun
- Performing, entertaining, sharing
- Immediately useful skills; practical know-how
- Learning through spontaneous, hands-on action
- Trust and generosity; openness
- Patterning themselves after those they admire
- Concrete, practical knowledge; resourcefulness
- Caring, kindness, support, appreciation
- Freedom from irrelevant rules
- Handling immediate, practical problems and crises
- Seeing tangible realities; least-effort solutions
- Showing and receiving appreciation
- Making the most of the moment; adaptability
- Being caught up in enthusiasms
- Easing and brightening work and play

INFJ

People-oriented INNOVATORS of ideas; serious, quietly forceful and persevering; concerned with work that will help the world and inspire others. Having Introverted INTUITION as their strongest mental process, they are at their best when caught up in inspiration, envisioning and creating ways to empower self and others to lead more meaningful lives. They value:

- A reserved outer life; spontaneous inner life
- Planning ways to help people improve
- Seeing complexities, hidden meanings
- Understanding others' needs and concerns
- Imaginative ways of saying things
- Planful, independent, academic learning
- Reading, writing, imagining; academic theories
- Being restrained in outward actions; planful
- Aligning their work with their ideals
- Pursuing and clarifying their ideals
- Taking the long view
- Bringing out the best in others through appreciation
- Finding harmonious solutions to problems
- Being inspired and inspiring others

INTJ

Logical, critical, decisive INNOVATORS of ideas; serious, intent, very independent, concerned with organization; determined, often stubborn.With Introverted INTUITION as their strongest mental process, they are at their best when inspiration turns insights into ideas and plans for improving human knowledge and systems. They value:

- A restrained, organized outer life; a spontaneous, intuitive inner life
- Conceptual skills, theorizing
- Planful, independent, academic learning
- Skepticism; critical analysis; objective principles
- Originality, independence of mind
- Intellectual quickness, ingenuity
- Nonemotional tough-mindedness
- Freedom from interference in projects
- Working to a plan and schedule
- Seeing complexities, hidden meanings
- Improving things by finding flaws
- Probing new possibilities; taking the long view
- Pursuing a vision; foresight; conceptualizing
- Getting insights to reframe problems

ENTP

Inventive, analytical PLANNERS OF CHANGE; enthusiastic and independent; pursue inspiration with impulsive energy; seek to understand and inspire. Extraverted INTUITION being their strongest mental process, they are at their best when caught up in the enthusiasm of a new project and promoting its benefits. They value:

- Conceiving of new things and initiating change
- The surge of inspirations; the pull of emerging possibilities
- Analyzing complexities
- Following their insights, wherever they lead
- Finding meanings behind the facts
- Autonomy, elbow room; openness
- Ingenuity, originality, a fresh perspective
- Mental models and concepts that explain life
- Fair treatment
- Flexibility, adaptability
- Learning through action, variety, and discovery
- Exploring theories and meanings behind events
- Improvising, looking for novel ways
- Work made light by inspiration

ENFP

Warmly enthusiastic PLANNERS OF CHANGE; imaginative, individualistic; pursue inspiration with impulsive energy; seek to understand and inspire others. With Extraverted INTUITION as the strongest mental process, they are at their best when caught in the enthusiasm of a project, sparking others to see its benefits. They value:

- The surge of inspirations; the pull of emerging possibilities
- A life of variety, people, warm relationships
- Following their insights wherever they lead
- Finding meanings behind the facts
- Creativity, originality, a fresh perspective
- An optimistic, positive, enthusiastic view of life
- Flexibility and openness
- Exploring, devising and trying out new things
- Open-ended opportunities and options
- Freedom from the requirement of being practical
- Learning through action, variety, and discovery
- A belief that any obstacles can be overcome
- A focus on people's potentials
- Brainstorming to solve problems
- Work made light and playful by inspiration

ISFJ

Sympathetic MANAGERS OF FACTS AND DETAILS, concerned with people's welfare; stable, conservative, dependable, painstaking, systematic. Having Introverted SENSING as their strongest mental process, they are at their best when using their sensible intelligence and practical skills to help others in tangible ways. They value:

- Preserving; enjoying the things of proven value
- Steady, sequential work yielding reliable results
- A controlled, orderly outer life
- Patient, persistent attention to basic needs
- Following a sensible path, based on experience
- A rich memory for concrete facts
- Loyalty, strong relationships
- Consistency, familiarity, the tried and true
- Firsthand experience of what is important
- Compassion, kindness, caring
- Working to a plan and schedule
- Learning through planned, sequential teaching
- Set routines, common sense options
- Rules, authority, set procedures
- Hard work, perseverance

ISTJ

Analytical MANAGER OF FACTS AND DETAILS; dependable, conservative, systematic, painstaking, decisive, stable. Having Introverted SENSING as their strongest mental process, they are at their best when charged with organizing and maintaining data and material important to others and to themselves. They value:

- Steady, systematic work that yields reliable results
- A controlled outer life grounded in the present
- Following a sensible path, based on experience
- Concrete, exact, immediately useful facts, skills
- Consistency, familiarity, the tried and true
- A concrete, present-day view of life
- Working to a plan and schedule
- Preserving and enjoying things of proven value
- Proven systems, common sense options
- Freedom from emotionality in deciding things
- Learning through planned, sequential teaching
- Skepticism; wanting to read the fine print first
- A focus on hard work, perseverance
- Quiet, logical, detached problem solving
- Serious and focused work and play

INDEX

Author Bios

The original authors of the latest edition of this book, Jane Hardy Jones and Ruth Sherman, are sadly no longer living. Dr. Sherman died in 1996. Dr. Jones, who died in 2009, was able to work extensively on the new edition but was unfortunately unable to see the project through to conclusion. The publisher would like to take this opportunity to thank the psychologists and experts on psychological type who volunteered to assist with some of the revisions in memory of Dr. Jones so that this important work could be brought to completion. We also want to thank Leslie Jones, Dr. Jones's daughter, who worked closely with her mother on revisions to the manuscript.

Jane Hardy Jones, Ed. D., was an educator, researcher, and counselor at the University of Hawaii. During her forty-year career she maintained a private practice that was primarily focused on individual, marital, and relationship counseling. She was responsible for introducing the Myers-Briggs Type Indicator® assessment to the faculty and staff at the University of Hawaii, where it is still used today. Dr. Jones was also a co-author of CAPT's Type for Life™ guide, Building Better Relationships: Using the lens of personality to help couples thrive.

Ruth G. Sherman, Ph. D., was a psychologist and a founding member of the Association for Psychological Type (APTi). Dr. Sherman wrote one of the earliest dissertations on marriage counseling using the MBTI® assessment in order to give couples the tools for bridging personality differences. Dr. Sherman was a well-known lecturer and author and trained a myriad of students on the use of the MBTI instrument in clinical settings. She worked closely with co-author Jane Hardy Jones at the Counseling and Testing Center at the University of Hawaii.